HER
Silent
BONES

BOOKS BY PAMELA FAGAN HUTCHINS

Seeking Felicity

Emily Bernal Series
Heaven to Betsy
Earth to Emily
Hell to Pay

Michele Lopez Hanson Series
Going for Kona
Fighting for Anna
Searching for Dime Box

Ava Butler Series
Bombshell
Stunner
Knockout

HER
Silent
BONES

PAMELA FAGAN
HUTCHINS

bookouture

Published by Bookouture in 2024

An imprint of Storyfire Ltd.
Carmelite House
50 Victoria Embankment
London EC4Y 0DZ

www.bookouture.com

ISBN: 978-1-83790-081-7
eBook ISBN: 978-1-83790-080-0

To my husband Eric who thrives in a family of strong, challenging women. I am grateful beyond my ability to express that you are who you are, and I love you about ten times that much.

ONE

With the steel toe of one boot, the man lifted the woman's face to see if she was still breathing. Blood ran from her nose and one corner of her mouth, only visible because of light coming down through the trap door. Blood and spit. It was disgusting. She was disgusting. A bubble formed in the pink glop on her lips, then they parted. Maybe she was alive, maybe she wasn't. He dropped her head. It made a soft *thunk* on the dirt floor of the cellar. Served her right for biting him. He touched his chest. His shirt was soaked with his own blood. The bright blue stone pendant, the one he'd stolen from her before he'd taken her, was slick.

He crouched beside her, close enough to feel the warmth from her body, to smell the coppery scent of her blood and her rank odor. Not that he couldn't smell it standing up. The whole place reeked of her. It hadn't taken long for her to go from exciting to repugnant.

She had been exciting, though. A little hellcat, actually. If she was representative of her kind, then Wyoming women were tougher than the Las Vegas girls he was used to. Sure, the Vegas women were more hardened. More streetwise. But this one took pain without a whimper and never quit fighting back. Stronger than she looked, too. Her arm was relatively clean, so he squeezed the bicep, testing the muscle tone under skin the color of a UPS driver's shirt. She'd landed a few punches on him. He could see why they'd left bruises.

She flinched. Jerked. Spat. "Don't... touch... me. He... will... kill... you."

He laughed. Maybe she was still a little exciting. Like a trapped desert rattler. You could cut their heads off and they'd keep trying to bite you for a good hour after they were dead. And she was dead, even if she didn't know it yet. He eyed her body. Clean, she was a good-looking woman, for the area. He imagined her in a sequined body suit with a peacock feather tail and headpiece, her feet high kicking in stiletto shoes. Yeah, she could have been a showgirl, with enough make-up. Without it, add a few pasties and she'd at least make a decent stripper. Although nothing about her attitude made her suitable for hooking. Men would have lined up for their money back after a few minutes with her.

God, how he missed his days in Vegas. Figuring out which of the girls were shooting up, which were corrupting men. Waiting for the signs—never without the signs. Only dispatch irredeemable women. His dad had taught him that, as his grandfather had done for his father, too.

And he'd delivered them to hell until it had all gone sideways.

He supposed he should be grateful for a second chance in a new place. The black web advice about careers for people with knife skills had been sound. Wildlife processing. It was like a meat market job, without having to wear a clean white smock and smile at customers over a sterilized counter. Kept him sharp. They even let him use his own knife.

But he hated that it was in Wyoming. And not even Jackson, Wyoming. Godforsaken, podunk, backwater Kearny,

Wyoming. In the middle of the state. Light years from Vegas. In the foothills of mountains no one had even heard of. The Bighorns.

Pfffft. He'd show them *the* big horn was in town if he didn't freeze his ass off first. For shit's sake, it was the third week of May and still below freezing every morning. If he saved up some money and let things die down in Sin City, maybe it would be safe to get out of here. Not back to his home. But to Atlantic City. Or Reno.

A man could dream.

He said to her, "How do you think I found you, sweetie?"

Her reply was too muffled for him to understand the words, but her tone still said she didn't believe him.

He put his cheek on the ground and turned her to face him. Her swollen eyes were open to slits. "You're dead to him." She'd shown disloyalty to the one friend the man had made in Kearny. "So, now you're mine."

"Rather... die."

"Oh, you will. Soon." If he squirted her off with a hose— no, pressure-washed the whole room—it might be fun to keep her around longer. Except that it would be against his personal rules. Rules were important. Delivery in two days after he took them. He made it a priority. A sacred duty. A mission.

His cell phone buzzed from outside the room. His friend's number. He'd had to install a signal booster and antenna the height of the damn Eiffel Tower to take calls at all.

He clapped his hand over the woman's mouth and nose. She struggled against his grip, but he was stronger. Probably her dehydration, hunger, exhaustion, and injuries didn't help. He answered the phone on his Bluetooth headphones. "Yes?" He looked up, taking note of the video monitoring equipment he'd installed so he could keep an eye on her even when he was offsite. "Always have the right tools for the job, even if you have to do the work yourself," his father had told him. He'd taken the words to heart.

With a quick snap of her jaw and teeth, she bit into his palm. He jerked his hand back. She screamed.

"What was that noise?" his friend asked.

He backhanded her, knocking her head away. She shrieked again. "Damn cat. Sorry."

"I didn't know you had a cat."

He said, "A feral one that's latched on to me."

"Show it who's boss."

"Oh, I will." He pulled his knife from his boot holster, taking a moment to admire the T1 blade he'd smithed and the oil-rubbed handle he'd crafted to look a hundred years old, down to carving the year of his grandfather's birth into it. 1915. The era he belonged in. Before the Congress in the U.S. gave women ideas. Then he dropped his weight on the woman's small torso. Her breath burst out of her. *They're still the weaker sex.* He pressed the knife tip into the hollow of her throat, locking his eyes on hers.

Tension radiated from her body. He knew her resistance wasn't squashed yet. *See what happens when they have* ideas?

His friend said, "You still working at the processors?"

The Bambi butchery. "No."

"Why?"

He looked down at the woman. His pulse quickened. "Busy with other things."

"Huh. Are you busy now?"

"Yes."

"I'll text you, then."

"That would be better."

"Are you all right? You sound funny."

The man smiled. "Peachy."

His friend ended the call.

The man bared his teeth at the woman. After he was done

with her for the day, he'd have to make some enhancements to the room. She'd nearly bested him a few times. If the next ones were as wild as her, he'd need more ways to control them.

It was also time to think through his revised methodology. In Vegas, the cops had picked up on his signature. It was an important element of his work. Was then, was now. But he had to modify his method. He didn't like it, but it was too risky otherwise. And he sure couldn't leave her where she'd be found when he was through with her, like he'd done in Vegas. That wouldn't be a problem here. Wyoming is desolate. Remote. Practically uninhabited. There are a million and one places to dump a body. Almost that many wild animals to dispose of the evidence. Without a body and with a different way of signing for delivery, no one here would connect him to Nevada.

"Was that him?" she asked, her throat pressed on the blade as she spoke.

He removed the knife and twirled the tip on the floor. "What do you think?"

She gasped breaths between sentences. "If you let me go, I'll leave. I promise. You can keep my necklace. I'll never tell anyone. I'll change my name. Never come back."

He raised his eyebrows.

"I swear."

"I'll think about it. But first, we're going to spend some more time together." The terror in her eyes tingled in his chest, his throat, his pants. It felt so good, he wanted to close his eyes and lean back. But he didn't.

"No. Please," she said.

"Okay."

"Really?"

"No," he said, lifting his knife and slicing her clothes off from the neck of her blouse to the crotch of her jeans, drawing a line of blood.

She started kicking and beating at him with her fists,

showing strength left in her body that he wouldn't have believed possible. Amazing. And, yes, exciting again. But futile.

He poised his knife, more than ready to leave his mark and send her on her way. And then find his next girl. And then the next one after her. His mission was endless. His work was never done.

TWO

TWENTY-FOUR HOURS LATER

Delaney Pace's emotions were blowing up bigger than her britches, tearing her self-control apart at the seams. She clutched the circle around the cold silver star in her hand, then shoved it into her purse. Crawling over glass would have been less painful than asking for her old job back, yet that's what she'd just done. She'd been recycling the moment at about five thousand RPM ever since. The apology she'd been forced to make for running out a decade before, on the department and her mentor, Sheriff Coltrane Fentworth. The smile on his face. The handshake and handover of her old badge.

"I've been saving it for you," Sheriff Fentworth had said as he pulled it out of his drawer like he'd always expected this, as if this was a happy moment.

The kicker? The promotion that he'd given her with it. What had that been about? A few extra bucks each week to buy a more cooperative and less vocal Delaney? *When hell freezes over.* As if reading her mood, Cheap Trick sang 'Ain't That a Shame' over the big box speakers mounted high in the corners of the bar.

She smacked a hand on a wooden bar top. The Loafing

Shed. Cleverly named after the three-sided run-in shelters used by horses, it was better known in town as the Loading Shed—the place cowboys go to get loaded on the eastern face of Wyoming's Bighorn Mountains. Well, she needed out of it now. Away from her big feels and unwanted memories. Away from her brother Liam's disappointments—failing bar to go with his failing construction company and failing everything else. She'd idolized the larger-than-life risk-taker, popular in a way Delaney had never been. For a split second, she felt bad for him. Not just because he'd died, but because she'd expected him to succeed like it was his birthright, not limp along through life.

Before the bar was Liam's, it had been her father's. Her second home and biggest source of embarrassment as a kid. Even more so as a grown-up, compounding her current professional humiliation. But now it was all hers to run, whether she wanted to or not. *I do not.* She planned to unload the Loafing Shed and all the rest of Liam's ventures the first chance she got.

But there was one thing her brother had left her that made up for all the rest. One person, rather. Her orphaned eleven-year-old niece Kateena, she of a head of black curls unruly in their natural state, big eyes, and a smile full of crooked teeth. A sprite of a girl. A sad smile crossed Delaney's lips and her heart seized. She knew too well what it was like to face the loss of parents. How could it be that in only two weeks, though, the girl had gone from being just another obligation to running away with Delaney's heart? Delaney knew she wouldn't be leaving Kearny any time soon. She'd stay as long as Kateena needed to be here. Hence the shiny badge in her purse that she had to come to terms with. Immediately. Like, before she picked Kateena up from school that afternoon. She wasn't going to inflict her inner turmoil on her niece. Wasn't going to repeat the mistakes of her own mother.

Delaney filled a glass with soda water and chugged it. The liquid didn't douse her emotions. Nothing but spinning tires and silence would give her peace, never had since the days she'd traveled with her dad in his beat-up travel trailer while he was racing his Chevelle SS, Shotgun Shelly. Normal, her childhood had not been. With an absent mother, no sisters, and life on a homestead outside of town, there had been no dolls and tea parties for her. Love was the countless hours she'd spent with her dad tinkering Shelly to perfection.

"We did it, Laney." She startled, hearing Rudy Pace's voice as clearly in the bar as if he was standing beside her, even though he'd shouted the words from atop the makeshift wooden podium at a dirt track race in Gillette when she was no more than ten years old. He'd given her the prize—a cheap, heavy medallion that read "Eastern Wyoming Dirt Track Champion" —and she wore it as a pendant low on her chest, even now.

After he was gone, the road became her escape, her therapy. Her sanity. Her tether to that feeling she lost when she lost him. Truth? There were times in the last ten years she'd missed law enforcement and Fentworth, but ice road trucking had been her version of an extended stay at a yoga retreat. An endless quest for a sighting of the aurora borealis. Bunking in a different town in Canada or the Dakotas every night if she bunked at all. Leaving all of the garbage inside her out there on the asphalt. Isolated from causing herself new problems.

Aloud, she said, "Enough. This place is a mausoleum. A damn memory crypt."

She rinsed the glass and put it on the drying rack a little too hard. The glass broke. "Crap." The break was clean, at least, and she picked up the pieces and tossed them in the trash. Her hand came away crimson, sliced open. "Double crap." She dabbed it with a brown paper towel and examined her wound. A glorified paper cut. She wrapped the paper towel around it.

Her phone buzzed. A text. She dug her phone out of her purse.

Chad. Her ex. *I miss you. I'm sorry. It's only because I love you so much. It will never happen again. Let me make it up to you, please.*

Sorry? That was funny. She stuffed the phone away without answering him. When she broke up with him, she thought he'd taken it well. Until she'd stood to hug him goodbye and walked right into his sucker punch. She was well trained to fight back. Skilled, and fit. It didn't hurt that she was also tougher than a rhino, or so her daddy used to tell her. She could best almost anyone in a fair fight, if it came to it, or outdrive them if she needed to run. But Chad had always fought dirty. She was the one who was sorry. Sorry she hadn't seen it coming.

She threw away the bloody paper towel. Her keys were in her pocket. Shelly was in the parking lot. Kateena was at school. The bar was empty. No one would miss her. She raised the bar flap, slipped through, and let it slam down behind her. "I'm outta here."

The *click-click-click-click* of toenails on hardwood reminded her she wasn't alone. *Dudley.* Kateena's French bull-dog. He had the look of a tuxedo-clad Regency gentleman, the attitude of a portly prize fighter, and sounded like the unfortunate mating of a pig and a chainsaw. He was also a trouble-maker who required supervision twenty-four-seven, so when Kateena was at school, that was Delaney's job.

She sighed. "Come on, Duds."

The dog grunted.

"Laney? Can I ask you something?" A woman's voice surprised her. The front door hinges were a little too well greased, apparently.

Delaney shot the woman a side glance. Long brown hair teased high over the crown. Thick eyeliner. Ten pounds of bling on the pockets of her jeans. One of the bartenders. Delaney couldn't remember the woman's name. She'd taken time off smack in the middle of Delaney's homecoming, so they'd barely met each other.

And she'd called her Laney. Delaney had dropped her childhood moniker the minute she'd left Kearny. "Sure. And it's Delaney, actually. Can you remind me of your name? Things have been a little frenzied—my brain isn't holding on to all the details."

"Sorry. Your brother called you Laney. I'm Mary Galvez." The woman stuck out her hand to shake.

"No problem." It was awkward, but Delaney turned back from making her exit and shook, arm long, smiling but keeping her distance.

"Your brother never worked out front." Mary let go of Delaney's hand and started picking at her own nails.

Delaney shrugged, sighed. "I had to tend bar in place of the no-show guy I'm going to fire."

Mary frowned. "He's never been reliable." She looked away.

Delaney followed Mary's gaze around the space that had once been a thriving watering hole. High ceilings. Empty tables. Stacks of cardboard and pallets left over from bottle delivery. An odor like sweaty jockstraps, stale beer, and neglect. Delaney's time in Kearny so far had been filled with moving and her niece. She couldn't afford help cleaning the place up, even if she would have been able to find the warm bodies to do it. With the influx of wealthy out-of-staters driving up property values, employers couldn't pay enough to fund housing for their workers. It was bad here and getting worse, with even the places that remained open chronically underemployed. There were fewer working folks around to frequent local hangouts like the Loafing Shed, too, which meant businesses losing revenue. Where would it end? Jackson's Target had closed for lack of staff. Not that Delaney wanted a Target. Give her the old Moms and Pops any day. *Like the Loafing Shed.*

When Mary let the silence stretch without an ask, Delaney prompted her. "So, what can I do for you?"

Mary made direct eye contact. "I wanted to see if I could pick up some extra shifts. My ex owes me a bundle in child support, and I could really use the money."

Delaney didn't have work to offer, unless she did fire the guy who'd skipped his shift. "I'll take a look at the schedule when I get back. I was just on my way out to, uh, run by Kateena's school." A lie. She needed to get in her car and test the sound barrier before she picked her niece up.

"I'll stay and cover for you now if you want. And, hey, nice pedicure."

Delaney nodded, glancing down at her sandals. Fire-engine red polish her father would have called war paint. A gold anklet with a dangling cross her mom had given her. Today Delaney was rocking a little heel, too. Her lifestyle had never lent itself to manicures or even clean hands. She compensated. "That would be great. Thanks."

And then she bolted out the back door, Dudley snorting and huffing behind her.

Shelly was parked in the afternoon shade of the building. Delaney ran her hand over the beautiful hood, bought and paid for by her ice road trucking savings.

The spend had been worth it. The car looked like new. Or Delaney thought it did. She hadn't been alive in 1969 when Grandpa Pace bought it. Its early days had been documented in faded Polaroids, and after Delaney replaced the hood, she'd recreated the original paint job. The only thing she hadn't been able to match from those pictures was the license plate, which was currently North Dakota and had been Wyoming back in the day, and now would be again soon.

And my niece thinks I am super cool when I drop her off at school in it.

"Am I ever glad to see you, Shelly," she said.

She opened the door and let Dudley hop over onto the passenger seat, then slipped behind the wheel. As always, the sense of her father's presence surrounded her like a warm hug. A familiar pain welled up and through her chest, but she didn't yield to it. The engine roared to life at the turn of the key, like the car had been waiting for her. The stereo pumped out a generic pop-country song from the radio. She pushed an eight-track tape into the player, one of the elements she'd left vintage. Luke Bryan's voice was replaced by Brian Johnson sing-screeching "You Shook Me All Night Long." The AC/DC *Back in Black* album. Her father's jam.

The she pulled down her visor and ran her finger across a photograph behind plastic. Eighteen wheels of black beauty on ice, back-dropped by high-piled snow. Her rig, a black 2006 Kenworth W9 with *Gabrielle* stenciled in a lacy script on its door, pulling a trailer loaded with explosives bound for the diamond mines of Canada's Northwest Territories.

She checked the time on a tiny dash clock, the old-fashioned kind with actual hands. Only two hours until she'd need to pick up Kateena from school. On time. Because she'd discovered on day one that schools and nieces frown on lateness. She shifted into gear. Gravel spun from under the wheels as she accelerated out of the lot, careful not to overdo it and damage the undercarriage. She turned onto the highway without a blinker. The late May sun had burned the chill off the air, but it was too nippy for the windows to be down.

Dudley woofed. He was standing with his feet on the armrest, staring out the window.

"Get in the back, dog."

He shot her an insolent look.

Delaney used the voice her grandmother had used on her during her pre-teen years. "Dudley Pace, get in the back seat right now."

Dudley slunk to the back. He circled three times before plopping down on the seat.

Delaney drove on, the road rising and falling on a serpentine path through grassland segmented by stands of trees, creeks, and enormous outcroppings. She enjoyed the mile to town from the Loafing Shed this time of year, driving Kateena to and from school. A memory arose. Running out of gas on the side of the road in Shelly, age twelve. Then Deputy Fentworth finding her and taking her to Buns in the Barn for a burger, a milkshake, and a gentle lecture about underage drivers who sneak out cars. *Don't get soft about Fentworth.*

She refocused on her surroundings. Even though the area was generally arid, the spring grass was mid-calf height and green. Canada geese and sandhill cranes flocked in the fields, intermingling with grazing deer and pronghorn antelope still fuzzy from winter. The dark outline of snow-crowned mountains loomed thousands of feet above, calling to her. The only road up into them was on the other side of Kearny, the town a stockade to her sanctuary. She wanted to be there now. Five minutes ago. Yesterday.

She drummed her fingers, slowed to thirty, eased through traffic lights, and braked behind turning drivers. Passing Kateena's school on the far side of town, she reduced her speed to twenty and scanned the surroundings. It was bare of kids.

Not bare of traffic, though. An old Chevy pickup that looked like most of the beaters in the area—old on the outside but usually meticulously cared for where it counted and jacked up a few extra inches for winter—burned rubber on a side street next to the school. *The road to the storage unit where Gabrielle sleeps.* The truck, carrying a four-wheeler in the back, plowed into the road in front of Delaney. She slammed on her brakes to avoid a crash. The pickup swerved onto the shoulder and fishtailed. When it regained traction, it sped up. Gravel from the shoulder of the road sprayed from its tires, peppering Shelly's new hood and windshield.

"Uh-uh. No way," Delaney shouted, throwing up an arm in a reflexive move to shield herself from the barrage.

Dudley yipped. She checked him in the rearview mirror. The dramatic dog was fine.

Thoughts pinballed in her brain. *Nobody's gonna get away with messing up Shelly.* And *so close to the school—what if Kateena or another kid had been running across the road?* Then *Kids, old folks, animals—that driver's an out-of-control menace to the town.*

And finally, *I picked up a badge today.*

True, she wasn't official until the next morning, but as a trained and experienced law enforcement officer, even an out-of-practice one, she couldn't ignore this. She had a responsibility to her community. An ethical one.

Ethics always won, in Delaney's world.

The pickup had pulled away from her. A Silverado. Bronze two-tone. Short bed with handrails. A vague impression that the dirty plate looked to be from Wyoming. She didn't have a description of the driver. She didn't even know gender. Race. Age. Basically, nothing.

She checked the road ahead and around her for other cars and pedestrians. Clear. Time to close the gap between the vehicles.

She accelerated. "Hold on, Duds."

She needed to call this in to the city police, who shared facilities and some services with the sheriff's department, like 911. She cut her eyes to the seat beside her. No purse. She groaned. Remembered putting the badge and the phone in it, inside the bar. Leaving in a hurry without it, satisfied that her keys were in her pocket. She looked one more time, risking a slightly longer glance. Maybe she'd forgotten putting her phone in the car? Dudley could have knocked it to the floorboard.

Nope. There wasn't a darn thing in here besides her worthless self and an equally worthless dog. And she was exceeding the speed limit without a license on the same day she'd signed back on with the sheriff's department. *Go, me.*

Shelly's engine growled louder. They gained ground on the Chevy. Biting her lip, Delaney weighed up her options. She could let the dangerous motorist go. *Not happening.* She could pass the truck, get a plate and a description of the driver, then head back to the school and call the cops from there. *At a minimum.* Or, after she got the info, she could attempt to slow the truck and if she wasn't successful, she could follow it and make a citizen's arrest. *Maybe overkill?* But if Kateena and her friends had been outside, they could have been hurt. *I have to at least try to stop this truck before it causes damage.*

With her mind made up, the accelerator mashed down almost of its own accord. Chasing down a lead-foot driver, she knew she had the advantage, especially on her home turf. These were the roads she'd cut her driving teeth on, in this same car.

Dudley poked his head between the seats.

"Back," she commanded.

He ignored her. She ignored him. *Kateena and the mutt are headed for obedience training.*

Shelly flowed along the road, through cottonwoods, aspens, and pines, around the curves, and onto a straightaway as they left the valley and creek bottom behind—always the anchor for small Wyoming towns—and headed toward the mountains through terrain that only appeared barren and flat. A closer look would reveal rugged gulches teeming with wildlife, snow melt run-off, and lush vegetation. But she didn't have time for a closer look. Shelly was bearing down on the truck at one hundred miles per hour—*how is that piece of junk making this speed?*

She drew close enough that she should have been able to read the Wyoming license plate but was foiled by thick spring mud. There were no other vehicles in sight. This was the time and place for Delaney to make her move.

"Let the horses run, Shelly."

The Chevelle surged forward, and Delaney eased into the oncoming traffic lane. When she was alongside the pickup, she slowed to pace it. The driver didn't so much as glance her way. She pointed at the roadside, hoping he'd look over and see that she wanted him to pull over. When he didn't react, she made a "down" motion with her palm and said, "slow down" several times to no one, since he was pretending she wasn't there.

Dudley growled. *My thoughts exactly.*

She made mental notes about his appearance. *Light-skinned Caucasian. Maybe late-thirties. No expression. No facial hair. Wraparound sunglasses. Baseball cap pulled low with gray hoodie over it, obscuring part of his cheeks and all of his hair. Mouth closed, no look at his teeth. No marks, birth or otherwise. No visible scars or tattoos.*

Completely forgettable.

The man lifted his middle finger, eyes still on the road. *Small hands.*

"Mr. Friendly."

Delaney asked the Chevelle for a little more speed. The car responded, and she maneuvered in front of the truck, preserving a safe following distance behind her. The last thing she wanted was damage to her vehicle, so she turned on her emergency flashers, too. Then she slowed her speed to eighty-five, eyes glued to the rearview. This probably wouldn't work, and she had to be ready to get out of his way if he threatened Shelly.

The truck flashed its lights, then the horn sounded in a continuous blast.

"Doesn't appear he's in a cooperative mood."

She throttled back another five miles per hour. Down to eighty. *Is he the ramming type?*

The horn stopped. The truck jerked to the left so violently that for a moment she worried it would flip. It recovered and sped up in the oncoming traffic lane. Delaney's eyes moved like a metronome from the road in front of her, to possible wildlife or vehicle hazards coming from the sides of it, to the truck behind her. Tick. Tick. Tick. Trees closed in on the road. Soon, the pavement would end and continue as gravel for the climb into the mountains. The truck would have the advantage on the rougher surface.

The pickup increased its speed.

Trying to coax him to stop hadn't worked. Following was now the better option. She decreased her speed. The truck rocketed past, engine straining. With inches to spare, it cut in front of her.

She stepped on the brake. "Jack wipe."

For a few seconds, she gave the driver time to break away. Then she matched his speed, pacing him from fifty feet behind. Her speedometer read one hundred again by the time Shelly's tires crossed from pavement to gravel. The chassis shimmied. The engine rumbled in protest at the change in incline. The washboard surface gave the tires and shocks a workout.

"Steady, girl."

Her heart thrummed. The truck didn't slow down. A smile pulled up the corners of her lips. Just because it was her duty to stop this guy didn't mean it couldn't be fun, too.

A *whoop-whoop* sounded behind her, nearly drowned out by the road and engine noise. She checked her side view, knowing what she'd find there. A Kearny County Sheriff's Department pickup, lights wig-wagging, right on her tail.

Delaney smacked the steering wheel. She didn't need this. But maybe the pickup was the deputy's target. She could slow down and let the fuzz fly on by. She pulled slightly to the right and removed her foot from the gas pedal. "Come on, buddy. Go catch the bigger fish."

Her ploy didn't work. The KCSD truck rode in behind Shelly's back bumper and stayed there. When Delaney kept coasting forward, the sirens started. Dudley barked in rhythm with the pulsing noise.

"Insult to injury." Delaney didn't have a choice. Hopefully, this would be someone from KCSD she'd worked with years ago. If she handled it quickly, the erratic driver wouldn't escape. She could give her information about the truck directly to the deputy. Let the law deal with the jerk.

She stopped in the grass, leaving plenty of room for other vehicles to pass in both directions. The truck pulled up, still putting on a light show. Delaney looked at the empty passenger seat again, where her purse should have been. She sighed. *Great.* In her side view, a uniformed deputy approached. He didn't seem familiar. She cranked down her window.

His voice was terse. "Do you have any weapons on you?"

Dudley amped up his barking.

"No, but I—"

"Exit the vehicle and keep your hands where I can see them."

The truck is getting away. But there's nothing I can do about it without creating an incident. She reached for her handle and opened the door, mulling his voice as he backed away from her. There was something in his accent. For sure not Wyoming. She thought she recognized west coast, from long hauls she'd made out there. It made sense. The influx of people from that area invading her home state lately was continuous. She was seeing it all over the country, though. Big city dwellers, especially coastal, relocating to smaller towns, a slower pace, and cheaper lifestyles.

So, how was this one going to react to her? She ticked off her transgressions. More than fifty miles an hour over the speed limit. No license with her. A vehicle registered outside Wyoming. If he was an out-of-towner, he wouldn't know her past or present. He wouldn't understand the small-town credos the locals lived by. Live and let live. Don't tread on me.

She exited, hands in front of her shoulders, palms facing him. Dudley leaped out the open door.

"Dudley! No!" She caught the dog before he hit the ground and shut him back in the car.

He continued his complaints from the front seat. If he wanted out badly enough, he could still jump through the window, so she blocked it with her body and turned to the wary deputy.

Now that she saw him up close, she was sure they'd never met. He'd be hard to forget. He had a beard like most of the guys in the state, but his salt and pepper fuzz accented sculpted cheekbones, a nose that had never been broken by an ornery steer, and eyes moraine blue. Rough like he meant to be but pretty like he couldn't help it. He turned away for a moment to speak into his radio. She exhaled softly, waiting.

"Control your dog. Turn around. Put your hands on top of the car. Stand with your feet spread," he said.

One of those things is next to impossible. The deputy sounded pissed. And it was about to get worse.

THREE

Leo's pulse raced. Day one with KCSD. Day one as a deputy, for that matter, although he'd logged nearly fifteen years between special operations for the Coast Guard and as an undercover cop in Narcotics in San Diego. He'd expected Kearny to be boring, but this high-speed traffic stop had gotten his pulse up. A late 60s or early 70s muscle car, with two thick white racing stripes over the hood and North Dakota plates, burning up a gravel road.

And the driver. A woman. Not just *a* woman. An extraordinary woman, and he'd seen a lot of them in California. He rubbed his beard, staring at her. Scratched at his short beard, really. Wished he hadn't been forced to grow it out when he was sent on this assignment. "To fit in," he'd been told. Why did men here do this to themselves? On the west coast, he'd been clean-shaven. His face tanned evenly. His skin was smooth and never itched. He'd worked out and jogged along the beach, swam and surfed in the ocean waves. Nature and humans had coexisted there without the need to sprout three inches of protective facial hair.

Get over it, Palmer.

Back to the woman. The face. Green peepers—glowing cat's eyes—which she fastened on him like he was prey. Light brown braids with streaks like lightning. A tall, lithe bod. Tight jeans and sexy red painted toenails peeping from her shoes.

A mountain lion, ready to pounce.

And she was about to be under arrest for driving like a psychopath. Pulling her over had probably saved her from dying in a fiery crash. Or, if his suspicions were correct about the person driving the truck she was chasing, in a domestic dispute.

She ignored his instructions and took a step away from the car. "Listen, this is all a misunderstanding. I need to explain. The man in that truck. I was—"

He blocked her path. "You heard me. Turn around, hands on the roof, feet apart." He could barely hear himself over the barking dog. The thing was a little terrorist.

Her glare was insolent and penetrating, but she did as she was told.

"I'm going to check you for weapons." He patted her down quickly. *Think about baseball, think about baseball.* No weapons. He backed up. "All right. You can turn back around, but no sudden movements."

She turned. *Those eyes.* "I'm Delaney Pace. I grew up here, but I only just came back. I work for the—"

He wasn't falling for some half-baked excuse from a femme fatale. This one would be by the book. Going off script had been his downfall in the past. "License and insurance, please."

Her eyes narrowed, lips thinned. "Fine. But I left the bar without my purse. I don't have any ID with me."

The bar? *Great.* A day-drinker behind the wheel. She was an even greater hazard than he'd thought. She didn't seem wasted, but some people hid it well. And the lack of her ID bolstered his theory that she'd taken off after the truck in a big hurry. Probably caught the guy in a bathroom stall with another woman, the way she was hell-bent on catching him. *What man in his right mind would cheat on this woman, though?* "Delaney Pace, you're under arrest. Please face away and put your hands behind your back."

Her voice was a hiss. "You'd better be effing kidding me."

The dog took it up a notch.

Leo wouldn't have thought that was possible. "I'm not."

"But the sheriff can vouch for me. I—"

"Save it for him, then."

"Deputy, you don't understand. I was chasing a reckless driver. He's getting away."

"Now, Ms. Pace."

She scowled. "Show me some ID first."

"Besides my truck and badge?" He tapped the metal on his chest. "I'm a deputy with the Kearny County Sheriff's Department." He tapped his badge.

"Name?"

"Leo Palmer."

"Great. Nice to meet you." Her voice dripped sarcasm. Then she lowered it to a mutter. "But before all this they will lay their hands on you and persecute you."

Has she lost her mind? "What did you say?"

"Luke 21:12."

A holy roller. He used to get accosted by them when he was undercover on the streets. They even worked the beaches, following the smell of marijuana to find marks to preach to.

She rotated and put her wrists behind her, still muttering unintelligibly and staring up at the mountains. He got the impression she'd segued from religion to his manhood and IQ. He had no reason to think she was violent, but if she wanted to resist arrest, there wasn't much he could do except tase her until he got her cuffed. His pat down had revealed muscles that were impressive without being masculine. And she gave off an electricity. The panther thing, he guessed. Leo wasn't a slouch. He lifted. He was in shape. He'd had combat training. But something about this Delaney Pace set off warnings inside him. He wished he had back-up.

Just do it and do it fast.

He slipped the cuffs around her wrists and clamped them shut. He noticed one of her hands was bloody. Defensive injury? Also consistent with a domestic.

"You've forgotten something."

That stung. Getting the details right had always been key to his success. He frowned. "What's that?"

"What are you arresting me for?"

Oh, that. "Reckless driving. Speeding. Driving without a license. Suspicion of impaired driving."

"Give me a sobriety test."

"I will. When we get to the sheriff's department."

"Fine. But did you not see the truck in front of me driving even faster than I was? The driver I was trying to stop before he hurt somebody?"

Irrelevant. But, again, his theory about a domestic dispute was feeling right. She was trying to get the guy in trouble. "I couldn't take you both at once. You were breaking the law." And she was the last in line and the one with out-of-state plates. North Dakota. Did people actually live there? He tried to picture where it was on a map. He hadn't known where Wyoming was before he was sent here.

"Deputy What's-your-face, I'll tell you one last time. You're making a huge mistake."

He shook his head. Implied threats wouldn't sway him either. "I clocked you going over a hundred in a forty-five. No mistake there."

She snorted. "You can't see the forest for the trees."

Whatever that means. "Let's go." He pointed at his vehicle.

"I'm not leaving Dudley or Shelly here."

"Who?" Was there a second dog? Or a kid in the car?

"My niece's dog. And my very valuable car."

He couldn't leave a dog on the side of the road in a car. Animal rights activists would run him out of town. He had to succeed here. "We'll bring the dog."

"That's a start. Could you send someone to pick up my car? My niece needs a ride home from school, too. And I want to speak to the sheriff, ASAP."

Why are the best-looking ones always the craziest? He didn't bother to hide his derision. "I'll get right on that, Ms. Pace."

FOUR

Jubey Smith was gassed. He'd gotten a late start from town—tourists renting bicycles right before closing time without calling ahead. Then he'd flatted and had to change a tire. He wanted to set up camp before sundown. So, he'd pushed harder on the ascent into the mountains than he usually did.

He stood up in the pedals for another incline, this one from the forest road onto the trail that would take him to his favorite site for sky-watching: Cliffside, with Kearny far enough below that it wouldn't interfere with the strawberry moon expected tonight. His wife, a nurse, usually came with him, but she had a night shift to work. He'd miss her, but it was still going to be cool.

He chanted with the rhythm of his pedal stroke. "Pick it up. Pick it up. Pick it up."

The trail was new, but he knew it well, as he'd consulted on the design. The entire path ran through the Bighorn National Forest. Built with mountain bikers in mind, hikers used it, too. It was wide enough for two bikes to pass safely, had bitchin' rollers, and featured some gnarly terrain and chutes, the best of which wound through a rocky hilltop that was like a maze.

Right now, though, what he liked about it best was the forgiving grade and switchbacks. *My quads are still on fire.* The length so far was four miles one-way—an out and back—but this summer their community land grant foundation was extending it. They had big plans. If they succeeded in them, they could turn Kearny into a mountain biking mecca.

Jubey forgot his heavy breathing and quads as he imagined giving competition to Colorado's Leadville 100. Then he noticed the four-wheeler tracks in the dirt. Dirt that he had helped shape. Back-breaking rock removal. Shoveling in blistering sun and sculpting to get the banks just so. In fact, he'd discovered his sky-watching spot the summer before during construction, only about one hundred yards off-trail. Motorized vehicles were strictly forbidden, and there was a large sign reminding visitors of this critical fact at its head. Motorbikes and ORVs could destroy their hard work. He navigated a switchback. Wide, aggressive four-wheeler tracks had torn into the bank. The soil above the track had caved in on it.

"Son of a bitch!" he shouted.

All thoughts of camp, the strawberry moon and view, the shish kebabs he'd constructed to cook over the flame of his mini propane stove, and the six-pack of beer were gone. He wasn't a big guy, but he was pissed, and he was scrappy. When he found the four-wheeler, he was giving someone a piece of his mind. And he was taking down the plate number. This would be reported to Kearny County and the National Forest Service.

Legs pumping, lungs searing, he rode as fast as he could, noting additional damage every few yards that stoked his rage. The tracks were easy to follow, ripping through mud and snowy sections. He sped through another switchback above a rock formation and into the forest. Just as he passed his turn off-road, he saw a four-wheeler ahead, parked in snow with two wheels off-trail.

He stopped so fast that his back wheel slid out to the left.

He dropped his bike in the middle of the trail and was running before it hit the dirt.

He shouted. "Hey, man, is this your four-wheeler?" He tried to sound less angry than he felt. He wanted to talk to this jerk, not scare him into hiding.

No one answered. He heard something, though, from the direction of his secret camp site. Footsteps? Breaking twigs? A big animal moving through the woods? It could be a deer. Or any of the other game that roamed the area. Elk. Moose. Bear. There were others, but they were stealthier. Mountain lion. The wolves that had recently moved into the area from western Wyoming.

His money was on a human, though.

He doubled back to the cut where he would have taken his bike, if not for the four-wheeler. Despite his labored breaths, he jogged. "Where are you, dude?" Huff. Huff. "I just want to talk to you."

The sun was sinking behind the peaks to the west. The eastern side of the mountains grew dark early. He stumbled. *Dammit. I'm going to be setting up in pitch dark.* A log loomed ahead of him. He'd have to go wide to get around it. Stopping to catch his breath, he listened for the human sounds. Nothing.

He trotted forward again, toward the log. Just as he was about to skirt it, he noticed the coloring. Dark, but also red. And the shape was odd. Did it have a split trunk?

And then the horrible reality became clear, like a macabre Rorschach test. It was a woman. A Black woman, totally nude, and covered in blood.

"No," he said. "No."

He'd stopped without realizing it. He forced himself forward, toward her. Had she been attacked by an animal? His eyes cut back and forth, searching for predators, until common sense took over. *Animals don't take people's clothes off.*

"No," he whispered.

The woman's eyes were closed. *She could be alive.* But something was horribly wrong with her midsection. *Her insides are on the outside.* His stomach heaved. He turned to the side. Vomited. Wiped his mouth.

He swallowed and licked his lips. "Ma'am, can you hear me?"

She didn't speak.

He moved to her side and knelt. There was almost no part of her that wasn't bloody. He lifted her wrist. His hands were trembling. He knew CPR. How to take a pulse. How to render first aid to cuts, burns, insect bites, and broken bones. But his heart was thrumming so hard and fast, he couldn't tell what was him and what was her.

"Calm down, Smith. Calm your shit *down.*"

He closed his eyes and tried again. Long seconds passed until he was sure. Her heart was not beating.

He put his hand below her nostrils and just above her mouth. Watched her chest. She wasn't breathing.

He heard a wailing noise. He jumped to his feet. *What is that?* But he didn't want to find out. He started running, back to the trail. Someone had killed her. He had to get out of here. He had to call 911. The nearest phone signal was three miles away, at the top of the mountain face. A spot that locals called the telephone booth because people went there to check their phones without having to leave the mountains.

And then he was flying forward. Falling. Landing, face first.

FIVE

Delaney sighed and rotated her neck, mulling her predicament and location. Booking—which was where Leo had parked her. The area wasn't cozy. Gray cinderblock walls that matched a gray concrete floor. Heavy metal doors. Ceiling tiles and fluorescent lights. No phone call. No water. No food. No coat, no blanket. And, after she finished here, she was facing jail for who knew how long. At least Leo had called Mary to pick up Kateena and Dudley. Delaney hadn't known who else to turn to. The bartender had agreed to let dog and girl spend the night if necessary. Delaney vowed to empty her wallet for this favor. Kateena was going to be pissed, though. They'd had plans to hole up and stream *Heartland* together until they fell asleep in front of the TV. Maybe Delaney still had a chance if booking moved fast, and she talked to the sheriff soon. He'd release her.

Kateena. What a horrible role model Delaney was. In jail, forced to send a bartender she barely knew to pick the girl up from school. She could tell herself it was because she'd been attempting to stop a reckless driver, but who's to say she wouldn't have been driving that same speed anyway? Just not in town in front of a school like the other guy had.

She had to do better. This wasn't only about her anymore.

The metal chair in the booking area was colder than her grandmother's heart. And that was saying something, given that Grandma Pace made the North Pole seem balmy. Once, she'd overheard her dad and grandmother fighting, and he'd accused her of freezing out Delaney's mom. Said his own mother was the reason his wife wouldn't stick around. Delaney banished the thought of her mother from her mind. She just wished she'd dressed warmer. She only had the clothes she'd been wearing when she left the Loafing Shed. Jeans, sandals, and a short-sleeved T-shirt with her medallion pendant hanging beneath it. She crossed an ankle over a knee and rubbed her foot for warmth, rattling her handcuffs and jostling her anklet cross. She eyed the cut on her hand. It stung, but it didn't look infected.

She leaned forward, watching a female detention officer seating and cuffing a male detainee who had arrived before her and just completed his glamour shot. The deputy's nametag read "Jones." She was tall and spare, with hair Marine-recruit short and a harried air. Jones returned to a computer at a desk in a row of two.

The large man was sitting similarly to Delaney except he was stripped down to his boxers. Gravity hadn't been kind to him, although he couldn't have been more than five or ten years older than her. She tucked her face into her shoulder to escape the stench of vomit clinging to him, striving for empathy. He was probably as cold as she was. Scratch that. He had a lot more personal insulation around his middle to keep him warm.

Jones was typing. "Skeeter Rawlins, as a frequent flyer, I have your information memorized."

"That's good," he said.

She gave him a sardonic smile. "Not really. Drunk and disorderly. Again."

"The disorderly's bullshit."

"Of course."

Delaney's stomach growled. It had been nearly twelve hours since she'd shoveled in hash browns and sausage straight from the pan at breakfast before hopping in Shelly to take Kateena to school. It seemed forever ago. Was the car safe? By and large, Wyoming wasn't a state known for car theft or stripping vehicles for parts. But who knew with all the new people moving in lately? Everything was changing.

"Hey," Delaney said. "How long is this going to take?"

Skeeter seemed to notice her for the first time and answered before Jones. "You a virgin?"

Delaney had worked for the county, but that wasn't her only experience with booking. She'd done a stint in jail in Mandan, North Dakota three years before. A watering hole outside of town frequented by truckers. A guy who wouldn't take no for an answer made one too many disgusting suggestions in her ear, the last one accompanied by his tongue. Instinct took over, and she swung her full beer bottle up and back, connecting with his face. Never mind that his tongue was sexual assault, his injuries—three surgeries later he'd been restored to his previous state of ugliness—resulted in her being taken in by a sheriff whose name she'd never forget. Crispin Allen. She was charged and spent two nights in the slammer. After hearing her story, the judge had declined to sock her with anything beyond a misdemeanor and the minimum fine in return for her guilty plea. But that incident had occurred on a busy Friday night. Law enforcement types had been in and out twenty-four-seven. The cells had been crowded. Today's arrest had been on a Thursday afternoon, in Kearny. Not exactly rush hour in a crime hub. More of a sleepy village compared to Mandan, even though the two towns were roughly the same population.

So, was she a virgin? Not in any way, shape, or form, not that she owed or would give him an answer.

"Just wondering." His voice was gravelly. "It's not so bad.

And they feed us the good breakfast sandwiches from Buns in the Barn." *A regular.*

"I'll get to you as fast as I can," Jones said to Delaney, not pausing her typing. "My co-worker is indisposed." She muttered under her breath. "If that's what cheating on me is called."

Uh-oh, dating on the job. Delaney closed her eyes. Imagined the hum of low-pressure tires spinning across ice at fifteen miles per hour. Could feel the cold of minus sixty degrees pressing against the window. How odd that in a profession where she couldn't lose her focus for more than a second at a time, the memory of it could soothe her like nothing else could.

"I said, what are you in for?" the man's voice boomed.

Delaney jerked out of a doze. "I drove too fast."

"I didn't think that was a federal crime."

Technically, it wasn't, and they were in county lockup, but she withheld the explanation.

"Name's Skeeter."

"So I heard. As in a skeet shooter?"

"As in a mosquiter. On account of how I used to make people itchy."

She considered asking what he meant, then decided nothing good could come of it. Wondered if he bit. *Ew.*

"Yours?"

Jones looked up from her computer. "Clearly we don't need to fingerprint you, Skeeter. What am I gonna find when I pull your records? Have you been misbehaving anywhere besides Kearny County?"

"No, ma'am," he said, fingers up like a boy scout.

Delaney asked him, "Where do you do your drinking?"

"Piece of shit bar. You've probably never heard of it."

"Try me."

"The Loading Shed. I do some of my best work there."

The Loafing *Shed. Doesn't anybody call it by its correct name?* "What do you do when you're neither drunk nor disorderly, Mr. Skeeter?"

"Just drunk." He sat up straight, pulling his belly off his thighs. "I'm a private investigator."

Jones snorted.

"Here? In Kearny?"

"Based here. But I go where the work is."

"You make any money at it?"

"Enough."

Enough to fund his drinking. And the bar. It wasn't like the place had a lot of paying customers. She assumed he paid, anyway. It was already a long night, and morning was hours away, if they held her over. *And I start my new-old job tomorrow.* The first thing she was going to do was give Deputy Palmer a piece of her mind. She humored Skeeter, amused by him. "How'd you become a PI?"

"Got hurt. Couldn't work out in the oil fields anymore. Met an old boy who was on a job. He told me that in Wyoming there are no licensing or training requirements for PIs. If you want to be one, you are one. I figured I was qualified to do that. Got some cards made up. Listed the business in a few places. Called it WYO Investigations." He grinned, proud of his originality, she guessed. "Started landing a few odds-and-ends jobs."

A phone rang. Jones said, "Shit," then, "This is Jones."

Delaney asked Skeeter, "Like what?"

"Domestics. Chasing down deadbeats and runaways. Gathering evidence in divorces. Mostly video." He said it "vi-dee-oooooooh" with a leer and a head bob.

Jones moved across the room, away from her charges. She curved like a C into her phone.

Delaney straightened and shifted her cuffed hands. Her fingers felt sticky after contact with the chair arm. She wanted to push hair out of her eyes, but maybe it was best she couldn't.

Her fingers might superglue to it with bodily fluids left behind by the last occupant.

"I told you about me." Skeeter said. "What's your name?"

"Delaney Pace."

"Pace—are you Liam's kid sister who just came back to town?"

That got her attention. An image flashed in her mind. Liam propelling himself off a cliff into the cold waters of Tie Flume Reservoir, his tanned, muscular body flying through the impossibly blue Wyoming sky. Her, arms wrapped around her shivering torso in a purple one-piece with bright red polka dots, watching nervously for him to reappear. Long seconds passing. Then, his head popping up out of the dark water. "Come on. You can do it. I'll be right here waiting for you," he'd shouted, grinning. Of course, she'd jumped, even as terrified as she was. And he had been there, that time. *RIP, big brother. I'm sorry for everything.*

Enough of that.

"Why do you ask? Are you a friend of his?"

Skeeter lowered his voice. "I've heard of you."

"From?"

He shrugged. "People. They say you're coming back to take over his businesses."

"For now. Everything's for sale if you know anyone who might be interested." *Because what better place to market the sale of the businesses than to a drunk in jail?*

"I've also heard that you're some kind of freaky badass driver."

"Not freaky."

Jones said, "Just get back in here and do your job or I'll report you, asshole." She straightened and put her phone in her pocket.

Skeeter added, "And that you witnessed your own father's murder."

Delaney stared back at him, eyes slits, not deigning to answer. Did he think it was okay for a stranger to just say that to her? That she'd want to give him the inside story?

He got the message. "Listen, I didn't mean to upset you. I just have a reason for bringing it up."

"I can't think of a good one."

"I thought you'd want to know what people say about him." He winked.

Delaney nodded. She did. She definitely did.

Skeeter's chest expanded. "Well, they say—"

Jones walked over, interrupting him, her cheeks slap-red. "Sorry about that. Let's go." She slid a key into Skeeter's cuffs, releasing them from the chair arm.

He stood and turned his back to Jones.

"What were you going to say?" Delaney asked.

"He's going to say bye-bye, now." Jones recuffed his hands behind him. Then she wiped one hand on her pants and held Skeeter with the other. "You sobered up yet? Feeling okay?"

Delaney growled softly.

He threw his hands up. "I'm fine. I was barely buzzed."

"Your puked-on clothes tell a different story."

"A bad kielbasa, that's all."

"What about me?" Delaney asked. "Maybe you want to just let me go home?" She added a hopeful lilt to her voice.

Jones didn't look her way. "Nice try."

"But I don't have anything to wear." Skeeter's voice was a whine.

"Sure you do. Free, on the county. Come on and we'll get you to Ned to bag your personal items, do your search, and suit you up." The woman gave him a push to lead the way.

He lumbered ahead of her, thighs rubbing together above knock knees, a slight bounce around his waist. His eyes cut back to Delaney. "Nice meeting you. Maybe I'll catch you at the Loading Shed."

"Don't go anywhere, Ms. Pace. I'll be back for you in two minutes," Jones said.

"Great." *As if.* Delaney was mulling the last thing Skeeter had been talking about before Jones had moved him. What had he been about to tell her? And had it been about her dead father or her dead brother?

SIX

Nearly two hours after he'd returned with Delaney Pace and the hell dog, Leo knocked on the frame of the open door to the sheriff's office. While the deputies and cops—the Kearny police department and KCSD shared the building—worked in modern, utilitarian cubicles, this office, the office of the police chief, and the conference rooms were decorated Old West. A hat tree stood inside the door. Ranch relics were interspersed with political photos of the sheriff with various state and local dignitaries. Barbed wire coiled and mounted on wood. A block of similar size with brands burned into it. The branding iron itself. Spurs. Horseshoe art.

Sheriff Coltrane Fentworth stood beside his enormous pine desk, holding a sheaf of papers up close to his face, almost to his handlebar mustache, his head tilt threatening the stability of his ten-or-more gallon hat. He was framed by a picture window view of snow-capped peaks in the distance. Leo caught a whiff of leather and Old Spice.

"You wanted to see me, Palmer?"

"Sheriff." Leo stood in front of his short, wiry boss. "Yes, sir."

"How was your first day on—" Fentworth frowned. "What in God's name are you wearing on your feet?"

Leo rotated his foot for a better view. His Reef Swamis. "Just some casual boots, since I'm off patrol."

"Those are not boots. These are boots." Fentworth pointed at his own feet, clad in cowboy boots. "Those look like they'd melt if you stepped in a puddle."

"They're actually pretty hardy."

"A piece of advice. Wear those at your own peril around here."

Leo raised his eyebrows. Was Wyoming really this backward? "Gotcha."

"Now, have a seat, Palmer. What can I do for you?" Fentworth sank into his own chair.

Leo sat in front of the desk and looked Fentworth in the eye. Literally, in his one eye. The right one. Fentworth wore a patch over the left. "I clocked a car doing a hundred in a forty-five. When I pulled the woman over, she didn't have a license, and she said she'd just come from a bar. I arrested her and took her to booking."

"Was she impaired?"

Leo grimaced. "I tested her for alcohol when we got here. She blew zeroes. Couldn't have been any lower. I don't know about other substances. Besides driving crazy, I didn't see any other signs she was messed up."

"So, what seems to be the issue?"

Leo pulled at the neck of his shirt. "She's demanding to speak to you. And demanding we send someone to pick up her 'very valuable' car. She also demanded someone take her dog home. And pick up her niece from school." He glanced at his phone to check his texts and got the confirmation he sought. "Apparently the niece is taken care of."

"Where's the dog?"

A female voice spoke from the door. "He left Dudley with me."

Leo smiled at Clara, the department admin. He owed her one. "I'm sorry about that."

Freckles galore smiled back at him. The white braid had probably been red, once upon a time. Clara had the look of a woman who spent most of her time outside. Browned arms, no make-up, and pressed blue jeans. She was holding one end of a leash. "Don't be. He's a little charmer."

Dudley was snuffling around the entrance to the office. He grinned up at the sheriff then gave Leo what appeared to be a withering glance. *The feeling is mutual, mutt.*

Clara moved aside. "This is Mary Galvez. She's here for Dudley. Mary, this is Deputy Palmer and Sheriff Fentworth."

The one who picked up the niece, too. The woman beside Clara could have been the kid sister of half the guys he'd met through the Bajeños, the crime syndicate Leo had infiltrated in San Diego. Latina heritage. Short. Curvy. A shy smile. "Sorry to be a bother."

"No bother." The sheriff walked to the door and shook her hand. "Nice to meet you."

Leo followed suit. "Likewise, Ms. Galvez. Thanks for picking up your charges."

"I wondered if I could drop off a purse, too?"

Leo nodded. "Clara, could you add it to the personal belongings of our guest?"

Clara made a kissing sound to the dog. "No problem."

A wraith of a girl in a shocking pink track suit suddenly appeared in the doorway. Her black hair was in fat braided tails on either side of a face with eyes electric with something. Energy? Intelligence? Trouble? "I'm Kateena," she announced, glaring. "You arrested my aunt. Dudley is my dog."

Fentworth cocked his head, studying the girl. "Sorry about that. Kateena, Dudley is a very handsome animal."

She nodded, the glare not wavering.

Clara put a hand on the girl's shoulder. "I'll see Mary and Kateena out. But I'm going to miss Dudley!"

The short-legged dog seemed to trot away a fraction taller at her words.

Leo and the sheriff sat back down.

"The friend seemed normal," the sheriff said. "The kid's cute."

"I'll grant you that. But the woman. She's something else, Sheriff. Gives off a dangerous vibe. Like maybe inside she's a Tasmanian devil." He remembered her quoting scripture to him. *Holy terror, more like it.*

Fentworth adjusted his patch. "Are we talking about Delaney Pace?"

Leo frowned. "How'd you guess? Is she a repeat offender?"

Fentworth sighed. "I recognize the niece and your description of the aunt. When Delaney was teetering on the edge of juvenile delinquency, I took her under my wing to help her manage her understandable rage."

"Did something happen to her?"

"Her father was murdered—knifed to death—right in front of her eyes when she was a little thing. Left her an orphan, since her mother had run off for good by then, not that she was ever around much. Losing their parents really did a number on the kids."

"Kids?"

"Delaney has an older brother. Liam. He and his wife died a month ago when his car crashed into a propane tank."

"Wow." Not an excuse for her actions, but it sounded like she'd been through a hard time.

Fentworth pulled his patch out a few inches and rubbed his eye socket, his other eye closed. "I hired her, back in the day."

"Dang. I'm sorry it was her tonight, then." The sheriff's words took a moment to register. "Wait—you hired her? Like, to weed your garden, or are you talking about her working for the department?"

The sheriff walked to a bookshelf and selected a framed photograph, which he handed to Leo. "I suspect the only reason she took a job here was to find out who killed her dad, but none of us has ever had any luck with that. She was a darn good deputy. Until she got pissed off at me over a difference of opinion ten years ago and walked out. Might have even been the best thing for her, leaving here. But dang, if I didn't miss her. The hell of it was that she was right. But so was I. I think part of her knows it, too."

Leo scrutinized the picture. A younger version of the sheriff with a few deputies, including Delaney. The woman's expression made her look like a porcupine about to plant its quills in the face of an unsuspecting victim. "What was the difference of opinion?"

The sheriff waved off the question. "She came to see me earlier today."

Leo handed the picture back. A cold dread coursed through him. The sheriff had mentored Delaney. More than that. It sounded like he'd been a father figure. And Leo had just arrested her on his first day. He cleared his throat. "She did?"

"I re-hired her. As of tomorrow morning, she's your superior." Fentworth positioned the photo, stepped back, moved it a fraction of an inch, then nodded.

Leo fought to keep the mortification off his face. His lip twitched. "She's... oh. I see. A deputy. Here." *Just shoot me. Shoot me now.*

The sheriff turned to Leo. "A deputy investigator, actually. Let me ask you—did she give you a reason for speeding?"

Leo closed his eyes. "She said she was chasing an erratic driver. But she didn't have her license. I couldn't confirm her identity. None of it fit."

Fentworth pursed his lips as he walked back to his desk

chair. "I don't like what she did. Driving like that in a civilian car out of uniform, she could have caused an accident. But I know Delaney. Her sense of justice is unwavering, even if her methods aren't always what I'd choose. I don't want her charged. Let's leave her in the clink for a few more hours to consider public endangerment." He leaned back in his chair, hands laced behind his neck. "Oh. And have someone go pick up her car. She's right. That Chevelle's a pretty valuable ride."

Frustration had been building and now overflowed from Leo. "Dude, she was breaking the law, and you want me to deliver her car to her?" He cringed. *Dude. How Spicoli of me.* It was hard to wash the vestiges of his last assignment away. His cover with the cartel had been to play up the Southern California stereotype, although his role was as a cyber expert.

"Dude?" Fentworth said in a voice like he'd bitten into something rancid. "Did you just call me *dude?*"

"Say that at my own peril around here?"

"Something like that." The sheriff grinned. "My orders stand. But she seems to have you worked up."

Leo felt heat in his neck, then his cheeks. "She could get under anyone's skin, I'd guess."

"You liked her."

"She leaves an impression."

"And she's beautiful." Fentworth beamed like a proud papa.

Beautiful, yes. But he'd made a horrible first impression, not letting her tell her side of the story, not radioing the sheriff from the scene. He made one last weak attempt to support his judgment. "Bottom line, um, sir, she did the crime. And I looked it up. She has a record."

"Not a felony and not in our county she doesn't. Send her home in her car, Palmer. Everyone deserves a second chance. Like the one I gave you."

Leo's stomach flipped. It was the first time the sheriff had alluded to the less-than-stellar circumstances that had brought

Leo to Kearny and the department. Getting booted off his assignment for attending the quinceañera of a crime boss's daughter. It had been bullshit, but he'd been unable to stop the train that ran him over. And he was sure it was why, although he had more experience than Delaney, the investigator role wasn't his.

The sheriff waved toward the door.

Leo stood to go.

The phone on the sheriff's desk rang. "Sheriff Fentworth." He paused, frowning. "Where?" Then, "On our way, as fast as we can."

Leo waited in the doorway. "What was that about, sir?"

"Let's go spring Delaney. We've got a dead body, and I need her on the case." He winked and pointed at Leo with his thumb raised, then cocked an imaginary pistol hammer. "Time to find out if you two can play nice together."

SEVEN

Rattling keys pulled Delaney out of a slumber. She rubbed her eyes and sat up. Jones was unlocking the cell with Sheriff Coltrane Fentworth—a head shorter—beside her. When she was a girl, Fentworth had reminded her of a frog. A wonderful frog who had hopped in and saved her when her world had fallen apart. Now, a frog holding a cowboy hat covering his midsection from belly to thigh.

His face was a smirk. "Delaney, you're looking no worse for the wear. How were our accommodations?"

"You're doing better than me."

"Any day on the right side of the dirt is a good day."

Or the right side of cell bars. "Didn't you hear I've been asking to talk to you for hours?"

"I wouldn't complain if I were you. You're lucky we're cutting you loose this quickly. The law gives us forty-eight hours to hold you."

"I wouldn't have minded so much if your new deputy had taken me seriously about the lawbreaker I was after."

The door to the cell opened. Jones pulled the keys from the lock and walked away. Deputy Leo Palmer appeared behind

Fentworth. He hadn't gotten any uglier since Delaney had seen him last. The thought galled her.

The sheriff tracked her murderous gaze. His grin put him in line for a throat punch, right after Leo. "Palmer, I believe you and Delaney have already met?"

Leo's face contorted as if looking at her was root canal-level painful. "Ms. Pace."

"Deputy Investigator Pace," she corrected him, trotting out her title like she hadn't been bemoaning it all day.

She stood and walked out the door. "Am I free to go?"

Fentworth pursed his lips. "Not exactly."

"What does that mean?" She put her hands on her hips.

"It means I need my deputy investigator. I've got to go ahead and swear you in. We've got a dead body on the mountain."

Her breathing slowed. A body. Intriguing. And her job. She couldn't argue that she was unavailable as both men knew Kateena and Dudley were cared for. Plus, she couldn't wait to get started taking Leo apart one dainty jaw-chomp at a time. She tried to sound aloof anyway. "Details?"

"Found by a mountain biker less than an hour ago."

It was growing harder to feign disinterest. "Accident? Animal? Natural causes?"

"Murder. Dispatch said the bicyclist told her the victim was carved up pretty good."

Delaney held up her hand to take the oath, abandoning her attitude. This is what she'd signed up for. Again. And damn, if it didn't feel a little bit good. "What are you waiting for, Fentworth?"

"That's Sheriff Fentworth to you, Deputy Investigator Pace."

She rolled her other hand in the "get on with it" motion. Fentworth recited the words, and Delaney swore her allegiance and agreement in all the right places, aware of Leo's eyes locked on her as she spoke.

As soon as Fentworth finished, she started walking away. At the end of the hall, she turned to the two men. "Are you coming or not?"

She didn't wait around to find out.

EIGHT

Leo was feeling the rapid change in altitude from desk to mountain trail in half an hour. Being fresh off sea level didn't help either. Literally, sea level, in a live-aboard catamaran still docked and waiting for him to come back. He tried not to breathe so hard that people in Kearny could hear him, but he didn't think he was succeeding.

The hiker who had found the body—Jubey—claimed it was a short walk to site. The man's nose was bloody and his front tooth broken, which he said had happened when he ran pell-mell down the trail, to return to cell reception and get away from the body and possibly the killer. The injury had Leo's attention. It made a good cover story for a victim fighting back if you discounted the efforts this guy was making to report and lead law enforcement to the body.

Jubey led the way, and Leo, the sheriff, and Delaney followed, wearing headlamps and carrying backpacks over-loaded with crime scene equipment, Delaney decked out in an ill-fitting uniform that Clara had hastily scrabbled together. The crime scene equipment was a necessity since the Wyoming state crime lab team from Cheyenne was not expected until the next day. The headlamps illuminated the path as they walked the fringe of the trail to avoid messing up any track and footprint evidence. Tree branches loomed on either side, reaching down for them. They'd already marked the unauthorized off-road vehicle prints on the foot-traffic-only trail and traced them back to truck tire marks at the trailhead. The remaining patches of snow and mud from melt-off were working in their favor for additional tracks.

"It's been a while since we've had a murder in Kearny County," the sheriff said.

Delaney said, "I think we only averaged one a year during my tenure." It was the first time she'd spoken since they'd left the department. The tension was palpable, but Leo was doing his best to ignore it. And her.

Leo wished he could say the same about San Diego. Not that he'd worked in Homicide. The Bajeños killed plenty of folks but were best known for trafficking drugs and people. And working undercover was only something he'd done because Narcotics needed a cyber expert for the assignment. A love of gaming, an undergrad degree in computer science, and a misunderstanding with the law over recreational hacking had led him to the Coast Guard and his first job in law enforcement.

Something incongruous caught his eye. He aimed his headlamp at the ground. *Blood.* He pointed at droplets. "Unless this was a wounded animal, it looks like the victim came through this way. Trying to escape. Or brought by the killer."

The sheriff grunted. "Good eyes."

"Did you see anyone else on the trail?" Leo asked Jubey. He was trying to keep the chatter out of his teeth and regretting his light jacket. The thermometer reading in the truck had been thirty-seven degrees Fahrenheit. Nearly freezing. And to think only a few days ago his life—such as it was—had been at an average temperature of sixty-five degrees.

Jubey's voice was dull. He didn't bother turning back to

them, and it was hard to understand him. "Not a soul, man. Just the four-wheeler and the body."

"What about on the road?"

"A few vehicles coming and going."

"Could you describe them?"

"I was on my bike. It was dusk. They were just headlights, you know?"

The dark had thickened since they'd arrived. "How'd you drive up the mountain?"

"Mountain bike."

From town? *Respect*. Leo wasn't sure he would have wanted to pedal the two-thousand-foot ascent. "Far out. What brought you here alone after dark?"

Behind him, Fentworth made a sound like a cat gagging up a live mouse. A lot was riding on him bonding with the sheriff. Why was it so hard to wash the California out of his vernacular?

Jubey said, "The strawberry moon. I like to sleep under the stars when I can, especially when Mother Nature puts on a show."

Leo glanced up. The rosy moon was enormous, like a Chinese lantern hanging so low he could have flicked it with his fingers to set it swaying. It was probably bright enough to hike by. Only the nature of their mission made the headlamps necessary.

Delaney said, "You always camp in this spot?"

"Lately. It has a great sky and town view." He stopped, facing them and pointed ahead, across a patch of snow. He was wearing a beanie with extra room in the top, making him seem far taller than he was. In point of fact, he was not blessed with height, maybe five foot seven. His hair was wiry and short, like his body. Even in the low light, Leo could see his ear discs and the bottom of sleeve tattoos above his wrists. "The four-wheeler was there."

"Did you get a plate?" Delaney said.

Note to self. Four-wheelers have license plates in Wyoming.

"No."

"Color? Make or model?"

"No, man. I was too pissed it was on the trail. I was looking for the driver to chew him out."

"Him?" Leo said.

"Or her." Jubey shuddered. "But I only found the dead woman."

"Did you ever see the four-wheeler again?"

"I did not."

"And no sign of a person?"

"I thought I heard something. That's how I found her. But I can't be sure what the sound was."

"Then what?"

"I left the trail here, zigging up where it zags." His voice grew raspy. "I found her. On the right side of the clearing."

"How far ahead?"

"Maybe a hundred feet. I nearly stepped on her. And I, uh, I tossed my cookies. Sorry."

"That's okay, son. It happens to the best of us," Fentworth said.

"I heard it again. The four-wheeler. When I was bicycling away. After I fell." He touched his nose.

"Sounds like you were too close for comfort. Why don't you take a load off here? We'll need to talk to you more after we take a look at her."

"Thank God," Jubey muttered. He sank cross-legged onto a rock on the downhill side of the trail.

An eerie sound, almost like a squalling baby, raised the hair on Leo's neck. "What's that?"

"Scared?" Delaney said, sounding happy about it.

"Probably a mountain lion," Fentworth said. "There are a lot of them in this area."

Leo was glad he had his firearm. "Do people hunt them?"

Delaney snorted. "Some. More like they hunt us."

Predators weren't something he'd had to worry about in San Diego. Sharks, if he was in the ocean. People, on land. But he'd learned to live with those threats. Wyoming could drive him to missing sharks.

Fentworth changed the subject. "The good news for us is that we won't have a pissing contest over this case. Her body's on private property. Federal jurisdiction ends fifteen feet off this trail and cedes to county."

Leo looked around for a fence or marker. There weren't any he could see. "I didn't know there was any private property in the national forest."

"Pockets. We're on the edge."

"Want me to go first, sir?" Leo asked the sheriff. He wanted to show initiative, but he felt Delaney stiffen. It probably came off as competitive. Or, worse, chauvinistic.

"Yes, but both of you go. Take it slow. We need to preserve the scene."

Great. Togetherness with Delaney. "Gotcha." Leo studied the area ahead of him. The ground was relatively clear, with what appeared to be an unmaintained trail across it, faint and narrow. *Game trail?* He felt Delaney's presence as he steered wide to the left and moved slowly, doing his best not to step on anything vital. Walking at this speed, each of his steps measured roughly two feet. That meant he should reach her in fifty, give or take. The dead woman. The *murdered* woman.

Delaney grabbed his arm to stop him. He pulled it free.

Her voice was a low hiss. "Listen—I don't like what you did to me today. I don't like *you*. But this is an important case, so let's talk it through."

"Fine." Now would have been a good time to apologize, but he couldn't force the words out. "What did you have in mind?"

"I'll go left and walk the scene. It sounds like the woman

will be to the right. You take the first look at her. I'll approach after I've made a first pass," Delaney said. "And try not to mess up the scene."

"Same to you."

He passed some snow and began counting off paces in time with his heartbeats as Delaney worked her way left. He didn't spook easily, but there was something eerie about approaching unseen violent death in dark wilderness. Imagining the killer hiding. Watching. Or a predator... eating. He slipped his hand to the grip of his holstered gun. *Aren't you supposed to make noise to scare off a bear? What scares off mountain lions?*

He stomped his feet and cleared his throat, digging for an excuse to speak loudly. "Should be almost there."

His step count reached forty-five. He tensed, dreading what was coming and yet somehow eager. Eager to do his job. To find the woman and her killer. A sour smell hit his nose. *Jubey's vomit.* He stepped around it.

Then he saw her. Not that he would have recognized her as human. Just as something long and dark. More like downed timber than a person. And, luckily, with no bear or mountain lion feeding on her.

"Found her." He stopped. Delaney kept moving slowly to his left like it was no big deal. "I'm about ten feet away. Want me to string some tape?" They'd secured the trail at its head already.

"Take a look at her first," the sheriff said. "Tell me what you see."

Leo donned a pair of gloves and booties and edged forward. He'd seen plenty of corpses. People dead in their homes from heart attacks and accidents. Gunshot victims on the street. A few overdoses. Bodies in morgues, cold and gray. A suicide by hanging once. Even a floater who had been in the water too long, partially eaten by fish. That had been the worst. But death was never something he looked forward to seeing.

The light from his lamp beams flooded the woman, shining off her bare, dark skin, absorbed by the blood. And there was so much blood. Blood on her arms and legs. Pooled on her filleted and lumpy torso and the ground around her. Her head and face appeared relatively uninjured, other than something that might be dried blood below the nose. Dirt or bruising on the exposed side of her face. It was impossible to differentiate even in the bright wash of his lamp.

His first murder investigation. It was different from the dead bodies he'd seen during his year on patrol as a beat cop before he went into Narcotics. It was night and day from sitting behind a monitor, like he'd done undercover and in Coast Guard special ops, physically separated from the visceral impact of experiencing crime. Computers didn't emit odors and drip bodily fluids.

He hadn't expected how personal it would feel. He was responsible for her.

His mind started searching for answers. Did the killer find her here? Force march her? Incapacitate her and transport her? Or kill her elsewhere? He remembered the blood droplets on the trail. Which proved nothing, yet. If she were carved up offsite, wouldn't she have gotten blood all over her in transit? And all over the murderer, too. He pictured a body bag or a tarp with an inert shape in it. Yet her legs and head weren't bloody. He supposed if the blood had already dried before she was moved she could have stayed clean, but then where did all the pooled blood on the ground come from? His pulse kicked up a notch with each question.

He took a deep breath. Time to slow his roll. Finish examining her and save the analysis for after he'd gathered the evidence. He studied her again. Thick dark hair. Brown skin. Delicate face. In life, beautiful. In death... but, wait—was she dead? She was on her back, naked, hands to her middle. Like she was clutching that destroyed abdomen. In pain. Eyes closed.

Could she still be alive?

He shouted back to Jubey. "You're sure she's dead?"

"Yeah, man. No doubt. I checked."

Still, Leo had to confirm it. If there was even the slightest chance to save her, he had to take it. He placed his feet carefully and crouched, then pressed two strong fingers against her carotid artery. It gave him a close-up view of the slice from the base of her throat and downward. All the way to her pelvis, where her insides bulged into her hands. It took all his self-control not to rocket backwards in a terrified crab walk. *Don't let this murderer get away because you mess up something crucial.*

He waited for a flutter, a sign of life.

NINE

"Is she gone?" Delaney asked. She shone her headlight at Leo's back.

"Gone." His voice sounded slightly deflated. Professional, but sad. She warmed toward him a degree, from arctic cold to mid-winter frigid.

"Sheriff?" a woman's voice called. It sounded like it was coming from below Leo. Back down the trail.

"Is that you, Dr. Watson?" Wentworth said.

"It's me. I heard you had a murder up here."

"I guess that would make me Sherlock then. Who called you?"

Leo turned to look at Delaney, shielding his eyes from her beam. She tilted her head to aim it away from him.

Leo whispered, "I thought the body would go to the coroner."

"Correct," Delaney put a finger to her lips, cocking her head to aim her ear at the trail.

Kearny County had a forensic pathologist and an elected coroner, but no medical examiner. The plan they'd made on the way up the mountain had been for the body to be taken down on a stretcher by EMTs, then on to the coroner's funeral home. The forensic pathologist would be called in only if necessary.

"I called her," Jubey said. "She's my mother-in-law."

Voices carried on the mountain. It was like Dr. Watson, the sheriff, and Jubey were standing right beside her and Leo, but they were each a hundred feet or more away.

Fentworth said, "I didn't know Amy was married."

"Not Amy. Annette," the doctor replied.

"Oh, nice." Then, "You better not be stepping on my evidence, Louise."

"I'm not an amateur, Coltrane."

"Can't be too careful."

Delaney smiled. Same old banter between Fentworth and Dr. Watson. The two were the best of friends. The doctor had even come to some of Delaney's races with him, years ago.

"Where's the body?" Dr. Watson said.

Leo stood. "Up here."

"Time to rope it off," the sheriff said. "I'll come up with the doc."

"On it," Delaney said.

Leo knelt down again and said softly to the dead woman, "I'm sorry."

Delaney set her backpack on the ground and tried to look like she wasn't listening to Leo, even though he had one hundred and ten percent of her attention. She wasn't sure why he apologized to the woman. Because they were too late to save her? Because of her brutal end? Because of the indignity she was about to endure in death? Maybe all of the above?

He spoke again. "We'll get the person who did this to you."

Delaney experienced another two degrees of thawing. *If he keeps this up, I'll be a damn puddle.* She reminded herself that he had arrested her without letting her explain herself earlier. It helped.

The sheriff and doctor were moving like ghosts under the

strawberry moon, their headlamps casting jerky kaleidoscopes on the ground. Leo walked uphill to join Delaney. He set his backpack down beside hers. The crime scene tape was on top inside his pack, from where he'd used it to rope off the mouth of the trail earlier. He retrieved it, handing a roll to her and keeping one for himself.

"I'll go left, you go right again?" Delaney said.

"That works."

She began staking out her side of the perimeter, keeping an eye out for clothes, shoes, a purse, footprints, blood, a tarp, a weapon—something sharp—or tape. Anything out of place in this natural setting. She saw nothing, though, the same as before. Maybe the crime scene guys would have better luck. They'd have the advantage of light for their work.

When she'd completed her half of the wide circuit with the tape, she rejoined the sheriff a few feet away from the doctor and the victim. Leo finished and moved over to the group.

The sheriff said, "Louise, this is Deputy Leo Palmer. He's new. Moved out here from Cal-i-for-nye-ay and just started last week. Leo, this is Dr. Watson. She's Kearny's forensic pathologist."

Dr. Watson looked up from where she was squatting beside the victim. Her headlamp illuminated a little of her face—almond eyes under dark, thin brows. "Welcome to Wyoming, Deputy. We don't usually get this much excitement. Is this you bringing an ill west wind our way?"

Leo grimaced. "No, ma'am. Nice to meet you, Dr. Watson."

Then she saw Delaney. She stood and threw open her arms. "Delaney Pace! Coltrane, why didn't you tell me?"

Delaney moved into the woman's embrace. She wasn't much of a hugger, but she could make an exception for Dr. Watson. "Great to see you."

The doctor released Delaney. "We'll have to catch up soon."

"Absolutely."

The forensic pathologist nodded. Then she squatted and returned her attention to the body.

"Any idea what happened to her, Louise?" the sheriff asked.

"I'm pretty sure she was murdered," she answered, her voice dry.

"Other than that, wise acre?"

"I'd hazard a guess she died of blood loss a couple of hours ago, but precise answers will have to wait for an autopsy."

The sheriff grunted. "I could have guessed that without your fancy degree."

"Also, her organs have been removed and then placed back in her body."

"They've what?"

"You heard me. The killer took her insides out, then put them back in. Or tried to."

He harrumphed. "She's going straight to the hospital for you to do your thing."

"It doesn't work that way, Coltrane."

He held up his radio. "It will do by the time I've talked to the coroner. We've got something strange on our hands, and it probably isn't a first-timer. I may even call the feds for help."

Delaney hadn't felt a need to scrutinize the body until Dr. Watson's revelation, but now she was drawn to it like a bug to a blue light. Dark brown skin—African American—and a beautiful, delicate face. A face she knew, mostly from pictures, but once from meeting her at a birthday party, which Delaney had attended because she was hauling through the area at the time. And because she looked so much like her daughter.

When her words finally found their way out, they sounded strangled. Like her throat was constricted. "Oh, no." She reached for her throat. Pulled her pendant up by its chain, let it fall outside her shirt, and squeezed it in her palm.

"What is it?" Leo asked.

Delaney licked her lips. "I know her. It's Lila. Lila Clement."

"It can't be." But then he moved closer to look at the woman's face, too. Fentworth closed his good eye and groaned. "Oh, Delaney, I'm so sorry I brought you up here." When he opened his eye, he squeezed her elbow.

"I don't understand what's going on," Leo said.

Delaney was numb. She was having trouble comprehending it herself.

Fentworth said, "Because that's her brother Liam's wife. And the kicker is that until this very moment, everyone believed she died with him a month ago."

TEN

The man buttoned his quilted flannel coat on the way to his truck. He wished he'd owned the jacket to wear it the night before on the frigid mountain. He'd warmed up fast enough, though, from sheer exertion. As light as Lila was, carrying her limp-but-alive body wrapped in a tarp and getting her strapped to the four-wheeler had been a challenge. Next time he had a body to get rid of, he was sticking to flatlands. No hiking and humping it up into a forest at that altitude.

He'd been lucky he hadn't seen anyone on the way up there. Well, he had seen that crazy woman who'd passed him and tried to get him to pull over. *Whatever that had been about—maybe women here are just aggressive when they see what they like.* A smile lifted one side of his mouth. But she hadn't seen what he had wedged in beside the four-wheeler in the bed of the truck.

The real problem, though, had been the mountain bike nut who'd found the four-wheeler and Lila. He'd never dreamed anyone would be up there. Not where he'd stashed her. Miles from town. Miles from paved road. Way beyond even a gravel two-track, and deep in the forest, off a trail. But she'd been discovered before he was even done with her. He'd stayed hidden until the guy left, but the quick discovery of the body was shitty luck. It had been genius to vary his signature. He'd worry about further modifications later. For now, he was still in the afterglow.

Walking slowly, his mind returned to the clearing he'd found for Lila's dispatch. To her naked body. His special knife, the one made for just this purpose. And the blood. Spurting at times. Seeping up around the blade. Trickling to the ground. Tracing the shape of her. Cherry-red against her bare skin. A dizzying warmth flooded him, everywhere, and he stopped, eyes closed. Savoring. He was glad he'd restrained himself back at the cabin, keeping her alive for another day. Finishing her out in the wilderness had been an even bigger thrill than he had hoped. Like taking her into God's house and giving Him the finger. *Created from man? I don't think so. Created to ruin man. Your work was done in seven days, but mine will never end.* Signing his work hadn't gone as planned, though, and that had been disappointing. The tool wasn't something he'd made himself. *Whatever you do, do it well,* his father had always told him. The man had been full of so much wisdom.

A blast of arctic wind hit him, and he opened his eyes and looked around. No one was watching him. He resumed walking and flipped up the collar on the jacket. He'd just bought the ugly-as-shit thing in the menswear section of the hardware store. The hardware store. Go figure. The rubes in this town bought their timber and toilets and hammers and whatever at the same place they loaded up on the latest mountain-man fashion. And it was open at six a.m. daily which was convenient given that he hadn't been able to sleep after the excitement of last night. He blended in now. Or he would if he wasn't the only man in a coat for a hundred miles. Since the four-wheeler was taking up the bed of his truck, he set his bag of purchases in the passenger seat. New tarp. Heavy duty chain. Two locks. An upgrade for the shoddy tool. He'd get it right next time.

He backed out of his parking space. Talk about blending. He snorted. He'd never be caught dead in a vehicle like this in Vegas.

With Lila done, it was time for his next dispatch. He was ready. More than ready.

He'd been following her on and off for the last twenty-four days, ever since he'd received the sign that she was the one. Seeing what her patterns were. Identifying who her people were. Her house. Her job. Figuring out where to snatch her and how. Dropping breadcrumbs to create a flight path to confuse law enforcement. He'd already taken a treasure from her house. It excited him to remember it, and he touched the plastic hospital ID bracelet in his pocket.

It would have been better if he had more time to watch her and plan. But, thanks to the mountain biker, he didn't. He had to collect her quickly. Hence this shopping trip. Not just to the hardware store, but the Walmart, too. He patted that bag. Dog bowls. Canned dog food. *Because I'm going to have myself a pet for two days.* He laughed out loud. A female pet. A female dog. A bitch. When he was over his amusement, he thought about the woman. Her pert face. Her short, curvy body. He was going to enjoy their time together.

He hit the gas. Stalking was over. Time for hunting. And, thanks to the reconnaissance he'd done at her house and work-place the day before, he knew just where to start.

ELEVEN

Delaney sat in front of Clara and signed the last part of the new hire paperwork in an illegible scrawl, her bleary eyes not registering the words, her tired brain not caring. All it cared about was the woman they'd brought down from the mountain. Her sister-in-law. Kateena's mother. *Kateena can't find out her mother died in that way.* But how was Delaney going to break the news to her and keep her from learning the horrific details? Or about the monster who had done unspeakable things to her? They hadn't seen Lila delivered to the hospital morgue until five a.m., after turning up no evidence at the crime scene, which had been adding insult to injury. Murder, no leads. Delaney needed a toothbrush and to refill to the McDonald's coffee she'd grabbed when they'd stopped there on the way to the department.

"Done." She stood, wobbled. "Anything else?"

Clara smiled at her. Her face looked well rested. "I'll be ordering you some equipment for your workspace, cards, uniform, and the like, but they won't be in for a few days. The sheriff said you could wear plain clothes until then if you'd rather." She winked. "I didn't know we were expecting a new deputy, or I would have been prepared. Anyway, the sheriff ran home to catch some sleep, although he usually starts at seven like the rest of the day shifters. He asked me to send you back to Leo. Maybe after that I could take you to put together a temporary duty belt?"

"Thanks. Do I have a work area yet?" Delaney withheld any further comment. She liked the woman. Would like her even more with a little sleep and less personal trauma. But inside her brain, she cursed Fentworth. Sending her to Leo? It was like he was trying to torture her.

"Let me work on that over the weekend."

"All right. And we can just do the belt then, too, if you want."

"Great. Oh, and I almost forgot." Clara dug in her drawer then handed Delaney a familiar ring of keys across the desk. "Joe and I went and fetched your car last night. I got to drive it. Vroom, vroom." She laughed.

"Yeah, it's something. It was my dad's. Thanks." She slipped the keys in her pocket and forced herself to exit and walk down the hall, weaving a little, fists clenched.

Her phone buzzed.

Mary: *Kateena is up. I'll drop her at school and take Dudley to TLS with me if that's OK?*

Delaney had texted her half an hour before with an update that she was out of jail and at a new job. How was she ever going to repay this woman? The kindness Mary was showing a relative stranger was humbling. Delaney walked into the kitchen, poured coffee black as pitch into her cup, and then stood, typing. *Thanks. I'll p-u Dudley ltr. Nap b4 Kateena gets out.* She sipped the coffee. It smelled like burned weeds and tasted worse, but it didn't scald her tongue. She gulped it down and refilled her cup. The acidy feeling in her stomach wasn't going to stop her. She sipped again.

All-nighter?

The worst.

Sry!

She took a deep breath and stalked out, then across the mixed city and county bullpen, holding her coffee aloft to keep it from sloshing out. The place looked exactly the same as when she'd last seen it a decade ago except for new mix-and-match patterned carpet squares in a range of tans and browns. Her coffee would blend, except the acid would probably burn a hole in it. A few heads turned toward her. She nodded indiscriminately, avoiding eye contact. If she knew any of the cops from the old days, she'd renew acquaintances later. Not now, when she didn't have the bandwidth for the inevitable questions and condolences.

"Delaney." Leo's voice. She turned to it. He was standing in a cubicle and waving her over. A night without sleep dulled the shine of his movie-star good looks but not much. She lifted her hand in acknowledgement. He sank back below eye level.

She ducked her head and hurried the last few steps to join him. He'd pulled up a second chair at his desk. She eyed the space. The quarters would be tight. "Maybe we should grab an interview room? Or one of the conference rooms?"

"We've got the phone and computer here," he said.

She took a seat and rolled as far away from him as she could, which was still close enough to feel something—heat? electricity?—from his body. *Good God, Delaney. Stop.* She swallowed some coffee. "Any progress while Clara was making me official?"

Leo leaned forward, a spark in his eyes, a determined set to his mouth. "Ever since you identified Lila, there's been a question burning a hole in my skull. Who is the other dead woman, the one who died with your brother?"

"It's bothering me, too."

"I ran a few searches for missing women similar in age and height to Lila in NamUS."

Delaney remembered the federally funded National Missing and Unidentified Persons System, although the ten years she'd been gone was like one hundred when it came to information technology. "Go on."

"I repeated it all in the National Crime Information Center, the Wyoming division of Criminal Investigation's missing persons database, and in each of the neighboring states. Colorado. South Dakota. North Dakota. Montana. Nebraska. Utah. Idaho. If there was consensus on how and where to log the information, it would make this exercise a lot easier. Someday when I run the world, there will be."

"What did you find?"

He sighed. "I haven't had a chance to comb through the results for matches to Lila or connections to her or Liam yet. It's not going to be a quick or simple process. And I'm a little worried I might have focused too narrowly. I saved it all and sent a copy to Fentworth." He looked her in the eye. "I didn't know how to get it to you."

"Clara's getting me set up. Send it to my personal email for now." She scribbled her address on a yellow sticky pad and pushed it to him. She was eager to dive into his research, but also feeling a little overwhelmed. First case back and it was a murder—of a family member. There were a lot of emotions to sort through and a lot to do on this one. The question was where to start.

Leo was typing her address when Fentworth's voice boomed in her ear. She jumped and coffee splashed onto her shirt.

She rubbed at the damp spot with her hand. Not that it would do any good.

Fentworth took a step back. His expression was a twinkly eyed scowl. "Are we gonna find a killer today or what?"

"I've been mired down with new hire paperwork." She gestured at Leo. "He's off and running, though."

Leo stood, towering over the small sheriff. "Already working on the missing person angle. Have you decided whether to call in the feds?"

"I reached out to the FBI resident agency in Casper. Bastards told me it was Memorial Day weekend. They said they can have someone up by Monday. Asked if I wanted a profiler. What did they think I was calling for?" He shook his head. "Feebs."

Delaney said, "Have you learned anything new about Lila?"

The sheriff motioned with his head for them to follow and the three of them walked out of the bullpen and into the quiet and greater privacy of the hallway. "Won't know until we get to the hospital. I got a call from Louise."

"Dr. Watson?" Leo asked.

"To you youngsters, yes. Without any other suspicious deaths on her dance card, Lila shot to the top of it. I'm invited to the autopsy. We don't get many cases like this one around here. Chances to attend are few and far between. I figured you two might like to join me after breakfast."

Like was not the word Delaney would have used about attending an autopsy.

"Oh, that would make my day," Leo said, using a Clint East-wood accent.

Delaney felt something almost painful in her cheeks and realized it was a smile.

Fentworth coughed into his hand, sounding like he was covering the word "bullshit." Then he tried his own Eastwood rasp and mangled a Dirty Harry quote back at Leo. "Everybody wants results, but nobody wants to get their hands messy."

Leo laughed. "Touché."

Delaney let her smile broaden. Fentworth mangling obscure Eastwood quotes back at Leo? He'd always been great on Trivial Pursuit night at the Loafing Shed, back in the day. "Nicely done, Sheriff."

He bowed. Then his mood changed suddenly. ""Dr. Watson works fast. Been at it since the second we delivered Lila to her. She's taking this one hard. We all are. Never seen anything like it around here."

"We need to find the person who did it before he does it again," Delaney said. "And we have zero evidence."

"Exactly. So, I'm counting on Louise."

Delaney reached for her purse. "Me, too."

TWELVE

Leo chewed on his gum with all his jaw strength as he took in the stainless-steel surfaces and glossy floor of the hospital morgue. It was too damn early for this. Combined with the Vicks VapoRub on his chest, upper lip, and the edges of his nostrils, he was minty fresh, even though Lila no longer was. His fried green tomatoes eggs Benedict over a discussion of the case at the Cowpoke Cafe had been outstanding, but he didn't want to taste them a second time. Or toss them in front of Delaney.

Fentworth stretched to his full five feet six inches and stuck out his hand. "Louise, lovely as always."

Dr. Watson held hers up in gloves. "I'll pass, for your sake. And you need to visit your optometrist. I'm in a medical gown with a mask, hairnet, and gloves."

"It suits you."

She turned back to Lila. "Do you want the CliffsNotes version, or should I stretch this out and sock the county with a bill that I attribute to you?"

The sheriff grinned at Leo and Delaney. No gum, no Vapo-Rub. "She's a pistol, this one." To Dr. Watson, he said, "The voters expect me to spend their money wisely. Tell us what we need to know."

"I'm not done yet. Some of the tests I'll be sending off may take a few weeks. I won't be releasing preliminary results until tomorrow."

"Tell us you're about to make our jobs easy today, Louise."

"Easier. First, the basics. You saw the wounds. She'd been sliced up pretty badly. But it had happened over a day or two. Some were starting to heal. The older cuts weren't life-threatening."

"She was being tortured, then," Delaney said.

Leo marveled at her stoicism. It had to be hard for her, as Lila was her sister-in-law.

Dr. Watson nodded. "As for cause of death, there's nothing inconsistent with it being blood loss from her numerous knife wounds. I'll enumerate the bases for my conclusions in my report. And she definitely died there. I'd estimate time of death no more than an hour before Jubey found her."

Leo drew in a sharp breath. Jubey had barely missed the killer. How easy it would have been to have ended up with two corpses on the mountain. Or for no one to have found Lila at all, for days. Weeks. Months. They'd been lucky in some ways, unlucky in others.

"Any fingerprints or biological evidence?" the sheriff asked.

"No fingerprints or fluids. I'll be sending in some fibers and hair to test. But I do have something interesting. Take a look." Dr. Watson gestured at Lila's pelvic region.

"Sexual assault?" Fentworth asked.

"No semen or lubricant. I can't confirm penetration. But that's not the issue. Look closer."

The area was held open by a pair of retractors, exposing the inside of the woman's hip bone. The cavity seemed empty, and Leo realized Lila's organs had been removed. More than that, he could see that the tissue around the bone had been pulled away.

Leo didn't think he could chew harder. He did. "Do you normally pull the meat off the bone like that?"

She nodded in approval at his question. "No. But the damage to the tissue above led me there. You'll recall that I told you someone had removed her insides and then tried to put them back in. Thus, it appears at some point the killer also had the bone exposed like we do, although it had retracted in the hours since his attack. It was a messy job. The lower intestine is out of place. There was tearing and separation. Cutting. And things weren't replaced precisely or completely. Uterus. Ovaries. Fallopian tubes. Think 'bowl of spaghetti.'"

Leo pictured Lila's body as it had been found on the mountain. It was too sick to contemplate. He hoped for Lila's sake she'd passed away before any of this had been done to her.

"But why would someone do this?" Delaney asked.

Leo leaned in, squinting, curiosity getting the better of him. "Excuse me?"

He realized he was blocking Delaney's view. "Sorry." He scooted over so she could see.

The look on her face said she wasn't his biggest fan.

Leo refocused on the bone. Despite the retracted muscle, there was still plenty of tissue on the surface of the bone. Pink over white. Yet there was something unnatural as well. A color. Brown, in a wavy pattern of lines. A healed fracture? An illness? An old injury? Or something worse? A coolness seeped over his face. His voice cracked when he spoke. "Is that a stab mark?" The sheer force needed to stab someone so hard that a knife embedded itself into bone was hard to fathom. But this wasn't a single stab. And bones don't bleed.

Dr. Watson looked pleased. "No, but follow that line of thinking."

If stabbing was close but not correct, it had to be worse than accidental. An intentional knife mark in bone, in a woman's pelvis... The pattern... "Is something carved in the bone?"

"Carving wouldn't have left the discoloration we're seeing."

Of course not. The horror was dulling his brain. Could it be pigment, like ink or paint? But it didn't look like paint. Paint couldn't have dried in a damp body cavity anyway. What else could leave a brown wavy pattern in bone? Then his stomach turned. He remembered two cadets who'd been unable to escape a ship boiler room and burned to death. One of the bones had escaped obliteration and while the flesh had burned away, the bone was intact. The fire had left it discolored. Brown.

"Fire," he said.

Now the small doctor outright smiled. "Yes. Burn marks. Very good, Deputy Palmer."

"I've seen decorative bone burning before," Delaney said. "On animal bones. Antlers. Similar to scrimshaw carvings. Really intricate detail."

"As have I. But this is not like that. These burns are less precise. No artistry."

"But how could someone even do this?" Leo frowned. "There was no evidence of a fire out there. And the body cavity was... is... so wet."

Dr. Watson nodded. "Do you have any background in the medical field?"

Leo straightened. He wanted to wipe away the sweat beading his forehead, but that would betray his anxiety. "None. This is my, um, my first autopsy."

"Why didn't you say so, Johnny Utah?" Fentworth clapped him on the back. "Do you need to take a break?"

Leo's teeth rattled from the contact. "I'm fine." *Johnny Utah?* It took a moment to place the reference. The movie *Point Break.* Actor Keanu Reeves in the role of FBI agent Johnny Utah, who'd worked undercover as a surfer. *Clever.*

Dr. Watson pulled a mechanical arm from the ceiling and lowered a lens. It projected a magnified image to her computer monitor. The doctor and three officers clustered in front of the screen.

Leo frowned. His lips moved as his finger followed the marks. There were five of them, nearly identical. He looked at Delaney. Sweat beaded at her hairline.

Fentworth swore under his breath. "Do we have some kind of satanic thing on our hands?"

"Why do you ask that, Coltrane?" Dr. Watson said.

"What other kind of sicko would drag a woman onto the mountain, disembowel her, and burn deviant symbols into her pelvic bone?"

"Not a normal human, to be sure. But there are other reasons for the evil doings of men than satanism."

Religion, for starters. The Crusades. 911. The Israeli-Palestinian conflict. Pakistan and India. Most of the wars in the Middle East. But Leo kept those thoughts to himself in favor of the case at hand. Five wavy lines. Each starting from the trough of a wave and lifting over one complete peak and ending at the height of a second.

"Do we know whether we're looking at the correct orientation?" Delaney asked

Dr. Watson clucked. She clicked a key and flipped the screen. "Better?"

Leo cocked his head.

"It's the same thing," Fentworth said.

Leo held up his hand. "No. The waves descend from height and end on a trough in this direction. They do the opposite in the other view."

"What the hell difference does that make?"

"I don't know."

"Either way, we have a surfing devil-worshipper on the loose."

As a surfer, Leo didn't think Fentworth's conclusion about

the waves felt right. "This isn't the type of wave a surfer would draw."

"What do you mean?" Dr. Watson asked.

"Surfing waves are more aggressive. Bigger. And they're usually artistically rendered as they're cresting." He searched for "image of surfing wave" in his phone's browser and showed them the images.

"Maybe," Delaney said, nodding. "It could just be a count of some kind. Like a body count."

"A serial killer. Let's hope not." Fentworth crossed his arms. His expression was peevish. "So where are we on this?"

Leo didn't know. "I don't understand how he burned her. We didn't see any remnants of a fire. This doesn't seem like something that could be done with one of those flame stick lighters."

"No, it isn't," Dr. Watson agreed.

Delaney said, "And I can't imagine someone transporting a blow torch and a live Lila up the mountain."

Fentworth's countenance brightened. "They make those mini soldering irons with rechargeable batteries these days. I've got a friend who has one."

"What in the world would you use it for?" Dr. Watson said. "Present instance excluded."

"My buddy uses it for small jobs like melting the ends of electrical wire and cutting into things. Soldering electrical connections. It's handy."

Leo tried to imagine the heat needed to leave these marks. "But would it be enough to burn damp tissue and bone?"

Fentworth shrugged. "That's why I hire experienced officers like yourself and Delaney, to figure these things out."

"There's a lot we can do with this information. Especially if the killer has done something like this before." Delaney was nodding. She sounded excited.

Fentworth patted her shoulder. "Delaney is back in action."

Leo's mind was racing. He needed to get back to his computer. Start searching the crime databases. "It sure doesn't seem like the work of a first-timer. Who even knows how to do the cutting and organ removal?"

"A hunter," Delaney said. "Anyone who has field-dressed an animal."

Leo had never hunted. He wasn't sure he ever wanted to after this. "Someone with medical training?"

Dr. Watson shook her head. "The way she was handled was too rough. Someone in medicine would have been more precise. The cutting was definitely not done with a scalpel. My guess would be a six-to-eight-inch blade with a non-serrated edge. Probably an outdoor knife. A sharp one."

"Butcher?" *Or maybe the killer learned it online. There's a video tutorial for everything these days.*

"Not a bad thought," the sheriff said. "Maybe someone who'd use one of these soldering doodads for work, too."

Leo wondered how that could be identified. Maybe just as a piece of information that made a suspect more or less likely to be the killer, although any schmo could buy one.

Delaney said, "I'd add that it's someone who didn't grow up around here."

"Why's that?" Leo asked.

"Because nobody native to Wyoming would think they were being stealthy driving a four-wheeler up a trail that prohibits motorized vehicles. Plus, he took a big chance murdering her so close to the trail. Locals would have known better."

"Maybe the risk is part of the thrill."

"Could be," Delaney agreed.

"Or it's someone trying to make it look like a non-native did it."

Fentworth cackled. "You sound like you're defending out-of-state citiots."

Leo wasn't familiar with the term. "Citiots?"

"Idiots from the city." *Which includes me.* "Anything else, Louise?" the sheriff said.

"I'll let you know if I turn up something else good. It's all I have for you to go on for now."

"This was gold. Disturbing, but gold." Fentworth turned on his heel, motioning Leo and Delaney to follow.

"Thanks," Leo called over his shoulder.

"I'll have my assistant pick up some of the rechargeable soldering irons and try them out," Dr. Watson said. "I should be able to give you an answer later this afternoon. But my initial guess is that it would be sufficient for the job we see here." The doctor lifted her hand, waggled her fingers, and turned back to what was left of Lila Clement.

THIRTEEN

Delaney put on her blinker and turned into the school parking lot, muttering curse words under her breath. Giant cottonwoods reached for brilliant blue sky behind the school, which backed up to the Cheyenne River. It was running high, thanks to heavy snowfall the previous winter. She'd played on its banks in her own schooldays here. Cold water, shocking her senses into overdrive. The heady scent of pine. Laughing until her sides hurt. Not all her Kearny memories were bad ones. At least not before she turned eleven.

But she wasn't here to enjoy the scenery. When she'd returned to the department from the morgue, she had discovered a voicemail from the school. Kateena had gotten in a fight before school had even started with a boy, apparently over kids taunting her about Delaney's stint in jail. *Thank goodness it wasn't about Lila. The word isn't out about her yet.* Delaney's presence was required to meet with the principal and to take her pugilist niece away.

She parked and jogged into the school. The death of her own father had made her an outcast here. She imagined it was the same for Kateena. But possibly having a jailbird aunt increased her coolness quotient. Beating up boys? Double that. Fighting wasn't behavior that paved an easy path long term, though. Delaney had to put an immediate stop to it.

She pushed open the vestibule doors, then the inner doors, and made a hard left toward the administrative offices. At the reception area, she gave her name and Kateena's to the gate-keeper and asked to meet with the principal.

Platinum eyebrows rose over watery blue eyes. Pale pink lips turned down. The woman pushed a nonexistent stray hair behind her ear toward her low bun. "Did you call for an appointment?"

"No. I'm Kateena Pace's aunt. I got a call from the school about an issue with her—"

"I'm aware of the incident."

Delaney forced a painful smile. "I came as soon I could. It's a situation I take seriously. Hence, my presence."

An almost inaudible sound escaped the woman's lips. Disdain. She lifted her phone, pressed a button, and turned away from Delaney, whispering into the mouthpiece. She hung up and pointed down the hall. "Your niece is over there." Then she went back to her computer monitor.

Delaney followed the woman's finger. Kateena sat on a wooden bench in silver tights, a long purple T-shirt, and purple Converse sneakers. A purple headband held back her gravity-defying hair. She was fiddling with an iPad and didn't spare Delaney a glance.

Delaney closed her eyes. When she opened them, she walked over to Kateena. The girl hunched over the iPad, ignoring her aunt even harder.

"Hi, Kateena." Delaney crossed her arms and eyeballed her niece.

Kateena didn't look up, but she answered in a huffy voice. "I thought adults were supposed to set a good example for kids."

"I was released. It was a misunderstanding. I am a good example. Now, what happened?"

"Other kids were making fun of me. About you going to jail." She looked up. Her voice was pouty, but her eyes were shining.

Double uh-oh. Suddenly, Delaney felt less tired. "And what happened?"

"I punched Jeremy Jerkface Peterson in his big fat mouth!"

Delaney winced. Possibly teaching Kateena how to hit the weekend before hadn't been the best idea. She'd discovered Kateena's wimpy punch when they'd been goofing around. What responsible aunt wouldn't have straightened her out? "Did the kids who taunted you get in trouble?"

Kateena oozed satisfaction. "Yeah. Jeremy is on suspension too."

"You're *suspended?*"

"For a week."

A week of suspension. When Delaney had just started her new job. "Hitting is not the way to solve problems. Or to stay in school."

"I hate school."

"That's not the point."

"But what am I supposed to tell the other kids, Aunt Delaney? Everybody's talking about you."

"Tell them the truth. I was trying to catch a bad guy. Because... I'm a deputy now." *The bad guy.* What had happened to him? With Lila's death, the earlier events had escaped her. *Ugh, I have to talk to Kateena about that, too.* Delaney pulled her badge from her purse. She flashed it at her niece.

"You're going to arrest people?" Kateena's tone dripped disgust. "Dad said people who do that can't find real jobs."

A sentiment Liam had expressed to Delaney once as well. Her big brother had strong opinions. She hadn't let it bother

her, and she didn't combat it now. "We're lucky the sheriff hired me back. We can't stay in Kearny unless I have a job."

"I wish it was a different job."

Time for a subject change.

A voice startled her. "Laney Pace. How nice to see you again."

She turned and saw a man. She took in his buzz cut of gray hair, standing straight up. Ice-blue eyes. A belly that screamed of too much wheat—probably in the form of beer. Outstretched hand.

"Mr. Rickets?" Delaney pulled the name like a wisp of fog from her hazy past. He'd been her middle school biology teacher. She'd suffered through many a detention written up by him.

"Principal Rickets. Come into my office."

"I'll be right back, Kateena." She followed the principal reluctantly, her previous visits for her own transgressions weighing her steps. The place wasn't as scary as in her memories, but it smelled the same. Sterile, like industrial cleaners, with an undercurrent of sweaty kid.

"Have a seat."

"Thank you. I heard you wanted to speak to me about Kateena and that she's on suspension."

He held up a hand. "Slow down. I'll get to your niece. But let's start at the beginning. Kateena came back to school immediately after the death of her parents."

"So I was told. I wasn't with her yet at that point."

"Last I heard, you'd quit the sheriff's department here and moved away. What have you been up to this last decade?"

"Ice road trucking."

"Oh, my." His tone wasn't complimentary. "Seems I read that in the paper today. Trucker. And now come home to run the family bar."

He knew what I'd been doing, so why did he ask? Delaney

didn't flinch or respond. But what was he talking about, paper? The writer had done some homework. But the information hadn't come from her. Who in town knew about it? A reporter had left her a voicemail the week before, asking for an interview. *But I never called back.* Right now, she cared more about helping Kateena than giving interviews. *Priorities.*

"Are you back for good?"

"I'm back for as long as Kateena needs to be here. Living in Kearny isn't my first choice."

"Will you be trucking based from here?"

"Not as a solo guardian. I've taken a job locally. Kateena's parents didn't leave anything solvent for her support. We have a house, a broke bar, and a failing construction business. And no cash."

"And you'll be working where?"

The questioning was beginning to feel like an interrogation. Like Delaney was the one whose behavior was under scrutiny, not Kateena's. She'd bear it for her niece's sake. Up to a point. "Deputy Investigator at the Kearny County Sheriff's Department."

His eyebrows rose—gray, black, and white hairs curling upward and a few down. Like a spider was trying to escape his face. "And how do they feel about your arrest last night?"

Delaney glanced at her feet to hide her smile. She'd changed back into yesterday's clothes before she left the department, including her sandals. Her nail polish was chipped on her big toe. "It was the first day on the job for a new guy who didn't realize I was in pursuit of a suspected felon. One that was driving recklessly, adjacent to the school." So, she embellished the story a bit. No harm for Kateena in that.

His round mouth made her happy. *Score one for Delaney.* "Oh."

"You didn't notice a Caucasian male in a two-tone Chevy

pickup in this neighborhood engaging in suspicious behavior, did you?"

"I, uh..."

"Anyway, they cut me loose as soon as they realized my colleague's mistake."

He regained his composure. "Well, I'm glad that worked out for you. Kids can be harsh, though. You heard what happened at school?"

"Some jerks mobbed Kateena about it, and she fought back."

He tsked. "Not as dramatic as that. I think her fuse is short. We've tried to make allowances."

"Like suspending her?"

"We do have a zero-tolerance policy on violence. And given her family history, well, I'm sure you know."

Delaney cocked her head. "Know what about her family?" Was he talking about Delaney? Liam? Lila?

"Pace is a name well known to this administration."

She seethed, fists tight. "What's your tolerance for bullying?"

"Zero on that as well, of course."

"So, all the bullies were punished?"

"Not every transgression is equal. And, you have to admit, it was your behavior that brought this on."

"I'll admit no such thing. I was briefly detained due to a misunderstanding. Your students bullied my niece, a young girl who'd done nothing wrong, and who has experienced an enormous amount of recent trauma."

"Is it possible that's your past talking? I seem to recall a young girl in similar straits and the trouble she caused."

Delaney counted to three. Then five. Then ten. When she was still angry after that, she let the emotion out. "Principal Rickets, Kateena needs and deserves protection from bullying while she recovers from a loss her fellow students can't begin to comprehend. She doesn't deserve to be sent home into isolation. What was the punishment for the kids who bullied her?"

"The boy she punched admitted to making some unkind remarks, and we sent him home."

"For how long?"

He pulled at the neck of his shirt. "Until Monday."

"Kateena is suspended for a week for fighting back when the administration didn't protect her, and he's suspended for two days, mostly over the weekend, for managing to rile her up by rubbing salt in her wounds?"

Crickets from Rickets.

Delaney stood abruptly. She addressed the principal from above him. "Kateena will be back at school on Monday, like the other boy. At that time, I expect the two of them to issue mutual apologies in this office in the presence of me and his parents. And after that time, if she is bullied again, I'll file a grievance with the school board. You remember me as a hurt young troublemaker. I won't argue with that. But I grew up. You'll find me even more effective at raising Cain now. If there's nothing further?"

Rickets pushed himself off the desk and rose. "I'll need to consult with—"

"Monday morning. We'll see you then."

"All right. Monday." He cleared his throat. "Ms. Pace?"

She froze. *No more Laney.*

"About that vehicle you were chasing. I do believe I've seen it on more than one occasion in the last few weeks. I'll call law enforcement if I see it driving erratically again."

Delaney nodded and marched out, tears threatening. Since the death of Rudy Pace, no one in her family had ever had her back. She damn sure was going to have Kateena's.

FOURTEEN

Music hit Delaney at the door of the Loafing Shed. Not her playlist. Something twangy with a pop vibe. Moving from the bright morning sunshine into the relative darkness of the bar, she put her arms in front of her so she wouldn't run into anything. Or anyone—if there were any people besides her employees here. After two weeks back in town, she had yet to arrive to find a packed house.

"What in the heck is coming out of the speakers?" Delaney said, by way of greeting.

Kateena lagged behind her.

"Delaney!" Mary sang out. "That's Maggie Killian. 'I Hate Cowboys.' A remake duet with Ava Butler. Maggie lives near Story with Hank Sibley."

The musician was a train wreck last Delaney had heard. She'd been a fan once upon a time. She'd assumed that Killian had died of a drug overdose long ago. Fame seemed to result in more than its fair share of second chances in her opinion. And she and everyone else around Kearny knew champion bull rider Hank Sibley. "I think Hank's Liam's age. Rival schools, though."

"This is my favorite song. Do you want me to change it?"

"No. It's fine. I owe you until the end of time, so you can play whatever you want." She pulled a wad of twenties from her wallet and pushed them across the bar.

Mary grinned, chomping at gum, and took them. "Thanks. Glad to see you're out of jail."

Her pronouncement coincided with the end of the song and echoed in the silence. "And now everyone knows I was in it," Delaney grumbled.

"Oh, it's all right, Delaney. There's practically no one here." Mary popped a bubble. It was probably some kind of health code violation, but, as Mary had pointed out, they didn't have to worry since there were no customers and no health code inspectors present. *Thank the Lord for small favors.* "What did they charge you with?"

"They didn't charge me with anything." Delaney plopped onto a stool at the bar and balanced her chin in her hands. Sleep. She desperately needed sleep.

"How's Dudley?"

Mary grinned. "Cutest dog ever. My little boy loves him."

Kateena sidled up to stand beside her aunt. "He ate one of Juan Julio's toys and pooped it out."

"Nice." To Mary, Delaney said, "Sorry. I'll replace the toy."

Mary said, "No need. He's in the office. In case, you know, he's not done."

Kateena grabbed Delaney's hand. "His tummy probably really hurts. Should we take him to the vet?"

Delaney kept a stern look on her face, even though she wanted to laugh and cry at the same time. "We'd better go see if he's okay."

"Can I get you something to drink?" Mary said.

"A gallon of water."

Mary filled a beer stein with water. "Seriously, what can I get you?"

Delaney took a long pull. Then another. Drank the whole

thing and pushed it back over. "A refill. I don't drink." Which was stretching the truth. She didn't *not* drink. She just didn't usually choose to. And it was easier to shut down offers with a declaration that was close enough to true. She'd grown up in this bar, with a front-row seat to the theater of the absurd things people did under the influence. She preferred to be in control of her damn self, thank you very much.

Mary snorted and handed over the refill. "And now you run a bar."

"Hopefully not for long." Delaney took a sip, then left it. "I'll come back for this."

"Hold up. Just so you know, Billy showed up late this morning."

"Billy?"

"The guy who no-showed his shift yesterday? I figured you'd want me to send him home for you. I did. He won't be coming back. But it's no problem. I can cover all his shifts. I even redid the schedule for you. Although, I can't work tonight. I have a date. A cowboy. His name is Chip." She blushed a little as she said it.

The unusual name rang a bell for a moment, but Delaney was too tired to access her memories. Or argue with Mary about the schedule. Not that she felt like it, much. Mostly she was relieved that she hadn't had to do it herself. "All right. Thanks. We'll talk later."

"One more thing?" Mary gave her a tentative grin.

"What is it?"

"You know Liam used to take all his calls on his cell?"

"No."

"Well, he did. People—customers—have started calling on the landline here to figure out who's gonna finish their work."

"Construction work customers?"

"Yes."

Delaney was going to nod and end the conversation until

she reminded herself that Mary was motivated and a problem-solver. "How do you suggest we handle it?"

Mary touched her clavicle. A smile played across her lips. "Seems like if we disappoint the clients, they go find someone else themselves. But you don't want to run a construction company."

"Not a single bit."

She nodded. "Let me make a few calls. Find you a contractor to refer the work to who'll give you a cut."

She deserves a promotion and a raise. One out of two wasn't bad. If she found a contractor, she'd get an exalted title. *Savior of Delaney sounded about right.* "Sounds good. Thanks, Mary."

Delaney waved and put a hand on Kateena's shoulder, steering her toward the swinging door that led to the kitchen, the storeroom, a back door, and the office. Her father's. Her brother's. Now hers, hopefully for a very short time. The office door was closed.

She opened it. "Dudley?"

The little Frenchie barreled at her, boxed her, licked her, and danced in a circle, chasing the tiny corkscrew that passed for his tail.

"He missed you," Kateena said. "Didn't you, Dudster? You missed Aunt Delaney?"

Delaney sighed. "I missed you, too, you little badass."

"Language, Aunt Delaney."

Delaney channeled her grandfather's stock response to her religious grandmother. He would quote one of the many passages in the Bible with the offending word. "Ass is in the Bible, Kateena. Look it up."

"Oh. Well, you said *bad*ass."

"Same difference." Too late Delaney realized she'd just given the girl permission to say the word herself. "But it's a grown-up word. It could get you suspended again."

Kateena's eyes sparkled like she was making plans for earning her next suspension already.

Delaney turned to Dudley. The floor was clean. The dog didn't look sick. "You're well. You don't need to be languishing back here in the office."

Dudley was too busy to answer, occupied in sniffing her to see what she'd been up to.

"What does languishing mean?" Kateena asked.

"Suffering."

"I don't think he was suffering. Sleeping and snoring are more like it."

"If he's well, he might as well be out entertaining people. Dudley, I hereby dub thee the official mascot of the Loafing Shed." When Dudley wasn't beating up on larger dogs or humping stuffed animals, he was the master of loafing. It seemed fitting.

Kateena cheered. "Dad never let him in. He said it was a health code violation."

Delaney should ground Kateena for fighting, on top of her suspension. So, was pleasing her niece now bad timing? Like rewarding her instead of being stern? Probably. Except that Delaney felt responsible for what Kateena had done. The girl had been having a tough time since losing her parents, something Delaney could relate to. Now Delaney had brought negative attention on her.

She winked. "Lucky for Dudley he's under the 'bad example' aunt regime now."

Dog and girl ran out of the office. Delaney followed Kateena's peels of laughter and the clicking of Dudley's toenails on the wood floor. Clearly, being suspended had not dampened Kateena's spirits.

"Hi, Dudley!" Mary said.

The dog checked her with some high chin, then made a lap of the bar, smelling the smells, and hoovering up anything resembling edibles. As in food, not marijuana. Or so Delaney hoped.

Food. The thought of it made her stomach rumble. She needed to eat and crawl into bed. "Kateena, gather your stuff. Time to head home."

The front door opened. A man lumbered in. Delaney barely gave the guy a glance.

Kateena used her whiny voice. "Ah, Aunt Delaney. It's boring at home."

Delaney pointed at the iPad, then the door. "We'll grab lunch on the way."

Kateena skipped to a table with her iPad, good mood restored.

Mary called out, "Welcome, Skeeter. The usual Bloody Mary and snit?"

Delaney only knew that a snit was a three-ounce ration of beer from her many years in this very bar, but she didn't often hear people use the term.

A rumbly voice replied. "Double down, Ms. Mary. It was a long night."

Delaney couldn't imagine more than one Skeeter in Kearny, Wyoming. She turned. *Yep.* It was her booking buddy. Getting an early start on today's drunk and disorderly.

"Are you working on my case today?" Mary mixed a Skeeter's drink with two shots of vodka.

"Remind me again what I'm doing for you?" Skeeter straddled a bar stool and slapped a newspaper down.

"Collecting child support from my deadbeat ex." Mary pulled a tall draft beer. *More like a quadruple snit.* Speed Goat Golden Ale from the Ten Sleep Brewing Company across the mountains.

"Right. When do you need it done?" He rubbed his temple.

"I thought you'd already started. I needed the money yesterday. I have rent overdue." She put the stiff Bloody Mary and snit in front of Skeeter.

"Sorry about that. I was held up on other cases. I'll get on it today."

Tears welled in Mary's eyes, and she ducked her face. Delaney scowled, thinking over Mary's straits. The woman had already asked for extra shifts. Not only was she dealing with a deadbeat dad but a deadbeat investigator, too. She deserved someone she could count on. Well, Mary could count on her, at least to go out and visit the guy once. It would be a way to continue repaying the woman for the above-and-beyond help of the last twenty-four hours.

She climbed onto the stool beside Skeeter's. "Hey, Skeeter. Remember me?"

The man squinted, looking lost, then grinned. "Liam's little sister." He pointed a crooked index finger at the paper. "I was just reading about you."

A sliver of memory worked its way to the surface. She had a question for Skeeter. He'd insinuated he had information about her brother. Or her dad. Or both. She couldn't ask him in front of Mary and Kateena, though. Belatedly, she wondered what he'd read about her in the paper, if he had. *The paper again.* Skeeter didn't seem like the sharpest pick in the icehouse.

"Hey, man, I owe you one," she said.

His eyes grew more vacant, and his mouth hung slack. "Why?"

"You helped me navigate the system last night. How about I pay you back by working Mary's case for you, just for today?"

"I, uh, I work solo. Can't afford to partner up."

Delaney held up her hands. "Gratis." His eyes didn't clear, so she tried again. "Free. As a thank you."

He looked skeptical. "You done this kind of thing before?"

As a deputy? And then some. "Enough. It would be my pleasure. And I could get started—" she glanced at her wrist as if at a watch, even though she wasn't wearing one. "—right now." The sheriff had told her to go home and sleep after she picked up Delaney. To come back to work on Lila's case when she was rested. Hopefully collecting from Mary's baby daddy wouldn't take long so she'd be able to sneak in the nap she so desperately needed before she returned to the department.

Mary wiped her eyes. "Really, Delaney?"

"Really. Just give me his name and address and I'm on it."

"Thank you so much! His name is Sicario Menendez. I'll text you his address and directions. I can't believe you'd do this for me. After you've been up all night. You're the best!"

"Thank me when the mission is completed successfully." Delaney had missed plenty of meals and sleep on the road. She turned to her niece. "Slight change of plans, Kateena."

I can sleep when I'm dead.

FIFTEEN

Leo leaned toward the screen and chewed the inside of his bottom lip as he typed. He knew he was sleep-deprived, but his need to make progress was stronger than his need for rest, other than the brief nap he'd managed after the autopsy. But he'd returned refreshed, and he was ready to tackle Lila's case.

His phone rang. The sheriff. He answered. "Yes, sir."

Fentworth's jovial voice was fast-paced as always. "I've got Louise on the line to update us on the tests her assistant did with the rechargeable soldering iron. I tried to patch in Delaney but she's not available. Will you update her?"

"Yes, sir." A conversation that would go over like a lead balloon, given that it would be coming from him. "Hello, Dr. Watson."

"Hello, Deputy Palmer. I have Ena Atul with me. She's going to describe her work. Ena, take it away."

A softer voice took over. "At Dr. Watson's request, I purchased a rechargeable soldering iron at our local hardware store. After it was sufficiently charged, I took it with me to Big Horn Meat Processors, where I had called ahead to arrange to test the instrument on a freshly slaughtered animal. They were able to oblige me with a swine that the county purchased so that we could skip the severing of veins and arteries for purpose of bleeding out the animal, as we needed to duplicate the situation you encountered with Lila Clement on the mountain."

Leo's forehead bunched up. He didn't know what he'd expected, but her words were still a jolt. She made sense, though.

She continued, her voice growing stronger. "I witnessed the butcher remove the organs and viscera to clear the inside of the pelvis. He blotted the area dry for me, then I attempted to recreate the pattern the killer left on Ms. Clement." She paused, and Leo could hear her swallow. Then she rushed onward, excited. "With my first attempt, I was unable to duplicate it exactly. But I tried again, stopping frequently to blot and wipe away fluid. It took some time, but I succeeded."

Leo shouted, "Yeah!"

The phone went silent.

"Excuse me," he said. "I meant to say, that's great."

Ena continued. "As with Ms. Clement, the burns are not especially dark, but they are clearly visible and quite similar to the marks inside her pelvis. We rearranged the organs, waited ten minutes, then removed them to recheck the pattern, and it was still there. While with more time, I can conduct additional tests if needed for a greater level of certainty, I concluded that the small rechargeable soldering iron could have been used by the killer. I cannot conclude if it was in fact the exact instrument that was used, however."

"Thank you," Fentworth said. "I believe that's enough for us to pursue the theory anyway. Louise, what's your recommendation for us?"

"I'll be consulting my counterparts around the country for ideas on other possible tools. But I can't come up with any other ideas to test. If you guys have them, send them our way. Thank you, Ena."

"Yes, ma'am."

"Yes, thank you both," Leo said. "I'll let you know if my research turns up other possibilities."

The call ended. He smiled. The speed and creativity of the small-town staff was heartening. And they had something. Not much yet, but something.

One after another, he logged into crime databases and searched for disembowelment, burned bones, killers who'd marked victims with wavy lines, and for similarly staged mountain murders. The federal Violent Criminals Apprehension Program, a.k.a. VICAP, through their Law Enforcement Enterprise Portal, a.k.a. LEEP—the feds loved their acronyms. Others for the adjoining states—again, he focused in on Idaho, Montana, North Dakota, South Dakota, Nebraska, and Colorado.

The results were voluminous, but he scanned through them, hoping for a miracle. A mountain murder of a young woman the previous year in Colorado seemed promising. He left a message for the detective to call him back. None of the others appeared on point without further digging, which could wait until later. He saved them to a file and sent a copy to Fentworth and Delaney, with a note about the possible similar case in Colorado. Leo had other things to set in motion, now that Ena and Dr. Watson had confirmed a possible tool. The highest priority was calling area hardware and home improvement stores. Maybe someone had purchased a mini soldering iron recently. He tried not to think of all the different places they would be sold online. Or how easily someone who bought one four states away could get in a car and drive to Kearny.

He wished Delaney was there, working with him, which would have seemed impossible twelve hours ago. And not just because he was drawn to her. She was prickly, but she was sharp and invested, like he was. He hoped she got the situation with her niece resolved and was back soon. How hard must her life be right now, he mused: new job, dead brother, murdered sister-in-law, and troubled niece. New colleague who arrested her and threw her in jail.

He stretched his fingers and sighed, feeling antsy. Rule number one in his years as a computer scientist and cyber specialist with the Coast Guard had been to get organized. Rule number two was to stay organized. He'd been sloppy today, letting himself be pulled from one task to another, first diving into missing persons, then similar cases to Lila. *Start with solid police work, done methodically. Organized thoughts lead to organized actions.* Logic. Like the computer scientist he was trained to be. It was time for an investigation plan. He started typing, compiling information in his own method.

Crime: Murder of Lila Clement (linked to murder of unidentified woman with Liam Pace?)

Victim: Lila Clement

Known associates: Liam Pace (deceased), Kateena Pace, Delaney Pace, others??

Family: See above

Employers: ??

Previous residences: ??

Record: ??

Issues: ??

Online presence: ??

Phone records: ??

Suspect: ?? Hunter? Drifter? Butcher? Someone who uses rechargeable soldering irons for their work? Possible repeat offender? Someone who works with fire? A knife enthusiast? Someone not local and unfamiliar with use of trails in mountains?

He typed a to-do list.

- Order phone records for Lila and Liam Clement
- Search Missing Persons for identity of deceased at Liam Pace death
- Analyze tire treads for four-wheeler and other vehicle; get expert opinion
- Search for similar crimes: in process
- Search for sales of mini soldering irons in area
- Find knife/murder weapon
- Review crime scene evidence
- Interview witnesses (Pace family and employees, friends, Clement family)
- Background and social media presence on Lila and suspects
- Call butchers in area
- Look for knife clubs
- Notify family members

The last one on the list made his teeth clench. Notifying family members. Did Lila have family other than Delaney and Kateena? He'd call Delaney and ask after he finished with the hardware stores. He put his fingers back on the keys and noted the status of the items in progress. Preparing the plan was a downer when information was so sparse, but necessary. Maybe once he called around he'd have something to add. Possibly Delaney could fill in some gaps for him, too.

"Making any progress?" It was the sheriff's voice.

Leo jumped. His arms fell to his sides. "Maybe." He filled his boss in.

Fentworth unwrapped a red lollipop. "It's a good start. Listen, I've got some paperwork related to the case that needs filling out, so I can update the mayor. Time sensitive. I'll email it over to you." He threw the wrapper in Leo's trash.

"Great," Leo said, not meaning it. It seemed like pushing paper around was eighty percent of a cop's job. He understood it was important for future court proceedings to establish a record, and for protection from possible lawsuits, but he chafed at it anyway. He preferred the "doing" part of the job. Possibly, that was why he'd liked his undercover work with the Bajeños. Sure, he'd had to create a log, but it was so much less time-consuming than what he'd done before or since. He wanted to learn all he could about the life and times of Lila Clement, interview witnesses, and follow up on the similar crimes research. Progress his task list. None of that could start until he finished killing the trees, though. *Bear down and buck up.* "Who else will be working on the case?"

"You, Delaney, and me, for now. The feds when one surfaces. Let me know if you get bogged down. We have a mutual aid statute in Wyoming, so we're all set up under agreements to help each other, even outside jurisdictional lines." Fentworth stuck the sucker in his mouth.

"Will do."

The candy came back out again. Fentworth's lips were stained red. "Oh, and the state crime scene team sent over their preliminary report. They cast some footprints as well as those tire tracks and they gathered blood evidence, but that's about it. They said it was a surprisingly clean scene. I'll send it on to you and Delaney."

Leo felt a twinge of disappointment pinch in his chest. "I'll read the report as soon as I finish your paperwork."

"I'm going to dig into it right now. I'll give you a shout if I see anything else useful. Then we can grab a burger and exchange updates before my meeting with the mayor, all right?" The sheriff saluted and returned to his office.

"All right. Talk to you later," Leo said.

Leo completed the paperwork faster than any he'd ever done and got back to the case. After he'd searched online and made a list of the possible stores in a fifty-mile radius, he started calling and asking questions about the soldering irons sold in the last month. Most of the time he ended up talking to assistant store managers, since it was nearly Memorial Day weekend, a prime time for people to be vacationing based on pecking order. He did learn they didn't sell a lot of the tools. Some were able to look up the information while he was on the phone. He found a store in nearby Sheridan that had sold one and was able to send him credit card information via email. At the largest stores, he was promised callbacks after the long weekend when they had sufficient staff to check data from their point-of-sale systems.

The email arrived for the credit card purchase and yielded a name. Irma Fielding. A search of driver's license records showed her to be a seventy-one-year-old woman living twenty miles north of Kearny. *This is not the crime of a septuagenarian female.* But she could have given the tool to someone else. Or procured it by request from the killer. He added a visit to Irma to his list.

The last store on his list was the small Kearny hardware store. From Leo's one visit, he knew it to be pricey and more like a general store than one for serious hardware shoppers. He was transferred to the manager.

Leo introduced himself and explained to the man what he was looking for. "Any sales like that?"

"Well, we've got two ladies who work the registers. Let me walk out there and ask."

Leo heard the man's breathing change and the sound of his footsteps. "That will work."

The man repeated the question to a woman he called Rosie. Her reply was inaudible.

"Yeah, she sold one a few days ago to a fella," he said.

"Could you put me on speaker phone?"

"Sure. Here you go."

"Rosie, this is Deputy Leo Palmer. Can you describe the person who bought the mini soldering iron?"

"He paid cash." Her voice was flat, and he couldn't hear her much better on speaker than off.

"Great. And how about what he looked like?"

"I don't know, sir. I barely looked at him. Other than he was white and normal-sized. He looked like every other man in Kearny to me."

"Rosie is very shy," the manager cut in. "She was raised in a culture where women don't make a lot of eye contact with men other than their husbands."

Leo squeezed his hands into fists. *Not helpful.* "How do you —? Never mind. All right, is there anything else you can tell me about him?"

"He had a funny accent," she said.

"In what way?"

"I couldn't place it. Not from the south or the east or west coast. I also recognize people from the Midwest and even up in Michigan and Wisconsin and thereabouts. Or from foreign countries. But not him."

"Did he sound old or young?"

She paused. "Neither? But he didn't walk old."

"Would you recognize his voice again if you heard it?"

"I think so. I remember voices pretty good."

"I'm going to leave my number. You call me if he comes

back in, as fast as you can, okay? I'll come right out to get my eyes on him." Leo thought for a second. Then he said, "Do you remember what else he bought? Or maybe have a register receipt with a record of it?"

The manager laughed. "We're not computerized like the fancy stores."

"I remember," Rosie said.

The manager's voice was jovial. "We'll never need computers as long as Rosie works here. She's got a brain like a bear trap."

"He bought rope and some bungee cords. A mess of clamps. Two tarps. A whetstone."

Leo asked, "Were those unusual purchases?" They would have been in San Diego. This sounded like a lead to him. A good one.

"No, sir. I figured he was needing to camp out and do some ranch work."

Maybe. Or maybe not. Still, Leo felt a rush of energy as the case started moving forward.

SIXTEEN

Mary's directions had been precise, but Sicario Menendez lived at a higher elevation—and in a more beautiful location—than Delaney had expected. It was a piece of property ripe to be picked up by buyers from the west coast, those with Wyoming mountain dreams. Trees ringed a lily pad-covered pond. A moose stood stomach-deep, its head under water. A moment later, the head rose, enormous antlers first, water and stringy green plants streaming from the animal's bulbous muzzle.

The rest of the place was an affront to its otherwise pristine surroundings. Not that the Pace family homestead was the Taj Mahal. But compared to the wooden pallets, shells of ORVs, pipe, snowmobile skids, and molded hay, it was close. She parked next to a beat-up bronze long bed pickup in front of a mobile home that sagged like a pot-bellied pig. No curb, no sidewalk, no driveway. She surveyed the rest of the grounds. A rusted propane tank. A crudely installed direct vent—probably to a freestanding stove for heat. There were no visible power lines, but she saw solar panels on a flatbed trailer with four flat tires.

Not a place most women would line up for a chance to inhabit.

"Cool," Kateena said, pointing at the moose. "But what a dump."

Delaney agreed but she didn't say so. The girl needed to respect adults more, not less. For that reason, she'd decided not to tell Kateena the details about her meeting with the principal. She turned her attention to the trailer. Was the owner even home?

"Wait here." She had no reason to expect Mary's ex to be dangerous, but she didn't imagine he'd be happy to talk about his financial obligations, and she didn't want to expose Kateena to him.

"How long?" Kateena's tone dripped attitude.

"Fifteen minutes, max." The temperature was hovering around fifty-five degrees. She cracked the windows an inch. "Keep the door locked. I'll take the keys with me."

Kateena rolled her eyes like Delaney had just said the dumbest thing *ever*. Maybe if she'd known her aunt had got up in someone's grill for her, she'd have been nicer. Or maybe not. As Delaney recalled, this was pretty age-appropriate behavior. But infuriating. "Duds needs to go potty."

"After."

Delaney palmed the Staccato C2 pistol from her purse and shoved it into the back of her jeans. She felt confident with it on her, in part because she practiced with it at least once a week. No self-respecting truck driver hauling in remote areas *wouldn't* carry. Hell, this was Wyoming. She didn't personally know any adults who weren't gun owners and proficient shooters. Owning a Staccato, though, probably put her in the category of gun snob. She could have a Glock for a third of the price, but she'd fallen in love with the high-capacity C2 for concealed-carry in her law enforcement days and had to have it, even though it had set her back two grand for a private purchase.

It had been languishing in her purse last night, though. Part of her wished she'd had it with her. The guy she'd been following could have given her trouble. Part of her was glad she hadn't. Leo would have added it to her list of transgressions.

Kateena bobbed her head in what might have been compliance regarding Duds and his potty break. "Fine. And I see your gun."

Delaney opened the door. "Fine. I wasn't hiding it from you." The girl and her sass. She shut the door a little hard, not quite a slam. *Be the grown-up.* She was trying. It would be easier with some sleep.

She marched to the trailer. Before she could announce herself, her Spidey senses started tingling. She stepped sideways, reaching for her gun. The door cracked open. A shotgun barrel slid out.

A strained male voice shouted. "Stop. What do you want?"

This was starting off worse than she'd hoped. She gripped the stock of her pistol, finger on the safety. "My name's Delaney Pace. I just want to talk to you. There's no reason for firearms. I have my young niece out here with me. Can we take it down a notch?"

"Pace?" The barrel didn't waver.

"Delaney Pace."

"Any relation to Liam?"

Delaney glanced at the car. Shelly's windows were up, and her doors were closed. "My big brother."

The barrel dropped. "You carrying?"

"Of course. But I'm not pointing it at anyone." She tucked the Staccato back into her waistband. Next time she was wearing her belly holster. She blamed forgetting it on the sleep deprivation. "I just put it away."

The door opened over empty space. Hopefully, there was another entrance to the trailer, because this one would be a challenge to use, seeing as the steps up to it were missing. The man who hopped to the ground was shaped like a bowling ball. She couldn't imagine him climbing back through the opening he'd exited.

"Your brother owes me money."

"I didn't catch your name, but I'm hoping it's Sicario Menendez."

Now that he was closer, she saw that he had a crumpled ear. Like a boxer. She imagined away the folds of fat around his eyes, recreating him from slovenly to athletic. He had probably been handsome in a dangerous way, but not recently. "Who told you where I live and what my name is?"

Delaney dodged his question, returning to his earlier point. "Sicario, my brother is dead."

"I guess that means you owe me now. Are you here to pay up?"

She snorted. "It doesn't work that way. And, speaking of money, Mary bartends for me at the Loafing Shed. She tells me you owe her some."

"Yeah, and I would have paid her if Liam hadn't stiffed me." *Because he is a stiff.* He bumped his forehead with his palm. "Wait. Mary sent you?"

Delaney locked eyes with him. "She's broke. Can't make rent. She works hard and takes good care of your son."

He ran his hands across his eyes. "Juan Julio."

"I could deliver some money for him. You know, from you."

"I don't have any cash. I lost my job. On account of your brother died."

"Do you have part of it? Anything to keep food on the table for him?"

Sicario leaned against the trailer. "I got a little."

"Why haven't you called her and told her to come get it?"

"No cell phone. I had one of them pay as you go phones, but it's used up. And her and me don't get along so good."

"What do you do for food?"

He gestured around him.

Living off the land. "Any job prospects?"

"I'm good at construction. But my truck is broke down. I can't afford to get it hauled off and fixed." He shook his head.

Delaney tried not to feel sorry for him. He was an unemployed dad not paying child support. But his sadness about Juan Julio seemed genuine. "What's wrong with your truck?"

"I don't know. It doesn't run. I'm not a mechanic or I would have fixed it myself. I don't even have internet to search YouTube, you know, for one of those DIY videos."

"I'm something of a mechanic. How about I take a look?"

He scowled. "Right."

Delaney was used to this reaction from men. "Don't insult me, Mr. Menendez. I'm the only one here, and I don't owe you anything. I just offered my help. If you don't want it, that's fine with me."

"It's not like that. I mean, I don't understand why you want to help me. I'm nobody. And I ain't done right by Juan Julio and Mary."

Delaney sighed. She didn't understand either, other than that maybe if she helped him, he'd be able to help Mary. "I'll tell you what, I have a toolbox in my trunk, but my niece and her dog are in the car. If they can get out and run around while I work on it, I'll see what I can do. Then, if I'm successful, you can deliver that money to Juan Julio yourself."

Instead of nodding or shaking her hand, Sicario barreled at her.

SEVENTEEN

An hour later, Delaney, Sicario, and Kateena carried burgers and fries toward a booth in Buns in the Barn, where they'd gone after a stop for Sicario to add minutes to his phone. After Sicario's rush at her had turned into a teary bear hug instead of an attack, things had gone quite swimmingly with the man, hence his presence with them for lunch. Which Delaney was buying, of course. She was also carrying a small burger to go for Dudley, who was waiting in the car. The greasy smell was intoxicating, and Delaney's stomach growled like she hadn't had a big breakfast at the Cowpoke Café. She thought about washing her hands again—she'd done it once in Sicario's trailer —since her fingernails were black from working on the truck. The bathroom here wouldn't have the kind of soap to get them clean, though. At least she still had girly toes.

"Great to see you, Laney," the proprietor called, waving from the cash register below the colorful lighted menu. Her hair stood on end in a gray dandelion poof.

Delaney had terrorized this place in her teens. She considered it a minor miracle that they still served her as an adult. "Always a pleasure, Martha."

"She called you Laney," Kateena said in a hiss.

"I don't correct my elders. Something you could learn from."

"I know how much you hate being wrong. I'm only helping you."

Sicario laughed, a coyote howl of a sound. He and Kateena had played with Dudley while Delaney had worked on his truck. He hadn't said much since they'd arrived at the restaurant, although he'd been effusive in his thanks when Delaney had fixed the distributor. Not that it had been tricky. She'd confirmed that the engine was getting gas and that power was making it to the spark plugs. While she'd been messing with the spark plug wires, the whole distributor assembly had turned on her. They tended to vibrate loose in old model Chevy trucks if they weren't tightened properly. After that "Aha!" moment, all she'd had to do was adjust the timing. She was aiming for about thirty-four degrees, basing it on the sound of the engine. Without a timing light she couldn't be a hundred percent sure she'd hit it, but she knew she was pretty close. And it was running now, passing the one true test of repair jobs. The vehicle always tells you if you get it right.

In her opinion, auto mechanics should be a required course in high school. A prerequisite to obtaining a driver's license. It was about more than keeping cars running. There were too many bozos operating dangerous, expensive vehicles with no idea what they were capable of and how that knowledge could help them avoid accidents, injuries, getting stranded, and even death. Partly she felt this way because of her dad, but years as a deputy and truck driver had hammered his lessons home.

Sicario slid into the red plastic booth and dug into his food like a starving wolf. Kateena took a seat across from him. Delaney sat by her niece.

Kateena nibbled ketchup-dunked fries in tiny bites, like a rabbit with a stalk of celery. "Where are we going next?"

Delaney swallowed a bite of burger. "Back to the Loafing Shed."

Kateena's horrified expression was made grotesque by blood-red ketchup dripping from the corner of her mouth. "Do we have to? Let's do something fun instead."

A booming voice interrupted them. "Delaney. I thought you'd be at home sleeping."

Delaney glanced up at Fentworth. Leo had walked up beside him. Delaney felt her face flush. It reminded her she wasn't supposed to like Leo. Damn her pheromones for making her forget it over and over.

"Delaney." His voice was less than enthused.

"Hello, Fentworth," she said. Then, turning her face so only Leo could see it, she gave him a steely look to make sure he knew she wasn't over him arresting her yet. "Leo."

Sicario took a sharp breath, then coughed. Was he choking on his burger? She glanced at him. His face had reddened, but he was breathing fine.

The sheriff touched his head. "Remove your lid, Palmer. You're riding for the brand."

Leo removed his baseball cap. "Dang, there's a whole lot of new rules to learn in Wyoming."

Fentworth grunted. "Seems like now's the perfect time to let you two know the good news. You're working so well together that I'm pairing you up for a while. I think it will be a good way for Leo to learn the ropes and Delaney to reacquaint herself with law enforcement."

Delaney ground her teeth like she was eating glass. She didn't do teams. And she'd only just wrapped her head around being paired by circumstances with Leo on Lila's case. Anything more official just felt too... official. "I thought deputies rode alone."

Leo said, "But, sir—"

"Well, I'm glad that's settled." The sheriff smiled at Kateena. "Nice to see you again, young lady.

Kateena glared at him. "My daddy didn't like you."

"Kateena!" Delaney said.

Fentworth nodded without a flicker of reaction to Kateena's words. "I sure am sorry your daddy's gone. It's my job to enforce the laws. Occasionally, people disagree with me about that. Sometimes you need sheriffs, though, even when you disagree with them. It's our job to keep the bad guys from hurting people."

She sniffed and turned to Leo. "You're the one who wasn't nice to Aunt Delaney. And you don't like Dudley. I got suspended from school because of you."

Having Kateena's back wasn't a one-way street. Delaney wanted to hug the girl. "She got in a fight with a boy about my arrest. She won. And got suspended."

"She takes after you," Leo said to Delaney.

Martha's loud, cheerful voice interrupted them. "I read about you being a trucker, Laney. I hadn't heard you were going back to working for Coltrane, though." Her eyes flitted away, and she called after a departing customer. "You come back now, sir!"

Delaney looked toward the exit. All she could see was Sicario's backside as he hustled toward his truck. She cut her eyes back to the booth. His burger basket and Coca-Cola sat unfinished.

Fentworth cocked his head. "Was that Sicario Menendez with you?" He pointed at the table.

"Aunt Delaney fixed Sicario's truck for him so he can go back to work and give Mary money to use for Juan Julio." Kateena beamed with niecely pride.

More information than necessary, but nice.

Fentworth whacked his hat against his leg. "Delaney, what the hell are you doing? That man's a drug dealer."

Delaney gnawed the inside of her lip. Neither Sicario nor Mary had provided her with that nugget of useful information. Trouble seemed to be following close on her heels ever since she'd returned to Kearny.

EIGHTEEN

The bell jingled in the gap between songs as the door opened. Normally, Mary didn't hear the sound of the bell over the music and hum of conversation, but the place was empty.

She was midway through writing an inventory of the liquor behind the bar. She scribbled on her notepad without looking up. WYO WSKY. They were going through the stuff like water. That spelled opportunity. She had ideas for this place. Lots of them. If Delaney would turn it over to her, she could get this bar in the black and make it no trouble whatsoever to her new boss. It had seemed like Liam *wanted* it to lose money. Like he hated it or something. And now Delaney didn't have the time or interest to rescue it. Mary decided to pitch a business plan to Delaney. Why not? She thought she'd made a good impression so far.

When the newcomer didn't speak or approach the bar, she glanced up. Smallish white guy with a smooth face. New clothes. A flannel jacket with a hoody, which he wore up. Dark sunglasses. No tan or wind burn on his skin. *Out-of-stater. He was in yesterday.* Had ordered one beer and not drunk it.

"Welcome back. Let me know what I can get for you," she said.

He didn't reply.

She went back to her inventory. The playlist advanced on Liam's old iPad. "Detroit Rock City" by Kiss. Ear-splitting with no one in the bar to absorb it. She turned it down. The playlist was new. Delaney had subbed in one with classic rock on her first day in town. No explanation. Just deleted Liam's contemporary country and hit play. Mary didn't mind classic rock, but she would have liked more variety for the patrons. Some Maggie Killian. Some Ian Munsick. Not music she'd listened to before moving to Wyoming, but she'd come around. She'd put that on her list of suggestions.

The man was walking around the bar, stopping to examine every photograph and memento, giving the place a real once-over. Even though he wasn't looking at her, she felt his attention. Was he wanting her to watch him? *That's not going to happen, hombre.* She'd given up the best years of her life to Sicario, attracted to the bad-boy side of him. Granted, he'd gone straight eventually, working in construction, but maybe if he hadn't he'd still be paying child support. Now she was stranded in Wyoming with no family and no help from him, the fat, lazy fool. He hadn't been fat when she'd met him, but he'd always been looking for the easy way out. Her next man was going to be a cowboy. Like the one she had a date with later today. There were no fat or lazy cowboys.

"Bathroom?" the man asked. His high-pitched voice was definitely out of state. He sounded slick. Citified.

She pointed to the back hall.

He walked toward it without thanking her.

Her phone rang. She answered on hands-free so she could keep working. "Mary Galvez speaking." Just the way her mamacita had taught her to answer the phone. It had stuck, unlike many of her lessons. She should have listened to the woman more. Maybe then she wouldn't be a broke-ass single mom with a former gang-banger's baby, getting ready to beg for a chance to run a broke-ass bar.

A man said, "You called me about the construction jobs."

She glanced at the screen. The caller ID read Ryan Hefler. Apparently, Ryan's mama hadn't taught him phone manners. She recognized the name, though. A general contractor she'd called. One whose name she'd seen in the paper before.

"I did. Thanks for calling me back. You know Delaney Pace?"

"Never heard of him."

"How about Liam Pace? He passed recently."

"Everybody knew him."

How to put this? She wanted to sound like she had the authority to make this call, not like she was just a bartender doing a favor for the boss. She took the phone off speaker and put it to her ear. "Delaney and I are looking for someone to take over Liam's customers. Are you interested?"

"Why don't I come in and we can talk in person? I'm in the neighborhood. I can be at the Loading Shed in five."

Before she could answer, he hung up. She scrolled back through her missed calls. None of the other contractors she'd left messages for had called back. She meticulously culled all her communications daily—she hated clutter—but she decided to leave the record of Hefler's call. The call before it in the list was from Liam, even though it was nearly a month old. She wasn't sure why she'd left it there. Maybe it was because it was the last time he'd called her and now he was gone. She'd picked up, heard breathing, and the call had dropped. She'd smiled, thinking it was a butt dial. It seemed like only minutes later deputies had shown up looking for a family member to notify about Liam's and Lila's deaths. Everything since then had been stressful. And sad. So deleting the phone record felt sacrilegious somehow.

A weight settled into a bar stool behind her, closest to the front door. She turned. Hoody man. She didn't want to initiate conversation, but she worked for tips. *Not if I become the manager, though.* "It looks like you beat the crowd."

He lifted his eyes and stared straight into hers, pinning her, it felt like.

She wanted to squirm away. "What are you drinking?"

He pointed to the bottle on the counter—the half-empty Wyoming Whiskey—and held up two fingers.

"Two fingers?"

He shook his head. "Two shots."

"A double?"

He shook it again. "Two. Shots."

She laughed, a tinny, nervous sound. "For you and your imaginary friend."

His gaze held steady. His mouth stayed closed. While she poured, he picked up the newspaper Skeeter had left behind. He rolled it up and tucked it inside his waistband. *Help yourself, mister.*

She set two shot glasses on the counter and poured. "That'll be ten dollars." She included an upcharge for him being rude and creepy.

He put a twenty on the bar top. She pushed the shot glasses over to him.

He slid one to her with the back of his hand. "Special delivery."

"I can't drink on the job."

"Not it. You."

"I don't follow?"

He pulled a piece of plastic out of his pocket. She frowned. A hospital bracelet. Tiny. Baby-sized. He held it up, turning it in the light. She caught a glimpse of the name. MENENDEZ.

From her house. Juan Julio's hospital bracelet. Her treasure from his birth. This man had it. *He knows who I am. Where I live.* He'd stolen it and brought it here, where she was alone with him, and suddenly everything made a horrible, awful sense to her.

She ran. As fast and hard as she could toward the back door and her car outside, thanking God that she'd left the bar flap open, regretting the heeled boots that made her ass look good and earned more tips, listening in terror to his bootsteps rattling glass behind her, only realizing as she reached the door and he grabbed her ponytail that she didn't have her keys and couldn't have escaped him anyway.

Her last thought was to wonder who would take care of her son.

NINETEEN

Still worrying over whether she'd just facilitated a friendship between Kateena and a drug dealer, Delaney pointed Shelly toward the Pace homestead, which was a few miles past the bar, off the highway toward the eastern buttes. Kateena slept beside her. Dudley snored in the back seat. Protective affection bubbled up inside Delaney. It was time to restore some normalcy to her two charges.

Still, she'd hoped to be escorting Sicario and his modest wad of cash to Mary at the Loafing Shed right now. His sudden departure had been peculiar. She wondered if there was a warrant out for his arrest. She'd check later. But, maybe after he'd left, he'd taken the money to Mary anyway. She hadn't gotten his number, so she couldn't reach him, short of driving back out to his trailer.

She pulled onto the tree-lined winding driveway, crossing a wooden bridge halfway to the house. The driveway ended between it and a big red barn. *The place needs some work.* Maintaining a house, pieces of which were over a hundred and twenty years old, wasn't easy, or cheap. Delaney would get to it when she had the time and money. White paint peeled from the wooden siding of the old homestead house, a compilation of original build and additions by later generations. The roof was short a few shingles, like an old timer who'd misplaced his dentures. Broken spindles on the porch drew the eyes away from the warped deck boards.

Kateena and Dudley awoke as Delaney parked Shelly in the barn. The child and dog climbed out. Delaney slid the car's cover on. While there was not currently any livestock at the place, the bats that roosted here left a mess, as did the barn cat and the rodents it hunted, but the risk of hail outside made it smarter to keep the car in the barn.

Girl and dog whooped and barked as they ran into the house ahead of Delaney. *Always so much energy.* Her steps dragged. She needed a bed and a nap. Even if it was the creaky four-poster in the main bedroom that had once belonged to the grandparents who chose not to raise her. The person in the family she'd truly counted on—her dad—had slept in his travel trailer, giving up the inside bedrooms so that his son and daughter each had one of their own.

Painful memories rushed over her, holding her hostage in the front yard. Her grandmother, brandishing a bar of home-made soap and screaming as she looked for her grandson. "Liam Pace, did you take the Lord's name in vain?" Her fifteen-year-old brother crushing a cigarette, holding a finger to his grinning lips as Delaney watched open-mouthed, and running off into the forest. Little Delaney helpless and the only target for Grandma's wrath. The taste of the soap when she wouldn't give up his location. The sting of her grandfather's belt on her bare skin. The pain in her knees as she knelt on pebbles reciting the Bible verse of the day in front of her grandparents until she got it right. The way her father pretended all of it was normal, which she guessed it had been, to him, growing up in this house before her.

She shook it all away. *So tired.*

The screen door slammed behind her as she entered the house, which still smelled like her grandmother was boiling lima beans and canning sauerkraut in the kitchen. Kateena was whipping Dudley into a frenzy in the living room. The dog careened into the free-standing rack of fireplace tools. Because they were a Rudy Pace special, they crashed to the floor, top-heavy. Dudley yelped, tucked his bottom, and scooted across the room and down the hall. Kateena's laughter reverberated off the walls as she ran after him. Delaney had to smile. Her father's welding skills were good enough for his car, but when he translated them to homestead art, the results were crude. Nothing could stop him making and installing his specialty in every place his friends and family built fires, though. This set had an old metal GMC emblem welded into the shaft of the poker.

"Aunt Delaney, what's for dinner? And are we going to watch *Heartland* now?" Kateena shouted from her bedroom.

"Ask me when I wake up."

Delaney stopped in the kitchen beside the shelves Grandpa had built because the pantry was filled with canning equipment, so Grandma could keep a week's supply of food handy. The root cellar housed enough of her food stores to last a hard winter, and it was conveniently located next to the equally well stocked gun safe. Both were accessible to what people these days would call a safe room. Delaney had revisited it all when she'd first returned. The underground footprint was nearly as large as the house above it, but the supplies had dwindled in the absence of her grandparents.

Sinking into one of the blocky pine kitchen chairs built by her grandfather, she pulled out her cell phone and speed-dialed the bar from her Favorites. She needed to give Mary a report on Sicario, if she could keep her eyes open long enough to do it.

A sloshy male voice answered. "The Loading Shed. Today's the day to get loaded with your bud Skeeter."

Skeeter is answering the phone?! "Let me speak to Mary please."

"Mary has run off somewhere. This is Skeeter, the temporary bar keep. Today's special is free whiskey for everyone." He shouted the last few words with glee.

If Mary was out and Skeeter was driving the bar closer to bankruptcy, Delaney's nap was going to have to wait. She rubbed her eyes. "You're not the temporary anything, Skeeter. This is Delaney."

"Who?"

"Delaney Pace."

"Oh! The jailbird who was doing the job free for me today." *Close enough.* "Same one."

"Did you get the money?"

"Maybe. Progress was made."

Skeeter said, "Could be the reason Mary took off? If she got the money, I mean."

Delaney felt the beginning of a wicked headache. The real question was how it had taken so long for one to develop. Mary didn't seem the type to skip town with fifty bucks, which is what Sicario had scraped up for her and Juan Julio. But how much did she know about the woman? She didn't show signs of being an addict, but maybe she needed a fix. Maybe she'd gone to one of the casinos on the Wind River Indian Reservation. Maybe she'd driven to Montana for some pot or edibles.

Or maybe she'd run to the grocery store for nutritious food for her son.

"Did she leave a note?" Delaney asked.

"Nope. When I came back from my mid-day siesta, the door was unlocked, but no Mary."

"I'm on my way."

"For the free whiskey?" Skeeter said.

"To shut the free whiskey down."

"But why? It's the best crowd this place has seen in years."

"I'm the one covering the tab for this party. Except for yours. I'm holding you responsible for that."

"Why would you do that? I can't even remember what I've had."

"I run the place, remember?"

Dead silence on the other end of the line.

"I'll see you in ten minutes."

"Uh, yeah. Anything you need me to do before then?"

"Pass a hat to defray my expenses. Anyone who doesn't chip in, get them out before I show up."

"But people are too drunk to drive."

"It's only a mile to town. Have them walk or call for rides. Just no freeloaders left on the premises by the time I arrive."

His answer was slow, his voice dubious. "O-kay." He didn't bother to put his hand over the mouthpiece. "Party's over everybody. The owner's on her way, and she's pissed."

The one running the place against her will. The owner was only eleven years old. But Skeeter had the sentiment right.

Delaney had left Kateena curled up on the couch with a *Horses of the West* coloring book and a brand new 120-count box of crayons. The girl was humming over Dudley's snores. Delaney smiled at the mental picture as she climbed out of the Chevelle, behind the bar. She'd never planned to have any children of her own, too afraid of repeating her past with a new generation. Kateena was hers for keeps, though. There would be no parade of foster families in the girl's future. And far less of the Loafing Shed. Bar-time hadn't done Delaney any favors growing up, and no matter how Kateena had been raised until now, there was a new sheriff in town—or, deputy investigator at least—and Delaney planned to do better. Better than had been done for Kateena so far, and better than had been done for Delaney herself. Which reminded her that she was going to have to figure out the school bus schedule for Kateena and find someone to hang out with her while Delaney worked.

She opened the back door to the bar. Then she paused. Mary's old Monte Carlo was parked in its usual spot. *That's strange.* Maybe she'd had car trouble. Maybe a friend had picked her up. Or maybe she'd returned since Delaney's call with Skeeter.

But why hadn't Mary called her? Delaney's number was on her phone. Unless she was a far different person than Delaney had experienced her to be so far, she wouldn't walk off and leave the bar unlocked and unattended without notice. If for no other reason than she needed the job. But the woman seemed smart and eager to make a good impression. Ripe for more responsibility.

Delaney walked the hallway. Raucous laughter and pop country music. As she passed the office, familiar terrors seized her. The walls closed in. She put a hand on one to steady herself. *No. No. Come on. Walk away from this.* But her leg muscles were unwilling or unable to move.

Time shifted into reverse, and she was a girl Kateena's age, standing in the doorway to the office. Her daddy had told her to stay in there and read her book. *On the Banks of Plum Creek,* but she'd read it a million times already. Daddy had gone to talk to someone, and he was shouting. Should she go see what was going on? Daddy's voice drew closer. She shrank back as two figures entered the hall. One was her daddy, but his tall body was blocking her view of the other person. It was winter, and Daddy had on his bulky Carhartt pants and a sweater. She couldn't see the other person at all.

Her daddy said, "Never. I've told you this. It's just not happening."

The other person laughed, then spoke in a whisper she could barely hear. "That's where you're wrong. Dead wrong."

She heard a footfall and swooshing air.

Her daddy gasped and leaned over. She saw the top of the other person's head, covered in a black wool cap. Were they punching her daddy? Something red—blood?—splattered on the walls, the floor. Daddy clutched his tummy. Delaney clapped a hand over her mouth. The person was hurting him. If she screamed, they'd hurt her, too. She felt the heat of her breath against her palm. She moaned and backed away. Should she call 911? Should she hide? She grabbed the phone and crawled under the desk. She punched in the numbers.

Someone answered. "911, what's your emergency?"

In the hallway, there was a thud. Grunting and thuds. Grunting and thuds.

"No one tells me no," the voice said. Raspy. Out of breath.

The operator repeated her words, "911, what's your emergency? Where's your location? I hear you breathing."

Footsteps. The person was walking away. Toward the front door.

Delaney said, "Help me. Help my daddy." Then she dropped the phone, left her hiding place, and ran into the hall to take care of him herself. His eyes were closed. The blood had been everywhere. His stomach. His legs. His feet. Bubbling from his lips.

In the present, Delaney made a keening noise and realized she was clutching her pendant. That had been twenty-four years ago. She was okay. Help had arrived, too late for her father. It had been too late by the time she'd made the call. But she was a grown-up and not a scared little girl anymore. There was no one in the hallway with her. Not her dad. Not the person who'd killed him and gotten away with it.

"Why can't I remember who stabbed you, Daddy?" Her words were a whisper.

She knew the reason. She'd never seen the killer's face. She'd barely heard the voice. It wasn't her fault. She'd only had her eleventh birthday the week before it happened. Her dad had swapped bedrooms with her so she could have a sleepover party with her girlfriends in the trailer. He'd brought them frozen pizzas that he'd heated himself, in boxes just like expensive delivery pizzas. When she'd opened the top box, she'd found a model of Shotgun Shelly that he'd built and painted himself.

"It wasn't my fault. I'm okay, and it wasn't my fault." She wiped tears from her eyes. It had taken her nearly all of the last two decades to teach herself those words, repeating them as wheels spun and road vanished beneath tires, even if she didn't quite believe them yet.

"Why did Liam and Lila have to die without wills and leave me responsible for this Godforsaken place?" she muttered. Technically, their daughter was their only heir, which still left Delaney with no choice but to give up her life to pick up the pieces of her brother's, because... Kateena.

It's the exhaustion. All these memories today. It will get better. She swallowed, then took a deep breath and pushed it explosively out of her mouth.

Using a firm inner voice, she coached herself aloud. "Roust the freeloaders, find a fill-in bartender, and figure out what happened to Mary. Do it, Delaney. Don't just stand here." She forced her legs to move.

When she reached the bar proper, Luke Bryan was belting out "One Margarita." She shivered in revulsion. Skeeter was shouting for people to leave. His hair was standing on end and his eyes wild. And the place was a wreck. Shot glasses, beer mugs, and cocktail glasses on every surface, some half full, along with wadded-up napkins, limes, olives, toothpicks, and sticky-looking spills. Chairs were on their sides. People were singing along to the music, arms around each other's shoulders, swaying back and forth, glasses in the air and contents sloshing onto the floor. There hadn't been this many people in the Loafing Shed at once since her childhood.

Mary was nowhere to be seen.

Delaney marched to the bar. The iPod was on the counter. With a few swipes and taps, she turned off the music. She pounded the bar top. "Party's over, people. Out."

Skeeter was wringing his hands. "I tried to get control of them. I don't know what happened."

Grumbling and complaints commenced.

Delaney gave Skeeter some side-eye. Then she shouted, "Out or I'm calling the cops. Now." Still, they didn't move. She set her purse on the bar top, climbed up, pulled out her badge and gun, and held them both in the air. "I'm Deputy Investigator Delaney Pace, and this thing isn't loaded with salt pellets. Don't make me chase you out of here with it."

Sixty seconds later, the bar was clear. Delaney figured she'd just sealed the fate of the place. Word would get out. No more would people come to get loaded at the Loafing Shed. Not with a deputy in charge.

Skeeter turned to her and shook his head.

"What?"

"Men will be lining up at the door to see a law woman on the bar with a gun."

Delaney didn't understand men, which probably accounted for her being thirty-five and single. And having dated Chad. "There's a coffee maker." She pointed at the machine. "Make some while I lock up."

"I, uh, I gotta go."

She laughed without mirth. "After we clean up, Skeeter. Or after you do, rather. I'm going to track down our missing bartender."

Skeeter shuffled over to the coffee maker, filled the water well, and added a filter with grounds from the canister below the counter. From his familiarity with the machine and supplies, it appeared he'd done it a few times in the past.

Delaney got out her phone.

Skeeter looked up from his task. "Are you really a deputy?"

"I am."

"Why were you in lockup, then?"

"A misunderstanding." She scrolled through her Recents and called Mary's number. *I should have done this half an hour ago. Damn sleep deprivation.*

Ringing sounded from inside one of the cabinets. A knot formed in the pit of Delaney's gut. She opened the cabinet and found a gold fringed shoulder purse. It was the source of the noise. She dug her hand into it and pulled out a phone. The caller ID said, "Queen Bitch of the Bar."

Delaney mouthed the words. It took her a hot second to accept that sweet Mary had set up her contact for Delaney under that name. When she'd swallowed it, she considered the possibility that Mary would have left the bar willingly, leaving her phone, purse, and car. *No way.*

Delaney clicked the phone to decline her own call. Then she dialed the sheriff's department.

Mary was missing.

TWENTY

Leo's desk phone buzzed. After coffee with his burger, he'd been too wired to sleep yet, so he'd come back to the department when Fentworth had gone to brief the mayor. He picked up the receiver. "Palmer."

"This is Clara. 911 just got a call from the Loafing Shed about a missing person. Are you available to go out and take a report?"

Delaney. An unexpected panic seized Leo. "Male? Female? Name? Age?"

Fentworth appeared, taking off his hat, blatantly eavesdropping.

Clara said, "A woman. I didn't get the other information. I just said I'd send someone out. Sorry."

Leo's eyes shot to the sheriff. "Hold on. The boss just walked in. Let me ask him."

"What?" Fentworth asked.

"Missing woman. The Loafing Shed is calling it in."

"Not Delaney?"

"I don't know, sir."

Fentworth adjusted his eye patch. "No one else is available to take it?"

Leo hit speaker.

Clara said, "Nope. Joe called in sick. Tommy's on a domestic. Want me to ask city to handle it?"

The sheriff shook his head. "I don't want to owe Chief Nelson any favors for something this routine. The man's a blowhard. You'll need to take this one, Johnny Utah. Lila Clement can wait."

So would sleep. "No problem."

"And call me immediately if it's Delaney."

Leo parked his department truck in front of the Loafing Shed. The building had a roadhouse look. Weathered wood, a neon sign above the door. Tin roof. Beer and booze posters on every window. It was the kind of place that would've had thirty immaculate Harleys belonging to a gang called Hell's Accountants in front of it in California. The lot was empty, though, save one car, so he didn't have to fight for a spot.

A breeze bit through his uniform as he got out. *You're not in Kansas anymore, Dodo.* He pushed through the outer and inner doors, the two sets a common feature, he'd discovered, of entrances in Wyoming, to keep the weather outside. His nose wrinkled. The place smelled like it had been mopped down with dirty water and whiskey. Delaney and a large, pasty guy were the only people inside. The man was sweeping, and Delaney was stalking around the bar depositing trash in a black bag. It was a relief to see she wasn't the missing person. He found himself watching her a little too long. *No, Palmer.* He couldn't further complicate his life with a co-worker. Especially one who sent flickers of something dangerous through his nervous system.

"Took you long enough." She set the bag down.

Earlier, she'd seemed to thaw some toward him. That was then. Now was different, clearly. Eventually her abrasive personality would cancel out her looks and electricity. It just hadn't happened for him yet. "You guys called in a missing woman?"

She moved behind the bar. "This is Skeeter. He's a witness. Skeeter, this is Deputy Palmer."

"I don't know nothing," the other man said. Louder, to her, he added, "I don't see why you're not just handling this yourself, Delaney."

"I told you. We're doing this official. And I'm a witness, too."

Leo took a seat at a stool, pulled out a notebook and pen, and set them on the bar top. It was sticky. "Wet rag?"

Delaney ran water from a tap on a rag that may once have been white. She tossed it to him. Leo caught it one-handed and rubbed down the sticky spot. He threw the rag back to her. The bar wasn't any cleaner.

"Tell me what happened," he said.

Delaney crossed her arms and leaned away from Leo. "My bartender went MIA today during her shift. Mary Galvez."

Mary. The nice young woman he'd met the night before. "What do the security cameras show?" He looked around the bar and didn't see any.

"Liam didn't have any."

"You should get some."

"Thanks, Captain Obvious. But this place can't afford them."

He averted his eyes from the heat of her glare. "Did she call off?"

"No call. She's just gone. Her purse and phone are here. Her car's still here. Skeeter called her sitter, and her little boy is still there."

"Who's the sitter?"

"Toni Perkins. She keeps him at her house."

Skeeter took a stool at the far end of the bar. "Delaney got Mary some money today from her ex. She's probably out partying. I would be."

"Without her ID?" Delaney shook her head. "And she needed that money for food and rent."

"Someone I knew left the bar without her purse, phone, or ID yesterday." Leo regretted his words the second they left his mouth. He considered ducking under the bar.

"*Someone* took her own car. Mary left everything of value here. *Someone* has financial means. Mary does not. She needs this job. The woman is broke. Fifty bucks isn't enough to change that." Delaney ticked points on her fingers, leaning toward him. "Besides, I don't even know if Sicario came by or not."

"Sicario?"

"Sicario Menendez. Her baby daddy."

Menendez. Menendez. It clicked. "The drug dealer from Buns in the Barn?"

"Former drug dealer. Also, former construction worker. He's been out of a job for a while."

"And he owed her money?"

"Yes."

"Was on his way here?"

"Maybe."

Leo nodded. "So, he came by, and they're getting reacquainted."

Delaney shook her head vehemently. "No way."

Skeeter said, "Mary hates Sicario."

"Love. Hate. Two sides of the same coin." Leo tapped his pen on the paper where he'd jotted down a few notes. "Listen, you know she's not officially missing yet."

Delaney's eyes were slits. "And you know that a missing person should be reported as soon as their people have concerns and don't know their whereabouts."

Of course, she was right. It didn't mean he was wrong, though. There were still plausible possibilities that could explain her actions. But a killer was on the loose. Being cautious about Mary was the right way to go. "All right. When is she due to pick up her kid?" He noticed a "Miller Time" clock touting Miller Lite beer, with the little hand at four and the big hand straight up. Leo jotted his interview start time at the top of his notes. Three forty-five.

Delaney said, "I only know that she was supposed to be on shift until four. She was working breakfast through lunch and handing over to the night shift."

"Breakfast? At a bar?"

Delaney pointed at a posted breakfast menu on the wall. "There's no cook right now, but there's a place down the road that delivers."

"How about this: if she doesn't pick up her kid, we open the case, in light of what happened to Lila."

"What happened to Lila?" Skeeter said.

Leo winced. They'd withheld Lila's identity from the press, pending notification of next of kin. Which was on his to-do list, as soon as he'd talked to Delaney about Lila's family. And he'd planned to do it next. The call about Mary had come in before he could get to it.

"I'm sorry to have to inform you of this, Skeeter. Lila was found murdered last night."

"She died in a car wreck a month ago."

"Delaney confirmed her identity. The woman in the car with Liam was not Lila. I need you to keep it quiet. The press doesn't know yet, pending notification of her family, which I was hoping Delaney could fill me in on."

Delaney shook her head. Her voice was heavy. "I'd only met her once. I don't know anything about her."

"Any ideas who I could talk to?"

"Kateena, gently, after I tell her. Mary, when we find her."

She jumped to her feet and began pacing back and forth, her face betraying her emotions and rapidly firing synapses. "Shit. Why hadn't I put this together yet? Someone just killed Lila, here in our county. She's roughly Mary's age. Both of them are connected to the Loafing Shed."

Leo held up his hand. "You can't jump to conclusions, Delaney."

"The hell I can't. This changes everything."

"Can we stick to the plan? See if she shows up to get her son?"

"Your plan, my friend. And my guess is she should be picking him up right now," Delaney said.

Skeeter jumped to his feet. "I can take you there. I pick up Juan Julio for Mary when she gets held up over here."

Leo narrowed his eyes at the man. He hadn't known Skeeter long, but his veined nose suggested a long-time heavy drinker. He gave off the vibes of a regular. Leo questioned the judgment of a mom who would allow her child in a vehicle with Skeeter.

Skeeter stood taller. "Since her and Sicario broke up, she didn't have anyone to help her."

Delaney grabbed her purse. "Take me there," she said to Skeeter.

"I guess we're done here then." Sarcasm bled through Leo's tone. "If you'd care to provide me her home address, phone number, and other pertinent investigative information at some later time, Delaney, be my guest."

His sort-of partner shot him the bird. "I'll text you. Right now, I'm far less concerned about you than I am about Juan Julio and his mother. And my niece, who's about to get some bad news."

TWENTY-ONE

The front door of Toni Perkins's tiny house opened onto a sunny yellow hallway with house plants hanging in pots at various heights. From the interior, Delaney heard a loud *cacaw* and then another. Two different birds, from the sound of it. The tall woman framed in the doorway could have blown away in a stiff wind, catching some air in her prairie-style maxi dress. Her white hair was scraped into a low, severe bun. But her eyes twinkled when she caught sight of Skeeter.

"Is Mary going to be working late today?" she asked in a voice as gritty as sandpaper.

A dark-haired two-year-old peeked around her, a thumb in his mouth and the other hand grasping her skirt. A globby purple mess on his face suggested grape jelly.

Delaney stuck out her hand. "I'm Delaney Pace."

"She's a deputy," Skeeter explained, hoisting the coffee he'd been drinking for the last hour. He seemed remarkably sober. *A lot of body to absorb the booze and a lot of practice.*

Delaney bit the inside of her lip. She wasn't used to hearing herself called a deputy again. "Mary works at my brother's bar— I mean, his former bar. Have you talked to her today?"

Delaney was fighting to keep her focus on Mary's disappearance. She'd just hung up from a call updating Kateena that it would be a little longer before she came home. The girl was fine, but Delaney needed to be with her. To find a way to tell her about her mother. Now that Skeeter knew, word was bound to get out. How many more blows could the girl take?

Toni's eyes cut back and forth from Skeeter to Delaney. "Um, not since this morning. But that's not unusual. If Juan Julio's not feeling well, she'll check on him, but otherwise, I see her when she's off work."

"When do you expect her today?"

Toni glanced behind her at a wall clock. "Now. She said she'd be here at ten after four. She likes to pick up this little cutie pie as soon as she can." The woman ruffled the boy's hair.

He grinned around his thumb.

Delaney licked her lips. "What's the latest you hang on to her son for her?"

"Oh, I'm alone these days. I can arrange my schedule any way she needs." Toni's brow mashed into lines like a folding fan. "What's this about?"

Delaney sped up the questions. People tended to be more open before they realized they were in the middle of trouble. "So, you don't keep normal business hours?"

"No. But—"

She pushed her next question on the heels of Toni's answer. "But it would be unusual for Mary not to pick up Juan Julio when she left the bar?"

"Very. Wait—"

"And it would be unusual for her not to call you if she needed you past the day's pickup time?"

"I can't imagine she would ever do that unless something prevented her from calling. A real emergency. She's a good mother, that girl."

"She is," Skeeter said. "A tiger mama."

Delaney's unease was growing by the second. "Does she ever have anyone else come for Juan Julio?

"Only Skeeter." Toni wrung her hands. "Where is Mary? Did something happen to her?"

Skeeter started to speak.

Delaney dug an elbow into fat, searching for his ribs. "We're just trying to figure out whether Skeeter should take Juan Julio now or wait for Mary. She forgot her phone when she left."

Toni drew in a shaky breath. "Oh, good. You had me worried for a minute." She licked her lips. "I'm responsible for bringing dinner to the bingo game tonight at the senior center. I have a casserole in the oven for it."

Delaney paused, thinking. On the one hand, Juan Julio was with a competent caregiver. On the other hand, Delaney strongly suspected that Mary had met with trouble, trouble that might end up on Toni's doorstep. She would let the woman fulfill her bingo commitment and take Juan Julio someplace unexpected. Her own place. "Oh, by all means, take that casserole to bingo. If Mary does swing by, have her call me. Delaney Pace. She's got my number. Juan Julio will be in good hands with Skeeter and me." Delaney patted the big guy.

He threw open his arms. "Come to Uncle Skeeter, little fella."

Back at their vehicles, Delaney strapped Juan Julio in her back seat. She knew kids his size had special car seats, but as a childless woman, she didn't own one.

The little boy's big eyes took her in, looking dubious about her skills and qualifications.

You have good instincts, kid. "We don't have far to go. You'll be fine. I'll drive really slow."

He didn't blink.

Behind her, Skeeter said, "I guess I'll take off now."

She whirled on him. "No sirree, mister. I need your help."

"Didn't that pretty boy deputy say he'd start investigating if Mary didn't show up?"

"That doesn't mean I'm going to sit around and wait for him. We're heading to my place to drop you and Juan Julio off with my niece Kateena. You're babysitting." *Kateena can supervise, but I need muscle there, too, in case of trouble.* "I'm heading to Mary's. Then Sicario's. And anywhere else you can think of for me to look for either of them."

Skeeter's eyes showed their whites. "I'm no babysitter. Uh-uh. No way."

Delaney grabbed him by the neck of his shirt. "You owe me. I haven't even calculated how much Wyoming Whiskey you gave away today. Besides, Mary trusted you for some insane reason." She released her hold and smoothed his shirt. "Don't worry. My niece will help you. It will be all right. Just follow me."

He nodded, wordless.

Then she remembered Skeeter had information about her father or brother. "You were going to tell me something. When we were in jail together."

His eyes clouded. "I don't remember."

"About my brother or my dad."

"Oh. Yeah. It was about your brother."

"So? What is it?"

"It was just a thing people said."

She made a rolling motion with her hand.

Skeeter cleared his throat. "They said he lived a charmed life because had the right friends."

"What did that mean?"

"I don't know. But I heard him say it before. 'It pays to have friends.' Ya know?"

She nodded. "Do you know what friends they were talking about?"

He shook his head.

Liam had always been popular. The cool one. As a kid he'd been the first to drink, smoke pot, and shoplift and always gotten away with it. Fifteen years had passed since Delaney had any idea who her brother hung out with. She was sure he was friends with every mover and shaker in the area. Probably godfather to half their children. Right friends or not, Liam's charmed life had ended. Dying in a car wreck seemed too pedestrian for him. Too normal.

But it hadn't been normal, had it? Because the woman who had died with him wasn't his wife, and a month later Lila had been murdered and his employee was missing. Delaney glanced at the little boy in the back seat. She thought about Kateena. And wondered who would be next if she didn't find Mary and stop a killer.

TWENTY-TWO

The man dropped Mary's body to the floor like a bag of concrete mix. She didn't wake up. Back at the shitty bar he'd yanked her over backwards by her shiny black ponytail, and her head had slammed into the wooden floor. It had saved him from having to use the stun gun. As long as she didn't die before he'd even gotten started, he didn't mind. Really, limp and quiet was better. And an empty bar—he couldn't believe his luck. He'd already known there were no cameras from his visit the day before. Then, she'd only received one phone call the entire time he was there. It had gone perfectly. Perfectly.

It was another sign.

He cocked his head, evaluating her. She didn't look that strong, but he'd underestimated the last one. Hence his upgrade in the cellar. Metal handcuffs attached by a length of steel cable to an eye bolt in the concrete wall. He knelt and snapped one side of the cuffs around her wrist. He'd still have to be wary and keep his knife hand ready, but she wouldn't be able to surprise him at the foot of the stairs or get away.

Two days. He had to keep her alive for two days. No more, no less.

He crouched beside Mary. He wondered if someone would be searching for her. Lila had been easy. The world believed she was dead. Mary was different. Missing. But from what he'd seen of her life, she didn't have anyone who would care she was gone. She was a loner. No friends. An ex who was never around, and who was going to be very distracted, thanks to clues he'd planted for the cops. No family except for a kid. Social services would pass the boy off to people who'd be glad to pull in foster care income for as long as they could keep him. The only person who concerned him was the Delaney fellow. He hadn't come across a Delaney when he'd followed Mary, and he didn't like surprises. It sounded like a work thing, but he'd have to make sure.

His phone rang. He answered. "Yes, Jefe?"

"Status?" His friend's voice was a snarl.

He stood. "Complete."

"You'll forgive me if I don't take your word for it after you botched Lila."

Fury rose in him like a gasoline fire. "Botched Lila?

"It's all over the news. Some biker found her body. They didn't give her name, but it was clear who it was."

"It was just bad luck. I dumped her in the mountains. Off trail. Remote."

"There's no such thing as remote to a Wyomingite."

He stayed quiet. He had to find out whether Jefe knew when Lila died. That it was two days later than he'd believed it to be.

Jefe's voice was calm. "The news said you left the body in the open. And mutilated."

No mention of when. That was good. He pulled his knife from his boot holster. He ran his thumb along the face of the blade. He frowned. It had a chip out of it. A big one. He wanted it pristine for his next delivery, but it probably wasn't fixable with a whetstone. He eyed Mary.

"Are you there? Lila is going to attract attention. I should have sent someone else to get Mary."

His rage flashed, intense. "No! She's mine."

"Is?"

"Was."

"Where is she?" Jefe asked.

"No one will find her."

"You've worn out your welcome." Jefe ended the call.

Some friend. He felt the flame rise in him again.

Mary groaned. Her handcuff rattled as she pressed her hand to her head. He watched her, his interest stirring.

"Where am I?" Her voice was thick. "Juan Julio?"

He caressed the knife blade. "You don't need to worry about those things."

She gasped and turned toward him, wincing in pain. "Were you just talking about Lila Clement?"

"You know her?"

"She was my boss's wife. She died in a car accident with him."

He stepped closer to her. "She's dead now. She was alive until I was done with her."

"What do you mean?"

"I mean I kept her here. Like you. The cops found her body last night."

"That's impossible."

"But true."

She jerked the cuff. Her voice rose an octave. "You can't keep me here. Delaney will see you on the video cameras. The sheriff's department will come for you."

Delaney. "You mentioned him on the phone. Who is Delaney?"

She stared at him unblinking for several seconds. "Lila was Delaney's sister-in-law. Delaney is a deputy and owns the bar."

"Delaney Clement?"

"Delaney Pace."

"Am I supposed to be scared?" He sneered at her.

"You will be if you're smart. You should let me go." Her sass was impressive, but futile.

"I'm smart enough to know there aren't any cameras at that bar. No one's coming for you. You're mine until it's time for me to send you on your way." He held his knife in front of him and advanced on her.

She shrank from him. "Who are you?"

"I am the Delivery Man." The words filled him with pride.

She mouthed his name. "Why are you doing this to me?"

"You need deliverance. All women do. You and I just got lucky that your time is now, and I am the one to do it."

"You're not making any sense." Her voice was shrill.

He liked it.

His father's words rang in his head. The lessons the man had painstakingly taught him, as he delivered his wives from their evil ways, with the help of his son. As his grandfather had done with his women as well. *What a man is made to feel and do by a woman is a spell she casts on him. It's not his fault, son. If you are drawn in by her temptation, do not feel guilt for what she forces you to do. Instead, know that she has proven it is her time, and that you are the one to deliver her, as I have raised you to do.* The Delivery Man had never married. He couldn't. Wouldn't. But he had continued his father's work. Improved upon it.

"Original sin. Continuing sin." Yes, in this case Jefe had led him to Lila and Mary. But the women put the temptation there, so he knew his father's words were true and that he had no choice.

Sobbing, she said, "But I've done nothing. I'm a good person."

"If that were true, then why would I want to do this?"

And then he showed her what he meant. Her screams told him that she understood.

TWENTY-THREE

The department was quiet when Leo returned from the Loafing Shed. He hurried to his desk feeling a new sense of urgency to work on Lila's case. He owed her his best effort to find her killer before he got pulled onto something else. Not that he didn't care about Mary. He did. But it was likely that the woman was picking up her child at that very moment.

He quickly filled out an affidavit of probable cause for a search warrant for Lila's home, vehicle, computer, and phone. Fentworth had given him the contact information for Judge Gregory with instructions for this type of situation. He shot off an email to the judge.

Then he consulted his bare bones investigation plan. He googled butchers in the area. Made a list. The day was nearly over, so he would start visiting them tomorrow. Next, he considered how to identify hunters. Were there local hunter associations he could contact? He discarded the idea. Almost everyone in the state of Wyoming hunted. It could be part of the profile of characteristics to evaluate if he had a suspect, but it wasn't useful as a starting place.

That left Irma Fielding as his strongest investigative lead, the woman who'd used her credit card to buy a mini soldering iron. He'd pulled her address earlier. He wanted to talk to her face-to-face, in her home. Calling to set up an appointment might result in a spooked subject. An unannounced visit would be better.

He pushed his chair back. A yellow message slip on the floor caught his eye.

Deputy Rick Collins from San Juan County Colorado returned your call. Out until Tuesday for the holiday. Emailed you his file. It was signed CB for Clara Bartholomew.

Leo re-opened his email and pulled up the message from Deputy Collins.

> *Case file attached. It should speak for itself, except for one thing. We had a suspect. A local elk-hunting guide who had dated the victim. He had an alibi, but I was never satisfied with it. I think the guy was from your area originally. He'd be worth checking out. My partner retired last month, and he's on a safari in South Africa. I'm camping for Memorial Day. No cell signal. Back Tuesday if you have questions.*

Leo sent a quick thanks. He'd read the file as soon as he returned from visiting Irma.

At the address for Irma Fielding, a wheelchair rolled toward the storm door, its occupant a man with a gray crew cut. Tanned face with wrinkles consistent with seven decades in Wyoming. Clean blue jeans. A pressed, collared shirt. Big shoulders, erect posture, hands firmly on the chair's wheels. Horn-rimmed glasses, through which he peered at Leo.

Leo nodded to him and tapped his badge. He raised his voice to be heard through the glass. "I'm Deputy Leo Palmer. Are you Mr. Fielding?"

The man shook his head. "There is no Mr. Fielding. Open that door so I can hear you better. Easier for you than me."

Leo obliged. "May I come in?"

"No reason not to." He reversed and turned around. "Cup of coffee for you?"

Leo followed him, walking slowly to examine the pictures in the hallway. A family of three. Man, woman, son. Or were they the boy's grandparents? Pictures of the boy, pictures of a teen, then a young man, all the same person. The couple in camo on a successful elk hunt. The man in military uniform—Air Force. The woman, many years earlier, on a horse leaning in, low to the ground as it rounded a barrel.

"Yes, please." *Always accept what's offered to set a friendly tone and extend the interview.*

"Black okay?"

"Black is fine."

The man entered a kitchen with a spectacular view of the distant mountains through the bay windows. "Have a seat."

As the man retrieved a coffee cup from a lower cabinet and filled it from a percolator on the stove, Leo pulled out a chair at the kitchen table. "Nice place. How many acres?"

"Five hundred. Enough to run our own cattle, before this." He gestured at his legs with his head. "Now I lease it out. Still a lot of work, though." He used one hand to wheel to the table and slide under the side with no chair.

Leo took the warm coffee cup extended toward him but didn't drink it. "Thanks. I didn't catch your name."

"Charlie. And I didn't catch the reason for your visit."

"I'm hoping to talk to Irma Fielding."

Charlie's face stayed slack other than a slight lip spasm. "You missed her."

"When will she be back?"

"She won't. Irma passed."

"My condolences." Leo paused. "This is a bit awkward

then. Her credit card was used to make a purchase at a hardware store recently."

Charlie waved his hand. "I gave it to our boy."

"Son?"

"Yes."

"You and Irma were...?"

"Husband and wife, although she kept her own last name since we came together later in life. Parented late. After I got back from Vietnam and out of the Air Force."

"I understand. Thank you for your service."

"Did you serve?"

"Coast Guard."

He smiled, although it didn't reach his eyes. "Puddle Pirate."

Leo smiled back, taking the familiar ribbing about his branch of the service in stride. "Worse than that. I was a Puddle Pirate who stayed out of the puddle. I worked law enforcement." He took a sip of the coffee. Licked the grounds from his teeth.

"I haven't seen you around before."

"I'm new."

"Let me guess. California."

Leo wished it wasn't so easy for people to identify where he was from. He brandished the cup. "Don't hold it against me, please."

Charlie stared at him without agreeing or disagreeing with the request. "What is it about Irma's credit card that caught your attention, Deputy?"

"We're following up on purchases of a particular item."

"Which tells me nothing."

Leo took his turn not agreeing or disagreeing. "I'd like to speak to your son."

"Me, too."

"Is he not around?"

"He was. But he left for town before I had a chance to give him my grocery list. Hasn't answered his cell phone."

"When are you expecting him back?"

"Now there's a question for you." Charlie sighed. "Charles Junior said he moved back to town to help me around the place. But honest labor's never been his strong suit. Is he in some kind of trouble?"

"I just need to talk to him about the item he bought."

"I'll ask him to give you a call when he shows up."

"Better yet, why don't you call me, sir? I'd like to speak to him in person."

"Fair enough."

Leo handed him a card. "And forgive my ignorance, but his last name?"

"Same as mine. Crawford."

A chill passed through Leo as he shook the widower's hand. *What was that about?*

TWENTY-FOUR

Delaney lifted a scrap of paper and stared at it as if the words had a hidden meaning to reveal, Shelly idling. She'd written Mary's address on the paper back at the homestead, but her mapping app was having trouble finding it. Between Kateena's emotions, Juan Julio's wails for his mama, and Skeeter's shell-shock at his babysitting predicament, there was a chance Delaney could have recorded it incorrectly.

She thought back on what she'd heard, divorcing her mind from her scribbles.

"No booze, Skeeter. I don't even have any here," she'd said as she laced up her tactical boots. The medallion pendant and cross anklet had gone into the jewelry bowl on her chest of drawers, the sandals into her closet.

He'd held his hands in the air. "Hey, now, give me some credit."

Delaney had, for about three seconds. She turned to Kateena and whispered. "You're in charge if he starts drinking."

"What's going on, Aunt Delaney? Is this about more than Mary?" Kateena said. The girl's emotional intelligence was spooky keen.

"A lot. I promise I'll tell you about all of it later. But right now, I have to find Mary. You understand that, right?"

Kateena nodded. Her pupils were dilated to deep black pools. Dudley was sitting in her lap, and she squeezed him so tight that he snorted.

Delaney pulled girl and dog into a hug. The dog scrambled out of it. Over Kateena's shoulder, she said, "What's Mary's address, Skeeter?"

He looked panicked at the question. "Uh, it's easier to give you directions than remember the address."

"Give me both."

And he had.

Not that it was doing her any good now. *Yeah, this address is crap.* Mentally, she ran back through his verbal directions.

He'd ended by telling her, "You can't miss it. It's the little blue box with her POS Monte Carlo out front."

"Except that's back at the bar."

"Except for that, yeah."

So, here she was on the right street, without the Monte Carlo to help her. But she saw the little blue box and pulled to a stop in front of it. The mapping app had been off by a block and had her on the wrong side of the street. Unfortunately, she'd left Mary's purse in the office at the bar. It hadn't seemed fair to move her phone, keys, and wallet, in case she came back for them. Now Delaney wished she had those keys. For a moment, she was frustrated that KCSD hadn't been able to fully outfit her earlier. She should have at least picked up a duty belt with its thirty pounds of useful gear. She'd never thought she'd look forward to lugging it around again, but here she was, and she did.

She parked in front of the house and called the department. No garage. No driveway. She hated leaving Shelly on the street, and this was the second time in an hour. It couldn't be helped, though.

A woman answered on the second ring. "Sheriff's Department. Clara speaking."

"Hi, Clara. This is Delaney Pace. Deputy Palmer came out to the Loafing Shed earlier to take a missing person report from me. He's expecting my call."

"Hi, Delaney. Why don't you call him directly?"

"Would you be willing to give me his mobile number? I have information for him on Mary's case."

"Mary?"

"Mary Galvez. She's the one missing."

"Oh, no! I met her last night when she was here to pick up Dudley. Such a nice young woman." Clara rattled off Leo's number. "I hope she's okay."

"Thank you." Delaney ended the call, reciting Leo's number. She typed it in as she got out of the car, purse over her wrist, and walked toward the door. When she'd been a deputy before, she hadn't turned in her lock picks and she'd used them since for her own good reasons—like reclaiming her stuff from Chad's when he wasn't home, because she didn't want another fist to the face. Today, she was glad she had them.

"Deputy Palmer speaking," Leo said.

"Leo, it's Delaney." She cradled the phone between her shoulder and ear as she got out her picks. "Mary didn't come for Juan Julio. I left him with Kateena and my, uh, babysitter."

"Well, damn. I'm sorry she hasn't turned up yet."

Delaney snorted. She knocked on the door. No doorbell, no answer. Then she used her shirt tail to protect the door from her fingerprints as she checked the knob. Locked. And cheap. "I didn't call for your sympathy. I believe this is the official start of the investigation." She wouldn't need her lock-picking set. A simple credit card would do. Where had this lock come from, a Cracker Jack box circa 1992?

"Correct."

She selected a credit card from her wallet. "So, I'm about to enter Mary's house."

"And you're just now calling me?"

"I was in the neighborhood."

Leo sighed. "Do you at least have what you need to enter?"

Did her credit card count? "That's about all I have."

"Damn. No gloves, no evidence bags?"

"No nothing."

"Wait for me. Don't mess up the crime scene."

Irritation prickled her. "You don't believe it is one."

His silence told her she'd thrown a bullseye.

"You there, Deputy?" she said.

"On my way. Please wait."

"Nope." She swiped her card in the door jamb. The lock released.

"Come on. We're partners."

"That's stating it a little strongly. We're collaborators. And I collaborate best on my own."

"You heard the sheriff."

"Hurry or I'll be done and gone by the time you get here." She hung up on him.

Her phone started to ring immediately. She checked the caller ID in case it was Skeeter, Kateena, or Mary. *Leo's number.* She shoved the phone in her back pocket unanswered. Then she put the credit card in her wallet and wallet in her purse, reached in the unbuttoned lower half of her shirt, and patted the Staccato in her belly holster. She might not have all the tools of the trade, but she had the most important one.

Using her shirt tail, she opened the door. "Hello? Mary?"

No one answered her. The house was eerily quiet.

She used her elbow to flip up the light switch. No lights came on. She thought about the small, powerful flashlight she kept in the glove box of the Chevelle. *And the one that would have been on a duty belt.* Her eyes were adjusting, though. The ambient light through the windows was enough. Plus, she had her phone. She could always go back for the flashlight later if she had to.

She took a moment to orient herself. A left-side kitchen and a living room on the right, open plan. Nothing overturned or left open. No blood or other fluids. The furniture was sparse. A highchair, a TV tray, and a folding chair in the eating area. A beanbag with a lamp beside it in the living room. A milk crate in the middle of the floor, a few toys and books stacked inside. Nothing on the walls, not even a clock. Mary hadn't been kidding when she'd said she needed money. But the house was tidy and smelled nice. No odor of a pet. No signs or sounds from one either.

A hallway split the back of the rooms. Delaney reached the corridor in three long steps and again used her elbow on the switch. Again, nothing happened.

No money for replacement bulbs? Power bill not paid? Outage on the street? Or something worse?

"This is Deputy Investigator Delaney Pace. I'm armed. Please identify yourself."

She set her purse down, drew her gun, and exhaled to release stress. *I'm out of practice.* Holding the Staccato in a two-handed grip, she pointed it at the floor a few feet in front of her then began advancing slowly down the hall, knees flexed. It only took a few steps for her to reach the back of the house. There were three doors—a bedroom on each side with a bathroom in between them.

She used her foot to nudge a partially closed bedroom door fully open. A crib with a yellow and brown blanket. A small chest of drawers. A window with a white fitted sheet serving as a makeshift balloon shade. A closet wide open, with nothing but an empty laundry basket inside.

She peered into the bathroom. Neat as a pin with only a zippered make-up pouch on the counter. A plastic shower liner but no shower curtain on the rod. Generic baby shampoo and a rubber ducky on the tub ledge. Two towels hanging from a rack. A window looking out on an unfenced backyard. Delaney walked over to it. There was no curtain or sheet to block her view of the line of pine trees about twenty feet from the house.

Pushing out another shaky breath, she left the bathroom and entered the final room. This one would be where Mary slept. If anything bad had happened in this house, Delaney expected to see it here.

"Anyone home?"

No answer.

One look and Delaney relaxed a degree. Empty, with nothing seemingly out of place. An air mattress on the floor covered by a threadbare white blanket and one pillow. A TV tray that matched the one in the kitchen, serving as a bedside table. A half-full water glass and a phone charger sat on top of it. A white top sheet hung over the window. Looking treasured but out of place, an antique vanity with an ornate, cushioned chair occupied a corner. It gave Delaney's heart a pinch. She walked over to it and used the back of her hand to touch a gilt-edged hand mirror and the handle of a brush. Then she turned to the dresser. Framed photos brought a smile back to her face. Juan Julio as a newborn, swaddled in a gender-neutral hospital blanket. Another of him beaming with a cake in the shape of the number one on his highchair tray. A third with his face pressed against Mary's, both of them laughing.

Ringing from her phone startled her. She glanced at it. Skeeter calling. She didn't want the interruption, but he had Kateena and Juan Julio. She answered. "Make it fast."

"Uh, Delaney?"

"Yes, Skeeter. I'm in a hurry. What is it?"

"What do you want me to feed the kids for dinner?"

She rolled her eyes. "I'll make you a deal. I'll forgive whatever you feed them for dinner if you only call me when it's an actual emergency."

"Can I text you?"

"For non-emergencies? Sure. We good?"

"We're good."

Delaney ended the call. *Where was I?* The dresser.

Using her shirttail as a glove, Delaney opened each of the scantly filled four drawers, bottom to top, by prying her fingers under the edge instead of using the knobs. Yoga pants and shorts. T-shirts. Pajamas—nothing sexy, suitable for Wyoming nights that ranged from chilly to frigid. And in the top drawer, where she expected to find a couple of bras and panties, nothing. She frowned.

Only the closet left to go. She stood to the side of the door, eyes closed, thinking it through. Then, again, she used her shirttail, turning the knob slowly, safety on but gun steady in her right hand at the height of an adult's mid-section, just in case. She pulled the door outward.

Crash.

The noise from inside the closet was explosive in the silent house. Delaney pressed her back against the wall, out of the line of fire. She tensed, waiting for a person to burst from the closet.

A box tumbled out, spilling its lid and a pair of black heels to the bedroom floor. She turned and peered cautiously into the opening. A short tower of shoe boxes had fallen over. She returned the heels— no scuff marks—to the box and replaced the box on the tower. On the shelf above the clothing rod, Delaney saw a shoe polishing and repair kit.

The rod wasn't weighed down with excess possessions. Just a few tops and sweaters, jeans, coats, and dresses. Delaney thought through the items she would have expected to find in a closet. Given the lack of other closet space in the house, where did Mary keep bags or suitcases? Juan Julio's diaper bag had been with Toni. But given Mary's financial straits, maybe she didn't own any others. *Unless she has one with her.* The woman seemed thrifty. In Wyoming, the grocery stores still gave away bags for free, and people by and large put them to good use for trash and transporting items.

Delaney frowned. The missing undergarments were a conundrum. She hadn't seen a washer and drier. They weren't hanging to dry in the bathroom. The hamper was empty. Was it possible that Mary had taken them to a laundromat? She would have to check the Monte Carlo for laundry when she got back to the bar. And for a suitcase. She didn't want to believe Mary would have abandoned Juan Julio, even for a short time. *I refuse to believe it.* But she'd verify her belief. It was the smart thing to do.

She shut the closet door with her foot. It was time to move outside. She exited the front door and made a lap of the perimeter, looking for anything out of the ordinary. While the lot had the nice pine trees she'd noticed earlier, there was no shrubbery along the base of the house. The yard had been left natural with hummocked grass native to the area. Bare earth showed through in spots. A quick search yielded nothing hiding in the grass, not even a garden hose or toys. In the back, there were only the three windows. Two of them with white sheets. In the center, the bare glass of the bathroom window.

Beneath it, the ground was mostly dirt. A disturbance caught her eye. Standing clear, she leaned in for a closer look. A footprint, toe facing the house. Tactical boot, it appeared. She pulled her phone from her purse and took a few close-up photos. She compared the print to her foot, clad in similar gear. Delaney may have prided herself on her feminine manicure, but her feet—and her hands—were man-sized. She could have left these prints. So, a woman with large feet or a man with small to medium feet had stood outside this window. And recently. It had rained three nights ago, and moisture would have obliterated the tracks. She eyed the wooden window frame. It was weathered and flaky. Not a great print surface, but better than nothing.

"There you are." Leo's voice interrupted her thoughts.

She controlled her startle reflex, turning to look at him. "Leo."

His face shone with a California glow. "What did you find?"

She pointed at the ground. "Peeping Tom. Can you get someone out here to cast this and print the windowsill and back of the house?"

He frowned, nodding. "Good catch." He stepped closer to look. His cowboy boots were so new the snake was still hissing. "That changes things."

"Nice boots. Where are you from?"

"Thanks. California. The sheriff strongly recommended I needed footwear that would fit in around here."

Wyoming people were serious about their boots, and Leo's were great-looking, but they weren't the kind to work in. She wasn't going to be the one to tell him. At least he was trying. "The house is pretty bare, but there may be prints on the top drawer in Mary's bedroom. The drawer should have held intimates, but it was empty. I couldn't find them elsewhere, either." She turned and scanned the ground. The new spring grass was crushed leading away from the prints under the window. She followed the trail, keeping her own feet wide of it.

"What are you doing?" he asked.

Without looking up, she said, "Tracking Tom."

"Let me get some techs out to work the scene. Then I'll come with you."

Leo spoke into his radio while she continued following the path of crushed grass. It led to the cluster of pine trees, where she lost it. The crime scene unit could take this further. She wanted to talk to the neighbors anyway. She headed for the house next door.

"Delaney? Are you leaving?" Leo called after her, radio at shoulder height.

She shook her head. "Neighbor interviews."

He nodded. "Someone needs to get on a computer, too, though. Learn everything we can about Mary. Her associates. Her jobs. Where she's from. Any trouble she's been in. Figure out if she has an online presence and check for activity. Order her phone records. Do the same thing with her ex. Break into her phone and check her texts and email. See whether she's had a stalker in the past. Check for any sex offenders or problematic people with access to her. Set up cameras here in case someone comes back. At the bar, too." He stopped to take a breath.

Delaney was impressed, with his ideas and his energy. Still, while it was all valid investigative work, nothing beat timely interviews with eyewitnesses. Someone might have seen this guy. Could give a description of him or his vehicle. Mary had disappeared hours ago. If someone had her—which was likely—every second that passed she could be further away and harder to find. "Sounds good. I'll call you if I find something."

"Wait!"

She turned. "What is it?"

"I'll, uh, I'll help you with this, then maybe you can help me with the other? You need back-up."

That will be the day. But she wasn't going to turn down an offer of help.

TWENTY-FIVE

Door to door, Leo walked, canvassing his side of the street while Delaney did the same on the other. He hadn't gone door-to-door since he was a beat cop, and not often then. So far, it felt like a waste of time. This was a working-class neighborhood, and most of the people he talked to had been away during the day. He knew it had to be done. But so did a million other things, on Mary's case and Lila's, too. The small size of the department was a real limiting factor. They needed more manpower. He glanced across the street at Delaney. Or womanpower.

With all but one of his interviews completed, Leo's phone rang. He stopped at the corner. It was Fentworth. At the sheriff's request, Leo updated him on Mary, including the footprint from the Peeping Tom.

The sheriff swore. "The mayor wants us full tilt on Lila Clement. Any chance Mary and Lila are linked?"

"Chance? Yes. Evidence? None." Leo leaned against a streetlight. It gave him a view of the entire street. Mary lived on a flat section at the top of a bluff, but it dropped away quickly toward the Cheyenne River a block later.

"We're going to look bad if it turns out Mary is on a bender, sleeping it off somewhere."

Leo looked across the street corner at Delaney. Her voice carried, calm and reassuring.

"Are you there, Johnny Utah?"

"Sorry. You're right. Especially if it pulls us off Lila's case. People get really worked up when young women are murdered."

"Even worse, women we've already declared dead."

Lila's case is going to create a media shitstorm when we release her identity. "Can we get more bodies on Lila's case, to keep it moving forward? Every second that passes, the odds decrease that we catch her killer. It would help to know who died with Liam Pace, too."

"As long as there's a chance Mary's alive, she has to take precedence for you and Delaney, so stick with her. I'll put Joe on Lila's case when he gets back in tomorrow. Maybe I can make some progress on the similar crimes research you sent in the meantime. And I'll get Clara started sifting through the missing persons information. She has an eye for that type of thing. What are you doing now?"

"We're going door-to-door interviewing neighbors to see if we can get a description of the Peeping Tom."

"We?"

Leo cleared his throat. "Delaney and me."

"Partnered up, are you?" There was amusement in Fentworth's voice.

Leo paused in front of his last house. The dirty white siding nearly blended with the gray slate roof. "We're not working *against* each other."

Fentworth chuckled. "Stay in touch."

"Of course, sir." Leo ended the call, slipped the phone into his pocket, and walked toward the house. Like most he'd visited, this one took up a fraction of its large lot. Unlike the others, it had a front walkway, some bushes in a bed against the house, and an attached one-car garage. And it was directly across the street from Mary's.

He knocked once. The occupant must have been watching him because the door opened immediately. The smell of cat boxes in dire need of changing assaulted Leo's nose. Standing in the frame was a Mr. Rogers lookalike. One in his gray-haired years, but whose youthful face suggested indoors work and great moisturizer. If he'd been a woman, Leo would have suspected plastic surgery as well.

Leo breathed through his mouth as he introduced himself. "We're talking to Mary Galvez's neighbors. I just have a few questions for you."

"Don't know her." Mr. Rogers moved to shut the door.

Leo pointed at the little blue house. "She and her two-year-old son live there."

The man's bitter expression eased. "The pretty Mexican woman?"

Leo felt a quickening of hope. This was the first neighbor who'd recognized Mary. "Yes. Mary is Latina."

"She sure has a bad-news boyfriend." The man made a *tsk-tsk* noise.

"I'm not sure what you mean," Leo said, even though he did.

The man nodded. "My name's Bert Raines. This place has been mine for decades." He stepped outside and gestured at two Adirondack chairs. "Have a seat."

Leo did as instructed and pulled out a notepad and pencil, jotting down the man's information. "Tell me about the boyfriend."

"He doesn't come around much lately. They used to argue right out the front. He's Mexican, too. Always had a sneer on his face. Out of shape, unlike her. Still looks like he could do some damage, though."

Sicario. "What did he drive?"

"A brown pickup. A Chevrolet. Old, back when they were the best thing on the market."

Leo wrote as fast as he could but kept asking questions. "Was he ever violent with her?"

"Just a little shoving. It seemed mutual."

"Did you ever hear him threaten her?"

"Oh, I didn't hear the words they said. Just the noise they made."

"When did he stop coming around?"

"A month or three ago. But I've seen a truck like his recently. Can't promise it was him driving it, but it might have been."

Leo paused, thinking. He rotated his neck to stretch it and saw the lens end of a spotting scope in Bert's window. It was pointed at Mary's house. *Was Bert the Peeping Tom?*

"You got any more questions for me?"

Leo made a show of stretching his neck in the other direction. "Yes. When did you see the truck most recently?"

"In the last day or so."

"Male or female driver?" He snuck a peek at Bert's feet. They were clad in low-profile hiking sneakers. He'd peg their size at about a nine. He couldn't rule them out as matching the prints outside Mary's bathroom.

"Don't know for sure. I assumed it was that boyfriend."

"Anything else—any unusual visitors? People coming at odd hours. People who you saw more than once. People who might have approached her home without going into it."

"You mean like a stalker?"

"That. Or just anyone you thought was unusual."

"Nah. Just the woman and her kid. And she seemed like she was good with him."

If anyone would know, it's the man watching them through a high-powered lens. But how could he not see the driver of the truck with that thing? He should be able to see freckles on an ant's ass. Leo handed Bert one of his cards. "If you think of anything else, call me, please."

"Sure. Is she all right?"

"Thank you for your time, sir."

Leo stepped off the porch. The interview had been promising. He headed toward the street where Delaney stood waiting.

Bert called out to him. "Deputy, one last thing."

Leo turned back. "Yes?"

"I just remembered something. When I was waking up from my nap earlier, there was a pickup like his here. About midday."

"Did you see the driver?"

"No one was in it. Is that relevant?"

Leo smiled. "Why, yes, sir. I believe it is. Thank you." Sicario the drug-dealing boyfriend. A neighbor who might be watching Mary. *Two suspects for the price of one.*

TWENTY-SIX

Delaney unlocked the back door of the Loafing Shed and jogged inside. Mary's purse was where she'd left it, in the safe in the office, its door ajar. Someday soon she'd have a new lock installed. Until then, it would remain open, in the same position since she'd had it drilled when she couldn't find the combination after her arrival.

She tucked the little purse under her arm and jogged back to the Monte Carlo, fringe bouncing. She dug in the woman's purse for keys. Found nothing. Dug again. Still nothing. She dumped the contents in the passenger seat of the Chevelle.

Her phone buzzed. Mary? She pulled it from her jeans pocket, glanced at it, and groaned.

Chad: *Why didn't you answer me?*

She stuffed the phone back in her pocket.

Leo was just pulling up beside Shelly, window down. "If I hadn't already arrested you for speeding once, I would have done it again on the way over here." He turned off the department pickup engine and climbed out, looking too good for the mood she was in.

Delaney pawed through the items on the seat. No keys. She

fumbled in the purse until she found a zippered compartment. All it contained was a tube of cheap lipstick in an orangey color. "Her keys aren't in her purse."

"Maybe they fell out? Or she left them in her car?"

Using her shirt tail, Delaney checked the door handle. It was locked. She tried the other doors. Also locked. She put her nose to the window. No keys.

"Just a minute."

She dashed into the building. Checked inside the safe. No keys had fallen out. She scoured her office. Still none. But she'd originally found the purse behind the bar. Scanning the floor for them with every step, she walked into the bar, lifted the bar flap, and began searching. None on the floor, the bar top, or in the cabinets. None stuck between bottles or glasses.

Where are they? Does someone have them? And why?

Leo had followed her. "Anything?"

"No. I found her purse in a cabinet here. Why would someone take her keys if they didn't want her car? Not that it's worth much, except to her."

"Maybe she had them in her pocket. She could have gone outside to get something from the car. Wherever she is and whoever she's with—all of that could have transpired outside."

It wasn't the worst theory she'd ever heard. And the more theories they generated, the better. "Or maybe someone came back and got them after they took her."

"You mean right then or later?"

Delaney snorted. "Those are the two possibilities. But I don't see evidence anyone has been here since Skeeter and I left." She walked to the entrance and pulled on the inner door. It was securely locked.

"You know Bert Raines said Sicario was at Mary's house this afternoon."

Leo had filled her in on his interview with Mary's neighbor. And that is not what she'd heard him say. "He *saw* Sicario?

I thought you said he saw a truck *like* Sicario's with no one in it?"

"Nearly the same difference."

"That remains to be seen. And Mr. Spotting Scope could have invented Sicario's truck to turn our attention away from himself."

Leo nodded slowly. "I wish we had enough to get a warrant for Bert's place. I don't think having a spotting scope will satisfy a judge."

"Not in Wyoming." Delaney returned to the bar and leaned against the top. "If someone took her keys, they could have used them to get into her house."

"What for, if she was grabbed here?"

"We don't actually know where she was grabbed from. Or where or when her keys were taken." The array of possibilities made her dizzy. "Mary's drawer that the techs are dusting for prints. It was empty. It should have held her panties and bras. I looked. They weren't in her house anywhere."

"You told me that. So?" Leo walked to the open bar flap. "Do you mind if I get a soda?"

She waved her hand. "So, they should be in her car."

Leo lifted a beer stein. "Or at the laundromat. Do you want something to drink?"

Delaney shook her head. "Did you see how poor she is? She wouldn't leave them there unattended."

"Fine. But why would a drawer of panties matter?" He filled his mug from the tap. Dark brown and bubbly. Coca-Cola.

"I don't know."

Leo rejoined her outside the bar. "One possibility—she could be leaving town." He took a sip of his drink, then coughed at the high carbonation level.

"She wouldn't leave Juan Julio." Leo started to interrupt. Delaney held up a hand. "But, if she did, she'd have taken more than her underwear."

"Maybe she did."

Delaney pictured the closet and drawers again. "Unlikely. No empty hangers. No half-empty drawers."

Leo drained his glass, then covered his mouth with a fist. After a moment, he said, "Then what's your theory?"

"I'm still working on it."

Someone banged on the front door.

"We're closed," Delaney shouted.

"Open the fucking door or I'll break it down," a man shouted.

Her eyebrows rose so far they stretched her forehead. "That sounds intriguing. Cover me in case he's as hostile as he sounds.

Leo shook his head. "Bad idea." He put his mug on a table.

Delaney pursed her lips. "What do you want to do?"

The voice bellowed again. "Mary, goddammit, let me in."

Delaney smiled at Leo. "Like I said, intriguing."

She opened the door. A red-faced man all cowboyed up with dusty boots, jeans, hat, and a pearl snap shirt threw a wadded-up piece of paper at her face. "Closed for a personal emergency, my ass. I went to—" A look of confusion came over his face. "Who the fuck are you?"

Leo appeared beside her, his hand on his holstered gun. "I believe I just witnessed the assault of an officer."

"And a bar manager," she agreed. Then, to the newcomer, she said, "Who are *you*? I run this bar, and you're the one charging in here like an asshole, so you owe me an answer first. And that better not be the closed sign I made that you just threw at me."

"I didn't hit you, man. Where's Mary?" the guy said. "And what the hell are you doing running a bar? Isn't that against some kind of law?"

Delaney said. "Technically, no. Ethically, still no."

"I know you."

He looked vaguely familiar to Delaney, but too young to have been a classmate. A name came to her lips. "Chip?"

"You're the bitch that got me sent to juvie," he said.

Now she remembered. The Crawford kid. He'd raped a drunk girl, although other boys had participated, too. One of them videoed it. The county attorney had declined to prosecute him as an adult, along with several of the other teens. Off to juvenile detention they'd gone. "I think you did that to yourself. What do you want with Mary?"

"It's none of your fucking business."

"Threatening language. Should I tase him?" Leo said. "I think I should tase him."

"I won't stop you." Delaney smiled.

Chip glared at them both. "We had plans. She wasn't at her house, so I came here. She stood me up."

Delaney remembered Mary talking about a date. Chip was the guy she'd been excited about. Sicario, then Chip. The woman had bad taste in men. "What kind of vehicle do you drive?"

He pointed at a Ram 3500 flatbed. All black. The engine was running, windows were down, and the stereo thumped with bass tuned too high. "What the hell does it matter? I ain't done nothing wrong. And where's Mary?"

The truck didn't rule him out. *Our vehicle witness is unreliable.* Delaney picked up her closed sign and threw it back at him. "You tell us. Because she's missing."

"Would I be here if I knew?"

"How would I know? Before right now o'clock I didn't know you were part of her life, and Mary and I are friends."

He sneered. "We just met yesterday."

"And you're this upset she didn't show? I'd hate to see how you'd act with someone you're actually in a relationship with." She ignored his growl. "Have you talked to her today?"

"By text this morning. That's when we made plans."

"When were you supposed to meet and where?"

"The Pizza Palace. At six. She said she had to bring her kid, so we were just gonna grab a bite to eat. A low-key hang."

"Uh-huh."

"I swear." Belatedly, he seemed to grasp the seriousness of the situation. "She's nice. And really good-looking. I hope she's okay."

"Give your number to my deputy friend. Don't leave town."

"But—"

"Assault on an officer," Leo reminded him.

"And bar manager," Delaney added.

Chip grumbled but went inside with Leo. Delaney picked up the crumpled closed sign. She smoothed and rehung the paper, then stood, thinking.

Chip bumped Delaney with his shoulder as he exited the building.

"Watch yourself," she said.

He didn't look back.

Leo came to stand beside Delaney as Chip backed out and left the parking lot. He slapped his thigh. "Is he any relation to Charlie Crawford?"

"Charlie is his dad."

"Did Charlie and Irma have more than one boy?"

"I don't know. Why?"

"Lila's case. I'm looking to speak to Charles Junior. I wonder if I just missed my chance."

"Is he a suspect?"

"Person of interest."

"And here he is, showing up in Mary's life on the day she disappears." Delaney stepped inside.

Leo followed. "I'll run background and question him in the morning."

"Sounds like a good idea. Ready?" Delaney turned the locks on the outer and inner doors.

"Born that way," Leo said.

"Come on then."

Delaney locked up the back exit on their way out. She hurried to Mary's car. The sun was sinking and they were losing the light. Leo was peering in the back. She did the same from the other side, double-checking for the laundry, the keys, a suitcase, or anything of interest. Nothing on the seat or floorboard. They did the same with the front seat. Empty. The car was as well cared for as Mary's house.

"Nada." Delaney sighed.

"Where does that leave us?"

She opened Shelly's driver's door. "Needing someone to break into her trunk and see what's in it. And me heading to Sicario's."

"We. And we should ride together in my truck."

Delaney would rather poke her eye out with a screwdriver. "No thanks."

"Then I could ride with you."

"Only if you spring for gas."

He sighed. "I'll bet this monster guzzles it."

Delaney grinned. "You have no idea."

Leo settled into Shelly's passenger side. Delaney got in, put the car in gear, and pointed it toward Sicario's.

His phone chimed with a text. "The techs tracked the Peeping Tom. His footprints ended where some tire marks began. We've got a photo of a tire tread."

She held out her hand. "Let me see."

"You're driving."

She pulled over. Leo handed her the phone. Scrutinizing the photo, she nodded and handed it back.

"That's a snow tire with studs in the tread."

He laughed. "Okay."

"You don't believe me?"

"There's a reason we have experts to analyze these photos."

"What do you think I learned driving a truck for ten years? Plus, I've been a mechanic since I was a kid. I do my own work. I watch other people work. I know tires. I know vehicles. And this is Wyoming. People have snow tires."

He threw his hands up. "Don't shoot, officer."

Being cute didn't make him less wrong. His not knowing something didn't mean she didn't. She hoped she hadn't just been partnered up with a chauvinist.

The defensiveness slowly drained from her. After a few miles of silence, she said, "I'll grant you, it doesn't make sense that someone is driving on a snow tire in May. But that doesn't change the fact that it is one."

"Thank you. A mechanic, huh? What can't you do?"

Despite her earlier hostility, a dry laugh escaped her. "Sing. Change of subject. What's your law enforcement resume?"

"Computer science degree USC. I was cybercrime with Coast Guard then undercover Narcotics with San Diego PD."

A light bulb went off for Delaney. "That explains it."

"Explains what?"

"All your great investigative ideas were desk jockey stuff. Because you've been riding one."

"Narcotics wasn't desk jockey work."

"Yeah, but undercover is mostly play-acting." She looked at him and winked.

"Should I be offended?"

"Only if you're a crybaby."

Now it was Leo's turn to laugh. "It's possible we may have skills that aren't redundant."

"I guess if Fentworth is making us pair up, non-redundant skills are a positive. We're here, by the way."

Delaney pulled in behind Sicario's truck, blocking it in. It was parked exactly where it had been the day before. The two of them walked to Sicario's door. The dusk made visibility limited. Delaney hoped she didn't trip over any of the junk in his yard and bust her teeth out.

She knocked.

"Let me do the talking," Leo said. "Since I'm the one who interviewed Bert Raines."

Delaney shrugged. She stepped to the side, moving her body out of the doorway.

"What are you doing?" Leo's forehead bunched with puzzlement.

"Last time I was here he met me at the door with a shotgun."

Leo jumped to the side.

"Who is it?" Sicario shouted. His voice sounded different than it had that morning.

"Delaney Pace."

"I thought I was doing the talking," Leo hissed.

Sicario said, "You didn't tell me you're a cop."

Delaney nodded at Leo, an apology for wresting lead away from him. "That's because I was helping Mary as a friend, not as a deputy."

"Same difference."

"It isn't. But that's not why I'm here. I'm looking for Mary."

"What the fuck would she be doing here? She hates me."

Leo opened his mouth, but Delaney shushed him with a zipping motion across her lips.

"Did you drop that money by for her?"

"I tried. Some fat dude was tending bar. I wasn't gonna leave it with him." He didn't seem to recognize the irony.

"Did you try to take it to her house?"

"No. She said she'd shoot me if I ever came back there. And she's a good shot."

"She has a gun?"

"She did. I don't know anymore."

There'd been no gun in her purse or house. It could be in

the Monte Carlo. If she'd had it on her, it seemed unlikely she'd been able to use it.

Leo shook his hands in frustration. *Apparently he'd like to say something.*

Delaney took pity on him. "I have another deputy here with me, Sicario. He needs to talk to you, too."

Sicario's voice pitched higher. "Why didn't you tell me? I don't like it. You're ganging up on me. You need to leave."

Leo took a deep breath. "Sicario, this is Deputy Leo Palmer. I was told a truck matching yours was seen at Mary's today."

"It wasn't me. I already said that, man. You need to get out of here."

"I'm told you've been around there more frequently lately."

"Who says that? They're lying. My truck's been broken down. I haven't left here in nearly a month until today. Ask Delaney. She knows."

Leo looked a question at her. It was getting hard to see him in the fading light. Not ideal circumstances if Sicario brought his shotgun back out.

She nodded. "I fixed it for him earlier. I can't vouch for how long it's been out of commission, but it wasn't drivable when I got here today."

Leo said, "You couldn't have told me that earlier?"

"It didn't come up. Sorry."

Leo shook his head at her, looking frustrated. He kept his voice calm, even placating. "Can we talk to you inside, Sicario?"

Sicario's voice rose in pitch. "You got a warrant?"

Leo grimaced. "Your turn."

He walked over to Sicario's truck and compared the treads to the picture on his phone. He waved for Delaney to join him.

"Just a minute, Sicario," she said.

"Just go."

At the truck, Leo showed her the picture. She did her own comparison.

172 PAMELA FAGAN HUTCHINS

"Not a match."

He shook his head. "I disagree."

"That would make you wrong."

"It's probable cause."

"What? To search the vehicle?"

"That. And to enter his house."

She shook her head. "The tires aren't a match. I'm going back to get permission to enter now." Without waiting for him to answer, she returned to the trailer. She lowered her voice and put a hand beside her mouth like she was sharing a secret. "Sicario, Deputy Palmer has a problem. Diarrhea. Could you please let us in so he can use your bathroom? If you don't know anything about Mary, we'll be out of here as soon as he's done."

Leo had followed her back to the mobile home. "Nice," he said under his breath.

"That's gross, man." The door cracked open. Sicario didn't appear. "You swear?"

"I swear. Just talk to me while Deputy Palmer is in the bathroom."

Leo glared at her.

Sicario poked his head out. "Fine. Don't mess it up, okay?"

"I won't," Leo said. "I promise."

To Delaney, Sicario added, "But if you're lying, you and me are done."

Delaney gave him an incredulous look. "After I fixed your truck for free?"

"That's the only reason I'm letting you in."

Delaney grasped the sides of the door frame and vaulted into the trailer over the two-foot gap where steps should have been and were not. She heard the thump of Leo's body as he followed her lead. The inside of the trailer was in total darkness.

"Any lights?" she asked.

"No. I don't have the power back on yet. I've got a little solar for daytime, but no batteries. When the sun's out, the lights are out."

"Okay."

"The bathroom's down that hall. Don't use all the TP. It's my last roll," Sicario said.

As he walked away with one hand on the wall as a guide, Leo mumbled something under his breath that sounded like, "I'm going to kill you, Delaney Pace."

Delaney lowered herself onto a love seat identifiable with the last of the outside light. Sicario sat with his knees open across from her. As her eyes adjusted, she could see he was on a couch. Compared to clean freak Mary with her bean bag and folding chairs, Sicario was rich but lived like a pig.

"What's going on, Delaney? Has something happened to Mary?" Sicario's voice was low. He sounded genuinely worried.

"She was working the bar alone today. She disappeared in the middle of her shift, and she didn't show to pick up Juan Julio."

Sicario jumped to his feet. "Is Juan Julio all right?"

"He's fine. He's with my niece Kateena and one of his regular babysitters." It was only a slight upgrade of Skeeter's actual status.

The bathroom door flew open. Leo rushed out, holding a plastic bag aloft in one hand and his phone with the flashlight function on in the other. The bag had a pink piece of fabric in it. "I thought you said Mary hasn't been here?"

"She hasn't, man."

"Then what were these doing on your bathroom floor?" Leo manipulated the bag until the contents were visible. It was a pair of women's panties with the word MARY stamped on the tush in peeling letters.

Sicario shook his head. "I ain't never seen those. I don't know how they got here. I swear."

Leo handed the baggie to Delaney. He removed handcuffs

from his gear belt. "Sicario Menendez, you're under arrest. Turn around with your hands behind you."

"For what?" Sicario screamed.

"Yeah, for what?" Delaney echoed.

"Kidnapping."

Sicario sprinted with a speed that belied his heavy frame and leaped through the door opening.

"Stop him!" Leo flew through the air after him.

Delaney bounded out the door, landing in a three-point stance. She paused to analyze the situation. Sicario was running past his truck and into the forest. She plotted an intercept and sprinted across the uneven terrain. With all of Sicario's attention focused on Leo and Leo running a direct chase pattern in slick-soled new cowboy boots, the takedown was anticlimactic. Sicario practically ran into her arms, and her momentum was enough to overcome his weight. The two of them crashed to the ground. Delaney had the element of surprise in her favor, so she was able to keep herself on top and grasp his arms, which she twisted and lifted as he struggled.

"Ow," Sicario shouted.

"Stop fighting me," she said. "You're adding resisting arrest and assault of an officer. Stop."

He quit thrashing. The sounds of their heavy breaths and Leo's pounding feet were all Delaney could hear.

She said, "Why did you run?"

"Because your partner has a hard-on for me. I could see it in his eyes. I ain't going back to prison for something I didn't do."

"You swear you don't know how Mary's underwear ended up in your bathroom?"

"On my son's life, Delaney. I haven't had any woman over since I've lived here."

"Okay." She believed him. "You behave for Leo, and I'll find Mary. Cooperate. Don't make this worse."

"There's one thing I want to tell you. When I went to the bar to give Mary the money, there was a man there."

"The fat bartender. You said."

"No. Someone else."

"Who?"

"I don't know. A man. He asked me if I knew Mary. I said yes. He wanted to know where she was. He said they had a meeting scheduled."

"Describe him."

"A white guy. Around forty. They all look alike to me."

A meeting. Chip Crawford or someone else? There would be phone or text records. And Delaney still had Mary's phone in her car.

Leo slid to a stop. His hands, knees, and snakeskin boots were covered in slimy mud.

Delaney pulled Sicario to his feet. "All yours, Deputy Palmer." Her tone was acidic.

Leo didn't look like "thank you" were the first words that came to his mind.

TWENTY-SEVEN

The Delivery Man pulled his truck into a cluster of pine trees about one hundred feet from the driveway of the Pace homestead. He turned off the engine, chuckling. After his first session with Mary ended with her passed out, he'd gone upstairs for a sandwich. The newspaper he'd taken from the Loafing Shed had been on the table, so he'd flipped through it. Inside, he'd run across an article about Delaney Pace. The Delaney Pace who turned out to be a she. The photo the paper used was old. Something from her teen years. Delaney and a short man with an eye patch standing beside a motorcycle. She was holding a trophy. The article explained that the death of her brother Liam and sister-in-law Lila—fake news, since Lila had not been dead when the article was written—had brought Delaney back to Kearny to raise Kateena at the Pace homestead, that she'd been a trucker and was on a reality TV show.

Kateena. Lila's daughter.

He'd decided to reconnoiter. Figure out if this Delaney woman was actually the threat Mary claimed her to be. He'd visited the bar first, parking in the woods behind it. He'd seen a woman beside Mary's car. Right place, right age to be Delaney.

She was attractive by society's standards, but tall and light-haired wasn't his type. He'd left when a Kearny County Sheriff's Department vehicle pulled in beside her. After he checked his video feed on Mary—still out cold—he'd gone to the Pace homestead, which had been easy to find online.

He lifted binoculars to his eyes and watched the house through the trees and across a bridge, thinking about what he'd learned so far. The woman outside the bar seemed familiar, like he'd met her in town before. He wasn't scared of one woman. He didn't like the idea of one working with someone from the sheriff's department, though. Especially since the sheriff's department would be investigating Lila's death, too. Hopefully, the misdirection he'd planted would slow the search for Mary down. If not, he could get more creative.

A Subaru hatchback drove out from between the house and a barn, up the driveway. He counted two heads in it. Maybe a car seat in the back, too? The driver was large. A man, although he hadn't found any information on a man living there. The passenger was small and dark-headed. Lila's daughter Kateena? *Yes, female. Young.* His skin tingled.

The car turned toward town. The Delivery Man didn't care where they were going. He was only interested in what he'd find in the house. He opened his door and hiked through the trees, a longer route than directly across the pasture but one that would keep anyone driving by on the road from seeing him. Five minutes later, he reached the cluster of buildings. The lights were all out inside the house, but on outside illuminating the grounds. The structure could have been a hundred years old, but seemed sound. He spent a few minutes searching for cameras, something he was expert at. When he didn't find any, he went to the back door and rang the bell with his elbow, prepared to claim his phone had died and ask to borrow one to call Triple A. But no one answered.

He donned gloves and jiggled the doorknob. It was locked.

In his experience, a window was almost always left open some-where, and, if there were kids, theirs were the rooms to check first. Since he didn't know which one belonged to the girl, he tested the one nearest the door first. Locked. He kept going, tested another. Locked. On to the next one. Locked. He tried again. Locked.

And then he tested one that slipped up easily, without a sound.

He smiled, raising the window to create the largest possible opening. After he checked inside it to make sure his landing area was clear, he hoisted himself, crouched with a foot on the sill, added the other, and then crawled onto a window seat and into a world of dark purple, black, and white walls, bedspread, and pillows. Some free-floating bookshelves held pictures. He pulled a miniature flashlight from his pocket and turned it on. A framed photo of Kateena with Lila and Delaney's brother. *Kateena favors her mother.* In the photo, the girl was young. Maybe only seven or eight. The paper had given her current age as eleven.

The Delivery Man didn't work with girls. It was too early for evil to manifest itself. Women were evil. Not little girls. But maybe he could come back for Kateena someday when she was older? That would be special—a mother and daughter. But he couldn't think about it now. It was too distracting. Too exciting.

He was here to learn about Delaney.

He barely gave Kateena's room another glance before taking off down the hallway. The next bedroom he came to was filled with boxes. "Kitchen" read one in black marker. "Garage", another. "Winter Clothes", a third. Delaney's things, from her recent move? But he wasn't interested in what she kept boxed up. He wanted to see the things so important that they were unpacked.

He continued to another bedroom. It was slightly larger in size than the last bedroom and held adult-style furniture and décor. The bed was neatly made with a navy-blue comforter and two pillows in matching navy and white cases. There were a few photographs, but none of Delaney. On the chest of drawers, a bowl of jewelry was centered in front of a mirror. He touched an almost masculine chain. A medallion slid on the chain when he lifted it. Delight rippled through him. This wasn't something Lila Clement would have worn. It had to belong to Delaney.

This was her room.

He swallowed, then removed the pendant from the chain. Reverently, he lifted a thick chain from his neck, unfastened it, and secured the medallion to it, along with the hospital ID bracelet from Mary's son and blue stone pendant from Lila. He refastened his chain, enjoying the weight of his treasures on his chest.

He turned to the rest of the room. A locked gun safe. One bedside table. He opened the drawers. Found bear spray and stuffed it into his back pocket on impulse. He turned in a circle, savoring his time in Delaney's private space.

But then something else caught his eye on the dresser. An envelope that read "Gabrielle; Storage". It wasn't sealed, so he opened the flap.

Outside, he heard a car engine. Someone pulling up to the house. Was the man already back with Kateena? Or was it Delaney? It wasn't time to meet them yet. He had to hurry.

He rifled through the envelope. A rental agreement for unit 101 in a storage facility on the outskirts of town. He'd seen it many times when he was driving to and from his other cabin—the one he kept for privacy. There were two keys in the envelope. They looked identical. He stuck one in his front pocket. The unit number wouldn't be hard to remember.

Car doors slammed. Voices outside. He jogged as quickly and quietly as he could back to Kateena's room. Her window didn't face the driveway or parking area, so he slipped back out, shut it, and stayed hunkered down until he heard the door to the house shut and the sound of voices inside. Then the lights outside winked off. He eased away from the house, staying close to buildings until he had the shortest possible gap to reach the trees again.

The visit had been a success. The medallion moved against his chest as he walked. As he neared his pickup, his mind was miles across town, in storage unit 101. He was dying to know what or who Gabrielle was. And he intended to find out, after he came back for Delaney. Because the signs were there. A woman with *ideas*. Guns, bear spray, the threat she posed to his safety. And wasn't he tempted toward her? Wasn't that the ultimate proof?

She needed delivery. And she needed it soon.

TWENTY-EIGHT

Leo pulled off his ruined boots and slipped his feet into the Swamis under his work desk. He propped his cheek on his palm, sighing with exhaustion. His eyes were crusty. His breath, stale. His brain in need of life support. It was one of the busiest days in his career and might become one of the most significant as well. If Leo and Delaney could prove Sicario took Mary—could tie him to Lila—they'd crack the two biggest cases in recent Kearny history.

Except that Mary is still missing.

And finding her was more important than proving anything. Rest would have to wait. He had two Bang energy drinks in the break-room refrigerator. If three hundred milligrams of caffeine couldn't keep him up cyber sleuthing, nothing could.

Delaney—well, she was pissed at him about Sicario's arrest. She was convinced the man wasn't involved in Mary's disappearance. He still felt the sting of the gravel from her car's tires when she'd dropped him back at his truck. He wasn't sure where she'd gone from there, but he wished she was here. He needed her help, and, perversely, he missed working with her. The woman was stubborn. Reactive. Uncompromising. But smart and capable. *Also, sexy and completely uninterested in me.*

First things first, though. He needed an investigation plan for Mary. Even if he hadn't gotten far on the one he'd started for Lila, it helped to organize his thoughts. He lifted his head, shook the cobwebs out, and started typing.

Crime: Kidnapping and possible link to the murder of Lila Clement?? Other Peeping Tom/stalker cases?

Victim: Mary Galvez

Known associates: Sicario Menendez, Lila Clement (deceased), Liam Pace (deceased), Delaney Pace, Skeeter Owens, Toni Perkins, Chip Crawford, ??

Family: Juan Julio Menendez, ??

Employers: The Loafing Shed

Previous residences: ??

Record: ??

Issues: domestic trouble with Sicario Menendez

Online presence: ??

Phone records: ??

Suspect: Sicario Menendez

Known associates: Mary Galvez, ??

Family: Juan Julio Menendez

Employers: ??

Previous residences: ??

Record: ??

Issues: domestic trouble with Mary Galvez

Online presence: ??

Phone records: ??

Other potential suspects: felon in neighborhood, Bert Raines (neighbor), Chip Crawford (date), stranger

He added street addresses and phone numbers for each person on the list. Then he stilled his fingers. The number of question marks was disheartening. He missed the warm bodies and help of his colleagues at SDPD and in the Coast Guard.

His mind went back to the overarching question. Was there a tie between Mary and Lila? They had known each other, and both had an association with the Loafing Shed and Liam Pace. The most likely scenario was usually the correct one, though, and that pointed to Sicario for the kidnapping of Mary. And Sicario wasn't a likely suspect for Lila's murder.

Stick to smart policing and let the facts guide me.

He worked on an itemized to-do list.

- Order phone records for Mary and Sicario
- Submit probable cause affidavit for warrant to retrieve data from the phones
- Break into the phones and check texts and email

- Set up/monitor cameras front and back of bar and Galvez home
- Check tire treads from Mary's house against those from Lila's crime scene
- Criminal, incarcerations, property, address, phone, and employment records for each
- Social media for each

First things first. He prepared the affidavit quickly and sent it to Judge Gregory.

He closed his eyes. This was going to take him all night. None of it was difficult. *Would be easier if Delaney was helping me like I helped her with the neighborhood canvassing.* Okay, if he was being honest, helping her amounted to nothing more than doing his job. But, dammit, he was only one human and this was a mountain of work.

His email pinged. It was the judge authorizing the warrant. *That fast?* There were some things about small-town life he could get used to. He'd have to follow up by filing the paper version at the courthouse Monday, but, otherwise, he was good to go.

His cell phone chimed with a text.

Delaney: *You forgot Mary's purse & phone.*

Her words were like cymbal clashes in his brain. She was right. His brain needed fuel and rest to operate at its best, but his caseload didn't give a shit.

Leo: *Thanks. How and when can I get them from you?*

Delaney: *I need call rcds, VM, text, email. Now, if you can hack a copy. Otherwise, tmrw noon.*

More cymbal clashes accompanied by fireworks. He could hack into that phone and make her a back-up in seconds. He even had the warrant already. But it was the principle of the thing. Had she hidden the phone from him to punish him for arresting Sicario? He wasn't being fair, again—even if she had, he should have remembered it.

Am I mad at myself for forgetting or at her for asking for a quid pro quo? Probably both. Two could play her game. What could he get out of it?

Leo: *If you'll help me for two hours, I'll hand you a back-up when you're done.*

Delaney: *That will work. But then I'll have to get home to Kateena and Juan Julio. Almost to front door.*

Leo hurried to meet her, practicing his most menacing expressions on the way over. He opened the door. Felt himself grin at her like an idiot.

She handed over Mary's purse. "Phone's inside. You've still got the wrong guy, but working together gets us to the right answer faster."

"Nice to see you, too, Delaney. Where have you been?"

"Driving around, thinking about the case. You've lost one minute on your two hours."

He rolled his eyes. "Follow me."

The two of them hurried through the deserted offices. At his cube, Delaney pulled a rolling chair from a neighboring station.

Leo pointed at his monitor. "I was working on a plan and to-do list. The double question marks are for any information I'm missing. I've done one for Lila, too. It's open in another window. Can you add your thoughts to them?"

Delaney read quickly. "Aren't you the organized one. Some of this I know off the top of my head. Others seem time-sensitive. Like putting up cameras before we miss an opportunity to capture evidence that we never get again. I can install cameras. Do we have some in the equipment cache?"

"Yes. I can get them for you and hack the phones."

She nodded. "I want six cameras."

"Six? I was thinking front and back doors at the bar and Mary's house."

"Six."

"These extra two better not be for something that will get me in trouble later. Like something we should have had a warrant for."

"Have a little faith." She sighed. Pushed hair off her face. "We really need help with Mary. I know you think it was Sicario, but we have to *find* her."

"How about I write to Fentworth and ask him to get us help?"

"Good. I'd ask for law enforcement and community search help. Also, I need tire prints from Lila's scene." Then her eyes bored into his. "You realize Sicario is not Lila's killer."

He didn't answer her. Didn't get a chance. She was already rolling her chair closer to the screen.

TWENTY-NINE

Leo's fingers flew over the keys as he typed an email to Fentworth and Delaney, the impact of his first Bang still buzzing through him. Delaney had left half an hour before, and the place was as quiet as if it was underwater. The only light in the room came from his computer screen, the only sound from his fingers on the keyboard. An odor hung in the air, and not a good one. Like someone had thrown away tuna salad in the cubicle next to him. It had not aged well over the course of the evening.

Boss:

Delaney and I would like to call in help on the Mary Galvez search. We're thinking local, state, federal. I know we talked about staffing for Lila Clement (thanks), but finding Mary is time-sensitive. We could run it as a task force. Get community help searching for her, too. And we need to stay informed on Lila Clement and keep you included on Mary. They may be linked.

He hit send. Based on the information to date, including from Delaney, Sicario was still his top suspect. He was feeling more confident about him all time. He added a few thoughts to his notes.

But before he could dig in on the work he had left to do for the night, Fentworth replied to Leo's email.

Sent requests for help to usual suspects. Please send me a brief written update on Mary. Nutshell on Lila: reviewed research on similar crimes. Nothing popped. Clara is combing through the missing persons research. No luck yet. Help—I'm on it with state and local. Task force—yes, with you in charge. This is too closely tied to Delaney. Community help with search— could start around bar and Mary's house, but after those places, the search area is too broad unless we can limit it somehow.

Leo dropped his head back. The sheriff's and Clara's progress on Lila's case sounded slow, bordering on sloth-like. Well, maybe some of Leo's work on Mary's case would be useful to them, too.

He stretched his fingers then lowered them and let them fly over the keys. He started with criminal background searches on his key players. As tempting as it was to focus solely on Sicario and Mary, he added Bert Raines and Chip Crawford. Bert, not only because of his spotting scope, but because a criminal record would have bearing on the stock Leo put on the man's information. Based on Delaney identifying California as the home state for Sicario and Mary, Leo added the California data-base to the "Wyoming and adjoining states" starting point he'd used on Lila.

He ran Sicario first. His record came as no surprise. Petty theft and possession escalating to burglary and distribution. If he'd printed it all, he would have used a ream of paper. He saved it instead.

Mary next. She was Snow White clean.

Bert Raines followed, without California. The man's record was unblemished. Just as he was about to move on, though, he noticed the address in the records didn't match the house across the street from Mary. Hadn't Bert said he'd lived there a long time?

Leo checked his notes of the interview. "Decades," Bert had said. *That doesn't make sense.*

He popped over to the property records for the county. The property taxes for Bert's house were mailed to, and apparently paid by, Tim Osborne, who'd owned the house six years, since the passing of an Ethel Osborne, and before her, a Jezekiah Osborne.

He ran the criminal background searches on Tim Osborne. They showed that Tim had pleaded guilty to possession of child pornography. He'd spent six years in the state penitentiary and was released five years before he took possession of the house.

Were Tim and Bert the same person? Next, he pulled driver's license photos, starting with Tim.

The photo was of the man he'd met that day. So it was clear that Bert—or, rather, Tim— hadn't lived in that house for decades, but even if he had, it couldn't have been continuous because of his stint in prison.

Lying to a police officer about one's identity is illegal in California. Leo wasn't sure about Wyoming yet, but he couldn't imagine that it wasn't some kind of interference offense, and it sure wouldn't add credibility to the rest of what the man had said. *It doesn't mean he lied about the truck, though.*

Leo thought about the lies, the spotting scope, and the possession of child pornography. Did that crime relate in any way to kidnapping adult women? He'd need an expert for that question. But it certainly kept him on the list.

His phone chimed.

Delaney: *Test cameras pls. 2 at bar, 2 at Mary's, 2 at my place. And set me up for access to them tmrw?*

Leo: *Six cameras are now working. No problem on access. I sent you an electronic copy of the full Clement file with the tread photo. What now?*

Delaney: *Home. Rvw files & Mary's phone. Sleep.* Leo had given her a thumb drive with the contents of Mary's phone. He'd cracked it and cloned it in less than sixty seconds.

Leo: *You owe me another half an hour.*

Delaney: *Put it on my tab.*

He smiled, energy renewed by just the brief interaction with her.

On to Chip Crawford, whose given name did turn out to be Charles Junior, who he also ran everywhere except California. Leo flipped through results. He'd expected the juvenile offense records he found, but Chip's adult record was a surprise. A charge of kidnapping that a former girlfriend dropped. He marked it for follow-up. It gave him pause, since Chip, a.k.a. Charles Junior, had also purchased the soldering iron. *But he's local and so is Bert/Tim, which may rule suspects out.* He wished he hadn't missed a golden chance to interview Chip earlier. *Tomorrow, early.*

Leo pressed on both his temples. He'd wanted this case to be easy. Instead, every person he looked at increased the complexity exponentially. He needed a flashing neon arrow showing him the way to Mary, not a bowl of spaghetti dropped on the floor with each noodle pointing him in a different direction.

A door slammed shut somewhere in the building.

"Hello?" Leo called.

Footsteps approached, but there was no verbal response. Leo's stomach knotted. A thirty-ish woman with a nose ring and neck tattoos walked in.

"I'm here to clean." She was pushing a cleaning cart with a broom, mop, and vacuum cleaner hanging from it.

Leo relaxed somewhat. "Don't mind me. Just burning the midnight oil."

"Could I get your trash? I'll try not to bother you."

He handed it to her. "The one in the next cubicle is especially bad."

"Got it."

"Thanks.

Leo went to the bathroom. Took extra time splashing water on his face and brushing his teeth. It helped. He retrieved his second Bang from the break-room refrigerator and returned to his desk. He'd forgotten his phone and noticed a text had come in while he was gone. He settled back in his desk chair and nodded as he read.

Delaney: *Sent you a file via email. Here's a screenshot of 3 numbers Mary called yesterday a.m. Calls short. VM? One called back ltr. Call 4 mins. Name's Ryan Hefler, a builder. Others belong to builders too. Mary looking for someone to take my brother's constr clients. I called all 3. No answer. Will try again in a.m. Reviewed call log, VM, email, photos, texts. Chip's date story holds up. Nothing references her leaving shift. She's organized and a deleter.*

Delaney had traded more than her missing half hour with this work. He sent her a *Thanks.*

He pushed his hair off his forehead. Downed his second Bang. Went back to a review of Sicario's phone contents and accounts. The first thing he noticed about the phone was that most of Sicario's data usage seemed to be dedicated to downloading porn. Virtually all of his email was either receipts for purchases or emails trying to lure him into buying more. The second thing was that Sicario hadn't used his phone for a month. Not for calls, texts, emails, or pictures. Nada. Before then, his communication with Mary was mostly fighting over money. He also had correspondence with her boss, Liam Pace. Some looked like it was related to construction work, but the communication was extensive. Were the two buddies? It seemed an unlikely friendship. And the interactions felt awkward, like they were written in code.

He added Liam Pace as a known associate of Sicario's and dry-swallowed two ibuprofen.

Next, he tackled social media. The only social app on Sicario's phone was Facebook. When Leo reviewed it, he saw that Sicario's profile was only half complete and his friend list consisted solely of Mary and their families. He hadn't made a single post.

Since Delaney had reviewed Mary's communications, Leo focused on her social media usage. Like Sicario, she had Facebook but didn't use it. Same with Snapchat and Twitter. She was active on Instagram, though. He scrolled through her posts. Something nearly every day—usually a selfie with a check-in at the bar or a picture of her son that didn't show his face. In fact, she'd posted a selfie from the Loafing Shed a few hours before she disappeared. The post said *Come get loaded with me at the Loading Shed ;-)*.

He snapped a screenshot and emailed it to himself and Delaney. He browsed back through more posts. Before Juan Julio was born, her photos had been far sexier and more frequent. He opened her notifications, looking for recent followers. Chip Crawford had followed her early that morning, after meeting her the night before. Another follower from the day before caught his eye. A cowboy-looking guy with a mustache covering half his face who claimed to be from the nearby town of Sheridan, Wyoming. He had posted a handful of pictures with his horse and dog, but none were more than a week old.

Ice formed in his stomach. Someone monitoring Mary's whereabouts from a fake account?

He typed it up in his notes. This was one he would dig into

more deeply. It didn't support his theory about Sicario's involvement—unless this *was* Sicario. Maybe the man had a burner they hadn't found and was trying to keep tabs on Mary.

Or maybe it was Tim.

Maybe it was someone they hadn't discovered yet.

Or maybe it was just a bot.

He put his head down on his folded arms. He was wiped out. He'd be no good to Mary if he collapsed. It was almost time to call it a night here. He could work until he fell asleep from home.

He checked his Apple watch—something he hadn't seen anyone else in town wearing. Midnight.

As he started to put his phone away, he saw the text from Delaney earlier. He'd forgotten to look at the email she'd sent. He'd do it, but that would be it for him. He pulled it up. She'd forwarded an email from Mary. A PDF was attached—a restraining order in SoCal complete with a picture. Five years before. It seemed irrelevant until he saw the name.

Jorge Perez.

Not able to believe what he was seeing, he accessed the criminal records in California. Looked up the social security number of Jorge. Found the records he expected from the last three years and a picture in the system of the same guy as the one Mary'd had trouble with.

He had to believe it because it was true. He knew the guy.

Three years ago, Jorge Perez was a punk harassing young Mary Galvez. But a few months ago, he'd been an enforcer for the Bajeños, the cartel Leo had infiltrated.

"Son of a bitch!" His voice reverberated in the quiet space.

"You okay in there?" a woman asked.

Leo startled, then remembered the cleaner. "Yes. Thanks." *No.*

He pounded his fist on the desk, cursing under his breath. If what was happening to women in Wyoming ended up connected to Leo's work back in California, he'd never forgive himself.

He texted Delaney. *We need to talk, ASAP. OK to call?*

He waited five minutes. No reply. He called anyway. She didn't pick up. Deputies didn't turn their phones off. They couldn't. Sure, it could have gone dead, but it was unlikely. She was at home. Probably with a charger right next to her.

A cold knot formed in his stomach.

He pulled up the video monitoring app and found the cameras for her place. He checked the logs. As expected, the cameras had each caught her as she secured them in place and activated them.

But there were two more captures at the back door. The first was of a man in a hoodie, his face obscured. The second showed him walking away. The man turned back. His face was pointed right at the camera. Caucasian, mid-thirties. Then he was walking away again. He tucked a rose and a note under Shelly's windshield wiper then walked toward the driveway and disappeared.

The cold knot became an iceberg.

Leo checked the time stamp. It had been an hour ago. He'd talked to her since the time on the video. But still, this was odd. Unsettling. He leaped to his feet. He'd just drive out to her place on his way home. It was out of the way, but he wasn't going to sleep without knowing she was safe.

THIRTY

TWO HOURS EARLIER

Delaney shifted Shelly into gear and drove toward the homestead, keeping an eye out for deer and a foot ready to brake. Farmers and ranchers called deer "pasture pests." The herds of hundreds treated the tended alfalfa fields like most of the truckers she knew did the all-you-can-eat buffets at Petro truck stops. But for a woman with a beloved Chevelle, they were more than pests. They were highway hazards, plain and simple.

When she parked by the barn, she took the last two cameras to the house with her. She spent fifteen minutes installing them by the front and back doors. Even if it was a long shot, it hadn't escaped her notice that she was linked to Mary, Lila, Liam, and the Loafing Shed. She texted Leo to confirm they were working.

At the door to the house, she peeked in the window. Dudley was waiting for her. He put his front feet on the door and barked. Skeeter was sitting in a wooden chair at the kitchen table, legs splayed, arms crossed, and head back, his snore rattling the warped glass in the windowpanes. The dog's yapping didn't rouse him. She eased the door open, then slammed it hard, something her dad used to find hilarious to do to her when she fell asleep in front of the TV. She felt a frisson of connection to him.

Skeeter shouted and fell to his behind on the floor. "Whozit what?"

Dudley ran in circles, lunging at him as he barked.

Delaney laughed. A real laugh that came from her belly and made her bend over her knees, hands bracing her weight.

Skeeter struggled to his feet. His composure shot, he avoided eye contact. "You find Mary?"

Delaney's laughter choked off. "No. I'll keep working tonight and be back on the hunt early tomorrow."

"Was that deputy with the crush on you any help?"

He doesn't have a crush on me. She wanted to deny his contribution, but the truth was the truth. "Yes."

Skeeter rotated his neck. It cracked like a gunshot. "Your girl's in bed. The little 'un is sleeping on a pallet in her room." He reached down and patted Dudley on the tush. The dog waggled his behind to help.

"Good." Delaney put her purse on the table. "Thanks. Listen, I'm going to need you again tomorrow."

"But—"

"I'm paying you, of course." She fished in her purse for her wallet. "What's your hourly rate?"

"For babysitting?" He looked incredulous. "I don't charge Mary nothing for that."

Delaney pulled out four twenties. "Will this cover today?"

Skeeter licked his lips. "What time you need me tomorrow?"

"Say... seven?"

He sputtered. "I, um. It's a long drive."

She pointed at the couch. "Make yourself at home. I can bring you a pillow and blanket."

He studied the couch. "That could work."

Dudley looked between the two of them. He ran over to the

couch, jumped up on it, and did a bicycle-legged back scratch, as if he was calling dibs.

After Delaney had given Skeeter his bedding, she retreated to her room. She took off her belly holster, locked the Staccato in the gun safe, and changed into a nightshirt. Then she settled into a nest of pillows and arranged a notepad, pen, her laptop, some files, and her phone around her, thumb drive clutched in one hand.

"Aunt Delaney?" Kateena swayed in the doorway. Her voice was gravelly with sleep.

Delaney patted the bed beside her. "Come say goodnight."

Kateena crawled onto the bed and snuggled up to her. "I had a bad dream."

"What about?"

"Mom and Dad."

Ugh. Delaney hadn't told her about Lila yet. She couldn't do that to her right now when she was already having bad dreams. *Later, but soon.* "Are you okay?"

"Yeah. I just... could I stay here with you?"

Delaney considered the work she'd be doing. Some of it wasn't fit for Kateena's eyes. She'd save that and start with the phone records. "For a little bit. Close your eyes."

Kateena's smile was beatific, and Delaney felt a strange pressure in her chest. The long lashes batted shut, but her niece's smile stayed in place.

Delaney inserted the thumb drive into her laptop's USB slot. Leo had backed up the text messages, phone records, voice-mail, and email to apps, and—without patronizing her—showed her how to use them. The world had changed a lot since she was hauling in drunks and passing out traffic tickets a decade before.

She pulled up Mary's texts first. One thing was clear quickly. Mary was as fastidious about keeping her text strings cleared out as she was about keeping her house and car clean. Only strings with texts from the last forty-eight hours were on her phone. One was with Chip Crawford, discussing their date that night. Another was with Skeeter asking him to help her get money from Sicario. Her mom made the list, talking about Juan Julio and family members Delaney didn't know. A woman that could have been a sister or good friend was there, too. That conversation was lively and filled with emojis and inside jokes. And Sicario. Those texts were one-sided—Mary asking for money and him not responding, which backed up his claim that he'd been phoneless for some time.

She thought about Sicario and the man he'd talked to at the Loafing Shed, the one who had come to see Mary. She'd hoped to find something on Mary's phone about who he could be if it wasn't Chip. But there were no texts to or from anyone about coming to the bar. None about Mary planning to go anywhere else either.

Delaney could come back to them later, but for now, the texts seemed like a dead end.

The email came next. Mary used a free Gmail account, like Delaney, and very sparingly. As Delaney would have expected, all except the most recent emails were filed appropriately. Bills in the Bills folder. Family, by name, in their individual folders. Sicario in his own, which was nearly empty. Friends in one folder—mostly chain mail. And then there was a Legal folder. That was interesting, but all Delaney found in it was a restraining order dated three years earlier in southern California. She sent a copy to herself and Leo, but she didn't hold out high hopes.

Mary's sent items were similarly filed, and her spam folder was empty.

Mary could teach Marie Kondo a thing or two about decluttering and organization.

Knowing the woman better by the second, Delaney opened her photos. She browsed folders. Admired pictures and video of Juan Julio. Of Sicario from happier—and slimmer—days. But, again, she didn't uncover anything that led her closer to Mary's current whereabouts.

Lastly, she pulled up the calls. Voicemail was empty, naturally, save for an angry message from Chip about her standing him up.

Delaney hit pay dirt with the call log. Mary had made three calls of less than twenty seconds each that morning. *She was leaving voicemail messages.* She'd received a call back from one of the three numbers about two hours later. That call lasted four minutes. Other than that, she'd cleared her call logs all the way back to the day Liam had died.

Delaney screenshotted the information and sent it to her phone. Checked the time. Ten forty-five. She decided to give each number a call but got only voicemail. Two electronic recordings gave out only the number of the phone. One provided a name, a man who identified himself as Ryan Hefler. It was the number the longer return call came from. Delaney hung up without leaving any messages.

A search online revealed that Ryan Hefler was in the construction business locally. Delaney repeated her search with the other two phone numbers. She found both attached to other local builders. The calls now made sense. Mary had offered to find someone to help with Liam's construction customers. Obviously, she'd followed up on it quickly. She'd try calling all three again in the morning.

Delaney texted Leo an explanation with the screenshot of the numbers and added a wrap-up of her progress. She yawned. Her eyes had been drifting shut off and on for the last half hour. She'd have to continue in the morning. Two nights with no sleep was too much when she needed to be at her sharpest, both physically and mentally.

Kateena jerked and shouted, "No, no, no!" She didn't wake up.

It was time to put the girl to sleep in her own bed. Delaney lifted her niece into her arms. She carried her into her bedroom and tucked her in, then pressed her lips against Kateena's cheek. She didn't stir. Delaney knelt and smoothed Juan Julio's hair off his forehead. He was sweaty. While he was too young to understand why his mother wasn't with him, he had to miss her. It hurt Delaney's heart.

Back in her room, Delaney cleared off the bed. She plugged her phone in to charge, then set the laptop on the chest of drawers. She turned to climb into bed, then froze.

An envelope from the storage unit. It was on the chest, and it had looked somehow different. She whirled around, getting a glimpse of her mussed braid and suspicious eyes in the dresser mirror. The envelope had been turned over. She knew she'd left it with the handwritten side facing up. *Gabrielle; Storage.* It made her feel connected to the freedom of her old life to see Gabrielle's name in black Magic Marker. She flipped it. The weight felt wrong. She'd left a key or two in it. She squeezed it. The key was still in there. Paper rustled inside. She relaxed.

She was making a big to-do about nothing. Skeeter had probably just done a little snooping. She would have in his shoes. She placed the envelope back on top of the chest. Smoothed it with her hand. That's when her eyes lit on the jewelry bowl. She didn't own many pieces. A few pairs of hoop earrings. A Wyoming Cowboy on a silver chain. The gold anklet her mother had given her. And her most treasured piece, the medallion pendant from her father.

But the pendant wasn't in the bowl. Nor was it anywhere else in the room, including under the chest of drawers.

It was gone.

THIRTY-ONE

Delaney was dreaming. It wasn't a good dream. In it, she was a child again. Her mother had slipped into her bedroom and woken her, big tears in her cat-green eyes. The moonlight streaming through the window caught them as well as something pretty and gold dangling from her hand.

A memory as much as a dream.

"My mother gave it to me when I was a girl. I was going to wait until you were thirteen to give it to you, but I've decided you should have it now." Mama smiled through her tears.

Laney touched the chain with a fingertip. She loved seeing it on her mother's ankle, but that wasn't often. Her mother was away more than she was home. And when she was home, she and Daddy mostly screamed at each other. Laney heard the things her grandmother said to her grandfather, too. *Something's wrong with that woman*, when she was being nice. *Bad wife and mother*, most of the time. *Godless tramp*, when she was angry. To Laney, her grandmother was wrong. Her mother was a beautiful will-o'-the-wisp. A northern light.

She'd rather have her mother than a piece of jewelry.

"Give me your ankle," her mother said.

Laney slipped it out from under the covers. Her mother clasped the chain.

"There. What do you think?"

Laney swallowed, and it felt like one of Grandma's dry, tasteless oatmeal cookies had lodged in her throat. Her voice came out a croak. "But what if I lose it, Mama?"

Her dad had walked in, smiling at her, ignoring her mother. "Just as long as you don't lose that medallion I gave you, kiddo."

"I won't, Daddy."

An explosion of barking jerked her out of the dream and awake into the cool of the old house at night. She licked her lips, opened her eyes. The moonlight of her dreams was blocked by closed curtains, leaving her in pitch darkness. *Dudley.* Then she bolted upright. Dudley was a professional sleeper. Nothing woke him. *Kateena!* Her breath caught in her chest.

Footsteps in the hall. *No.* In the doorway to her room.

Instinct took over. She rolled away from the door, flowing onto the floor soundlessly like a ripple across water. Away from the gun safe with her Staccato locked behind a four-digit keypad. *Shit. I need a weapon.* Her bear spray in the bedside table. She reached up and pulled out the drawer, felt inside, thankful for the silent runners and short height of the piece of furniture. But she didn't find it. She groped and walked her fingers. Still no bear spray, and she was going to make noise if she kept it up. *Dammit.* She slid her arm under the bed, sweeping, feeling. Her fingers bumped something solid. She grasped it. Cylindrical. Metal. Long.

A baseball bat. *Thank you, Liam.*

Weight pressed into the mattress above her. Dudley's barks moved to the entrance to the room. He was loud but unwilling to come any nearer the intruder. The mattress rose and fell as the person on it crawled around, searching.

The intruder was going to lose interest in an empty bedroom. She had to block access to Kateena's room. She lifted the bat above the rug under the bed and pulled it toward herself, praying for silence.

Scritch.

The sound of it scraping the metal underside of the bed frame invaded the silence.

Above her, the intruder froze.

Delaney abandoned stealth, jerked the bat out, and leaped to her feet. She raised the metal over her head and swung it down toward the mattress.

Thwump!

A person grunted. Not the scream Delaney had hoped for. She'd connected with soft tissue. Dudley's barking intensified.

"Somebody in there?" Skeeter called.

Delaney didn't have time to answer him. She cocked the bat back to try again when something launched itself from the bed with a twang of mattress springs. The force of the collision with her midsection knocked the breath out of her. Her bat caught soft tissue again, this time at close range. Ineffectual, but she hung on to her weapon. Arms wrapped around her, and the weight of her attacker slammed her backwards into the window.

Crack!

The glass gave way as Delaney felt the sill catch the back of her knees, the heavy drapes close around her body, and her head fly through the space beyond where the window had been, landing in a bed of iris. The attacker was on top of her, head bumping hers, the curtain cocooning their bodies together. Her hand still gripped the bat, but it was useless, trapped, and her other arm was, too, under her hip. She sucked in smell of body odor. Sweat. Fetid breath. Her heartbeat thundered in her ears. She had to untangle herself.

She bucked and twisted, trying to roll out from under the intruder. Glass crunched underneath the drapery barrier, digging into her like razors, but the attacker didn't budge. Warm skin pressed against her face. She used the only weapon left to her, opening her mouth as wide as she could, catching flesh, biting down, and clamping her jaws tight.

"Bitch!"

The scream she'd failed to elicit earlier rang in her ears, followed by another sound. Something approaching on the driveway. Tires. Light bouncing off the side of the barn. She didn't have time to think about it. Life or death was right here, right now, with this person. Man? Woman? Impossible to discern. Not from the voice, the weight, the feel, or the scent of the creature writhing and panting on top of her. But one thing she could tell. She had bitten into earlobe. And her attacker would have to sacrifice it to escape her.

Hands slapped at her face. Fingers reached for her neck. Nails bit into her skin. She didn't let go. And then the sound of an engine—across the yard, lights flooding her face.

"Delaney?" *Leo, thank, God.* But she couldn't answer him.

Spittle pelted her face. "This is the final sign."

Whatever that means. Skin gave way in her teeth, blood spurted over her chin and into her mouth, the weight on her body lifted. She gagged, released the bat, and wiped at her face with her suddenly free arms.

"Don't let him get away, Leo." Delaney struggled to rid herself of the drapes.

Hands were on her, pulling at the fabric, reaching for her, lifting her.

"Are you okay?" Leo pulled her to her feet and held her in front of him, his eyes sweeping over her, horror on his face as he took hers in. She had to look like a vampire.

For the briefest of seconds, she wanted to dive into his arms, but the urge was replaced by a burning hot need to go after her attacker. "It's not my blood. Which way did he go?"

He pointed with his head. "Around the house."

The door to the house opened. The outside light came on.

Skeeter stood framed in it, Dudley beside him, no longer barking. "Everything okay out here?"

"Back in a minute, Skeeter," Delaney said. "We had an intruder. You stay with the kids."

"But your face—"

She scooped up the bat and sprinted into the dark, conscious of Leo behind her. Once, she'd known this land. She was still familiar with the lay of it, but not the small changes rendered by time and weather. A broken ankle would be catastrophic. She slowed as they crossed in front of the house, searching for movement in the moonlit pastures.

She spoke brokenly between heaving breaths. "He'll have driven in. Be heading for the road. Fastest to run the driveway and avoid the creek."

"Got it," Leo said.

She cut across the yard and the gravel road, speeding up. Stones dug into her soles. Her footsteps slapped on the wooden bridge. Her lungs burned. But hard as she tried to get there first, an engine roared to life a hundred yards ahead, along the road to town.

"There!" she shouted.

Brake lights flashed red, then she heard engine strain as the driver accelerated out of a stand of trees and disappeared.

She slowed, slumped over her knees. "Did you call it in?"

Leo stopped beside her, breathing heavily. "No. I didn't know it was anything."

She stood. "What are you doing here, then?"

"I think that means thank you, so you're welcome." He exhaled hard. "You weren't answering me, so I checked the video feed for your house and saw a man on it. He left, but I thought I should come investigate."

She frowned. "He left?"

He pulled out his phone and in a few keystrokes, he was playing a video for her. "Do you recognize him?"

Delaney stared at the screen. A man in a hoodie, face obscured. He appeared to be Caucasian, in his thirties, and of medium height and stature. Like her attacker.

As he got closer, he pointed his face down.

"No," Delaney said.

"Could it be the guy?"

"Him or any other average white guy."

"Chip?"

"Same answer."

"What about Tim Osborne?"

Delaney couldn't have been more surprised if Leo had shot her in the face. She stopped the video. "What did you just say?"

"Tim Osborne."

"How do you know that name?"

Leo's forehead bunched like the grill of an Audi. "Bert Raines lied about his name, and I figured out his real name was Tim Osborne, a parolee for—"

"Whoa. Tim Osborne is on parole for possession of child pornography, and he should have been put away for more."

"Was he one of your cases?"

"That was before my time. He was one of my foster parents. And I was the one who turned him in to Fentworth."

"No shit?"

"Lots of shit. He was a horrible person. But I'm not making this up. He's Mary's neighbor? That's not where I lived with him."

"Were you... I mean, did he—"

"No. I was already older than his type. He lied about his situation to get me, though. There was a woman who claimed to be his domestic partner so that he could keep a few hard-to-place kids with him. We funded his habit."

"I'm sorry, Delaney."

She swallowed a lump in her throat. "It was a long time ago." Then her mouth opened and closed.

"What?"

"Do you think it's him? That this is payback against me?"

He blew out a surprised sound. "Wow. I don't know. Does he have a connection to Lila or Mary?"

A cold shiver raced up her neck. "Me."

"Could that be him in the video?"

She stared at the screen. Her bunched shoulders relaxed. "This guy looks younger than him. And the person who attacked me—I couldn't say for sure, but unlikely. I don't think we can take him off the list, though."

"There's one more clip. A better face shot."

He played another video for her. In this one, the man was leaving the house.

She said, "That's his back. So, he didn't try to go in? What was he there for?"

"Wait for it."

The man turned back.

Delaney was staring at a familiar face looking back at her into the camera. Then he stopped to leave a flower and envelope under Shelly's windshield. She'd left the car outside when she'd turned in for the night, too tired to bother with putting it up in the barn.

She closed her eyes. "That's not my attacker."

"How do you know?"

Humiliation made her angry. "Because I think if I've been sleeping with someone for a year that I'll recognize the voice and body on top of me."

"What?"

"The guy on the video? That's my ex. And I told the asshole to stay five hundred miles away from me. Apparently, he doesn't listen."

She turned and stomped across the grass toward the house.

THIRTY-TWO

Mary opened her eyes to darkness and pain. She was lying on her side. Her confusion gave way to panic. The same panic she'd felt every waking moment since she'd been kidnapped. She moved her arms. The handcuff clanked. She was stiff and the cuts burned. The dirt floor was unforgiving. Next, she tested her legs. She moaned. Her legs hurt worse. She pushed up to sit and cried out. Her mid-section was worst of all. How many times had he cut her? She'd lost count, then she'd lost consciousness.

She needed to get her bearings. She knew she'd been taken around midday. But was it still the same day? That night? It could be days later. With no windows, she couldn't tell what time it was or mark its passage.

And the stench. The place had smelled bad when he'd dumped her in here. Now she was naked, cold, bloody, and filthy. One time he'd woken her and given her a bucket to relieve herself in. She'd used it before he'd taken it away. But when she was unconscious, what had she added to these smells? The humiliation made her weep.

It would have been better if she'd remained asleep. Remembering the way he had sliced her, she almost wished she was dead. Except for one thing. One very important thing. Juan Julio. He needed his mother. No way was she leaving him to be raised by Sicario.

"*Hijo de puta!*" she yelled.

Who was this person, and why did he pick her? Tears flowed down her cheeks. Frustrated, scared tears. *Stop it, Mary.* What she needed to do was save her energy to find a way out of this dungeon. An escape. And to be ready to fight back.

Fight back. The one time she'd resisted, he'd threatened her with his stun gun. He was bigger. He was stronger. He was meaner. He'd knocked her out at the bar. He'd cut her, over and over. How many visits now? Three at least, and each time she was more delirious than the last. Fear. Exhaustion. Hunger. Blood loss. Pain. Thirst.

She ran her hand along the smooth length of the cable from her handcuffs to the wall. Explored a cuff with her fingertips. It was old-school metal. Something she'd never felt around her wrists before but had seen several times on Sicario as he was led to a cop car. Her left wrist was the one enclosed. The right cuff dangled from a few links of chain, clamped shut. During his visits, he cuffed both her wrists behind her and removed the cuffs from the cable.

Having her hands restrained had made her feel more vulnerable when he assaulted her. Pebbles had dug into her face. Dirt had been shoved up her nose. At one point, he had smashed her face into the ground. She'd thought she was going to suffocate. Those things, and all the cuts, had been bad. Worse, though, was that she couldn't do what she'd dreamed of —wrap the cable around his neck and use her body weight to cut off his air supply.

But the cable had still been in the room. For sure, if she got close enough, she'd try to use it.

It's a big if. He's careful.

She tried to stand up, and her hand hit something light and plastic. She sank back down to her hands and knees. What was it?

She probed its shape. A plastic water bottle. He'd brought her mushy food in a Styrofoam bowl with a plastic spoon, plus a liter of water. He'd left the bottle. She picked it up and shook it, hopeful, but it was empty. She let it fall back to the ground.

What if she filled it with dirt? Then she could use it like a club. An image of a heavy bottle smashing into the man's head flashed through her mind. His body crumpling to the ground.

She grabbed the bottle and moved to the farthest corner from the ladder. Using the cap, she dug up a small amount of dirt and dumped it into the water bottle. The plopping sound was depressingly soft. She grasped the right cuff with both hands and dug harder. A more satisfying amount of soil broke loose. She plunged her hands into it. Rocks. Mostly small. But some were large enough to do damage. She began scooping the dirt into the bottle. She dug faster. Scooped faster, afraid he would show up before she finished. She needed to fill the bottle and hide it in the hole left behind.

The weight of the bottle was increasing.

A scraping noise above her sent her heart into her throat. She shoved the bottle into the hole as far as she could and piled dirt on top of it, then crawled back to the middle of the room and curled up. The door swung open. She tried to slow her heavy breathing. *Why didn't I keep my rock and bottle?*

Next time. Next time she would be ready. No matter what, the next time he came through the door, she was going on the offensive. All she had to do this time was survive.

The trapdoor in the ceiling creaked open. The Delivery Man climbed down the ladder one-handed, leaving the door open above him. A slight breeze moved the air. The bad smell lessened. In one hand, he held the bucket. Something was banging around inside it as he climbed down. She saw another water bottle under his arm. She looked up. His head was bandaged. And the expression on his face was one of pain and fury.

He said, "I can't watch you eat. You're too disgusting. I'll be back in an hour. Don't do anything stupid while I'm gone."

She lay in a fetal position, watching him. *Look submissive.*

"I don't have to feed you or give you water. I could let you soil yourself."

She stared, unspeaking. A strong emotion was taking hold of her. Anger. Another—hate.

"Aren't you even going to say thank you, ungrateful bitch?"

She swallowed the dirt that had gotten in her mouth as she dug. Dry. So dry. "Thank you." Her voice sounded weak and crackly. But inside, she felt stronger by the second.

"Try to clean yourself up before I get back. I like a clean woman for delivery day."

What does that mean? It sounds bad. She had to be ready when he came back. He looked like he expected an answer. "Yes, sir," she whispered.

But inside, she screamed, *You're in for a surprise, pendejo.*

THIRTY-THREE

Delaney flipped a pancake onto one of the four tall stacks she'd piled on her grandmother's platter. She turned off the flame and removed the skillet from the stove, tripping over Dudley as she turned to put it in the sink.

"Out of the kitchen, beast." She tried to sound stern, but she owed him one for his early warning last night.

Dudley scooted back an inch to let her by.

"Breakfast," she shouted.

It was only six a.m., but she'd been up most of the night, chilly from a sudden cold front and unable to sleep except in fits and starts after Leo and the crime scene team had left, even though she'd nailed a slab of plywood she'd found in the barn over her window, to keep out the chill as well as repeat visitors. *Leo. He worried about me. He came.* She could count on one hand the people in her life who would have shown up like that for her. She'd have to think about that—him—more later. For now, her mind was consumed with what-ifs. Kateena's window had been wide open. The intruder had made ingress through her room, although she'd slept right through it. What if she hadn't? What if she'd been hurt?

Kidnapped? The thoughts were far more chilling than the inescapable conclusion that Delaney had been the target. And her strong conviction that whoever had come for her had taken Mary and killed Lila. Plus, the Tim Osborne connection had her rattled. *He's too old. And he's local. It can't be him.* Or was that just wishful thinking, because of how desperately she didn't want to be the reason Lila was dead and Mary gone?

She had to look through the evidence again and see if she'd missed something critical. She needed to go back to the place Lila had died. Been murdered. Revisiting a crime site further into a case had often helped her in the past. She couldn't think of anything better to ground her in the case and in this person who was doing horrible things to women Delaney knew. To her.

"Brr. Ain't you got a heater in this place? I thought you said seven. And I didn't barely get no sleep." Skeeter's grumbles were muffled by a blanket over his face.

"Join the club. I assumed you'd have eaten, be showered, and arrive here by seven. Up. You and I need to talk. Then you need to get Kateena and Juan Julio."

"But the kid part isn't until seven. You just said."

She walked into the living room, waving a spatula in the air. Dudley hovered under it in case it splattered food. "I just cooked a homemade country breakfast for your sorry butt, even after the night I had. Get it moving, Skeeter."

He lumbered off the couch, shirtless, his skin pimpled with cold. It wasn't a sight she'd soon forget. Belly hanging two inches over the waistband of his jeans. Patchy black hair. A scar under his ribs that looked like he got it in a knife fight. And when he passed her, shirt in one hand, more of his butt cheeks and crack showing than anyone should have to stomach this early in the morning.

"You need protection. In case our intruder returns."

He stood taller, shoulders back. "I know how to fight. But I don't expect he'll come back after you practically bit his earlobe off."

"I barely pierced his ear enough for an earring." She hoped Skeeter was right, though. Plus, the intruder had been after her, and she wouldn't be here.

"Still pretty gross."

"Not one of my top ten moments." But it had been his ear or her. "Can you shoot?"

"Is that a serious question?"

She walked into the bedroom and retrieved a shotgun and box of shells from the gun safe and brought them back to him. "Load it and unload it."

He made quick work of it, even replacing the shells in the box. "I been hunting birds since I was a boy. First with a pellet gun, then with a twelve gauge. Nice gun."

"Thanks." It had been her father's. "I'm trusting you with the most precious thing in my life. And in Mary's."

His face was solemn. "They're safe with me. You can count on that."

"Can you keep the gun at the top of the coat closet unless you need it?"

He nodded and lumbered to the closet. He opened it and shoved the weapon out of reach of the kids, then put the box of shells on the floor.

"Perfect. And Skeeter? Let's not talk about what happened last night in front of Kateena."

He nodded. "I'll get the little 'uns now."

She went back to the kitchen, feeling a little better. Cooking soothed her, which she sorely needed. Reminded her of times with her grandmother. The woman had come alive in the kitchen, sparkling with creativity and good humor she showed at no other times. She was still strict—requiring Delaney to be exact, economical, and obedient—but there was no kneeling on rocks. The two of them had canned, baked, and pressure-cooked every fall. The fruits of their labors had been stored in the root cellar, which is where Delaney had wandered into around dawn. It was finding the last jar of huckleberry syrup, labeled twenty-five years before in her grandmother's precise handwriting, that had inspired the breakfast.

Delaney placed the syrup in the center of the table, butter beside it. She'd tested it earlier, and it was delicious after all the time that had passed since it was made. She chewed a piece of bacon and eyed the spread. Cheesy scrambled eggs, what was left of the bacon after her sampling, pancakes, milk, juice, and coffee.

Kateena slumped into her normal chair, arms around her torso, facing into the kitchen. "Why am I up? I don't have school today."

"Good morning to you, too."

"Can I go to a friend's or something? It's so boring here."

"Uh, no. If you're suspended from school, you're suspended from a social life."

"But you never said that!"

"I'm saying it now."

Kateena crossed her arms and stuck out her bottom lip.

Skeeter took a seat beside her, Juan Julio in his lap with his eyes closed and head buried in Skeeter's chest.

"Good morning, Juan Julio." Delaney ruffled his hair.

He shook his head but then turned his face toward her with a smile. Skeeter helped him wriggle around to face the table. Then Skeeter grabbed a stack of pancakes with his hands. He stuffed one in his mouth, tearing at it like a caveman.

"After grace." Delaney didn't admit she'd eaten bacon already. "You guys look sleepy, so we can go with the short version." She took Kateena's hand.

Kateena held Juan Julio's. Delaney bit the inside of her lip and took one of Skeeter's mitts.

They recited in unison. "For health and food, for love and

friends, for everything Thy goodness sends, Father in heaven we thank Thee. Amen."

"Amen," Juan Julio repeated.

Delaney smiled at him. She served herself quickly, as did Kateena and Skeeter. Kateena made a plate for Juan Julio, cutting everything into tiny pieces. He stuffed food in his mouth with his fingers, making "um um" sounds as he chewed. He and Skeeter were a good match.

Between bites, Delaney asked her niece a few careful questions. "Did you sleep good last night?"

"Yes," Kateena said.

"You didn't wake up?"

"I don't think so." She put her fork down. "Why?"

"My, um, my window broke. I thought it might have woken you up." She'd locked Kateena's window herself last night, so she didn't mention it. They'd talk about safety later. Right now, she didn't want to raise any alarms. "Hey, did either of you happen to pick up my medallion pendant yesterday? It was in the jewelry bowl on the chest of drawers in m—" she'd almost said my, forgetting for a moment that to Kateena it was her parents' "—the main bedroom?" She wanted to believe her attacker hadn't taken it in an earlier scouting visit. She wanted it badly. But the missing bear spray—she'd confirmed its absence last night—added to the missing jewelry and altered placement of her storage records made it hard.

Kateena spoke with her mouth full. "The one Grandpa won at that race in Gillette?"

Dudley had stationed himself by Kateena. Delaney saw her niece's hand slide under the table. Dudley made gulping and smacking noises.

"Yes, that one. And don't feed the dog at the table. Do you have it?"

"Yes, ma'am. No, ma'am. I don't."

"Skeeter?"

He shook his head. "Don't look at me. Ain't seen one." He drank and set his glass down, oblivious to his milk mustache.

"Could Juan Julio have taken it?"

Kateena baby-talked to the boy. "Juan Julio, did you take Aunt Delaney's pretty pendant?"

He giggled.

But Kateena turned to her aunt with a serious expression. "He couldn't have taken it. I kept your door shut, like you always ask me to, on account of your gun safe."

Good girl. The freestanding gun safe weighed a ton, but it moved everywhere Delaney went. The prime rule of gun ownership was safety first, no matter what. "All right, then."

"When was the last time you saw it?" Kateena asked.

"I took it off and put it in the bowl when Skeeter and I brought Juan Julio over. Did you have any visitors at the house yesterday?"

"Just Skeeter and Juan Julio."

Delaney rolled two pieces of bacon in a pancake and dunked it in the huckleberry syrup, playing it cool. "Skeeter, did you have to get anything out of that bedroom? Some stuff was moved around. It's no big deal, I'm just trying to figure out what happened."

"Nope. The young 'uns kept me too busy to do anything but tend to them from the time we got here until we went to town, and after we got back. Then I fell asleep where you found me."

Delaney hadn't known they'd left. But pieces were falling into place. The intruder had unfettered access. "When were you gone?"

"Around dinner time. We picked up diapers and such at the Albertson's and grabbed some Taco Bell."

"Did you notice anything disturbed when you returned?"

"You're scaring me, Aunt Delaney," Kateena said.

Delaney leaned over and kissed the crown of her niece's head. She picked up the last bite of her pig in a blanket. "Don't be scared. It's probably nothing. I could be remembering things wrong. Just keep the doors and windows locked, okay?"

Skeeter saluted her.

Delaney got up, chewing, and put her plate in the sink. "I've got to run."

"Is Skeeter staying?" Kateena said.

"Yes. Do what he says. Have a good day everyone."

Kateena slumped. "Impossible. I'm stuck at home."

"You'll survive. And next time, think about how boring home is before you punch someone." Delaney had already packed up. Weather-appropriate outerwear. A makeshift crime scene fanny pack in place of a duty belt and department backpack. Her gun and ammo. Her purse with her phone and her laptop. She didn't normally carry the MacBook, but it would save a trip home if she needed it later.

Leaving Kateena was harder than usual. *The attacker was after me, not her. And the best thing I can do to protect her is find him.* Maybe if she repeated it enough times, she'd believe it.

She waved as she exited, feet crunching frost—this was why her grandmother had never planted outside before June first—but no one looked up from their food again. It was a compliment, she supposed. She grabbed the rose and card from Shelly's shield and threw them on the passenger seat, started the car, and turned on the heat and defrost. Only then did she read the card. *Delaney, I'm sorry. I miss you. I'll be staying in town for a few days. I want to talk to you. I love you.* Damn, Chad. Hell would freeze over before she'd talk to him.

Delaney shot a text to him. *Never again. Do not ever again show up at my house.*

She felt a little better. But if he hadn't pulled this stunt, Leo wouldn't have come to the homestead, and she didn't know how things would have ended. She shuddered. The intruder hadn't even appeared on the video, not at all, since he'd accessed the house through Kateena's room instead of the doors. And the only evidence he'd left was his blood. That wasn't nothing. If there was a DNA match logged out there for him somewhere, they'd identify him. Or catch him later if he did something else and left trace.

It was her job to make sure he never got another chance.

By the time she was pulling out of the driveway through the fog, she had her phone out. It was early, but people in construction didn't work bankers' hours. She went to Recents, found the number for Ryan Hefler and called. Voicemail. Same result with the other two numbers Mary had called the day before. Nothing to do but move on.

Her phone rang. A quick glance at caller ID told her it was Fentworth. She answered on speaker. "You're up early."

"I just got the news about last night. Why no one called me is going to be a point of discussion today. Are you all right?" His voice sounded concerned. Almost panicked.

"I'm fine, Fentworth. Really."

"I just hate that I wasn't there. That some pyscho attacked you and is still out there. I just got you back."

A wave of emotion engulfed her. Their old disagreement had quit mattering a long time ago. Why hadn't she realized it? She wrung her hands on the steering wheel. "And you're still stuck with me. Leo came."

"He's a good one."

Less bad than I'd thought. Her voice thickened. "Thanks for calling. See you at the office."

"Be careful."

She exhaled long and slow, ending the call and giving Shelly more gas. *Let your horses run, pretty girl.* The first of the lupine and yellow balsam root had started to bloom, covering the south-facing hills around the homestead in a blanket of color that was visible now as the fog was lifting. The wildflowers didn't mind the cold. Driving the Chevelle on these roads in the early mornings brought back memories of riding with her father. To school. To activities. To the bar with him. It was bittersweet. He hadn't been the best father in the world, but he'd loved her, and he'd wanted her for the right reasons. *No one has before or since.* Not her grandparents, her brother, the mother who'd left her, or the parade of foster families she'd lived with briefly until her eighteenth birthday.

Soon, she'd reached the base of the steep, rocky gravel road up the mountain. She glanced back. The fog was pillowy-white below, but dissipating, its blankets turning to ribbons. She hated taking this car—her father's pride and joy—to Lila's crime scene, but she didn't have a better option. Liam's truck had burned up in the crash. Lila's Lexus convertible was in for repairs, or it would have made no more sense than the Chevelle. And Gabrielle was all wrong for the road.

She took things slow on the climb, cursing each rock that pelted Shelly. The road wound back and forth up switchbacks and around one side of a jutting face onto the other. The valley spread out below with the town and buttes to the east. The view was a jaw-dropper and a heart-stopper, with impossibly steep sides sheering away at the edge of the road. Delaney knew better than to look. *Where the eyes go, the wheels follow.* The car gained elevation rapidly, and her ears popped. After cresting the top of the face, she pulled over. She had one last chance for phone signal before she lost it in the mountains.

She had received a voicemail and texts. She checked the texts first. Several were from the night before. Things that she and Leo hadn't talked about at her house.

Leo: *Chip Crawford has a past arrest for holding an ex-girl-friend hostage. Charges were dropped. I'll make it a priority to interview him this morning first thing. Mary is active on Insta-gram. She has a new follower with a fake account. Could be a stalker? The guy she had the restraining order against in CA is bad news. Mexican cartel. She has no record. Sicario does, home invasion and drugs. Did you review the Clement file? Call me when you're up.*

The guy wrote novel-length texts. Too late to have him come with her to the scene. *Although seeing him would be a good start to any day.* She went on to his next text.

Leo: *Check your email – I copied you on all of this, but here's the summary: no progress has been made on Lila, although Fentworth has a deputy on it and Clara helping, too. Fentworth is going to get us state and local help finding Mary. We're setting up a task force and community search volunteers.*

She'd read the email later. Theirs was a tiny department that covered over 2500 square miles, with an even smaller police force for their town of fifteen thousand people. A task force would help, but they'd still be constrained by lack of manpower. And none of the local officers had significant experience with this type of crime. Kidnappings and murders were rare. Well, they were if you didn't count the missing Native American women. Those crimes were underreported and undersolved. That didn't change the experience level of her fellow officers, though. And, once a task force was established, there would be protocol, procedure, and mind-numbing rules to follow. *Ugh.* She needed to figure out a way to work around them. They'd only constrain her and slow her down.

Delaney: *Thx. For all of this and last night. KMP.* At the last second, she decided it wouldn't hurt for another human to know her location in case things went south. *On the mountain. OMW to re-visit crime scene. Sry. Back in a few hours.*

She felt positively like a team player. Next, she played the voicemail.

The voice was brusque. "This is Ryan Hefler. Quit calling me at ungodly hours. Your voicemail says you're Delaney Pace. Maybe you can explain why Mary Galvez wasn't at the bar yesterday when I made a special trip to talk to her about your brother's clients, at her request. I'm still interested in the work, with some conditions. I expect she told you about them."

No other messages or missed calls.

She called Ryan back.

"Ryan Hefler."

"Mr. Hefler, this is Delaney Pace."

"Don't you ever sleep?"

"Sometimes. You were going to meet Mary at the Loafing Shed yesterday?"

"Yeah. I talked to her five minutes before I came, but she'd left by the time I got there. Did she have some kind of emergency?"

"Something like that. Did you see anyone else there?"

"The place was empty as a tomb." *An apt description most days, but an eerie one given the context.* "Except for the drunk bartender. That can't be good business."

Oh, Skeeter. "What about outside?"

"A heavyset Mexican fella. Didn't know him, but we said hello."

Bingo. Sicario had been telling the truth. He had come slightly after Hefler and seen Skeeter, too. If Hefler had arrived within five minutes or so of talking to Mary and Skeeter was already behind the bar, then Skeeter had only been seconds or—at most—minutes too late.

"Any vehicles? Either in the parking lot or on the road?"

"Hmm. Now that you mention it, I did see a Chevy pickup headed toward town."

Sounded like Sicario. "Model, year?"

"Silverado. Early 80s."

"You're sure?"

"I used to drive one like it in high school. Brown. Short bed. Thought I was quite the stud. Girls did, too." His laugh was self-satisfied.

She looked out her window at the peaks, thinking. For a

moment, they called to her, like they always had. The forces of destruction it took to create the rock giants. Upheaval. Heat. Pressure. *Not much different from the forces that shaped me.* She gave her head a shake. *Focus, Delaney.* "This one was just like it?"

"Well, not a hundred percent. I think the paint job was two-tone."

"Brown and what?"

"Beige, I think."

Sicario's was brown with a long bed. Not two-tone. "Did you see the driver?"

"Nah. Just glanced at the truck long enough for a trip down memory lane."

"So, no passengers?"

"Couldn't say. But you know what was strange? That fella I talked to in the parking lot? He had one, too."

"Chevy Silverado?"

"Yep. Now that one was a long bed. I got a good look at it. Why all these questions about trucks?"

"Same in all other respects?"

"Mostly. More beat-up. Listen, I do want to talk to you about those clients of yours."

Delaney couldn't help herself. "My brother's."

"What kind of cut do you want for me to take the business off your hands?"

"Don't you even want to know what types of jobs he had?"

"I've been thinking about that. What does it matter? My guys can do anything."

"What are you offering?"

"How about a five percent referral fee, after expenses?"

All Delaney wanted was the whole mess off her hands. "Sold."

"Great. I can come by on Monday to grab the files and talk about how we handle the books."

That sounded odd, but this wasn't the time to get into the details. "Fine. Talk to you then."

"Wait. Now you've got me curious. Why all the questions? Did you guys have a break-in at the bar?"

Delaney pretended like she hadn't heard him and ended the call. It had been a useful conversation, and she could research Hefler's background back at the department. There was a second truck like Sicario's. Its presence near the bar within five minutes of Mary's disappearance was an important piece of information. Especially since the pickup the neighbor said he'd seen at Mary's could have been the second truck—if the neighbor's story could be believed at all. Eyewitness testimony was notoriously unreliable. Eyewitness testimony from someone nailed for lying, even more so.

She reached for the shifter to put Shelly in gear, then froze with her hand on it. Why hadn't it dawned on her before? She'd seen a truck like this. Similar, anyway. The one she'd chased up the mountain two days before, with the unreadable license plate under a thick layer of mud. She hadn't jotted down a description, but she had a photographic memory for vehicles. Bronze and beige two-tone short bed with handrails. How many vintage Chevy Silverados could there be in the area? And that one had been headed toward the kill spot the night Lila was murdered. Maybe Delaney was the witness to provide a description of the killer. Caucasian. Male. The appearance of the skin she had seen suggested a man in his mid-thirties to forties, depending on how he lived. Hoodie and sunglasses. No visible scars or tattoos. She tried to recall his face. Anything that made him stand out from other white guys of about his age. But he'd never looked at her. All she could picture was an impression of his lips in profile. Angry. Scornful.

And she had zero impression of the intruder the night before. Nothing to compare him to at all.

Fingers flying, she texted Leo: *Confirmation from witness of truck like Sicario's near bar. You & I have seen one like it. The guy I was chasing when you arrested me!* She threw her phone in the passenger seat, shifted, and took her foot off the brake. Shelly rolled forward, and Delaney pressed the gas pedal, anxious and apprehensive about revisiting the site of her sister-in-law's murder.

THIRTY-FOUR

Leo's phone blasted Jack Johnson's "Upside Down." He slapped around until he shut the alarm off, cursing under his breath. He'd been at Delaney's until four and staring at the ceiling in his rental house worried about her until five. That added up to two hours of sleep after none the previous night. An image of Delaney on the ground grappling with the intruder filled his mind. Then her face, covered in blood. He'd wanted to fold her into his arms and never let go almost as much as he'd wanted to kill the son of a bitch who'd attacked her. Now he would worry about her safety as well as finding Mary and whoever killed Lila.

It was a lot. Today was going to be tough.

He palmed his phone and walked to the kitchen, dodging suitcases and boxes straight off the moving van. The house was like a deep freeze. Coffee. His brain wouldn't work without coffee. He put a cup under the Nespresso, popped in a pod, and pressed the brew button. While the machine worked its magic, he scavenged the refrigerator. He'd eaten out for every bite of food he'd consumed since his arrival three days before. Nothing in the refrigerator. The pantry yielded a crunchy peanut butter

Clif Bar left by the previous tenant. *Good enough.* Besides the protein bar, the place had come partially furnished with disposable-looking items. And the owner hadn't even charged extra for the dead flies on the windowsills, nail holes in the drywall, or scuff marks on the white paint.

His phone rang. Fentworth.

"Good morning, boss."

"Morning. Thank you again for working through the night. And for being there for Delaney. I don't know what I'd do if something happened to her."

Leo knew it. And he'd begun to suspect Delaney felt the same way about their boss. "You're welcome."

"Everything okay this morning?"

"Haven't heard differently."

"Good. Because the first meeting of the task force to find Mary is in two hours. We've got officers from the state police, Kearny, and Sheridan."

"No word from the feds?"

"They managed to reach their agent. He'll be here late today."

"What about Joe? Was he able to work on Lila?"

"He picked up a copy of the file. He's still under the weather, but he'll do all he can from home."

Leo didn't like it, but he couldn't come up with a better solution. "All right."

"I'd like you to do a press conference with me half an hour before the task force kick-off, asking for help from the public. I know it's early, but we've got to get it rolling. Clara put up the first request along with Mary's picture on social media last night, but we have to expand the ask. The volunteers will be run by Search and Rescue, reporting to the task force."

"You've been busy."

"Thanks. For everything."

"I'll see you soon."

Fentworth ended the call.

Leo took the sketchy bar, his phone, and the coffee to the bathroom. His phone chimed. He turned on the shower then glanced at his phone.

Delaney: *Thx for all the info and last night. KMP. OMW to re-visit Lila's crime scene. Back in a few hours.*

He closed his eyes, trying to decide whether to go after her. His timeline leading up to the press conference was tight, especially since he really needed to ambush Chip Crawford—Charles Junior—before the man was gone for the day. That didn't leave time for chasing after Delaney. She was strong, capable, and he knew she'd have her gun. And she'd be so pissed if he showed up that she might use it on him.

But why in the world had she gone back up the mountain? And why by herself?

He stepped into the hot spray for the world's fastest shower. *Dammit, Delaney. Everybody needs back-up. Didn't you learn that last night?*

THIRTY-FIVE

Delaney parked fifty yards from the fluttering yellow crime scene tape at the trailhead. She knew there'd been traffic up here since her last visit. Probably lots of it. But it never hurt to be cautious, especially with this heavy freeze to preserve the tracks. She considered the weather. It was cloudy out and cold enough for snow, but there was nothing falling from the sky. That was good—Shelly didn't handle snow or mud well.

She turned the car off, relishing a moment of silence and a chance to catch her breath. She wished she'd had a relationship with Lila. The only time she'd met her was at Kateena's eighth birthday party, which Delaney had attended because she was hauling through the area at the time. It had struck her then that the beautiful black woman was out of place in Wyoming where the African American population was one in a hundred and in Kearny where it was less. She seemed like a righteous woman, someone Delaney's grandparents would have approved of. Why had she fallen for Liam? How had the two met? They were questions Delaney would never know the answers to, she guessed.

She wiped tears from her eyes. "Okay, Delaney, get it

together," she said aloud, then took a few deep breaths. Twisting awkwardly, she donned her jacket, hat, and gloves. The interior had cooled down quickly.

She got out of the car, buckled her fanny pack of supplies, checked her weapon, and ducked under the tape strung between sawhorses. Her breath created a condensation cloud in front of her face. "Blowing smoke" her dad had called it, and Liam had showed her how to pretend she was smoking a cigarette and exhaling the vapor. It had made her feel so adult. So Olivia Newton-John in *Grease*. Her smile was sad and grim. He had been a cool big brother.

After a hundred yards hiking, she bent over. It would get easier when her muscles were warmed up and oxygenated. Most of her childhood she'd spent in the bar or on the road to races, but she'd still logged enough mountain time to have faith in her body's ability to adjust. From her position with her face near the trail bed, she stared at the four-wheeler tracks. The truck she'd been chasing had a four-wheeler in the back. She needed to look at the photographs of vehicle treads in Lila's file —she hadn't gotten to them last night. Compare them to the one on her phone from Mary's house and a photo she'd snapped of Sicario's tread. She should have done it when she was parked at the trailhead. *Don't fail me now, brain.*

She straightened and hiked without another stop. When she made the turn-off, she heard an engine revving high in the distance. Someone driving up the steep road to the trail. They'd be in for a surprise when they reached the dirt parking area and found the trail blocked off.

She walked carefully, outside the scene tape, thinking, thinking, thinking. Someone—the man she'd chased?—had brought Lila up this trail on a four-wheeler, presumably after transporting her up the mountain in a larger vehicle. She'd been alive. Injured from days of torture. Awake? Terrified? Delaney hoped not.

Her brain seized on a thought. The same fate, for the same type of woman. Loving mothers. Good souls. Beautiful women, in their twenties. Not white. Attracted to the wrong men. In some ways, Delaney was the same, in others different. She reached the clearing and stood on the near side of it, breathing deeply, sinking into its feeling of absolute silence and remoteness in a location locals would consider accessible.

She decided to search again for anything she and her colleagues might have missed. Each set of eyes on each pass improved the chances of finding evidence. She paced, walking an outer-perimeter pattern, working inward. Her eyes scanned the forest floor. Her brain recycled the facts she didn't want to think about. What this animal had done to Lila. Carved her up. Marked her. The horror sent her mind to men who hated women. To symbolic markings in death. To the wavy lines left deep inside Lila's bones. What did they mean to the killer?

She felt light-headed and stopped, breathing deeply, stilling her mind. When she'd regained her equilibrium, she restarted her search and her brain restarted its frantic review. The tools this killer had used included a knife—a sharp outdoor-use blade of about six inches, per the pathologist—and a burning tool that may have been a soldering iron. She was looking for remnants from those items as well as from the body or clothing of the killer or Lila. Maybe something suggestive of a bag to carry his tools. Even better, she might find a cigarette or chewed gum. Wrappers. A receipt. Anything that wasn't a part of nature here.

And nature owned this clearing. Spring growth was pushing up through a thick layer of pinecones and needles. Broken twigs and branches littered the ground. Rocks. Animal bones and feces. Every day, a new deposit was laid down, covering what had been. In time, the forest would hide forever anything there now.

Suddenly, the silence triggered an explosion in Delaney's

head. The vehicle headed toward the parking area and trailhead —she'd never heard it turn around and leave. Why had whomever it was stayed? Sweat popped out on her neck and chest, despite the cold. Sure, there were valid reasons. Like a mountain biker or hiker headed in the opposite direction. Someone enjoying a breakfast picnic. Someone... she was out of ideas that didn't involve killers returning to murder scenes to relive them.

She'd have to be more watchful.

The adrenaline rush spurred her to work faster. Her grid was closing in on the spot where Lila had died, marked now by tape in the outline of her body position. That would be the area most combed over, but the one most likely to yield results.

She stumbled on a rock, dislodging it from the earth. The sun glinted off an object flying through the air. She tracked its landing and hurried to it, trying not to get her hopes up. The glint could have come from the rock itself or something that flaked off of it. Gold. Pyrite. Mica. Chalcopyrite. Just a few of the possibilities she'd become familiar with in her previous stint as a deputy.

She knelt where the object had fallen. As her knees hit the ground, she winced, the inner Laney expecting pain. A Bible verse crossed her lips, warding off the punishment. "Ask, and it will be given to you; seek, and you will find; knock, and it will be opened to you. Matthew 7:7."

But the needles were soft and forgiving. She leaned forward onto her hands, spreading her fingers wide and propping up her body weight, like a modified push-up. The Bible verse seemed fitting. And like a prompt. All that prayer in her childhood had made an impression on her, although not in the way her grandmother had intended.

She raised her voice. "Hey, You up there. Help a girl out. Give me something that helps me find Mary and the sick son of a bitch who has her before it's too late."

That prayer would have earned her a bar of soap in her mouth from her grandmother, but she and God had come to an understanding long ago. Whatever way she came to the Creator seemed to be fine with Him, as long as she kept showing up. *Take that, Grandma.*

She sucked in a calming breath. When she felt inner stillness, she started a visual sweep. Anything out of the ordinary. Anything shiny. Anything with a sheen or glint to it. As with her walking pattern, she moved her eyes methodically, this time like a typewriter down a page. Left to right, up to down.

From this vantage point, the glittery object seemed to have disappeared. Sometimes looking from a different angle helped. She rotated her body ninety degrees and tried again.

Nothing. Another ninety degrees.

Nothing. Another.

And there it was. A silvery something, about an eighth of an inch square, embedded in the needles. Probably invisible to the naked eye on a rock, given how much it looked like mica. Using a small metal flag from her fanny pack, she marked the location by inserting it beside the object. She used her iPhone to take a picture, close up, then further away to show the location and flag. She got out a plastic bag and used a tongue depressor to flip the item into the mouth. Never taking her eyes from her treasure, she closed the zip-lock securely. Finally, she planted another flag roughly where the object had been before she kicked it. She took a picture showing both flags in place.

Then she examined her prize. Metal. Her heartbeat was thumping in her chest louder than a blown tire. There was a smear of something brown. Blood? Had the knife blade broken? *The killer used a knife, and I found bloody metal.* The odds of finding such a tiny fragment were low.

"Hey, Big Guy in the sky, thanks for the luck and the assist."

She dropped the baggy and depressor in the fanny pack and zipped it closed. She had to get it down the mountain. The blood could be analyzed for DNA. The knife could be inspected for identifying marks and the alloys could be tested for composition. She needed to—wanted to—update Leo.

A branch snapped behind her. In her excitement, she'd forgotten to remain vigilant. *The attacker. Last night. He's back.* She spun around.

A mountain of a man was standing five feet away from her.

THIRTY-SIX

"Delaney Pace." A man in a wool cap pulled low with a scarf around it walked to the edge of the clearing. Was he covering a damaged earlobe? *He's bigger than I thought the attacker was.* Although some of his size was due to his head and outerwear.

Delaney knew this man. "Chip Crawford."

Chip's past arrest for kidnapping an ex combined with his presence at the place Lila died made Delaney uneasy. His truck was a new black Ram 3500 flatbed, though. Nothing like the vehicles seen by any of the witnesses, including Delaney. And what connection did he have to Lila? She'd have to think those things through later. Now, his presence felt threatening. This man had brutally raped a girl in his youth, and he blamed her for the years he spent locked up. Her mind raced and her eyes flitted around the clearing looking for her best escape route. He was blocking the narrow path through the boulders back to the trail. The rock made exiting on either side of it a difficult and slow climb. She could take off through the woods, but she was likely to face similar obstacles no matter which way she went.

She held her ground.

He circled the clearing, staying outside the crime scene

tape. "You left Kearny about the time I got locked up. Now we're both back."

He'd cleared the path of her getaway route. But she wasn't running yet. "What are you doing here, Chip?"

He stepped over the tape. "Curiosity. I've been following you."

"Stay outside the tape!"

He didn't stop. "I read about you in the paper. A trucker? What kind of woman drives a rig?" He laughed, a mirthless sound.

She wished Leo was with her. What was it he'd said yesterday? That everybody needed back-up? *I'm closer to conceding the point.* She put her hand on her belly band. "Stay back. I'm armed."

He laughed again, still advancing. "You don't scare me. You think I'm not?"

"You think I care?" *God, save me from assholes.* She could almost hear the answer. *You've got this one all by yourself, Delaney.* Drawing on Chip would escalate things. Maybe de-escalation would work. She dropped her hand. "Whatever. I was done here anyway."

The look of confusion on his face was priceless. Then it vanished. "Done with what?" He stopped. Licked his lips.

"Paying my respects."

"Did the murdered woman work at the bar?" He slipped his jacket hood off his head. It made him seem several inches shorter.

"Did you know her?"

He shook his head. Took a step forward. "I wouldn't say that."

"What would you say?"

"That you're nosy as well as pushy."

"Well, she was my sister-in-law."

His rapid blinking suggested more confusion. Chip didn't

strike her as a probable MENSA member. He stepped closer, again licking his lips. *Definitely not MENSA.* "My condolences for your loss."

Delaney considered arresting him. But for what? Murder? Kidnapping? She had no evidence of either. Tampering with evidence? It seemed low payoff for the risk she'd run by trying. She could wait for him to assault her, but that didn't seem like a good idea either. Nor did asking him to remove the scarf so she could see his earlobe. She could push his buttons—ask him about his past arrests or where Mary was—but that seemed like the worst idea. He really might have Mary. He might have been the person who broke into the Pace homestead last night. If so, she needed him to lead them to the woman. Not run because he thought she was on to him. So, she'd let him go and follow him instead.

She nodded, then turned and began walking down the trail.

"Hey!" he shouted.

She ignored him. Kept going.

The sound of his heavy footsteps raised the hair on her neck. They sped up. He was running after her.

She wheeled, gun drawn, safety off, and aimed at his center mass. "Don't ever chase down a law enforcement officer. Especially not a female one in a remote location where she will rightly feel threatened. It's a good way to get shot."

He put his hands up. Her fanny pack was dangling from one. "You forgot this."

When had it fallen off of her? She swallowed. "Just drop it on the ground and back away."

"You didn't say thanks."

"Thank you."

"For my condolences either."

"You haven't backed up."

He grinned and started taking slow, exaggerated steps backward. He stopped.

"Farther."

He took two more steps.

It wasn't great, but it was good enough. She snatched up her fanny pack. "If I hear you behind me again, I will turn and fire without another word."

He laughed. "I've been tracking and hunting my whole life. If I wanted to sneak up on you, you'd never hear me coming."

That was exactly what Delaney was afraid of.

THIRTY-SEVEN

Leo stomped back into the office and dropped heavily into the chair at his desk. Delaney had ghosted him, despite his five texts. Basically, all the same. *Where are you, why aren't you answering me? Are you okay?* He was fifteen minutes away from initiating a search for her if she didn't contact him before then. Meanwhile, his morning had been fruitless. He'd been unable to reach Chip by phone, and when he'd dropped by the ranch to speak to him, Charlie Crawford had announced that Chip lived in town. The elder Crawford hadn't been all that nice about it either. Leo had rushed over to Chip's place. The younger Crawford wasn't there. He'd given up, for the time being.

Now he had only forty-five minutes before the press conference, so he would make every second count. He pulled up Jorge Perez's criminal record, muttering to himself. Like a lightning strike, he remembered the email from the deputy in San Juan County, Colorado. He'd never read the similar case the man had sent him. *Too damn much going on.* Nor had he forwarded the email to Fentworth and Delaney. He opened it and re-read it quickly.

Case file attached. The file should speak for itself, except for one thing. We had a suspect. A local elk-hunting guide who had dated the victim. He had an alibi, but I was never satisfied with it. I think the guy was from your area originally. He'd be worth checking out. My partner retired last month, and he's on a safari in South Africa. I'm camping for Memorial Day. No cell signal. Back Tuesday if you have questions.

The file was a voluminous one. He flipped through it until he found the information on the elk-hunting guide suspect. Ice replaced the warm blood flowing in his veins. The name of the guide was Charles Crawford, Jr.

Did he have the wrong guy locked up, when the right one had been in his grasp only last evening? Was Chip the one who had attacked Delaney, too? The troubling connection to Jorge Perez might be only a terrible coincidence. He forwarded the email and file to Delaney and Fentworth with a note about Chip. He hated she was up in the mountains alone, with Chip at loose ends. He hated that they hadn't found Mary. And he hated not being able to work on Lila's case. He thought of his to-do list for Lila, languishing. Yesterday, he'd planned to be visiting butchers this morning. Where might that have led? He had to let the dead woman down, for the possibility of keeping the other alive.

"Johnny Utah, give me good news." Fentworth's voice made him jump. The man managed to sneak up on him every time.

"I just emailed you with a lead on the Lila Clement case." Leo shoved Jorge Perez's criminal history aside. "And it connects to Mary."

"Is this an official meeting of the good old boys' club?" The female voice quickened Leo's pulse and made him feel woozy with relief. *Delaney.*

Fentworth wheeled to face her, a look of relief on his face. "You don't look any worse for the wear."

Delaney and Leo made eye contact over Fentworth's shoulder. Her cheeks were still bright pink from the cold.

"I really am fine. I promise," she said.

Fentworth said, "I'll leave you two to catch up then. Leo, meet me out front in half an hour." Fentworth ambled off.

"Yes, sir," Leo called after him. He turned to Delaney. Before he could stop it, his worry about her burst out in the worst way. "Where the hell have you been?"

Her response was a whip crack. "Why the hell didn't you respond to my text about the truck?"

"What text?"

Delaney opened her text messages on her phone. She punched at the screen. Frowned. "Oh. It didn't send."

"I believe the words you're looking for are, 'I'm sorry, Leo.'"

"I believe the words you'll be uttering next are, 'Thank you, Delaney.'" She dropped a plastic bag on his desk.

"What's that?"

"A piece of metal from exactly where Lila was carved up. Maybe part of a knife blade."

"How'd you find that?"

She made a peace sign then pointed it at her eyes. "And I ran into one of our friends up there. Chip Crawford."

"What?"

"He barged right into the crime scene. Said he'd been following me. He was pretty threatening, too. I had to pull my gun on him to get out of there."

"Holy shit. Do you think he was the one who attacked you?"

"Can't say. He had his ears covered, and since I was alone, I decided not to ask him if he'd had one bitten off recently. Damn weather. I think we need someone following him, though."

"It's more than that. I just sent you an email about a mountain murder in Colorado. Chip was a suspect. He alibied out, but the deputy there always believed he did it."

She shook her head. "So much about him doesn't make sense, but so much does. He's shot to the top of my suspect list. What about Sicario?"

"We don't have to make up our mind yet about charging him, so he can sit tight."

"I don't like it."

"Humor me a little longer?"

She heaved an enormous sigh.

He took that as assent. "The first task force meeting is in less than an hour. I need to—wait! What does Chip drive?"

"Black Ram 3500 flat bed. But the truck in Mary's neighborhood is just one piece of circumstantial evidence from an unreliable witness."

She was right. He'd just like to hear this could be wrapped up with no loose ends and tied with a big red bow. "Does Chip have any connection to Lila?"

"He says no. But he was at her death scene. He could have been making it up about following me. Which reminds me." She picked up the baggie, shook it, and put it back down. "Do you mind getting testing underway on the metal chip? I've got to do something."

He jotted: *Chip connection to Lila?* "Okay. I don't have to be at the press conference," he looked at the time on his phone, "for another ten minutes. The first task force meeting will be half an hour after. Will you be there?"

She was walking away. Over her shoulder, she said, "I'm curious about the metal." She turned and walked backward. "There's blood on it. Might be identifying marks. If nothing else, an XRF test could identify the composition. The alloys could help us match it if we find the weapon."

She would have made a great admiral.

And then she was gone without answering his question, sucking half the energy in the room out with her. Too late, he wished he'd asked where she was going. He'd assumed the break room, but, with Delaney, he was learning assumptions were dangerous.

Leo marked the metal chip into evidence and logged it. He probably had time before the presser to get it processed. He'd wait to present the information to the sheriff and Joe once he got it in motion. They'd agree with the need for speed. He called the local crime scene unit and reached a woman he'd met the night they'd found Lila's body. Sugar Kuhk. People called her Sugar Cookie. Leo couldn't bring himself to do that yet. Sugar was hard enough for him to utter. He explained what he needed.

"I can't believe between us and the staties that we missed that. Good catch," Sugar said.

"Delaney Pace found it."

"I remember her. I was always a little terrified of her, to be honest, but she's good. Okay, we can check for marks here. The blood scrapings will go to the state lab for DNA testing. That won't be fast."

"I understand."

"The XRF will be slow if we send it to the state, too. But there's a lab out of Gillette, a private company, that can do the work if you don't mind. They're a lot more expensive, but they've been known to do a same-day turnaround. Maybe a uniform could drive it over."

Leo didn't think the sheriff would balk at the price. Not on a case this big. "The faster the better. We have one woman dead and another missing." *And Delaney attacked.*

"I'll make it happen. Are the cases connected?"

"I wish I knew. But we have a task force for Mary Galvez kicking off at the top of the hour."

"Palmer!" The sheriff's voice boomed down the hall. "Where the hell are you? The press is waiting!"

"Gotta go. Thanks, Sugar."

"No problem. Wait—did anyone tell you yet that the team

found long brown hairs in Sicario Menendez's bed? I thought you'd want to know."

More damning evidence on Sicario. "That's great. DNA test them for a match with Mary Galvez?"

"Already on it. When I know, you'll know."

He just hoped what they learned would come soon enough for Mary.

THIRTY-EIGHT

Delaney parked in the shade of a tall cottonwood and cranked her window down, engine off. Out of her driver's side window, she could see metal yard art, kayaks, and grilling equipment at a feed store geared up for summer—its patio area operated like grocery store endcaps, but for ranchers who were dreaming of leisurely days off they'd never actually be able to take.

On the other side of the car, she had a good view of Chip's house. It was a one-story, aging white clapboard, with a front driveway and no garage. He lived behind the middle school, not far from where she'd initiated her pursuit of the speeding truck a few days before. A truck that looked nothing like his. That truck and that man had been heading in the right direction at the right time. As she had with Leo about Tim Osborne's eyewitness account, she reminded herself that the encounter was just one data point. And there was far more than one leading her to Chip.

From her angle, it looked like no one was home at his place. It was worth missing the task force meeting for this chance. For a split second, she thought about texting Leo and telling him what she was up to. *He's got a lot going on.* It wasn't remote here like on the mountain. She would be fine.

Taking only her phone and keys, she locked the car and strolled down the block. Her plan was to duck around a house—one with no dogs to alert the neighborhood to her presence—swing along the rear of the houses and slip into Chip's back yard. The creek burbled just within earshot, a nice sound. It would have been a pleasant day and location for a walk, to enjoy the flowers and mild weather. Hopefully that was what it would look like she was doing.

She chose a house with its lights out, no cars in front, and no backyard fence. Behind it, she found a little-used dirt alleyway five feet from the back property lines, which were mostly marked by fences. She walked quickly to Chip's yard. It was fully enclosed with chain-link fencing and a double-wing gate, big enough to drive a truck through, but padlocked. No second truck matching their suspect vehicle was parked there. No tracks marred the deep green of the new grass.

I might as well take a peek inside. She glanced at the neighbors' back windows on either side. No faces or eyes, no twitching curtains. The fence was an annoyance—she'd have to climb it. Once on top, she paused with a leg on either side. She clutched the metal top rail between sharp wire points, prayed her butt wasn't being captured on home security or wildlife cameras belonging to neighbors who'd call Chip, swung her other leg over, and yanked her boots out of the small spaces one at a time, moving from a standing split to the ground in an awkward dismount.

Delaney tromped across the thick grass, glad for it—she'd leave no footprints, and crushed grass was hard to spot. She climbed the concrete steps to the rear door, tented her eyes, and peered inside. The interior was dark. No movement. No sign of Mary or any other woman. Just a Formica-topped table and matching chairs in an L-shaped kitchen. While dingy, the space was tidy. No items on the counter that would suggest two humans were living inside. Or even one.

She abandoned her vantage point and climbed onto a picnic table outside one of the two curtainless windows. All the lights were out. She didn't need light to see the mess inside, though. It appeared to be Chip's bedroom. An unmade bed. Clothes heaped and covering half the floor space. An open closet door with a pile of boots and shoes but nothing hanging. Fast-food wrappers, bags, and cups littering every surface. *No wonder the kitchen is clean. He doesn't use it.*

She hopped off the table. The last window was trickier. It had damp earth beneath it and nothing to stand on. *Like Mary's bathroom, except I'm the peeper now.* She wasn't worried about being arrested, but she was worried about spooking Chip. As she was pondering her options, she heard an engine rumble to a stop. It sounded like it was in front of the house. A vehicle door slammed.

She sprinted for the back fence, this time with enough speed to plant her hands and side vault it like she'd learned at the police academy. The top of the fence caught her pants. She went down on her hands and one knee on the other side. Fabric ripped. The stiff metal snagged tender skin, but her leg came loose and caught up with her. She clamped a hand on the wound, wincing. No time to fuss over it.

She leaped to her feet and took off, cutting back through the unfenced yard. In the side yard, Delaney slowed to a walk, trying not to limp. She snuck a glance four houses down. Chip's black truck was parked in the driveway. She heard a door shut, sounding like it was from his house. He appeared to have gone inside.

Because she had been in a hurry to get away from him in the mountains, she hadn't slowed down to look at his truck tire treads there. She had another shot at it now. She'd have to move fast, but she could catch a picture or two. The truck would provide cover. She could be back in her car fifteen seconds afterwards.

She strolled down the street. No gutter, no sidewalk. Just asphalt and a curb. She readied her phone, pretending to be scrolling social media. When she reached the truck, she paused long enough to focus the lens on the tread, stilled her hands, and snapped pictures on burst mode. There was no sound from Chip's house. She turned and walked across the street to the Chevelle, a picture of nonchalance. Too late, she wondered if all four truck tires were the same type. Odds were yes, but it wasn't a given. She should have taken pictures of them all.

She exhaled and climbed into her car. Her phone was at five percent battery charge, so she plugged it in. Only then did she take a look at the gaping hole in the thigh of her jeans. She peeled the denim back, exposing a deep gash with some fatty tissue showing. A fair amount of blood. *I need stitches.* She'd learned in her years on the road that a wound could be stitched up twenty-four hours after an injury, though. The ER could wait. She had rubbing alcohol in Gabrielle, which was just down the road in the storage unit. Close enough to walk from here, and the key to the unit was on her ring. One, anyway—she'd had extras made. Her storage unit was even on the street row, facing Chip's house. She could still monitor him. Possibly get back to her car fast enough to follow him if he left.

She headed toward the facility. It was worth the risk. Adrenaline had masked her pain earlier, but now her leg hurt worse with every step. The storage facility wasn't fenced—this was Wyoming—so she walked straight up to 101, unlocked it, and slid open the door.

She sucked in a breath. The sun glinted off the metallic black paint job of her beauty. She'd never brought Fentworth into her trucker world. Maybe he'd like to come out and see how she'd spent her exile.

"Oh, sweet Gabrielle, how I've missed you." She put both hands on the front bumper. *Freedom. Power. Peace.*

Behind her, she heard tires on gravel and squeaky brakes. A vehicle parked. *Probably the site manager.* She ignored whoever it was in favor of getting alcohol on her thigh as fast as possible. The door was locked, but she grabbed the spare key from a magnetic box underneath the fifth wheel coupling. She let herself in the passenger side—leaving the key on the dash—crawled through the cabin and into the sleeper. Her custom-assembled first aid kit was strapped to the wall. It was well stocked, but it paled in comparison to her toolbox for maintaining and fixing the tractor. She had always been her own medic and mechanic, out of necessity. She unfastened and lifted the lid. The box was the size of an ice chest and filled with the items she couldn't travel the ice roads without, tucked into slots in the foam interior she'd built for it.

The bottle of isopropyl alcohol was right where it was supposed to be, half full, with its lid tight. It made her feel warm. Secure. She might be off the road, but she and Gabrielle were still a self-sufficient team. She pulled the alcohol out along with some cotton balls and anti-bacterial cream, then went to work on her leg.

The alcohol entered the wound. Pain stabbed her like hot needles.

"Son of a motherless monkey!" she shouted.

"Are you okay in there?" a man's voice said.

At first, she tensed, ready to reach for her gun. *Had Chip followed her—again?* But no, that wasn't his voice. The vehicle, she remembered. The site manager.

"Yeah. Doctoring a cut. Thanks. Out in a sec."

When she'd finished, she replaced the supplies, secured the kit, and took the soiled cotton balls. Grabbing the key, she climbed out. As she was locking the door, she realized a man was standing a few feet away from her. His face was shadowed in the darkness of the storage area. He was wearing sunglasses, too, which wasn't unusual, given the sunny, brisk day. But his raised hoodie was a little much.

"Hello," she said. She didn't like him invading her personal space. And Gabrielle was about as personal as her space got. "Can I help you?"

"Just admiring your rig."

Delaney threw the cotton balls in a trash can she kept in the unit. Then she stepped past him, out of the storage area. "You a trucker?"

"I'm in delivery."

An old pickup was parked close, blocking the mouth of her bay. *Bronze and beige. 1983 model Chevy Silverado short bed with rails.* Something was hanging from the rearview mirror, so near and dear to her heart that she couldn't miss seeing it.

A heavy chain with things dangling from it, including a medallion. *My pendant,* she thought, just as something sharp and painful bit her in the back—*wasps?*—followed by the most intense, blinding pain she'd ever experienced. *Not wasps. Stun gun.* Her muscles spasmed and she crumpled to the ground. She tried to scream. To fight back. To do anything but convulse.

It was futile.

Five long seconds passed. By the time her tongue cooperated and she was able to shout the F-word, it was into the gag he'd shoved in her mouth while she was incapacitated. Before she could scramble to her feet, a heavy blow hit the back of her head.

The world went black.

THIRTY-NINE

Delaney awoke to her head bouncing on an unforgiving surface and the sensation of being in the core of a tornado. It only took a few seconds to realize where she was, though—the bed of a pickup with the wind swirling around her. Not just any truck. *The* Chevy. And it sure as hell wasn't Sicario's, and hadn't been him who'd hit her with a stun gun. Plus, she'd heard the man's voice. It wasn't Chip.

She was the captive of a sadistic killer who kidnapped, mutilated, and burned his victims—the man she'd chased to the mountain face. It had to be.

Nausea roiled inside her. Her head was pounding. Her wrists were bound with zip ties. But the binding was in front of her, and not the police-strength version, praise God. She had limited use of her hands, enough to yank out the gag in her mouth but not enough to touch the back of her skull.

She gasped air then tried to move her legs. Zip tied, too.

My gun. She checked her belly band. The Staccato was gone.

This man had used a stun gun on her. Knocked her out.

Taken her weapon. Restrained her. Was transporting her. *Way to go on the deputy work, Delaney.*

And this was no random snatch. It had to be the same man who had attacked her last night. He had her medallion pendant. Her most treasured keepsake. A physical link to her father. He'd been in her bedroom, in the house where Kateena lived. Her most treasured *person*.

But why was he after her?

It didn't matter now. What mattered was that when this truck stopped, she was in big trouble. Trouble she must escape, or he might return for Kateena. Mary would be left in the hands of a killer.

She had to free her hands. *Think, Delaney, think.* An old truck bed would have a sharp surface somewhere. She slithered on her belly like a snake to stay out of his rearview mirror, searching first nearest the cab, high and low. Halfway around the passenger side of the bed, she found a rusted-out section of metal. She ran her finger across it, happy that this truck wasn't taken care of like her Chevelle.

The edge was like a dull serrated knife. *This will do.*

She shoved the back of her wrists into the space. Wriggled them to get the restraint as tight and high on her hands as she could. Made contact between the metal and the plastic. Began sawing fast and hard. Unfortunately, she couldn't avoid sawing into her fingers some, and every time the truck hit a bump, she lost contact and had to start over. Blood dripped onto the cracked bed liner and her already bloody pants. She didn't feel the pain. Seconds passed. She didn't count them. At about half a minute, the "knife" won, and the cuff split.

No time to celebrate. The ankle restraint was next. She put her feet up to the jagged metal. The space was too small. She couldn't make contact.

She searched the truck bed again but found nothing better.

She put a hand in her pocket. Her keys might be sharp enough, but they weren't there. She patted her back pocket. No phone. She'd left it in the Chevelle. But she had an idea. The severed zip tie. She slid to it on her back, rolled over, and grabbed it, then took the pointed end and inserted it into the locking ratchet of the ankle restraint. Working gently, she shimmed it open and off.

It had been so easy, she was horrified she hadn't remembered the trick immediately. *I'm dangerously out of practice.* She sat and leaned against the front of the bed, back-to-back with her abductor.

She had to turn the tables on this man. Escape was vital, but first she needed information. If she got away without it, he might disappear... with Mary. She held up the intact zip tie, staring at it, thinking. It could be useful. She stuffed it in her breast pocket, examining the back window to the truck. Four panels. She was familiar with the dual sliders. They had a latch lock from the inside. Maybe it wasn't fastened. But she couldn't plan for luck. The back window had to go. From her years of experience with auto glass, she knew older trucks were less likely to have safety glass, so she hoped this window was original. The best window to start with was the one behind his head, where it would be hard for him to reach around and grab her, and close enough that she could slip her ankle-length zip tie around his neck.

The easiest way to break it was to strike it in the upper corner with concentrated force. She had carried a tool for that every day as a deputy, right on her belt. A fist might work, with enough adrenaline, although it could also break her knuckles and render the rest of her mission more difficult. The point of her elbow was better. Both ran a high risk of serious cuts and bleeds.

A sharp object would be far better. Sometimes rocks, hardware, or tools slid underneath bed liners. As quickly as she could, she knelt, ripped the liner up, and tossed it over the passenger side of the bed, then dropped back to the floor.

If the man had seen her, she was ready for combat. He didn't stop, though. Hadn't been watching. *You've got way too much self-confidence, buck-o.*

With the bed exposed, she surveyed the detritus of years on its surface. Pebbles, small screws, hay, dirt, a bungee cord, and, only one foot away from her, she hit the jackpot—a multitool. She palmed it, opened it, and found the bit driver with its beautiful point.

She looked up at the window, paused for a few deep breaths and powerful exhales, turned, and slammed the bit driver into it. The glass spider-webbed. The man jumped. The truck swerved, but she was ready for it and holding onto the edge of the bed with her left hand. Poised like a cobra, she struck again, even harder.

The glass shattered. She dropped the multitool to the bed and stepped on it to hold it in place. She battered the glass out and onto him with her flannel-clad elbow.

The truck bucked and braked. His head whipped around to look at her, his eyes wide. Then he ducked. *That ain't gonna save ya.* She pulled the long zip tie from her pocket, made sure she had the proper orientation, and snared his neck with it, quickly feeding the pointed end into the ratchet and pulling. Her tie wasn't deathly tight yet, but it wasn't going anywhere. Fabric covered his neck. She realized he was wearing a balaclava that covered his face except for air holes at the mouth and nostrils. *Still can't see that earlobe, but I know this is the man who attacked me.*

The man released the steering wheel and clutched the binding, filling the cab with inhuman bellows. The truck swerved toward the shoulder. The terrain off-road was steep and unforgiving.

She screamed into his ear. "Drive, you idiot, or you're going to die."

He kept scrabbling at the zip tie with one hand but resumed steering with the other. She could work with that. She tightened the zip tie. He choked and sputtered, wrenching against her counterweight. Not letting go, she leaned down and picked up the multitool from underneath her foot. She held the bit driver against his temple and made eye contact with him in the rearview mirror. His eyes bulged, and he gasped for air.

"Where's Mary Galvez?" she shouted.

He shook his head.

"I'll cut you lose if you'll tell me."

His voice was muffled through the fabric, but she could make out the words. "Can't... have... her. Next for delivery. Not... ready... yet."

"You're torturing her like you did Lila?"

He jerked his head at Lila's name.

She pushed the knife into his skin. Blood beaded. "You think I won't kill you because I want to find her, but you're wrong. You have no idea how far I'd go." Although after last night, he should have a better idea of what she was capable of.

"You... you're the one... who... chased... me."

"Yes, I am." And he'd had Lila in that truck with him. *I'd have caught him if Leo hadn't pulled me over. I'd have found her. Saved her. Killed him instead.*

The man locked eyes with her in the mirror. She saw him scheming, evaluating. Anticipated his next move and drove the bit driver into his cheek just as he was jerking the steering wheel to the right.

He bellowed with pain and rage. The pickup went airborne off the road.

Delaney grabbed the side rails of the bed. The truck crash-landed and bounced several feet off the ground. Delaney crashed and bounced, too. She used the momentum to leap clear, one foot pushing off the side rail, arms and legs windmilling through space, as the truck started to roll. Her regrets flashed through her mind. *I won't be the one to raise Kateena. I'll never find my father's killer. I won't see my mother again. I won't know what it's like to kiss Leo.*

She landed on her hands, face down. One of her knees struck stone. Her arms buckled, and the force of her impact drove her flat into sage brush. The woody limbs of the plant dug into her skin. Her ears and head rang like metal struck with a hammer.

The crashing, crumpling noise of the truck came to a stop. The quiet was sudden and complete. She tried to get up. Failed. Put her head back down. Time passed. Not much of it, but some. The light dazzled her eyes. Wind blew grit into painful places on her face. Birdsong tinkled in the air like bells.

"Oh, my God. Oh, my God. Are you okay, ma'am?" a young male voice said, close to her head.

She looked up into the face of a boy in his teens. "Help," was all she could manage, and then she gave in for the second time that day to darkness.

FORTY

Leo barreled through the hospital doors, shouting when he was still three yards away from the reception desk, catching himself with both hands on it. "Delaney Pace. Where is she?"

The woman at reception clutched her plastic bead necklace. Her eyes were buggy behind thick lenses, her red lipstick garish and outside the lines. "Uh—"

He gulped air and slowed himself. "Delaney Pace. She's been in a car accident. A motorist called it in and brought her to the ER."

She released the beads. "Oh, right. That one."

"Where. Is. She?"

"Still in the emergency room, Deputy."

"How is she?"

She lowered her glasses a bit and mouthed something as she read her screen. "Her injuries aren't serious, it appears."

"Which way to the ER?"

"I can't let you back there unless you're family."

He scowled at her. "I'm her brother." When she looked dubious, he flashed her his most disarming smile.

She mirrored the smile back at him. It was like looking in a fun house mirror. "Her niece is already in there with her. And her little boy. And your other brother." Laughter lines and crow's feet crinkled. "Your family doesn't favor each other much."

He had a good guess who the other family members were. Winking, he said, "We're multicultural."

"I'm with him." Fentworth's voice boomed right behind him. Leo jumped. The man had to be one hell of a hunter.

"Let me guess. You're Delaney's father?" the woman sounded skeptical.

Leo clapped him on the back. "Hey, Dad." To the woman, he said, "Law enforcement is in our blood."

"I'll escort you." She pointed to her left.

"Thanks." Fentworth touched his forehead. His hat was already in his hand.

The two men met her at a door then followed her down the hallway to the ER. Leo hated hospitals. The antiseptic smell, the colors that were supposed to be soothing, the sterile corridors, the subdued voices, the food that smelled like everything was boiled. He could picture diseases hiding in corners, waiting to jump to a vulnerable host. Most of all, he hated the memories of loss. Too many people he loved had breathed their last in a place like this one. He shoved the thought back into the deepest recesses of his mind.

Metal rings sang along a rod as their guide opened a flowered curtain. It revealed a square white box of a room with white walls and two metal chairs on either side of a bed.

The hospital worker said, "Delaney, I have more of your family here for you."

Delaney was in the process of kicking blankets off and to a heap at the foot of the bed. Her palms and a few of the fingers on her left hand were wrapped like she was auditioning for a remake of Michael Jackson's "Thriller." A bulky bandage protruded from under the hem of her hospital gown. Both knees sported square adhesives. An IV was taped to her wrist and fluids dripped from bags on a stand behind her.

But it was the face grimacing at Leo that knocked the wind out of him. The beautiful green eyes were intact, but otherwise, it was a mess. Abraded, scraped, cut. By tomorrow, he was sure it would be bruised, too.

"It's my lucky day," Delaney said, gesturing to the crowded room. Kateena was standing as close to her aunt as she could get. Skeeter leaned against a wall, Juan Julio on one hip.

"Thanks again, ma'am," the sheriff said to the woman.

She beamed at him, closed the curtain, and walked away, her thighs making a high-pitched grating noise like cricket wings.

The sheriff reached Delaney first. He put knuckles against a bare spot on her cheek. "Are you trying to put me in an early grave, Laney?"

Delaney pressed his hand into her face with her own. "Never. Sorry."

Fentworth grunted and moved a few feet away where he seemed to study her to make sure all her pieces were in place.

Leo moved to Delaney's bedside. He wanted to touch the bandages. To touch her. He didn't do either. "We came straight from the search party meeting as soon as we heard."

Fentworth said, "Palmer drove out of there so fast he ran into a boulder. Popped a tire and bent a rim on his department truck."

Delaney said, "Note to self: never let Leo in the driver's seat when I'm with him."

Leo shook his head. "I just wanted a reason to drive my amazing rental car." *Not.* Then he said to Delaney, "What the hell happened?"

She pointed at the curtained door. "Skeeter, can you take your charges to the snack machines?"

"Sure." Skeeter moved away from the wall. "Come on, Kateena."

The girl shook her head, her face mulish. "No. I won't leave Aunt Delaney."

Delaney softened. "This is grown-up talk."

"I know bad things happen. They happened to my parents. Something happened to you. Stop treating me like I don't know anything!"

Delaney stared into the girl's eyes. Leo could see her shoulders drop as she relented. "Okay. Kateena can stay. But, Skeeter, when you leave, take them to your place, okay?"

Skeeter saluted. "Anything you say, boss." And then he was gone.

She nodded at him and turned to Leo. "I found our guy. Or he found me, I guess. At my storage unit."

Leo's heart slammed against his sternum. "Who is it?"

"I'd been watching Chip Crawford at his house—"

He pumped his fist, interrupting her. "I knew it was him. But why did you skip out on the task force? That's—"

She ran right over him, too. "I cut my leg going over his back fence, so I went down the street to where I keep my rig—"

"Your what?"

"My tractor."

"You keep a tractor in town instead of at your farm?"

"Tractor as in the thing that pulls a semi-trailer. The front end of an eighteen-wheeler. It's big and expensive, and I keep it there. Oh, and our homestead is technically a ranch, since it was traditionally used for raising livestock, although right now it is an out-of-commission ranch."

Leo had always thought he was sophisticated compared to country rubes, but he was uncomfortably less certain of it all the time. "Oh. Gotcha."

"I have a first aid stash in the rig. I fixed myself up, and when I came out, he was there."

Was she driving him crazy on purpose? Leo's voice rose. "*Who* was there?"

"I walked out and saw his pickup. I had barely registered that it matched our witness's description when I saw my medallion pendant hanging from the mirror."

"Whoa. What of yours?"

"Her medallion." Kateena's face had gone red. "He took it from our house?"

"Yes, sweetie." Delaney's voice was soothing. Leo noticed she didn't mention that the man had also attacked her there. "I'm afraid it burned up in the crash."

"The truck didn't burn." The sheriff was holding his hat in front of him with both hands. "It was empty when the first responders got there. I'll radio and ask for them to look for an... an anklet you said?"

"A medallion with 'Eastern Wyoming Dirt Track Champion' engraved in it," Kateena said helpfully.

"He wasn't there? That's impossible! That truck bounced and rolled all the way down the ravine. And it's deep." The space between Delaney's wounds turned as red as the rest of her flesh. "The kid that rescued me couldn't even get to it."

The sheriff bounced the hat on his thigh. "It appears he was thrown clear. There were footprints down the ravine. He climbed out at an easier stretch. The tracks ended at the road."

"Someone picked him up?" Leo said.

"Best guess. Did you ever get a look at him, Delaney?"

She shook her head. "No. He was wearing a balaclava."

Leo groaned.

"The one person I can assure you it wasn't, though, is Sicario, since he was locked up."

Fentworth's radio crackled. He pulled it from its holster and pressed the talk button as he exited the curtained room. "Go ahead for Sheriff Fentworth." He disappeared into the hallway.

"Do you think it was Chip Crawford?' Leo said.

"The voice was different. I really don't think so."

"Tim Osborne?"

"Probably not. This guy seemed younger. Plus, I think I'd remember his voice."

"Is it possible he disguised it?"

"Anything's possible. You know that."

"Okay. We need the DNA evidence and prints from that truck." Leo was getting excited. They had their guy. "The vehicle registration. Insurance card. There's bound to be plenty in there to identify him. And we've got to get someone out to your storage unit. He might have left trace there, too. What's the unit number?"

"One oh one," Delaney said. She looked lost in thought.

Leo typed, thumbs flying, sending a message to the task force about the storage unit. "Is it okay if we cut your lock?"

She shrugged. "No problem. Anyone that messes up my tractor is a dead man, though."

Leo typed her message verbatim. He didn't consider her the type to make threats lightly.

Delaney said, "This guy all but admitted to me that he had Mary, and I'm sure he killed Lila. Sicario didn't do *either*."

Before Leo could respond, Fentworth re-entered the room. "Well, remember how I said that truck didn't burn?"

"Ye-es?" Leo said.

Fentworth said, "It exploded. The whole thing incinerated five minutes ago."

Leo shook his head. "But it's nearly an hour after the crash. That makes no sense."

"Remote detonation. Has to be. I've got to get out of here." Delaney jumped to her feet. She swayed and grabbed her IV pole. Then she stopped. Her eyes grew moist. "I thought I was getting my medallion back. Now it's gone again."

The pressure in Leo's chest was painful.

"You're not going anywhere," Fentworth said. Calm, firm.

"Give Leo everything you know, and then rest. Take care of your family. And yourself. That's not a suggestion from your old friend. That's an order from your boss."

Delaney marched around the room dragging the IV, grabbing bloody jeans and hopping on one foot to get the other in the pants leg. "But he was in my house. He has my jewelry. He knew where my storage unit was. He killed Lila. He has Mary. My family is at risk until he's caught."

Kateena pulled at the hem of her sweatshirt. "Mama died in a car crash."

Oh shit. Leo was thankful it was Delaney who'd slipped and not him.

Delaney froze, her face crumpling.

The sheriff knew when to make an exit. "I'll go radio the team. Delaney, I mean it. Go home. And have Skeeter standing guard with a shotgun." He slipped out of the curtain.

Delaney walked over to Kateena, IV in tow, and pulled the girl into her arms. "I'm sorry, honey. There's some news about your mom." She closed her eyes. "A couple of nights ago, someone found her in the mountains. She'd been killed."

Tears welled and rolled down the girl's cheeks. "I don't understand."

"We don't either. But she didn't die in the crash with your dad. Someone did, but we don't know who it was. The man who took me today may be the person who hurt her. And he may have Mary. At least that's what I believe."

Kateena's back heaved. Sobs wracked her thin body.

Over the girl's head, Delaney looked at Leo. "He wouldn't tell me where Mary is, but he could have been taking me there, too."

Leo nodded. It was a good assumption, although he wished he understood why the guy had targeted Lila, Mary, and now Delaney. Not only would that information possibly help the task force find him, but it might also keep another woman safe.

"I need to update the task force. We can deploy the search team in that direction."

"As soon as I can get these clothes on, I'm out of here."

Kateena ripped herself away from Delaney. "No! You can't! I won't let you!"

Delaney frowned. "What's the matter, honey?"

Kateena threw herself across the hospital bed, her face in her hands.

Leo cleared his throat. "I think she needs you to take better care of yourself."

Delaney sat beside Kateena, holding the IV pole in one hand. "I'm tough, Kitty Cat. You know that, don't you?"

The girl nodded but didn't show her face.

"I'm not going to let him hurt me."

"He already did."

Delaney's voice was light and confident. "These are just scratches. I'm fine. And I'm going to bring Mary home and take care of you."

"You say that. But you didn't save my mom!"

Leo turned away. Emotions crashed inside him like a tsunami. The empathy he felt for Delaney was so strong, it threatened to pull him under. He fought against it. He'd swum in waters very much like the ones she was in once upon a time.

"I would have if I could have. I promise." She stroked hair away from Kateena's wet face. "And now I have to do this, to protect us. You and me."

Leo mulled his options. He wanted to throw Delaney a life-line. The sheriff would be upset if Leo knowingly helped her return to work today. The old pirate cowboy might even fire him. He had a soft spot a yard deep and a mile wide for Delaney. But she was Leo's partner. He needed to trust her, and she needed to trust him. Their lives would depend on each other.

Besides, Kateena needed to know that she wasn't the only

one looking out for her aunt. "How about you don't do this by yourself?" he said to Delaney.

"You sound like Fentworth." Delaney turned to look at him. "You can't talk me out of this."

"Not trying to. I just want us to work together, even if we do it... quietly. Without telling the sheriff. For everyone's sake." He nodded at Kateena's bowed head.

Delaney squinted, mulling it over. Then she nodded. "All right with you, Kateena? If I work with Leo?"

"That's better, I guess."

Leo nodded back at Kateena. "I won't even let her drive."

"Lucky for you, I don't have my car." She lowered her voice. "Or gun."

Leo winced. The perp had her gun. That was bad.

"Kateena, you're with Skeeter."

Kateena nodded, looking very adult. "The cafeteria. I know. I'm on my way." She kissed Delaney on the cheek and walked out.

"Go straight there!" Delaney called after her.

"Yep," Kateena hollered back.

Leo liked that kid. "You're in my vehicle, Delaney."

"Like hell I am," Delaney said.

"Would you rather I rat you out to the sheriff so he can lock you up?"

She made a grumbly noise.

He smiled. "That's what I thought. Let's spring you from this joint and put you back to work."

FORTY-ONE

HALF AN HOUR EARLIER

The Delivery Man hitched a ride back to the feedstore. He'd never felt such utter, unadulterated rage. *That bitch Delaney messed me up.* As he got out of the truck, he said, "Thanks for the lift," to the geezer who'd picked him up from the side of the road.

"You sure I can't take you to the ER?" The man's voice shook.

At least the old guy had attributed all his injuries to the wreck. There was enough of those, mostly on his left side, where he'd landed when he dived out of the pickup. A dislocated shoulder, which he'd fixed himself, sitting on a rock in the ravine. His face and side were scraped up. His wrist was sprained, he was sure, along with a limp that could be from damage to his ankle or knee. They both hurt. Then there was the stab wound to his cheek and the abrasion mark around his neck from the zip tie, which he'd sliced off with the tip of his knife. That would have been worse without his balaclava. And he wasn't even counting the hole she'd bitten in his earlobe the night before.

He glanced down at his boot. His knife was secure in its

holster. That knife was his best friend. His only friend after the way Jefe had treated him. If only the Delivery Man didn't limit his mission to women, he might send Jefe on his way.

The old man started to repeat himself. "I said, are you—"

He leaned back in. "My woman will take care of me for free."

"Suit yourself." The old man saluted him and drove away.

The Delivery Man waited until the pickup had disappeared around the curve toward the school. He pulled an object from his jeans pocket—a satellite phone—and opened an app. Thank God it had survived the crash. He pressed a button.

"Boom." *That will take care of any evidence in the truck.*

Then he walked to Kearny Storage, next door to the feedstore. After he'd knocked Delaney out, he'd taken her tractor keys from where she'd stashed them under the fifth wheel coupling. *Right in front of me. She's not so smart.* He was going to pay her back for what she'd done to him. First, he was stealing her tractor, although it had been a toss-up between that and her sports car. Because he had those keys, too. All her keys, actually. And her gun. But the big rig was hidden in a storage unit. Less recognizable as Delaney's.

Then, after he delivered Mary, Delaney was next. Immediately next. The signs were in neon letters ten-feet tall. And he was going to enjoy every second of it.

A flurry of cop vehicles sped past, lights flashing and sirens blaring.

He thought about Delaney. He'd have to accelerate the timeline. Get her quickly. Take her to a town with less heat. He congratulated himself on having driven her toward his bugout place. *Because I'm not about to overnight in a cabin with only an outhouse.* If the police searched in that direction and found the cabin, there'd be evidence of him there, but none of the women. He kept them on the far side of town.

And they sure wouldn't be looking for him in this showy Kenworth.

He took a moment to get his bearings in the cab. The shifter had eighteen gears. He'd never driven anything like it, but he wasn't the kind of person to let that rattle him. He knew how to operate a stick, and his right side wasn't injured. He'd make do.

He fired up the engine, shifted into first and cursed from the pain that coursed through him. When he had recovered, he rumbled out of the bay, stopping to close and lock the storage unit door. Back in the tractor, he turned right out of the parking lot and onto the road, where he upshifted rapidly. The low gears were *really* low. He was moving slow and noisy at first, but he got the hang of it. He heard air coming in from windows behind him. He decided he didn't care.

A young girl approached, walking on the sidewalk. She was looking down. Crying. She was African American. Elfin. He knew her. Lila's daughter.

Delaney's niece.

Temptation flickered. *But Kateena is a child. I don't deliver children.* Delaney, though, deserved additional punishment beyond delivery for all he'd done to her. Steeling her rig wasn't even enough. What better way than to take the girl?

He jerked to a stop and rolled down the passenger window. "Kateena!"

She paused. Peered up at him, where he knew the angle and distance made it difficult to see his battered face. Luckily, his injured earlobe was on the far side. "Yes?"

"I'm Robert. I was close to your mother. Sorry to hear about her passing."

"You heard?"

He nodded. "Horrible. Where are you headed?"

Kateena looked both ways. *She's not supposed to be here now.* "To my aunt's work." Then she seemed to notice the tractor for the first time. "She doesn't let anyone else drive Gabrielle."

"Yeah. But she asked me to take a look at a few things that need fixing. I was just about to stop by and talk to her about it."

"Weren't the cops coming to look at it?"

He clenched his teeth. "Were they? Because of what happened?"

Kateena nodded solemnly.

"Darn it. All the more reason to talk to her first then. Hop in, I'll give you a ride since we're going to the same place." He smiled at her. He hoped it looked normal.

The girl paused.

"You wanna call her first and make sure it's okay for me to give you a ride? Or I can call her for you?"

"No, no. That's okay."

She doesn't want Delaney to know where she is. "Suit yourself."

She licked her lips, then nodded. "Okay."

Using every bit of self-control he could muster, he ignored the pain, leaned over, and opened the door. The face looking up at him from the sidewalk was even more like Lila's than in her pictures. He'd never felt such delight. Such excitement. "Watch out. First step's a doozie."

Maybe his luck was improving.

FORTY-TWO

Delaney texted Leo from the conference room furthest from the sheriff's office, where she was hiding from Fentworth. It had been refreshed since she'd last worked for the county. Same Old West motif, a few coats of paint, new Keurig coffee maker.

Delaney: *Done. Ready. Tell me you've released Sicario.*

She held her head in both hands, pressing to stop the throbbing. The Toradol she'd been given in her IV had worn off. After she'd updated Leo on every detail of her abduction, she'd had a Zoom meeting with a sketch artist. The last half hour was a blur, and it didn't help that she was beyond tired. She would have traded Shelly or Gabrielle for a pile of Excedrin in a hot second.

Leo: *Out-processing right now. And I'm on my way.* He poked his head in as she was reading his text.

She raised her eyebrows, then was sorry she had. It hurt. "That was fast. You must have been lurking outside the door."

"Almost. I just came from talking to the leader of the search team. The state police brought drones to expand coverage and get to hard-to-reach places." He held up his phone. "I just texted you a link so you can look at footage if you want."

"Thanks."

His phone rang in his hand. He glanced at it. "It's, uh, Sugar. I think it's about the knife."

She made a rolling motion. "Answer it already."

He put the call on speaker. "Palmer."

"Hi, Leo. Ready for an information dump on your piece of knife blade?"

"Hit me."

"DNA analysis is underway. No usable prints, no markings on the sample. You already knew that."

"Right."

"The lab called. They identified the alloys in the metal. The person I talked to said to tell you that the main thing that jumped out was that it seems like a blade made for extreme heat, which could explain why it broke in our climate. I'm emailing the report to you now."

"Thanks." He ended the call. To Delaney, he said, "I wish I knew more about knives."

"I know a guy. Print me the results and I'll call him."

Leo nodded. "Be right back."

She scrolled through her contacts for Duggan Irwin, a fellow trucker in North Dakota. Once, she'd pulled him out of a foot of mud in a ditch, and they'd been friends ever since. He made and sold knives in his spare time, and he was as odd as a 1970 Gremlin. She pressed his record to call him.

"Delaney. D, as in delightful. Or Xena, X, as in excellent. How are you?" he answered, referring to the trucker handle given to her by her colleagues.

His gravelly voice brought a smile back to her face as did the use of her handle. "D as in dumb when it comes to knives. I thought maybe you'd help an old buddy, if you don't mind me skipping the niceties and going right to it."

"Damn straight. Whatcha got?"

"A very small piece broken off a knife blade that may have been used in a murder up in the mountains here."

"Good God, woman, what are you into?"

"I've gone back to work as a deputy."

"D as in deputy. The bad guys better watch out. I'd guess you're trying to learn more about the knife in hopes that it will lead you to a killer?"

"You watch a lot of crime TV, I take it."

"Nah, I consult with law enforcement in our area. That and a ten-spot will buy me a six-pack of beer. Tell me what's you've got."

Leo returned and handed her the printout.

Delaney changed the phone output to speaker. "I have you on with Deputy Leo Palmer, who just handed me the results from the various tests run on it. Leo, this is Duggan Irwin."

"Hello, Deputy Palmer."

"Mr. Irwin. Thanks for your help," Leo said.

Delaney continued. "No fingerprints, no markings. We've done an XRF test on it. The tester said it was a blade clearly made for extreme heat."

"Good. You used a non-destructive test in case you need to take it further later. What are the results?"

"Carbon. Chromium. Molybdenum." She stumbled on the word. "Vanadium. Manganese. Silicon." The names meant nothing to her except a flashback to learning the periodic table in high school.

"That's T1 high-speed steel. And it's odd."

"Why?"

"T1 is a pre-World War Two throwback. For those looking for high-speed steel, M2 is used more commonly in its place since then. And even an M2 wouldn't be what I would have expected you to describe. It's used a lot for power tools."

She nodded at Leo.

He said, "The pathologist believes it was straight, non-serrated knife. But we're not even sure this sample we found at the scene came from a knife."

"Was the scene somewhere people would use power tools?"

"No," Leo and Delaney said in unison.

"You said the murder took place in the mountains of Wyoming?"

Delaney said, "Yes."

"What kind of knives do you normally see people carry around there?"

Delaney answered quickly. "Hunting knives. Utility knives."

"Outdoorsman knives, then."

"Yes."

"And they'd be rated for extreme cold if I had to guess, too. Aluminum or titanium alloys."

"Seems like that would be smart."

"All right, then. Since I can't imagine someone taking a kitchen knife up in the mountains to kill someone or using something as small as a pocketknife, I'd say you're looking for a custom knife built by a T_1 enthusiast. And I don't think it would be owned by a hunter or rancher or even someone who lives in the area unless they fall into that T_1 enthusiast category."

Delaney summarized her understanding. "Custom knife. Not from a cold weather climate unless a T_1 enthusiast."

"Right. Do you know anybody like that?"

Her lips puckered as she thought about it. "No. But I've been gone for ten years."

"One more question. Any notes about unusual composition on your results?"

Delaney scanned downward. "Nothing more."

"Okay. Here's what you do. Get on 'knife forums dot com.' It's a place where knife enthusiasts talk about knives. You might get lucky."

"I'm on it. Thanks, Duggan. I'll send you some beer money."

"Why break my hot streak? I've got a ten in my pocket and I ain't afraid to use it. But I have an idea. Why don't I post for you? You don't have an account. And if you set one up, you'll stand out as someone new posting on an unusual topic."

"True. We've got to be careful not to tip this guy off. But would you mind instead giving me your login?"

He laughed. "L as in Lager. Now you're going to be sending me beer money."

FORTY-THREE

The Delivery Man checked his sideview mirror. Smiled. No one following him. He looked back at Kateena. Smiled again. Completely immobile. He'd used his stun gun on her as soon as she was in the truck, then tossed her in the sleeper, where he'd sat on her until he'd trussed her with duct tape and tied her to the sleeping net, thanks to Delaney's well-stocked boxes of supplies. He'd even moved the box out of the girl's reach, congratulating himself on his attention to detail. Adrenaline had kept his pain at bay.

It couldn't have gone better if he'd planned it.

The pain was coming back as the road grew steeper and rougher. The big rig bounced and whined. He ground his teeth to keep from crying out, more than once. He had some drugs in the cabin—the good kind—and he planned to take a double dose.

He turned the tractor in an arc in front of the cabin where he had Mary restrained in the cellar, leaving the vehicle facing uphill for a quick getaway. It was what nostalgic people called 'cute.' Not him. He was a student of early twentieth-century history, but he didn't believe in living like people had back then. In his opinion, the place was an inconvenient shithole, although it had a few positive attributes. An updated root cellar that suited his needs. The location an adequate distance from the creek so no fishermen had bothered him. The NO TRESPASSING signs he'd added probably helped.

"How you doing back there, little Lila?" he said, amusing himself.

Funny squeaking noises came from the sleeper as she tried to answer.

"You'd like to stay out here in the truck, you say?" He nodded. "I appreciate that. Save me from having to unload and reload you. You just take a nap. I'll check on you later, pet."

This time the sounds were more like screams, but he didn't care.

He rotated his body and hopped out of the truck onto his right leg, propping himself on the door. Pain ricocheted through his body. He grabbed his left arm, cursing, then hobbled to the cabin.

"Honey, I'm home," he shouted.

There was no sound except the rushing creek water.

He spent the next half hour tending to his wounds and napping. Sleep gave the hillbilly heroin time to take effect. When his alarm went off, to remind him to feed the dog, it was hard to get up. But deliveries were serious business. He'd have to consider how to work his injury into the delivery schedule for Delaney, once he got her. It didn't seem fair that the clock would start when he wasn't ready. Maybe he could calculate it from arrival in a new town. It seemed reasonable to him. Even the post office faced emergency delays every now and then.

For now, he couldn't let Mary starve. He emptied a can of wet food into a bowl. With his injuries, it was all he could carry.

He lifted the trap door. "Move back," he shouted.

There was a rustling noise below. It sounded like she'd

complied. He grabbed the bowl and a plastic spoon and carefully descended the ladder.

When he neared the bottom, his phone rang. Jefe. He lowered the bowl to the floor and shoved it toward Mary with his foot. He pulled out his phone. Holding it to his ear hurt, so he put it on speaker and retreated up the stairs, wishing he hadn't left his Bluetooth in the detonated truck.

After climbing two steps, he felt like he was going to pass out. He sat heavily on a rung. "Jefe, how are you?" Maybe Jefe had called to say he was sorry.

"Are things taken care of?" His tone was sharp.

That didn't sound like an apology. "I already told you they are."

"You have no idea how important this is to me. To my *friends*. I'll ask you one more time. Is that a yes that my problem is taken care of?"

Maybe this friendship had started on the wrong foot right back when Jefe was a customer at the wildlife butchery. Jefe had asked for special favors. Product inserts into packages. Of course, the Delivery Man had said yes. He knew his Spanish—the man called himself "Jefe," as in boss. Bosses were good people to make friends with. Or so he'd thought. It appeared Jefe had friends. The Delivery Man just wasn't one of them. "Yes."

"I want you out of town now. Out of the state."

"I'm out of here." *As if I'd stay.* "I get it. You're a bad guy. You work with bad people." *And you're not my friend.*

"Don't make me prove it to you. Pack your shit and get out. Do it now." The call ended.

The Delivery Man rolled his eyes. Fine. He would speed up the timeline. Anything over twenty-four hours since he'd taken Mary counted as the second day. He needed one last session with her before her dispatch, though. He needed to be sure. It didn't matter that Jefe had led him to Lila and Mary. That had been the first sign, with each of them. But he always gave the women plenty of chances to show him they would stop tempting him with their evil. He was an honorable man. It had never happened, but if it did, he would stop. Return them to their lives.

But damn, those oxy. Maybe he'd taken too many. After a nap would be soon enough to work with Mary. He looped his arm through a rung, put his head on the one above it, and closed his eyes.

FORTY-FOUR

Mary stood in the center of the cellar, her heavy water bottle in one hand, a sharp stone in the other. She couldn't believe it. She'd been ready for him. The phone call had pulled him back up the stairs before he got close enough for her to attack. The *pendejo* had no idea how close he'd come to death.

She set down the water bottle and pulled with all her strength on the cable. The Delivery Man was snoring on the stairs, looking like he'd been wrestling with a mountain lion. This was her chance, but she couldn't break free. The moment ended and left her weak. She slumped to the ground, her face in her hands.

Another emotion caught up with her, something partway between grief and shock. She thought she'd recognized the voice over the speaker phone. The man who called himself Jefe.

The words he'd spoken were ricocheting through her head, over and over.

"Are things taken care of?" he'd said.

The Delivery Man replied, "I already told you they are."

"You have no idea how important this is to me. To my

friends. I'll ask you one more time. Is that a yes that my problem is taken care of?"

Mary shuddered. It had sounded like he was talking about *her*. That Jefe had set her up to be tortured and killed by this freak of nature. She didn't know who was worse—Jefe or her captor.

More of the conversation replayed in her mind.

The Delivery Man had said, "I'm out of here. I get it. You're a bad guy. You work with bad people."

Jefe's words had chilled her, then and now. "Don't make me prove it to you. Pack your shit and get out. Do it now."

Mary sat up, rocking. Even if she escaped, Jefe would be out there. If she was right about his identity, wouldn't Jefe still want her killed since she knew who he was? What he was?

She'd never be safe as long as he was alive.

Never.

FORTY-FIVE

"There." Delaney posted her message in an established Q&A thread titled "Experience With T1 Tool Steel." She'd chosen the thread on Duggan's advice and drafted the message with him to get the voice right. They didn't want to spook people who knew him online. Leo provided input on the content, too, and watched over her shoulder. Luckily, Clara had been able to retrieve Delaney's laptop from the Chevelle while Delaney was working with the sketch artist, so she was able to do the work on her own machine. "Thanks, Duggan."

"Anytime. Catch you later."

Delaney ended the call and admired their handiwork on the screen.

LOOKING FOR T1 KNIFEMAKER

My buddy wants a T1 knife. I told him T1 is shit for knives, but he's got a bug up his butt about it and won't listen to me. Anyone out there drinking the T1 Kool-Aid who can help him? Advice or knifemakers, either one. TIA, assholes.

She pushed back from the conference room table and walked over to the Keurig. It was the third cup she'd made. The caffeine was helping with her exhaustion, but not with her nerves. "Since we know now that Lila and Mary were taken by the same person, I'm going to re-read Lila's file while I wait for a fish to take the bait on this T1 stuff."

Leo said, "I'll be checking in with the task force. Theoretically, I'm in charge, although Fentworth lurking around makes that hard."

"He can't help himself."

"Once the FBI guy shows up, it's going to get a lot worse." Leo shook his head.

Delaney sipped her coffee, watching him as he walked out. Okay, she'd admit it. He was more than just a pretty face, and working with him was less than awful, too. *Look at me, going soft.*

Her phone buzzed with a text. Her home screen read SKEETER. He'd promised he'd only call if it was an emergency and text if it was more like begging her to take the kids off his hands or send emergency Wyoming Whiskey. She'd look at the text later. There was too much to do right now.

She took a seat back at the conference table and pulled her laptop over. An hour passed while she combed the files, honing in on the bone marking—the angle she'd thought about the least until now. Most of the similar cases Leo had pulled involved markings of various types, like knife markings on bone and burn marks on flesh. He'd searched for lines, too. None of the cases he'd found involved five lines. A few had wavy lines but were otherwise dissimilar.

But there were no cases with marked *pelvic* bones and none with *internal* bone burns whatsoever. She considered Lila's burns. While they had barely gone deeper than the viscera on the pelvis, the pathologist believed he'd shown an intention to burn the pattern into bone.

A light bulb flashed on in her mind, a result of her knife forum posting. She could post the five wavy lines on a tattoo forum. Maybe someone would recognize the pattern there. And she could do an online search. She couldn't find anything in the file that suggested one had been completed. She tried Google, combing through the results for "image of five wavy lines." The images didn't resemble Lila's at all—they all related to surfing, music, and weather. She sketched the lines, took a photo of it, and posted it on EverythingTattoos dot com, along with her request for information.

A tone sounded on her laptop. She had a notification of some sort. She moved to the knife forum tab she had opened earlier. Her skin prickled. She had a reply on her post.

GRAYGRIZZLE45: *Hey, you ole sumbitch. You're better at talking women out of their panties than your own buddy out of T1?*

EDGARSCISSORHANDS: *I don't know shit about T1. But there used to be a guy who'd post all the time about it. He was obsessed with it.*

Delaney wiggled her fingers, excited. *Tread carefully. He could be watching. He could be one of these guys.*

DUGCAN1RW1N: @GRAYGRIZZLE45 *That's my problem. I was never any good at that either.*

DUGCAN1RW1N: @EDGARSCISSORHANDS *That's what I need. Someone obsessed. Send me his way.*

A reply came quickly.

EDGARSCISSORHANDS: @   DUGCANıRWıN
Haven't heard from him in a few months. Seems like he drove a delivery truck in Vegas. UPS or something. Wish I had his contact info. He might like me to throw him the opportunity, since nobody else uses it. His handle is @PRIORITYMALE

DUGCANıRWıN: @EDGARSCISSORHANDS *Vegas? Almost as bad as ND. I'll message him, but my friend is in a hurry, so I'll try to track him down IRL, too. Before I go on a wild goose chase, tell me you're sure he lives there.*

EDGARSCISSORHANDS: @DUGCANıRWıN   *I cannot tell a lie. But he told me that once he made a delivery to a showgirl who answered the door naked as the day she was born. And he said what happens in Vegas stays in Vegas.*

DUGCANıRWıN: @EDGARSCISSORHANDS *Figures you can't remember his name, but you remember the naked girl. Thanks, man.*

A smile spread over Delaney's face.
She called Leo. "We have a lead. A good one."

FORTY-SIX

Kateena gritted her teeth, trying to hold her tears in. Her nose was getting stuffy, and she couldn't breathe with the gag in her mouth. She had to stop crying and think about ways to escape.

She looked around her for the thousandth time. Her eyes had gotten used to it, but it was dark in the sleeper, except for some light coming in the side windows. A breeze wafted in one, too, and across her face. The man had pulled a curtain shut earlier when he'd left her in here. A curtain like a door, so she couldn't see into the cab or out the front windshield at all. And the sleeper was tiny. Small enough that it didn't take long to see everything she'd already seen, none of which would help her, because she was stuck and couldn't do anything but lay here on the bunk.

Her shoulders ached. The man had shocked her with something that hurt worse than anything in her life. She hadn't even been able to move. While she was helpless, he'd taped her wrists a bazillion times then tied her arms above her head onto a net that he'd buckled into place like a seatbelt. Under it, she was an animal in a zoo, the net criss-crossing in front of her—bars on a cage. Not that she'd ever been to a real zoo. She'd never been anywhere cool. And if she didn't figure out how to get loose, she might never go anywhere else again. She'd even be glad to go back to school if she got out of this.

It was going to be hard, though. He'd taped her ankles, too. Once, she'd watched a scary show while her parents were fighting and not paying attention to her. A woman had been kidnapped and she'd untied herself with her toes. That wasn't going to work for Kateena since he'd put the tape on around her socks.

She pulled at her wrists. The net moved like the Jacob's ladder at the school playground, but it wouldn't pull loose from the wall. Her wrists were raw from the times she'd struggled against the tape. Although they weren't as bad as her throat. She'd screamed her lungs out. After a while, she'd realized that there were no sounds, wherever they were, except for nature sounds. Wind. Birds, Water. No humans to hear her calling for help. And, truthfully, she wasn't very loud because of the gag.

Nothing she had tried had done any good. She was trapped. She was a prisoner. She might die. Like her dad. Like her mom.

And all because she'd been so stupid. Her parents had taught her better than to ride with strangers. Her dad would have whupped her good for it, if he was still alive and found out what she'd done. She'd known that bad things were happening in Kearny, too. But the man had been so nice. So normal. And he'd been driving Gabrielle. She'd only ever gotten to ride in Gabrielle once, when her aunt first arrived. Honestly, she'd been kind of excited about it. Plus, he'd said he was friends with Mom and Aunt Delaney. *Obviously that's not true.*

She turned her wrists over so that her watch faced her. Not a smart watch—her parents had said not until high school. But it did tell the date. She didn't know exactly when she'd climbed into Gabrielle, but she'd been in here a long time. Long enough that she had to go to the bathroom so bad that she was afraid she'd wet her pants.

Tears threatened again. She gritted her teeth harder.

But no matter how long it had been, she needed more time. Time for Aunt Delaney to figure out she was gone and come looking for her.

Because the man who had taken her was mean. A million times meaner than Jeremy Jerkface Peterson. And if he came back, she knew it was going to be for something very, very bad.

FORTY-SEVEN

The Delivery Man's phone dinged. He raised his head to read the notification, wiping drool off his cheek, his neck screaming in pain. Everything screaming in pain. He scowled. What was he doing asleep on the ladder into the cellar?

He looked at his phone. Two notifications from knifeforums.com. He hadn't been on the site in a while. He clicked the first one. It pulled up a thread where someone named DUGCANɪRWɪN was looking for a Tɪ knifemaker. He opened the guy's profile. A crusty dude out of North Dakota. But then he read what EDGARSCISSORHANDS had posted in reply. His breathing grew ragged. The guy was giving up information on him. His handle. Where he lived. What he did for a living. Things the Delivery Man hadn't meant to actually tell anyone but clearly had. *Son of a bitch.* He stuffed his phone in his back pocket.

Then he reined in his thoughts. This was no threat to him. He was far away from Vegas and his old life. Besides, this was a compliment. He considered answering DUGCANɪRWɪN. Maybe when he'd finished his Wyoming deliveries and relocated he could smith a blade for the guy's friend. He missed having legitimate reasons to work with blades.

He looked at a lump at the foot of the ladder. Mary was lying at the bottom. He stepped down a few rungs, moving softly and clutching his arm. The pain had come back some, especially in his face, but based on his ladder nap, more oxy was a bad idea. He'd take a handful of ibuprofen when he got back upstairs. Mary looked like she was asleep. As he got closer, he saw that the food bowl had been thrown at the wall. Dog food was splattered everywhere.

Wasteful, disrespectful bitch.

Just as he leaned down to grab her, she exploded up at him. Something heavy smashed the side of his face where Delaney had stabbed him. He bellowed and crashed to the floor at her feet. She leaped on him, banging him in the head with a sharp object.

He was dazed but quickly regained his senses. Enough was enough. If this kept up, she was going to kill him.

He grabbed her, throwing her off him and into the back of the room. He pulled the blade from his boot and stalked after her. She was going to pay for this. While she was at it, she could pay for what Delaney did to him, too. *Don't kill her. Save her for her delivery.* He wasn't sure he was going to be able to stop himself.

Fifteen minutes later, the Delivery Man was done with Mary and left her locked in the cellar. He climbed the stairs, took a few pills to wake him up, and stopped in the kitchen to clean his blade. Afterwards, he put the knife back in his boot holster, took eight ibuprofen, and grabbed the tractor keys. It was time for Mary's delivery, and he needed a pickaxe for it, which he would have bought earlier if he hadn't been in so much pain. And while he was shopping, he should buy a few things to disguise his appearance. He'd be going after Delaney later, and she was the one person who might recognize him.

He hobbled back to the tractor, clutching his stomach, which suddenly burned. No way was he risking his life by leaving Mary above ground, no matter how much he hated hiding his work. Making it difficult to discover was one thing but making it *impossible* was another.

Because what was a delivery without someone to receive it?

Muffled groans and thumps from the sleeper stopped him in his tracks. Then he remembered. The girl. No way was he dragging her back into town with him. Even secured, she might figure out a way to attract attention he couldn't afford. He climbed up through the passenger side and into the sleeper.

"Shut up, kid." He untied her arms, unbuckled the sleeping net, and slid his hands under her armpits, his groans louder than hers. The drugs were helping, but it still hurt like a son of a bitch. Lucky for him, she was a runt. Scrawny and light.

She writhed in his hands. He looked down. Tears streaked her cheeks, but her eyes were feral. Like if he hadn't gagged her, she'd bite a chunk out of his hide and leave him with rabies.

"You're wasting your energy."

He maneuvered her over the passenger seat, not giving a shit that he was rough. He lost his balance and fell backward off the running board. He landed on his ass, which had been just about the only part of him that didn't hurt, until then.

"*Oof!*"

Kateena remained in the seat. *Enough of this.* He grabbed her again, this time pulling her out and letting her fall to the ground like he had. The thud of her torso hitting the dirt filled him with pleasure. The sight of her rolling around in pain almost made his own bearable.

He considered where to put her. Not the basement. He didn't want Mary waking up and letting the little hellion loose. Maybe in the outhouse? Too cramped. He'd just leave her upstairs in the cabin. Catching her wrists, he dragged her up the step onto the small porch. He turned the knob and kicked the door open. Then he hauled her the rest of the way in and to the center of the room.

She whimpered. *Good.*

As secure as the duct tape was, he knew he had to anchor her to something, somehow. He was running out of gas, though. He paused to catch his breath and think. The lines he'd used to tie Kateena to the sleeping net? Maybe. *But Delaney keeps bungee cords in her toolbox.* He'd seen them when he grudgingly admired her tool and supply kits. Ones she'd outfitted herself. *She's not so different from me.* A shame, really, that the signs she'd given him were so clear that not only must he deliver her, he had to punish her. Cursing, he returned to the truck for two bungees. When he made it back into the cabin, the little demon had already inch-wormed herself to the door.

He laughed in her face. "Not happening."

Snaring her wrists, he pulled her to the wood-burning stove. Its black cast iron legs would be perfect. He snaked a bungee cord between her arms, catching the layers of tape, then wound it several times around one leg until he could fasten the end hooks to each other without leaving slack. He repeated the process with her ankles. He finished and surveyed his work. Kateena was on her side in the fetal position, facing the stove.

He crouched so he could make eye contact with her. "Try getting away now."

The snarl and the look she drilled him with gave him a moment of pause. She was just a child. She couldn't hurt him, could she?

FORTY-EIGHT

Leo shouted, "Hell yeah!" He let his head fall back against the chair in the conference room he was using as central command for the task force. Finally, a lead.

"What is it, Johnny Utah?" Fentworth was examining Leo as if he'd slipped a gear. *How come the man is always lurking?*

Leo couldn't tell the sheriff Delaney was still working the case instead of in bed under armed guard. "Got a lead about a custom knifemaker in Las Vegas for our piece of steel."

"Good work."

"I'm calling the Las Vegas PD."

"Ask for Stan Heigl. Tell him I sent you."

Leo waved his thanks and left the conference room.

Then he hurried to Delaney in the smaller conference room. "Hailing up Las Vegas PD now."

"Put it on speaker," she said.

"You take the lead. You're the one who figured out the connection."

A head poked in the door. Clara. "Hi, guys. Do you have a minute?"

Leo felt resistance. They needed to make this call. But

something about the expression on her face stopped him. "A very short one. What is it?"

Clara walked to the table and handed each of them a missing person report. "I found someone who could be the woman who died with Liam. The sheriff said I should bring it to you."

"That's great," Leo said. His eyes dropped to the paper.

"Physically, she's a match. Age, height. The timing works—she went missing the same weekend Liam died. She lives in Casper, so she's close enough to have ended up here. Casper PD has the case. I called the officer mentioned in the file. She said that the boyfriend is actually a suspect and seems to be on the run. The detective on the case has a lead on his where-abouts. Domestic issues in the past and such."

"Or they could have run off together," Leo said.

"Or gone on a crime spree à la Bonnie and Clyde," Delaney said.

Clara chewed her lip. "True, both. I just wanted you to see this record because, given that there was enough of the woman left in Liam's car for the coroner to say it was Lila, this is really the only person I can find from our area who's even close to a match."

"We need to check her out, but it also looks like it's time to expand the geographic area of our search, then. Nice work, Clara. I'll get someone on the task force to coordinate with you on all of it. Thanks."

Clara waved as she exited, answering over her shoulder. "You betcha."

Leo said, "Let me just assign that out before I forget." His fingers flew.

"No problem," Delaney said.

When he was done, he said, "Hey, Siri. Call the Las Vegas, Nevada Police Department."

A few seconds later, Siri promised she was on it. The phone

rang and was answered by a robotic-sounding human who transferred Leo at his request to Stan Heigl.

"Detective Stan Heigl."

Leo couldn't believe they'd finally reached someone who worked Memorial Day weekend.

Delaney rolled closer to the phone on the table. "Stan, I'm Deputy Investigator Delaney Pace with the Kearny County Sheriff's Department in Wyoming. Sheriff Coltrane Fentworth sent me to you."

"That lazy son of a bitch. Is he doing anything but polishing his boots these days?"

Leo said, "I'm Deputy Leo Palmer. Does assigning his work to poor schmucks like me count?"

A booming laugh. "What can I do for you?"

Delaney said, "We have a murder case where a guy burned a mark on a woman. We have reason to think we should be looking for a similar signature in your jurisdiction."

"Where was the burn?"

"Inside the pelvis. After he disemboweled her."

"Jesus. Sick fuck." Leo heard clacking keys. "No, we don't have any bone burns."

"Okay, what about five wavy lines? Left on a vic using any method?"

More clacking keys. "I'm coming up empty on that, too."

Leo looked at Delaney. Nodded.

She said, "What about murders committed by someone who drove a delivery truck. Maybe for UPS. Maybe for the post office. Something like that. He would have been a knife enthusiast. Possibly made custom blades. I have a description and really lean sketch-artist rendering if it would help."

"Why didn't you just ask me that in the first place? We had a creep here carving up girls. Some kind of early twentieth-century crime history buff. And he was a delivery guy. He did off-books deliveries, not UPS, though. We believe he was making drug drops."

"That might fit. We have a chip off his knife blade. It's T1 high speed steel. The kind that was popular before the Second World War."

Stan whistled softly. "Give me an email address. I'll send the file."

Leo recited his.

Keys clacked again. "Sent. We thought we had this guy. Then he disappeared when we went to pick him up. No more killings in the last few months—that's good—but he got away. We have his prints, his name, his social, everything but him."

"Got the email, and I sent you a copy of the mark on our victim," Leo said. "I'm pulling yours up."

Delaney leaned in for a closer look.

"Flip forward a few pages. He liked to carve up their bones."

"Ours was bone burns," Delaney said.

Leo looked at a circle. Or something round and roughly a circle. "And wavy lines."

Heigl said, "Our guy marks bones still inside the body, though. Who does that?"

"True. I couldn't find a match."

"We had him dead to rights. Maybe he decided to change things up a little." Then, "I just got your photo."

Delaney said, "Who were his victims?"

"Showgirls. He was picking them out at customer locations. That's how we found him; we discovered the girls who died and had these marks worked for places where the same dealer was delivering product with the same delivery man. We went after the dealer. He rolled on the delivery guy, but it was too late. He was a ghost. You don't happen to know where he lives in Wyoming, do you?"

"No." Delaney pointed at one of the photos. "If you

combined the round mark he was leaving in Vegas with what he did to Lila, what does it remind you of?"

Leo shook his head.

"I don't know," Heigl said.

"A cancelled postage stamp. Vintage style. He uses a pre-World War Two custom steel knife and marks his victims with elements of old-timey cancelled postal stamps."

Leo stared at her. Could she be right? It made sense in a creepy way.

Heigl whistled. "That's not bad, Delaney."

Delaney's phone rang. She didn't even look at it. "He's not local, so his use of a four-wheeler on a fairly public trail fits better than it would for someone from around here. And when I asked him if he was a trucker, he told me he makes deliveries."

Stan's tone changed to one of excitement. "Wait—you've talked to him?"

Leo broke in like a proud parent. "He abducted her. She escaped him. Twice."

"Holy shit, lady. No one has ever gotten away from him before. Not that we know of. You must be an ass-kicker."

Delaney ignored the praise. "He identifies himself as someone who makes *deliveries*. He uses cancelled postage symbols on the women as if he has *delivered* them."

Heigl laughed aloud. "We all just thought he couldn't carve worth a crap, so he did something simple. Damn, Delaney, if I wasn't already married, I'd propose."

Delaney said, "If we catch this jerk before he kills the woman who's missing here now, I won't even tell your wife you said so."

Leo frowned. His fascination with Delaney felt a little unoriginal. Did she have this effect on all men? He thought about the guy who'd left her flowers and a note in the middle of the night. *More than a few, at least.* But, more importantly, they now had the suspect's name, right from the Las Vegas file.

Robert Brighton. His prints. His picture. His social security number. They knew his MO.

What they didn't have was the man himself or Mary. The first twenty-four hours after a kidnapping is critical to successfully finding and bringing the victim back alive. And that time period had elapsed.

Thinking about timing, Leo asked, "How long did he hold onto his victims in Vegas? Did you ever get a feel for a pattern with that?"

"Oh, yeah. We found four women we believe he killed. We were on to him after the third. From the time they went missing, each of the autopsies showed death between thirty-six and forty-eight hours. His timeline was quick. By the time the fourth woman disappeared, it was almost a guarantee she'd be dead in two days."

Delaney's line of thinking took hold in Leo's brain. He said, "And this guy calls himself PRIORITYMALE, m-a-l-e, on the knife forum where Delaney found the lead on him." His stomach felt like the killer's knife had just plunged deep inside it. "Shit. The USPS guarantees two-day delivery for priority mail express, m-a-i-l."

"He's guaranteeing their delivery date!" Delaney said. "Mary's time is almost up."

That was exactly what Leo was afraid of.

FORTY-NINE

"What has the search party turned up?" Delaney jiggled her knee.

After they'd ended the call with Heigl, she felt claustrophobic. The conference room was like a prison cell, something she had a clear memory of thanks to her first meeting with Leo. Mary was running out of time. She had to get out of this place. Take action on their new information, push progress forward, and drive, drive, drive until she found Mary.

"Not a damn thing yet," Leo said. "I just hit send on an update about our progress here, though. Maybe it will knock something loose."

She knocked her chair back and started pacing the small room. "When does the Feeb get here?"

"Some time tonight."

Delaney's phone buzzed with a text. Skeeter again. She'd have to check his messages soon. Mary first, though.

Leo's phone rang. He answered it on speaker. "Palmer."

"Deputy Leo Palmer?" The voice was hesitant. A whisper.

"Yes. Who's this?"

"Rosie from Kearny Hardware. You called here asking

about a fellow who bought one of them mini soldering irons with the rechargeable batteries?"

Leo waved Delaney over. "Yes, Rosie. Thank you for calling me back. Have you seen him again?"

The voice dropped even further. "He's in the store right now with a full cart. I ran out to the parking lot to call you. He looks awful. Something got after his face. And he's limping something terrible."

Delaney's eyes widened. "Let's go," she mouthed. Relief flooded her senses. *Yes. This is right. Get on the road. Follow him. Go find Mary.* She grabbed her purse and started stuffing her laptop into a bag.

"Stall him if you can," Leo said. "But don't risk getting yourself hurt. We're on our way." He ended the call and shoved the phone in its holster.

"I'm driving," she said.

The two of them rushed for the door, Delaney favoring all her injured parts, but suddenly not as much as before. The adrenaline of the chase was an effective antidote to pain.

"God help us that I think that's the right decision," Leo said.

Clara stepped in front of her.

"Excuse me, Clara. We've got to go." Delaney moved to pass around her.

"Wait. I have a call for you. From Skeeter."

"Can you handle it?"

Clara put her hand out and grabbed Delaney's arm, then dropped it. Her eyes were wide. "Delaney, he can't find Kateena."

Delaney's world stopped spinning. Kateena's beautiful face filled her mind. Her knees buckled. She caught herself on the credenza next to the door. "What does that mean, can't find her?"

"He said he hasn't seen her since he left her in your room at the ER."

"That's impossible! Why didn't he call me?" But he had. She didn't ever want to check her texts or voicemail again. She knew what she'd find. *How can I be so horrible at keeping the people I love out of danger?* Her father's face replaced Kateena's.

"Robert Brighton has her," she whispered. "Because of me."

"Who?" Clara said.

Leo pulled out his phone. "I'll pull people off the task force. We'll find Kateena. There's no reason yet to believe he has her."

"But what if he does? I've got to—"

"You've got to drive me to catch Brighton. He has Mary, for sure. And he's at Kearny Hardware *right now*. If he has Kateena, that's our most direct route to getting her back."

He was right. She turned nearly blind eyes on Clara. "Tell Skeeter we're on it."

Clara sounded close to tears. "I will, Delaney. Anything else?"

"No," Delaney said, her voice a whisper. Then, louder, "Pray."

"You can count on me for that." And then Clara was gone.

Leo was on the phone, barking orders. "Start from the hospital," he was saying. Then he gave her description.

The only eleven-year-old black girl in Kearny, Wyoming. Delaney dragged him out of the conference room by the arm. "Do you have weapons in your car? He has my gun."

He put his hand over his phone's mouthpiece. "Not enough."

She led him to the weapons locker, willing her brain to stay with her. She needed to be sharp now more than ever. Kateena. The tiny spitfire who had captured her heart. *She has to be okay. She just has to be.* Leo entered his code and opened the door. Delaney put on a holster and slipped a gun into it, then selected rifles and ammunition.

When she had managed her armloads, she marched Leo

onward, as fast as she could go without dropping Fort Knox to the ground.

Leo's call ended by the time they reached his Equinox.

He threw her the keys. "Don't get us killed."

She opened the back end, and they secured their rifles and ammo inside. Then she got in the driver's seat and fired the vehicle up. Something low-key and beachy oozed out of the speakers. She turned off the stereo, then surveyed what she had to work with. This thing was barely an adult vehicle compared to Shelly and Gabrielle. The engine shrieked as she wound it up in neutral. She jammed it into drive, and it whined and shuddered out of the parking space. She barely paused before asking the SUV to give everything it had. Its wheels squealed as she turned out of the parking lot.

"Jesus H. Christ, Delaney!"

"You've gotta know what's under the hood. You'll thank me later."

She cut the driving time from the department to the hardware store from five minutes to three.

"I'm not sure how we're going to know which guy is him. Hopefully his face will be uncovered, and he'll look like the picture Heigl sent," Leo said.

What Delaney saw in the parking lot was traumatic second only to Kateena's disappearance. She mashed the brakes, emitting a piercing, angry war cry.

"What is it?"

"We're not going to have any trouble IDing Brighton."

"Why?"

"He'll be the guy headed for my rig. The bastard took my rig."

"What do you mean?"

She jabbed her finger. "I mean that beautiful black Kenworth belongs to me and was in my storage unit earlier today. He has my wheels and my niece. Even my medallion.

He had my sister-in-law and has Mary now." She was breathing so hard, she was afraid she was going to hyperventilate. She had to get control of herself. She'd always kept her cool when everyone around her was going up in flames. But that had been before a deranged killer had come after her world.

A man ducked out of the hardware store, arms wrapped around large bags. A pickaxe dangled from one hand. His flannel hoodie was up and sunglasses on. But the stab wound to his face was still clearly visible, as was his limp. Gabrielle was parked with the driver's side toward the store entrance, and he disappeared from view. After a few seconds, the engine fired up noisily.

Leo said, "Are you absolutely sure the truck is yours?"

Delaney shot him a WTF glare. "Tractor. And I thought you had people searching my storage unit. Where it was parked."

"I did. They're finished. I didn't tell them they were looking for a giant black tru— tractor. But I get it." He jerked forward, pointing. "Now I need the Danica Patrick version of you. The one I first met. He's leaving."

"I'm better than Danica Patrick," Delaney snapped.

"And modest to boot."

She wasn't in the mood for humor. She might never be again. She stared intently at Gabrielle. The man turned her tractor toward the opposite end of town, away from where the teams were searching for him.

Leo said, "That's the wrong direction. Where's he going?"

Delaney spun her wheel and eased after him, keeping her distance. It wasn't like a rig the size of Gabrielle was hard to follow. "If he's leaving town, there's no way we can follow him off road and not be seen. Get us the drones."

"Good idea." Leo made a call. "Clint, where are you? We need the drones on the opposite end of town." He nodded.

"Heading southeast on Highway 29. Hurry." He ended the call and put his phone in his pants pocket.

"Is he coming?" Delaney felt like a piano wire, taut and ready to vibrate into a scream at the slightest touch.

"Better. He was already in town grabbing dinner, and he has the unit with him. He's two minutes behind us. He'll deploy on our command at the last possible second."

"Why can't he put it in the air now? I could fall farther back. I don't want Brighton to make us."

"Battery life and range limitations."

"Which are?"

"It has about forty minutes of airtime, and Clint can get it out about three miles from us."

"Got it."

"We need units for back-up, too, and everyone is northwest of town. I'll get them moving in this direction."

He made another call. Delaney didn't listen. Her mind bounced back and forth between where Kateena was now and what Brighton had done with her. To her. She bit down on her lip, tasting blood. Robert Brighton. She hated that the man had a name, as if he was a normal person. He was anything but normal.

They passed the Loafing Shed. The CLOSED sign was still taped in place. She hadn't given a thought to the bar since the second time she'd taped the sign up. She'd driven this road a thousand times. By the time she was fourteen, she'd memorized the curves, the stands of trees, the creek crossings, and the areas where deer congregated to catapult themselves in front of drivers. If she was blind she'd still be able to drive it. Past the few ranches and some prime antelope hunting and great fishing spots.

But that was all there was out this way. It was the least populated side of Kearny.

"Where's the bastard going?" She pounded the steering

wheel. "Unless he's heading south to Bernard there's nothing on pavement out this way."

"It's okay. We're going to get her back, Delaney."

She lost control. Her voice reverberated in the small space, loud and scared. "You don't know that."

"I know she has you and me. And I believe in us."

After a long pause and a few deep, slow breaths, she said, "Yes," her voice softer.

Ahead, the black beast turned toward the mountains.

"No, no, no!" Delaney groaned in frustration. "That road is crap. And the line of sight is great for him, which is terrible for us."

"Is there an alternate route?"

"To where? It runs for miles with only a few offshoots to ranches and river properties before it dead-ends up there." She pointed at the rock cliffs ahead of them. Then she had a thought and nodded. "The one thing he won't be able to hide, though, is that dust trail. If we hang back half a mile or so, I can stay out of his sight but still see where he's going." She brought the Equinox to a halt.

"I need to give our back-up directions. What do I call this road?"

"You call it 'stay put at the Loafing Shed until we need you.' We lose all element of surprise if twenty cars start barreling after us."

"No."

"Yes."

He thought about it for a few seconds, then called in exactly what she'd asked for.

A camo-green Jeep Rubicon pulled to a stop beside them. The driver rolled down his window on the passenger side. Brown skin, dark hair, dark eyes. Bold cheekbones and an uncompromising jaw sandwiched deep dimples. Delaney lowered hers.

"I'm Clint Rock-Below, with state. You got Leo in there?"

Crow Tribe. Delaney had gone to school with some Rock-Below kids. Most of them had been younger than her, though.

Leo leaned forward and waved. "This is Deputy Investigator Delaney Pace."

Clint grinned. "Well, dadgum, it sure as hell is." To Delaney he said, "You were two years ahead of me in school. I live just down the road in Casper. You married?"

She pretended she hadn't heard him. Law enforcement types could find humor at times other people might think was highly inappropriate. It kept them sane. He didn't know her niece and friend were missing and that her sister-in-law was dead at the hands of the guy they were tracking. But she still needed to hurry him along.

"We're following a black tractor—the kind for pulling a semi-trailer. But no trailer on it. That dust trail is his. If we start to lose him, how fast can you deploy the sky cop?"

"Thirty seconds."

"I can't signal you. We may not have cell out here."

His face contorted into an expression of "duh."

"Can I count on you to send it up when we're in danger of losing him, like when he turns or speeds up?"

His eyes twinkled. "Yes, ma'am, Delaney."

"I'll be staying a half mile back unless his trail gets faint. You're armed, right?"

"Heavily."

"This guy has a gun. His name is Robert Brighton and he's out of Nevada. We suspect he has two hostages, hopefully both alive. One of them is a minor. Give me 250 yards before you follow." She gave him a two-finger forehead salute. "See you when we get wherever we're going."

Then she gassed the Equinox. The rig was at the end of her sight range, so she accelerated steadily, until she was at a gap-closing speed, but not so fast it would draw Brighton's attention.

The road was bumpy and rutted. Leo braced himself on the ceiling. Delaney hoped the Equinox hadn't flattened like a soda can by the time they caught up to Brighton. Caught up to Kateena, and hopefully Mary.

The grade started increasing.

"The creek bed is getting steeper," she said, wrestling the wheel as she navigated from side to side, to minimize the impact of the ruts from snow run-off and spring mud.

"Bull!" Leo shouted.

A cow and calf ambled slowly across the road.

"Not technically." She wanted to beep the horn at them, but they wouldn't cross any faster if she did. It might even make them turn and run up the road, blocking their path longer. She went around them on the right. The mother and baby scampered into the green pasture. Delaney watched in her rearview mirror as they trotted to join a herd of about fifty head. She also saw Clint, who was keeping pace with the Equinox, a few hundred yards back.

"Should we call someone and tell them about the loose cows?" Leo asked.

Delaney looked over at him. "They're grazing in a pasture."

"But there are no fences."

"It's a big one, granted, but we crossed a cattle guard when we took this road, remember? There was a fence there. The cattle are fine."

They continued up into the foothills, crossing a small washout of rocks in the road. Delaney decreased her speed.

"I've lost sight of him," Leo said.

Delaney had, too. She felt her niece slipping away from her. The rig—with its heavy suspension, high clearance, and better tires—could outrun the Equinox on a road like this. Run laps around it. But then she saw dust in the air, in front and to their right, and she felt light-headed with relief.

"I think he turned." Her windows were still open. An angry

buzz swiveled her neck and drew her gaze skyward. The drone had taken off. It gave her a sense of comfort. *You aren't getting away from us, Brighton.*

Leo said, "Clint's on it. Eyes are up."

The drone accelerated. It topped out at twice the speed they could make on these roads. Soon, it was just a dot in the sky. Delaney bore toward the end of the dust trail where she believed the rig had headed down toward the river. She frowned. Memories assaulted her. Scaling fish for Grandma to fry on a wood-burning stove. A mama bear and two cubs across the creek, watching her. Roaming the woods with her father and brother.

"I know this area." A feeling of speeding toward a nightmare she didn't understand took hold of her, a sensation above and beyond her worry for Kateena and Mary.

"That's what you said."

Her mouth was cottony. She glanced at the console. No water bottles. Her mind would have to best the emotions that were ramping up inside her. "No, I mean I am personally familiar with the road he took. There's an old fishing cabin down there. It used to belong to my grandparents." Was her voice trembling?

"You're kidding me."

"I wish I was."

"Does it still belong to them?"

"I assume they sold it when they moved to Arizona, but that was more than twenty years ago. I was a kid. No one told me stuff like that."

Leo looked perplexed. "Why is he heading to a place connected to you?"

"That question is literally ripping my guts out right now."

He turned to her. It felt like he wanted to hold her hand. She clutched the steering wheel tighter.

"Describe it," he said.

"Steep road. The turnaround will be tight with Gabrielle taking up most of the space. The cabin faces downstream at an angle to the water. It's about a hundred feet or so off the creek. One room. An outhouse. Summertime plumbing."

"Which means?"

"They piped in water from the river. Also, there's a root cellar. I think they used this place as a secondary storage location, in fact. They were preppers before being prepared was called prepping. Back then, it was just smart to have a cabin where you could live off the grid if you needed to. Like your family had for generations."

"Were they religious?"

The turn-off was just ahead. She eased off the accelerator. "Why do you ask?"

"You've been known to trot out the occasional—"

BOOM!

Delaney kept her grip on the wheel and the speed steady, scanning for the source of the noise.

"What was that?" Leo shouted.

"If I had one guess, a shotgun. If I had two, death to a drone. It appears Brighton has more than a knife and my Staccato."

Leo hit the dashboard. "And he's on to us."

"Correct. No way are we driving one foot down that exposed road toward the cabin." Delaney stopped the Equinox. Her phone rang. "I can't believe we have signal out here. Check who it is."

Leo picked it up, fumble-fingered. "I think I accidentally answered it."

Skeeter's voice boomed through the cab. "You found her yet?"

"Put it on speaker." Louder, she said, "Talk fast, Skeeter. We're in pursuit of Lila's killer. We think he may have Kateena and Mary. And we're about to run out of cell signal."

The man sounded congested, like he'd been crying. "I'm sorry, Delaney. You trusted me with her."

His voice brought tear prickles to her own eyes. "Not your fault." She was the one who'd kept Kateena in her hospital room, then let her walk alone to meet Skeeter in the cafeteria. "I'll let you know when we have her." She ended the call.

Clint pulled up beside them. "Something shot my bird out of the sky."

"We saw," Delaney said. "I'm, uh, sorry about that."

"That's okay. You're going to owe me, though. I'm thinking I'll get to take you to dinner."

Leo muttered, "Is this guy for real?"

"Follow me." Delaney accelerated gradually to avoid making noise. When she was up to speed, she whipped the steering wheel one way and then the other past some rocks. "I'll pass the driveway. There's another one heading in the opposite direction about fifteen yards further. It leads to the old Sturgeon place. I want him to think we're headed there. Maybe even question whether we were after him or not. Then we'll come back on foot."

They shot past the driveway to the old Pace fishing cabin.

He nodded. "Can you get us down to the cabin? It looks rough."

"It's steep and rocky with thick undergrowth. I can get me down there. Clint should be fine. You, I'm less sure about, especially if you're wearing your snazzy shoes."

Over the bumps, Leo's voice vibrated. "My footwear is fine."

"Hang on." She turned left without slowing, and the Equinox displayed exceptionally bad shock absorption over the washboard.

"Time to call back-up since he's on to us. Agreed?"

She nodded. Leo made the call from his radio.

Fifty feet later, she slammed on the brakes, threw the shifter in park, and was out and digging ammo for her gun out of the back end before Leo had his seatbelt off. She slung a rifle over her shoulder by its strap and added an extra magazine for it to her holster.

Leo appeared beside Delaney and took out a rifle and his ammo. Clint pulled in behind them, then turned his Rubicon around. He got out and grabbed a rifle out of his trunk, slinging its strap over his shoulder, then pat-checking his holster.

Delaney was already running stiff-legged toward the drop off to the creek and cabin.

"Doesn't appear she's waiting for us, man," Clint said.

Leo stuffed an extra magazine in his pocket. "Delaney is not someone to disappoint." He jogged after her.

Clint laughed. "You forget I knew her back when. She's practically housebroken now compared to her younger days."

"Do you think I can't hear you, Rock-Below?" Delaney turned and flipped him off, then she ran on.

She heard Leo's voice. "The minor with the suspect? It's Delaney's niece, Kateena. She's only eleven. This is personal for her."

Delaney felt a rush of emotion and stumbled. For a split second, she lost her breath. Her rhythm.

Clint's light tone evaporated. "Got it. We're here for Kateena. Let's go."

Heavy footsteps pounded behind her. She slowed to allow them to catch up. Without breaking stride, she coached, "Do not roll an ankle. Do not make a sound. Stay with me. Tight. Clint, take the rear."

Between breaths, Leo said, "You sure you weren't in the military?"

Delaney ignored him. Ignored everything but the mission in front of them. Across the road ahead, she saw a very faint trail going over the side of the ravine, into the underbrush. In a whisper, she said, "Animal trail. Stay low." She pointed, then eased down to an awkward jog.

Deer weren't known for taking circuitous routes—mostly straight down—but the trail traversed the hillside. *Cattle*, she thought. It wasn't wide enough for her to pass without the rifle jostling the thick buckbrush on either side, but wider than if a deer had made it. Lucky break for them. Leo kicked a rock behind her.

She wheeled on him with a finger to her lips.

Clint's voice was barely louder than a breath, "You sound like a stampeding bison. You gotta stop that or you'll get us killed."

She slowed to help Leo move more quietly. Better to take a minute more than be dead. She sidled to avoid a branch. The path undulated, and on a rise, she saw the cabin only twenty feet ahead.

She put her hand up to signal the men, then switched to a deliberate tiptoe. There was a rock outcropping directly behind the cabin. She used to hide behind it when her grandmother was in a mood. She crouched there now.

Leo joined her. His breathing sounded like Dudley's when the dog got wound up. Delaney wanted to clap her hand over his mouth, but she understood. He was coming from sea level.

"What now?" he said quietly.

Clint knelt beside Leo.

She heard something. A voice. She put a finger to her lips.

Faintly, she heard it again. A man's voice. He wasn't trying to be quiet. She strained to hear better. Robert Brighton? Had she tracked him down? Her senses were pinging and zinging. Her motor was running in high gear. She believed it was him, but she wouldn't know for sure until she saw his face and whether it matched the photos Heigl had sent.

"Jefe, for once, shut up and listen. I'm telling you, there are cops coming for me at the cabin. I know you want me gone.

Help me to help you." Silence. "For the last time, of course I took care of Mary."

Delaney's heart sank.

"But if you don't help me out of here, they might connect us. I promise. You don't want that."

Connect us? He hadn't had anyone with him either time he'd attacked her. But it sounded like this Jefe was Brighton's accomplice. And if the partner wasn't here now, how long would it be until he showed up?

FIFTY

Delaney leaned between Clint and Leo, her voice barely audible to her own ears. "You guys heard him?"

They nodded.

"We have to take him now. Before his help arrives."

"I don't like it," Leo said.

"We can do this. Right now, it's three of us and one of him. I like those odds."

"He has two hostages, which divides our attention. That's not an advantage. We should wait for our own back-up."

"We could lose him. Or the hostages. I can't accept that." She shook her head.

"I'm wondering where the hostages are," Clint whispered. "Are there any other structures on the property?"

"An outhouse downhill a bit from the cabin. And he has Gabri—I mean, he has that big tractor he was driving. It has a sleeper in it, and I believe it's likely he snatched the minor—" she couldn't bring herself to say Kateena's name "—and transported her in it. The cabin itself is one room above ground and a root cellar below. The only door is around front. Two windows in front, one on each side, one in back."

"How do you see this playing out?"

"I think we should check the outhouse and vehicle before the cabin."

"That, at least, I agree with," Leo said.

"Clint, can you cover us?"

Clint's face was stoic. "No problem."

"Leo, we'll tackle the outhouse first. If it's empty, then Gabrielle." She gave up on self-correcting. The tractor had a name to her. She was going to use it. "When we finish up, assuming they're clear, we meet back here."

Leo shook his head. "Where I vote we wait for back-up."

"He's injured. I stabbed him in the face and bit his ear. He was in a major car crash. You saw how he was limping. We can do this together. But he's still strong enough to kill the hostages if we don't."

"He has your gun. And a shotgun."

"He can only shoot one at a time."

Leo nodded, although he didn't look convinced.

Delaney drew her gun and dropped it by her thigh, then held up her other hand and counted down from three with her fingers. Then she took off in a crouch, barely favoring her injuries as her rifle bounced against her back. The outhouse was on the downhill side of the cabin, with the door facing it. She pointed at the window that Brighton would be able to see them through, if he became aware of their presence. Clint sprinted ahead of her and behind the building. He took cover behind a stand of sturdy ponderosa pines.

Delaney positioned herself beside the open door and flicked off the safety on her gun. Leo put his hand on its latch, closed his eyes for a split second, then pulled it open as he stepped out of the way. Delaney entered, following her drawn gun and extended arms.

The small space was empty, save for a chipmunk that protested the interruption with angry chirps. Otherwise, the outhouse showed years of neglect. Gaps between boards, a woodsy odor unlike the one she remembered from childhood summers, and a thick layer of pine needles on the floor. Delaney made a hasty retreat, and Leo shut the door silently. The chipmunk's sounds might draw Brighton's attention, depending on his familiarity with wildlife behaviors. It would have alerted her to an unusual presence in the area. She sucked in a deep breath. They had to move fast, away from the chirping animal.

"Hurry," she whispered to Leo.

"Right behind you," he said.

She bent down and ran as fast as she could toward Gabrielle, both hands clutching her gun, taking care with her footing. If she fell, she'd shoot her foot off. Or worse. She stole a glance toward Clint. A rifle barrel peeked from between the pines. The side of his head and one eye were visible behind a trunk. Then she was focused on her own path again. With only yards to go, her leg buckled. Her heart slammed in her throat, and she fell forward, catching herself on one of Gabrielle's rear tires. Her other hand managed to hold on to the gun. She pushed herself upright and lunged behind the protection of the tractor's bulk. Leo was right behind her. *You nearly ruined everything, Delaney,* she chided herself.

He put a hand on her shoulder. "Are you okay?"

"Fine." She didn't mean to snap at him, but the word came out harsh. "Fine," she repeated in a calmer tone. "You've got the door again." She moved into position, then nodded at him.

He tried the handle, but the truck door didn't open. "Locked."

Delaney thought about the keys on the ring, back in her purse inside the Equinox. *Fat lot of good they're doing us there. Dammit!* She and Leo couldn't risk entry through the passenger side except as a last resort, since it faced the cabin, and she wasn't about to bust out the window or shoot the lock. But there might be a solution. She took a step back and looked at the sleeper window. She'd left the windows on both sides propped open for ventilation while in storage. If Brighton hadn't closed them, she could get in that way.

And he hadn't.

She pointed at the window and shrugged out of her rifle strap, then set the long gun on the ground. "Get me up there? I can crawl in through the window."

Leo didn't bother answering. He moved to stand under it, bent one leg with his hip and knee turned out, and held up a hand. She put the safety back on her gun and holstered it. While she'd never been a gymnast or cheerleader, she'd climbed to stand on plenty of shoulders during water games in the town swimming pool. She could do this. He turned to look at her. Their eyes locked, and she had trouble ripping her gaze away. Then she gripped his hand and climbed from his thigh to stand on his shoulders, with her other hand braced against Gabrielle. She popped out the screen and pushed the window up, then hauled herself in. The wounds that her adrenaline had quieted screamed at her. She shoulder-rolled onto the bed, landing in a squat on the floor. It took a second for her eyes to adjust to the lower light. When they did, she saw a roll of duct tape and some rope on the floor and the lid to her toolbox open. She checked the inventory. The duct tape was missing, and it seemed light on bungee cords and rope.

Kateena. He held Kateena in here.

"Kateena?" she whispered. There was no hiding space in the cab or sleeper, though. The girl wasn't in here. *If he brought her here, she's inside the cabin.*

POP! POP! Rifle fire? That would be Clint.

CRACK.

Gunshot! Brighton was on to them.

"Oof!" The voice was right outside the sleeper window. *Not Leo!*

Delaney's heart did a swan dive. She heard a thud. His

body hitting the ground? She didn't dare call out. She scrambled to the passenger side door and searched for Brighton. No sign of him between Gabrielle and the cabin and outhouse. Not in Clint's direction. *He must be uphill on the driver's side.*

POP.

Clint's answering fire from the rifle.

She opened the door as quietly as she could and slipped out and down to the ground, leaving the door open as a shield for her head and torso.

CRACK. THWUMP.

A shot had hit her door. *At least Clint and I are drawing him away from Leo.* Stealth was no longer an issue. "Leo, are you all right?"

"Flesh wound." His voice was strained.

"Are you covered?"

"Enough."

Thank God.

CRACK. Another *THWUMP* into the door. Lower this time. His next shot might take out her legs. She edged low around the back of the rig.

POP. POP. POP. Pause. Clint providing covering fire. Now was her chance. The cabin or Leo?

Kateena. She bent over and barreled toward the front door. Only ten yards. Halfway there, she heard a *CRACK.* Log exploded on the cabin's exterior, peppering her with small hunks of wood. *POP. POP.* She ran pell-mell toward the door, slowing to twist the handle. Then she kicked it open and dove inside, down and to the left, landing hard against a bed frame and the wooden floor. The dark cabin interior was a fleeting impression of dust and memories.

BOOM!

That's not a handgun. Or a rifle. That's the shotgun.

BOOM! Pause. He was chambering a shell. *BOOM!*

A scream from Clint's hiding place. The hair rose on her

neck. Then silence. She was on her own. Brighton was out there, and he'd be coming for her. A sound from the other side of the room tore her thoughts away from Brighton. Muffled shouts. She rolled over. Saw Kateena's back. The girl was curled around the base of the wood burning stove that doubled as heat source and cook top. Remembering the duct tape and missing bungee cords, Delaney crawled to the small kitchen area where her grandmother had stored cutlery, plates, and cups. She pulled out the single drawer, peered over the lip, and reached in for a knife. She found a table knife. It would have to do.

"Coming, Kateena. I'm coming." She stayed on her hands and knees, conscious of the low front windows. But she had only feet to cover in the small space. She knelt over her niece and began unhooking the bungee cords. It was a quick job, and when Kateena was free of the stove, she rolled toward Delaney, huddling into her. Delaney felt as if her heart was shooting fireworks. She willed herself to work faster and started to work on the girl's ankles. *If nothing else, she'll be able to run away.* The serration on the old blade was dull. Delaney put her weight against it, sawing as hard as she could. How many layers of tape had Brighton used? She became conscious of Kateena trying to speak through some kind of gag, but she kept sawing.

BOOM!

Bits of splintered wood rained down on her from inside the cabin. His shot had gone high. His next one wouldn't. The tape gave way. She shoved the knife in her pocket, certain it wasn't sharp enough to do her harm. Then she jerked the rag out of Kateena's mouth.

"Get behind the stove. Quickly."

Delaney rolled to her side and aimed through the open door toward where she imagined Brighton would be coming from. Then she whirled and fired at the side window on the downhill side. Glass cracked and shattered outward. She rushed over to it and knocked the rest of the glass out with the butt of the pistol.

"Come on," she said and held out her free hand.

Kateena leaped to her feet. "What are we going to do?"

"I'm sending you out this window, then I'm coming after you."

"But my hands!"

"No time." Delaney hoisted her up and out the window, watching her catch herself like a cat on her feet and bound hands. *Youth.* She feared she wouldn't be as graceful. To avoid any glass remnants, she planted her jeans-clad butt and flannel-protected back in the window frame and swung her legs out. She scooted off the ledge, feeling a snag as glass ripped at her pockets, but no pain. She landed on her feet.

Now what? She had fallen colleagues out here and Mary was likely in the root cellar, if she was still alive. But she had to get Kateena to safety. That was the most important first thing. She could come back for the others. Again, she thought about cutting Kateena's wrists free, but she didn't dare risk it. Brighton was out there. He would be coming after them.

"Put your fingers around my belt and follow me."

"What if I can't keep up?" Kateena's eyes were huge.

She crouched and cradled the girl's face for the briefest of moments. "Then I'll slow down. But you can do it. You can."

Kateena nodded. Delaney turned and the girl slid fingers around her belt. Delaney set off for the back of the house. She'd take Kateena out the way they'd come in. She sped up, feeling pressure against her belt. Kateena stumbled but held on.

BOOM!

The shot was coming from inside the cabin.

Psych, sucker. Delaney gathered more speed as they started the climb. Kateena was panting, but she was keeping up.

A male voice bellowed from behind the cabin *He's outside again.* "You can't get away from me, Delaney."

BOOM!

Shot peppered the trees, shredding leaves and embedding

into dirt. He'd aimed to their right, on the downhill side. Kateena whimpered, but Delaney didn't dare make a sound to draw Brighton's attention.

CRACK.

Handgun fire? Was it Brighton, Clint, or Leo?

CRACK.

"Run, Delaney!" a male voice shouted.

It was Leo. His voice was thready. She wanted to go to him, but she couldn't. He was on his own.

BOOM!

This time, no underbrush or trees shook around them. Brighton had fired back in Leo's direction. Her partner's diversion had worked.

"Delaney." A whisper.

She froze.

"It's Clint." His face appeared in the underbrush from where he'd forced his way through.

"I thought you were hit?" she whispered back.

"My gun hand. Let me take Kateena. I'll get her out of here. You can go back for Leo and Mary." He was shirtless, with the garment wrapped around a hand the size of a club. Blood had soaked through the fabric.

Delaney gathered Kateena in her arms for a short hug. "This is Clint Rock-Below. He's a police officer. Go with him. Do what he says."

"No! Don't leave me." Kateena's eyes flooded with tears.

Delaney smoothed the girl's flyaway hair from her face. It sprang back immediately. "You'll be fine. And I'll be right behind you with Leo and Mary."

"You can't promise that."

Clint laughed. "Oh, yes she can. Didn't you see your aunt in action back there?"

Kateena nodded, still looking doubtful. Delaney heard another volley of gunfire behind them. She needed to help Leo.

She held up two fingers. "I promise. Now get."

"I love you, Aunt Delaney."

"I love you, too." She kissed Kateena's forehead.

Kateena stepped toward Clint. The one small step ripped away a piece of Delaney's heart. She hated letting her go with him. She had to let her go with him.

He put a hand on Kateena's shoulder. "I'll take care of her like my own, Delaney. Here, let's get your wrists free, Kateena."

She had business to finish back at the cabin, and she was going to need clear eyes and a clear head to see it through.

FIFTY-ONE

Delaney pressed her back against the downhill exterior wall of the cabin, stepping gingerly on the glass she'd sprayed outward earlier. The gunfire between Brighton and Leo had ceased, and she didn't dare call attention to her position. Mary was the next priority. Stealth was paramount. She snuck a look through the shot-out window.

A man was peering out the front window farthest from her, a shotgun propped on the windowsill pointed out and swiveling back and forth.

She memorized his position and withdrew her head. Closed her eyes. Drew centering breaths in and out. Then, moving as quickly as she could, she inserted her gun hand into the window and fired at him, following the shot with her body, diving to the floor.

She heard a grunt as she landed. *I hit him.*

She had to get as far away from the window as she could, because, if she hadn't disabled him, he'd likely return fire in the direction from where her shot had come, out of reflex. She rolled toward the back wall where she recalled from her childhood days that there was a small table. Only the table wasn't where she remembered it. It was pushed away from the wall. She crashed into it, knocking it over. She looked up, confused. A chest was standing against the back wall. She crawled toward it.

And then she realized her shot hadn't done much damage, because Brighton was moving—not that there was a lot of space in the cabin. He was on his feet, shotgun still in his hand, and he lunged toward the stove. She tracked him with the gun. If he took cover behind it, she couldn't fire. Her shots could ricochet back at her. She pulled the trigger. He screamed and dropped the shotgun, crumpling to the floor. The gun discharged toward the door. Wood chips were flying in every direction. She'd got him. But was it enough to stop him this time?

The sound he made was like an angry bull. He rose to his feet and charged her. Her shot had only wounded him. She drew a bead on him and fired again. Training told her to take the center mass shot, but she wanted answers from this man. She lowered her aim to his thigh.

"*Oomph.*"

She'd hit him—which wasn't hard since he was five feet from her. But he still didn't stop.

She tried to roll away toward the front door, but he landed on her like she was a rodeo steer, and he was the wrestler. *This man has been stabbed and shot multiple times. He lost his shotgun. He's unstoppable. How could he keep going after all his injuries?* She'd seen this before with suspects cranked up on drugs. Could he be under the influence? *And he has another gun somewhere, and a knife.* Her head jammed into the shelves. Metal clanged then rained down on the floor around her. Glass shattered. His weight slammed her gun hand into the floor, into the bite of broken glass. She lost her grip. Wriggled her fingers for it. Ignored the tortuous glass. Touched it. Couldn't grab hold of it. Knocked it out of her reach. *Under the shelves?* He clamped his hand on her wrist. One, then the other. No more contact with her gun. She bucked and kicked wildly. They were about the same size. Maybe even the same strength. But he had the advantage on top.

Her instincts told her to fight, but her brain broke in. *Lull him into a false sense of security, then strike.* She ceased struggling.

The face staring down at her with malevolence was a stabbed, scraped, shot, bitten, and bruised Robert Brighton. She was sure of it. It was electrifying to finally see the man she'd been hunting. But there was something about his face... What was it?

"Not so tough without your gun, Delaney?" he said.

Her name from his lips was vile. His weight was a boulder, stealing her breath. Something hard was digging into her chest. She forced words out anyway. She wanted him talking, not reaching for that knife or her own gun.

"I didn't have one when I bit your ear or zip-tied your neck and stabbed you in the face earlier, Robert."

From their close quarters, Delaney felt him grow preternaturally still. Then he lifted his face and spat in hers.

Brighton said, "I killed your partner. You're all by yourself now, and I have you."

His words hurt, but she held onto her strength. The strength of her mind and her resolve. Leo might be gone, but Mary needed her, and Kateena probably wasn't to safety yet.

"You gonna carve me and my bones with the T1 knife you made? Or stick with your new burning technique?" Delaney tried to scan the room for weapons without moving her eyes. It was difficult, but she caught sight of something large and black in her peripheral vision. A rack of fireplace tools. Now all she had to do was turn the tables on Brighton to reach them.

His mouth dropped. Then his cheeks flamed. "I'm going to make you my next delivery. Because you can't stop me. And because you're making me want to."

She smiled at him, trying not to think about his slime oozing into her eye from her forehead. "This is me not shaking in my boots."

"Funny lady. You know, we're not so different, you and me."

"We have nothing in common."

Brighton was the one smiling now, but she sensed a slight lowering of his guard. A softening of his grip. "Your mom left you when you were young, just like mine. Well, mine didn't just leave. Maybe your father delivered your mother to her fate, like mine did."

Don't react. Don't give him the satisfaction. "You think you know things about me, huh?"

"I've been in your room. Driven your rig. And I read a really nice piece about you in the town paper." She felt his muscles relax.

When Delaney got her hands on that reporter, she wasn't going to be gentle. "What a coincidence. I read a really nice file about you from Las Vegas."

Three. Two. One. Now! Without tensing first, Delaney exploded into a powerful twist, wrenching her wrists from his hands and her body to the side and over. She had to get onto her stomach. She had no power on her back. Brighton reacted quickly. He threw his weight onto her and clawed for her arms. Delaney was able to roll to her side, but he held her there. They grappled for a few seconds with no sound but their panting breaths and grunts. Delaney kicked. She elbowed. *Wrestling. I should have learned wrestling.* But she had played soccer. She threw her head back.

CRUNCH.

"Argh!" Brighton screamed. His hands lifted to his face.

Delaney's vision exploded with stars. *Do not stop.* She rolled to her stomach and, calling on all of her muscles from calves to core to chest, she pushed up and got a knee under her with Brighton still clinging to her back. Straightened her arms.

Began to feel hopeful. She looked up and eyed the fireplace tools—she had to get her other knee up. Make a lunge for them.

Delaney spurted forward and grabbed the poker she'd watched her father make from an old tire iron and sharpened to a lethal tip. Rough, ugly. Homemade with love. *Thank you, Daddy.* Brighton still had hold of her waist. The weight of his body was trapping her legs. But she didn't need those for what she was going to do. Careful not to twist all the way onto her back, she rotated her upper body, propping herself on one hand, moving fast as he came for her. With her other hand, she raised the poker and brought it crashing into the top of his head, just as he lunged for her. Flattening her.

THWACK.

She felt the blow pass from Brighton to her. His proximity had decreased her power, but it was still hard enough. His head landed on her face, nose digging into her cheek, forehead cracking her nose, then he didn't move. She shoved him and scooted out from under him. Blood dripped from her nose onto the floor. She climbed to her feet, using the poker for balance, breathing hard. He'd come to quickly. She hadn't hit him hard enough to do more than stun him. She had to secure him somehow.

She looked up. Kateena stood beside Brighton, staring open-mouthed at Delaney.

What was she doing here? Where was Clint? Delaney had to get her out of here. Her voice was an urgent shout. "Get out! Now, Kateena!"

The girl stared at Brighton, unmoving. *Shock?*

Delaney scanned the floor for her gun. Didn't see it. Remembered it sliding under the shelves, across the field of glass. "It's going to be okay. But you have to go."

She glanced back at Brighton. He was stirring. When he woke up, he'd go for Kateena first. The girl Delaney would do anything for. Anything. And he knew it.

Delaney was out of options. All she had was the poker. She took a heaving breath, then drove the poker into the back of his hand as hard as she could, pinning it to the floor. *Maybe that will buy me time to find my gun.*

Kateena shrieked. Brighton roared and starting writhing like an injured snake. Delaney wiped his spittle from her face with the hem of her shirt, then grabbed another tool from the fireplace rack. It was a small shovel. The working end wasn't useful to her. It was the heavy handle she was after.

She turned back to Kateena. "You have to get to the cars. Now. It isn't safe."

Kateena's bottom lip jutted out. "I don't know where they are. And Clint can't show me. He fell and broke his ankle."

Delaney swallowed. This wasn't good. "I understand. But go wait outside. I'll be there soon."

Brighton lifted his shoulders like a cobra ready to strike. He let out a supernatural scream. "I'm going to send you to hell. Straight to hell." Then he slumped to the floor. His whole torso heaved.

Kateena shook her head. She tore her eyes from Brighton back to her aunt. Tear tracks streaked her face, but her eyes were dry, and her voice was determined. "I can't leave. You're all I've got left."

Delaney could barely speak over the lump in her throat. "You're so grounded when we get home. But I love you." She couldn't stop to toss Kateena out, not with Brighton only partially restrained. "Hand me your belt."

"What?"

"Your belt. Take it off and throw it to me."

Kateena fumbled at her waist, then pulled her belt out of her jeans. She tossed it to Delaney.

"Thanks. Now, all the way outside. On the porch. I mean it."

"But why? She's unconscious."

"He. For now. Stand outside the door."

"Okay." *Kateena doing what she's told? A first time for everything.* "Do you know who she is?"

Brighton roared again. He reached for the poker. Delaney brought the handle of the shovel down on his head. That silenced the roar, and he fell back to the floor with a loud thump.

Delaney moved to his feet with the belt. When she slid it around the back of his ankles, she saw the handle of a knife inside a boot holster. She threaded Kateena's belt through its buckle. *Holes in the wrong place.* She cinched the belt like a noose, holding it by the tongue, then pulled the knife out. It looked like an antique. But she didn't care about its age. She was more interested in the chip missing from the wicked six-inch blade. She shuddered. *This is what he used on Lila. Probably Mary, too. And would have used on me. On Kateena.* She poised the knife tip against the leather and dug it in. Then she fastened the buckle to the hole. Tested the restraint. *Just the right length. Nice and tight.*

Delaney ran the few steps to the kitchen, knife in one hand, fireplace shovel in the other. She rifled drawers in the small cupboard and came out with a burlap apron with long muslin strings. Her grandmother had worn the utilitarian garment every time they'd visited the cabin. She held both strings in one hand and cut them off with a slice of the knife.

"Take the shovel." Delaney handed it to Kateena, who was standing just outside the doorway. Having a weapon was good, even if the situation was far from ideal.

"Okay." She cocked it over her shoulder like a baseball bat.

Delaney knelt by Brighton and pushed the knife out of his reach, toward the black iron stove. Suddenly, the girl wasn't alone. A male figure staggered to a stop beside her. Delaney started to go for the knife again until she realized it was Leo, looking a lot worse for the wear, standing on one leg and leaning against the door frame. One entire side of his pants was soaked in blood. But her heart soared. *He's not dead.* She stood, unable to stop herself.

"Leo!" Kateena cried.

As if in slow motion, Delaney saw it play out. Brighton's eyes popped open. With his one unrestrained arm, he reached behind his back and pulled her Staccato from his waistband. *It had been there all along?*

She threw herself at him, sure that she was about to be shot point blank.

POP.

The bitter, burned powder smell, the ringing in her ears. He hadn't shot her. *Oh, God. Kateena!!* Delaney landed on his arm. His finger was still inside the trigger guard. She grabbed his wrist and struggled, shaking, until the gun was aimed away from Kateena and Leo. Then she banged his wrist against the floor until he dropped the gun. She paused, still holding onto him, panting. His eyes had closed.

How easy it would have been for him to put a bullet in her temple while he was holding her down. Or to shove his knife under her ribs. *No more than forty-eight or less than thirty-six hours after they were taken,* Heigl had said about the time of Brighton's victims' deaths in Las Vegas. *Had he believed he couldn't kill me yet?*

"Aunt Delaney!" Kateena's voice was a wail.

She turned toward her niece. The girl was kneeling over the crumpled figure of Leo.

FIFTY-TWO

"Leo!" Delaney stuck the gun in her waistband and sprinted to her unconscious partner. Brighton had been shooting at Leo, and his bullet had found its mark. "Where did it hit him?"

"I don't know. I don't know." Kateena rocked back and forth.

"That's okay."

Delaney knelt beside Leo. Not a head wound, thank God. Ninety percent of those were fatal. *Check the arteries first.* The iliac in the groin didn't appear to be hit. His neck and carotid seemed uninjured. She pulled open his shirt. Blood seeped from his left shoulder. Panic seized her. She ripped off her outer shirt, balled it up, and stuffed it into the wound.

Leo moaned and jerked.

Not the heart. Please not the heart. It wasn't gushing. That was good. But she couldn't tourniquet the area. She needed to keep him from bleeding out before they could get help.

His eyes opened. His voice was a croak. "Delaney."

"Hush. Can you put your hand here and hold it against yourself, hard?" She positioned his opposite hand across his chest to the wound and her shirt.

"I'll try."

That wasn't good enough. "Kateena, could you push down on Leo?"

Her mouth fell open. She shook her head. But she said, "Yes."

"Good girl. Like this." Delaney put Kateena's hand over Leo's. "Press together, okay?"

"But I'll hurt him."

"I'm fine," Leo said. But the pallor in his face said otherwise.

"Did you call for back-up yet?" Delaney asked.

"After I was hit outside. On their way."

"Good." She returned to Brighton, snared his free hand, pulled across his body, and started tying it to the other.

Brighton jerked awake. "You bitch. You evil, evil bitch. That hurts." His eyes drilled into Delaney's.

Delaney leaned over and gave him a tight smile. "Should be nothing to a tough guy like you. A man who hurts women for fun. And certainly nothing compared to what you've done to them."

"What I've done? Don't you realize the evil of women?" He swung his legs around, trying to kick her.

Delaney scooted behind his head and wound the apron strings tighter. She made circuits until she only had enough string left to knot. "You're not going to go back to the whole apple in the Garden of Eden debacle, are you? Thanks to my grandparents, I'm well-schooled on the subject."

"People act like only men can be evil. Study the female serial killers." Again, he attempted to catch her with his bound legs, but this time the attempt was feebler.

She could see now where the bullets had struck him. One in his right shoulder, two in his right thigh. *I need some range time. I'm pulling left.* "Not something I make a habit of." She tried to knot the strings and lost her grip. The strings unwound.

He slumped to the ground, seemingly giving up, but that only made her more wary. "Ilse Koch. Ma Barker. The Blood Countess. Dagmar Overbye. The Chocolate Cream Killer. Amelia Dyer. Belle Gunness. Aileen Wuornos. Tillie Klimek. Madame Blanque. Leonarda Cianciulli. The Little Old Lady Killer. The Torture Mother. People try to say that most serial killers are men. *Read a little history.* I'm saving the world, one woman at a time."

Some of the names sounded familiar. Delaney wished she had a recorder. The amount of crazy Brighton had just exhaled was a thing to study. She hurried to retie him.

Leo was shaking his head. He caught her gaze and widened his filmy eyes. Apparently, he was having similar thoughts. She was amazed he was alert.

Kateena said, "Why would a woman say that about women? That doesn't make any sense."

Delaney had almost forgotten her niece was there listening to this man spew. Brighton's insanity had been mesmerizing.

Brighton said, "The mother wasn't as smart as her daughter. The aunt isn't, either."

Delaney froze in the act of crossing the ends of the strings to tie them. *Oh, Kateena.* But what was he saying? Kateena had called him a girl. Delaney stared at the man she knew as Robert Brighton. The lack of facial hair. The shoulders no broader than Delaney's own. The slight curve of the hips. And, yes, the face. That's what she had seen earlier. He was pretty enough to pass as a girl.

A *girl.* Robert Brighton was a woman. They'd have to add another name to that list of female serial killers he'd given her.

"So, why?" Kateena said, uncowed, still pressing both hands into Leo's wound. The girl's face was flushed. Brighton had just admitted to killing her mother. But the expression she wore was one of pure, determined intensity.

His face crumpled. "My father knew what to do."

"What do you mean?" Delaney finished her knot but stayed crouched beside him. Something was hanging from a heavy chain around his neck. He shifted, and it tumbled out from under the neckline of his shirt. A blue stone pendant, a hospital bracelet, and... her medallion. She heard a rushing in her ears, but knew it was coming from inside her. She snatched for the objects, breaking the chain.

"Hey! Those are mine."

She scooped the items from the floor. The medallion. Her dad. Her relief was so great that for a moment she froze with the pendant safely tucked in her hand. "Answer me and I may give some of them back." *I won't.*

"He knew that if I was a girl, I'd have to be delivered from my evil. That my grandfather would insist on it. The things I would make him and my father want to do wouldn't be their fault."

Bile rose in Delaney's mouth. She'd never heard a more eloquent pitch for the evil of men.

"My father delivered my mother instead and raised me as a boy. He saved me. He taught me. I am his life's work. His mission is mine."

"So, are you a man or a woman?" Delaney asked.

"I am who my father raised me to be."

A man who kills. *Kind of like a pit bull whose owner raises it to fight to the death.* It was never the fault of the animal. *But human beings grow up and can make their own choices. Can't they?*

"But why my mother?" The tears Kateena had held at bay were falling now. The reality of who this person was and what he—or she?—had done to Lila was a heavy load for an eleven-year-old. How Delaney wished she could restart this day and prevent this psychotic creature from kidnapping her niece.

"I wait for the signs."

"Which are what?" Delaney asked.

"If a man seeks me out for the delivery, it is a sign. If she makes me want to do bad things, it is proof."

Seek him out? Like, what, *hire* him? "Did someone hire you to kill Lila? And Mary?"

His voice seemed weaker. "The same man who will kill you soon."

Delaney felt dizzy. These were hired hits? *Jefe. The man on the phone. Not an accomplice. An employer.* There was someone awful enough out there to hire this depraved person and manipulate him into doing the dirty work? "What's his name? Jefe?"

Brighton shook his head. Her head? Delaney's own was spinning.

"What's *your* name?" she asked. "The one you were born with. Is it Robert? Or something else?"

Silence was the only reply. The killer stared at the wall, eyes glazing over. It was a miracle Brighton was still conscious. Still alive.

Delaney stood, backing away.

"You can't leave me like this," Brighton whispered.

"Sure, I can." Delaney picked the knife off the floor and set it on the iron stove. Retrieved her Staccato from behind it. She jammed it into the back of her waistband, like Brighton had done. Then she reached under the shelves and felt around until she found the department gun. She put it back in her holster.

She leaned down and patted Robert's back. Nothing more there.

Brighton said, "If you leave me, I won't tell you where Mary is."

Delaney didn't need him for that. It was time to find Mary. To find out if Mary was even still alive.

FIFTY-THREE

Delaney walked straight to the chest on the back wall and moved it aside, revealing the trap door to the cellar.

"How did you know where to find the door?" Brighton's voice was a wheeze.

"It's a small town. This cabin belonged to my grandparents. I did a lot of climbing up and down that ladder, getting things from that root cellar when I was a kid." She yanked open the trapdoor. "Mary?"

"You're too late." Brighton coughed weakly.

She refused to accept that. "Mary, it's Delaney. I'm coming to help you." Delaney grabbed a battery-powered lantern from the top of the chest, switched it on, and started down the ladder. When she reached the bottom, she turned.

She gasped and covered her face with her forearm.

The woman on the floor was a bloody mess—unmoving—and the smell in the cellar was putrid. She lowered her arm and shone the light on her. *So much blood. Maybe I am too late.* But as bad as she looked, it was clearly Mary. Delaney sank to her knees and grabbed Mary's wrist, feeling for a pulse. Just when she was about to admit defeat, the woman's eyes fluttered open. Then they widened.

"Delaney," she whispered, her voice a croak.

"You're alive! Thank God."

Mary closed her eyes. She was silent for a few moments. Delaney shook her gently. The eyes opened again. "Did you kill him, The Delivery Man?"

"Next best thing."

"Good." Mary smiled, revealing bloody teeth.

"The Delivery Man—is that what you call him?"

"That's what he calls himself. Get me out of here, please?"

Delaney smiled back at her. "No problem."

Mary's eyes drifted shut again. This time Delaney didn't rouse her. She put her arms under the smaller woman and hefted her over her shoulder. She sent up a silent, fervent prayer. *If you're listening, big guy, please send an able-bodied helper of legal age before Jefe delivers reinforcements.*

Then she began the thigh-burning climb up the ladder.

FIFTY-FOUR

Delaney looked back from the sleeper into Gabrielle's cab at Leo in the passenger seat. His head was back, his eyes open. His bleeding had slowed, and Delaney had changed out her shirt for gauze from her medical kit, both for his shoulder and his leg. He'd insisted he was well enough to sit. Elevating his wound over his heart was a good idea, but she'd keep an eye on him. He was stiffening up and hurting. It was written all over his strained face. She was, too, but she didn't have bullet wounds to the shoulder and thigh. "You okay?"

After Leo—her most critical patient—she'd assisted Clint, Mary, and—very grudgingly—Brighton. Triage. It would have gone faster with help, but theirs had a long trip to make from north of Kearny to south and off-road. She expected the cavalry any minute. And Jefe.

Delaney and Kateena finished tucking Mary into the tractor's sleeper bunk. Kateena snapped the sleeping net into place over her. The trip into the rig had been tough on Mary and not so easy on Delaney and Kateena. Mary looked like the target in a knife-throwing contest, but she had improved some with painkillers from Delaney's first aid tub and sips Kateena had been giving her from a water bottle. But the turning point for Mary seemed to come when she woke up in the cabin and saw the person she called The Delivery Man speared to the floor. Delaney hadn't removed the poker, on the theory that the wound might bleed worse if she did.

She shoved her shirt behind her gun for even easier access, just in case. She nodded at Kateena. "You're doing a great job. Can you keep holding Mary's hand? It will make her feel less scared and alone." *And it will keep you in the sleeper where it's safer in case of more trouble.*

Kateena nodded. She leaned down and whispered, "I'm here, Mary. You're going to be okay."

Mary had fallen asleep again. That was the best painkiller of all.

Delaney pulled her medallion pendant from her pocket. It was unscathed. *I'll do better keeping it safe from now on, Dad.* She reached in front of Leo, opened the glove box, and placed it inside. Then she heard a vehicle coming down the road. She scrambled into the driver's seat and looked in the sideview, tense and ready.

It was the sheriff's truck.

She let out the breath she'd been holding and turned to Leo. "Back-up has arrived. Fentworth. And an ambulance behind him."

Leo's hand was on his gun, but he dropped it. "Good. Maybe he can give that sicko a ride to jail. Properly restrained."

She nodded. "I hope so. I don't want to put EMTs at risk. Are you good to keep an eye on Mary and Kateena?"

He gave her a tight nod. She knew he wanted to do more. She would have in his shoes. But he'd done plenty, dragging himself around on his injured leg to engage and re-engage Brighton during the heat of the battle, which had allowed her to get back to Kateena. He was good back-up. Better than good.

She jumped out, greeting the sheriff and a city cop she

hadn't met before as they exited the truck. "Glad to see you guys."

The sheriff's lips puckered. "I'm tempted not to return the sentiment, since you were supposed to be home resting with your family. But, given the outcome, I suppose I'm on the losing side of this argument."

Delaney smirked, glad he wasn't angry at her. "That's not unusual, sir."

The sheriff clapped her on the shoulder, then pulled her into a quick side hug. "This is Officer Ted Cross with the Kearny PD. Ted, Delaney Pace."

Ted, a ginger-haired behemoth, stuck out his hand. "Nice to meet you, Delaney."

"You, too." She shook his hand and addressed her mentor. "There's a chance more bad guys are on the way, so we need to move out."

The sheriff nodded briskly, jarring his hat loose. "Tell me what you need."

"Mary is alive. Leo was shot twice. I've got them in my rig and need to get them to hospital ASAP."

"And Kateena?"

"Unharmed, physically. Probably headed for years of therapy." *Or life as an ice road trucker.*

"Thank God she's safe."

"Brighton is waiting for you inside the cabin, a little worse for the wear. And Clint Rock-Below from the state police took a bad fall on the hill. He's got a compound fracture in his leg. I gave him water and painkillers. He'd already stabilized the leg and stopped the bleeding himself. But he needs help."

The sheriff pursed his lips. "Sounds like Clint needs a ride from the EMTs so we don't make him worse."

"I'll tell them how to find him."

"All right. Ted and I will take Brighton. I'll let the units behind know to come secure the scene."

"Also, both Leo's and Clint's vehicles are parked on the road to the Sturgeon place."

The sheriff raised his brows. In a dry voice, he said, "Oh, is that all?"

Her smile was grim. "It's been tough sledding, sir."

"I look forward to hearing all about it. I'll treat you and Kateena to a burger and a milkshake tomorrow after you've rested."

"Perfect."

The sheriff shooed Delaney aside as the two officers loaded and secured Brighton's limp body into the back seat of the sheriff's truck. She didn't want to admit how badly she hurt, but she was glad for the respite. She used the time to get the EMTs en route to Clint.

When she returned, the men were finished. Fentworth walked her back to Gabrielle. "Nice job, Deputy Investigator."

"Thank you, Sheriff. For everything, I mean."

He smiled and handed her a cold bottle of water. "See you in town."

FIFTY-FIVE

Leo felt a sharp pain in his chest when he lost sight of Delaney that didn't ease until the driver's door opened.

Kateena leaned out of the sleeper and whispered, "My aunt is a badass, isn't she?" Then she looked worried. "It's okay to say that, you know. It's in the Bible."

Leo smiled. "A definite badass."

The sheriff did a K-turn to reverse directions in his truck, and headed up the hill.

Delaney bounced into the driver's seat. "Everyone good?" She fired up the engine.

"Yes."

Good." She shifted gears and started the tractor up the hill. The low gear made for slow but powerful climbing. It was Leo's first time in a vehicle like Gabrielle. She was almost as impressive as her owner. "How is Mary?"

Kateena said, "Asleep. Snoring a little. I'm still holding her hand."

"Good. That will help more than anything. Get Leo some fresh gauze, please. And pressure, Leo. I don't like your color."

"I've felt better," he said.

The drive toward the highway was just as bumpy but much less hair-raising than the one in. Leo gripped the arm rest and tried not to let his pain show. Figured he would pass out soon and that it would be a blessing.

"I don't dare go any faster," Delaney said. "The ride in the cabin can be uncomfortable even when you're not hurt."

Leo winced. "No problem."

One after another, law enforcement vehicles passed them heading out toward the fishing cabin. Delaney and Leo waved to each as they went by. Ten minutes later, they rumbled over the cattle guard at the mouth of the road then rolled onto the smooth pavement of the highway.

"Is that better?" Delaney said.

He ungritted his teeth. "I didn't say a word."

"You didn't have to. Now that my adrenaline is wearing off, the bumps are hurting me, too."

A slight vibration shook the rig's frame. In the distance, Leo heard a sound, like an impact. It was hard to tell over the engine and road noise. He looked at Delaney. She was frowning.

"What do you think?" he said.

"I think there's a collision ahead." She backed off on her speed as they entered a sharp curve through a forested area.

When they hit the next straightaway, Leo spotted smoke over a group of trees. "I think you're right. I'll call it in." Getting his phone out made him see stars, but he was relieved to see reliable, strong signal. Communications would have been easier with his police radio, but since it had been pulverized by Brighton, he put the phone on his good leg and punched in 911.

Delaney navigated an S curve and then braked hard. Leo gasped in pain.

In front of them, the road was blocked with the remains of two trucks. One, a white sheriff's department pickup. The other, what looked to be an old brown and beige Silverado.

There was no human activity outside the vehicles. No movement that Leo could see inside them, either.

"No!" Delaney shouted. She pulled the rig to the side of the road, put it in park, and turned off her engine. Somehow, she had the presence of mind to turn on her hazard lights.

"911, what's your emergency?" a woman's voice said in Leo's ear.

Delaney was out the door and running.

"Aunt Delaney?" Kateena shouted.

Leo said, "This is Kearny County Deputy Leo Palmer. There's a very serious vehicular accident at..." He looked for a mile marker and gave it and the highway number to the dispatcher. "I need to get out and work the scene."

"I'll let Sheriff Fentworth know. He's in the vicinity."

Leo's eyes burned. "I'm sorry to have to say this, but his appears to be one of the vehicles involved in the collision. Send help. Fire. Rescue. Ambulance. Officers." He ended the call and threw open his door. He turned back to Kateena. "You stay here with Mary. I cannot stress that enough. We need you to take care of her. No matter what. Your aunt will be fine."

"But—"

He made his voice hard as rock. "No buts. Promise me."

Her lower lip trembled. "I p-p-promise."

He had no choice but to trust her. He climbed down from the tractor, woozy, stepping first onto his uninjured leg. He shouted as loudly as he could. "Wait, Delaney. The vehicles could—"

One fireball shot into the air, then another, as the two vehicles ignited. Delaney kept running toward them without slowing down. There was no way he could catch her. He wasn't even sure he could get to her at all.

"Delaney, no!" he shouted.

"Help her!" Kateena screamed behind him.

Leo hobbled after Delaney. She'd never hear him. He saved

his breath. But he couldn't stop the voice in his head. *Please stop, Delaney. Please stop.*

The dual explosions were close to simultaneous. Debris shot toward him, along with a wall of heat and pressure. He turned his back toward the inferno and put his right arm up to shield his face. Something hot stung his neck. *Delaney.* He moved toward her, lopsided, as the shockwave dissipated, limping but gaining speed. At first, all he saw was smoke and fire. Then he saw her. She was one hundred feet away from the burning vehicles, crumpled on the ground.

No. No. NO.

He tried to walk faster. *Do not pass out. You cannot pass out.* It felt like it took an hour to reach her, like he was fighting his way against a flow of molten lava. He touched her back, afraid to lower himself to the ground in case he couldn't get back up. "Delaney!" *Don't let her be gone. Please don't let her be gone.* No movement. He started to sink to his knees when she groaned and rolled over. He only thought she'd looked bad after being thrown from the back of a pickup. Now she was worse. Her face was blackened and her brows singed. Her eyes blinked open, though, and she coughed. One of her hands reached up and pressed an ear.

"Fentworth," she choked out. "Sicario."

"Sicario?"

"His truck."

He stared into the flames. Sicario had been released a few hours ago. But he didn't live out in this direction. Sirens wailed. The ambulance Fentworth had called earlier for Clint Rock-Below approached from the direction of the fishing cabin. Delaney pushed herself up on one arm. Then she sat. He reached for her hand to help her, but she shook him off. He felt something trickling under his shirt. His bleeding was getting worse again.

"I'm fine. You're not." She stood, then limped closer to the inferno, hand tenting her eyes. She stiffened. "I see something. In the undergrowth, clear of the wreckage on the left."

She limped faster. He followed her at his own tortured pace, his right hand now pressing his shirt into his wound. She dove to her knees beside some huckleberry bushes, their new leaves blackened like Delaney's face. Feet were sticking out of the bushes. Leo watched Delaney as she lowered her ear to the mouth of the person on the ground.

Fentworth. Maybe he's alive!

But it wasn't the sheriff. The body was longer, the belly thick and round. Sicario. He was speaking, lips barely moving. Then he went limp, like the effort had taken everything he had left in him.

Delaney shook her head. Her eyes were glazed over.

"What did he say?"

"He asked me to take care of Mary and Juan Julio. And to tell Jefe that he's sorry." She met Leo's eyes. "Remember Brighton on the phone asking Jefe to send help?"

Leo nodded. "And Sicario was the help?"

"That would be my guess. Although I can't understand why Sicario would be involved with a man who'd hired someone to kill the mother of his child."

"And it ended like this for him." Leo gestured with his chin at the lifeless man in front of them. At least he hoped it was the end. It would be so much better if it was.

"But maybe not for the others." Delaney was up again, heading for the burning rubble.

He struggled after her, nearly spent. He knew she had to check. But he also knew what she'd find, and he couldn't let her be alone for this.

She stopped five feet from the flames, her hand shielding her face from the heat. She stretched on tiptoe, looking inside the burning truck. When he reached her, the strongest woman he'd ever met turned herself away from what she had seen and folded herself into him. Her scream buried itself deep in his chest, vibrating into the core of him. He put an arm around her and absorbed her pain, forgetting his own.

"Fentworth." She gasped, sobbing. "He's in there."

"I'm sorry. So sorry."

"I can't get to him. I can't save him." Her head reared back. "I saw him. He's gone." Her teary eyes were vacant. "He's already gone." And then her body shuddered. She laid her head on his uninjured shoulder and cried like the young girl she'd been when Fentworth had saved her.

FIFTY-SIX

ONE WEEK LATER

Delaney opened the door to Mary's hospital room and slipped inside with Leo. Mary was propped up in bed eating applesauce. Her body was a minefield of stitches, bandages, and red wounds left open to the air. Her eyes seemed haunted. Her dark hair looked freshly washed, though, and was wound into a top knot.

"You're back." Delaney smiled at her. It was the first time she'd been awake when Delaney had visited.

"Barely." Mary's voice was hoarse.

She had survived her ordeal, and, physically, her prognosis was good. So was Clint's, a few surgeries and screws later. Clint hadn't uttered a word of complaint. He'd survived. Two of his colleagues in law enforcement hadn't. He was feeling well enough in fact that he had already asked Delaney for a date as soon as he was released from the hospital.

"Is now an okay time to visit?" Leo said.

"Sure. Don't expect much. But thank you both. And Clint and Kateena. So much."

"Of course." Delaney took a seat by the window.

Leo leaned against the wall. "You're welcome. We're glad you're improving."

Mary shrugged. "You were injured in the rescue?"

Leo was wearing a sling and still walking with a pronounced limp. But he'd been lucky. The bullets hadn't struck anything vital, and he was on the mend after surgery to repair his shoulder. "Not too bad."

"I need to tell you something that I didn't include in my statement. Before I get too tired." She was staring at Delaney.

Delaney sat forward. "What is it?"

"I think the Delivery Man worked for someone. A bad guy." She paused to rest.

"Bad guy?" Leo said.

"That's consistent with his MO in Las Vegas. Is it the man who calls himself Jefe?" Delaney asked.

Delaney and Leo had talked at length with Heigl about the possibility that Brighton had been hired for the kills in Nevada and Wyoming, his gender, and his childhood raised by what sounded like serial killers. She'd shared with both of them that she'd received an email from a forum member of everythingtattoos.com. The former Nevada USPS worker sent a photo of his tattoo —a cancelled postage stamp. The marks left by Brighton on his victims, if Nevada and Wyoming were put together, were identical to the tattoo. When Delaney wrote back to the man, he verified that he'd been a co-worker of Robert Brighton's, and that Brighton had mentioned admiring the tattoo.

With Brighton dead, no one would ever be able to learn anything more from him. But Heigl had tracked down a home birth certificate in southern Nevada for a Robert Brighton. No female version of the killer had ever officially existed. DNA tests of the remains had confirmed biological gender as female, though. Cadaver dogs had searched the vicinity of Brighton's childhood home and pinpointed a veritable killing field. Delaney had no doubt they'd find the mother of Robert

Brighton amongst the victims buried there. No information had been released to the press about Brighton's past yet. For Mary's privacy, her information had been withheld from the public, too. An enterprising journalist would blow the story up eventually. It was inevitable. There was so much there.

It was still hard for Delaney to come to grips with the evil that had shaped Robert Brighton, or, as he had called himself to Mary, the Delivery Man. And it was terrifying to think that the person who'd hired him to murder at least two women was still at large, possibly in their area.

"Yes. Jefe. And I think I know who he is," Mary said.

Leo stepped closer, his eyes intense.

"Who?" Delaney asked.

Her phone rang. She glanced down. It was an unknown number, something she'd usually ignore, but her gut told her to answer. She held up a finger to the others and walked into the hall, turning to face Mary's door.

She leaned against the wall and pressed Accept. "This is Deputy Investigator Delaney Pace."

"You always did think you were better than everyone else, including me," the male voice said.

Her breath caught in her throat. It sounded like... it couldn't be... "Excuse me? Who is this?"

"If you come after me, I'll be coming for you next."

"Liam?"

The line went dead. She dropped her phone. It skittered across the floor and into Mary's room.

"Are you okay, Delaney?" It was Leo's voice.

Delaney put a fist to her mouth and sank to rest her weight on her heels. Liam. The connection to her grandparents' fishing cabin had been bothering her for a week. It was too big a coincidence. Her mind was reeling. Her brain refused to stay in the hospital room. It took flight back to the homestead. To a conversation she'd overheard from the door of the room that now belonged to Kateena, between her twenty-one-year-old brother and her grandparents.

"We're not staying in Wyoming another winter. Bought us a place in Arizona," her grandmother had said.

Liam's voice was bored. "Well, I'm not going. I have business here."

"The bar." Her grandmother said it like she was holding a rotten lemon in her mouth.

"Amongst other things."

"Well, you've got Delaney to attend to as well. We're not taking her with us," her grandfather said.

Delaney had felt a surge of hope. *Yes. She could live with Liam! Not the grandparents who didn't love her. And she'd be right where she still felt her dad's presence, and where her mother would come looking for her someday.*

"Good for you. But she's not staying with me. Find her somewhere else."

Delaney slumped to the floor. She hadn't expected Liam to refuse. How could he? He was her brother. She loved him. She didn't want to move to Arizona.

Her grandmother spoke again. "We figured as much from you. This means we'll turn her over as a ward of the state."

"That's better for her than being with me, and we all know it."

Liam had walked out, the screen door slamming behind him. Delaney pressed a hand to her mouth. Her parents were gone. Her family didn't want her. She was going to be given to strangers. People who might be worse than the family she already had. She jumped up and ran back to her room, put on her medallion pendant, climbed out the window, and sprinted, stumbling, crying, out to the barn where the old Chevelle lived under a tarp. She knew where her dad's old keys were hidden, on a nail inside a stall door. She snatched them up, ripped off the cover, jumped in the car, and tore out of the barn, intending to never come back. To never speak to the brother who'd abandoned her ever again.

Coltrane Fentworth had found her out of gas on the side of the road an hour later.

She shook off the memory. Even if it made some sense, Liam was dead. It was crazy to think the caller could have been her brother. It had to be someone else who sounded like him. Who knew her from before. Who had her mobile number. Because her brother might have refused to raise her, but he wouldn't have any reason to threaten her or to pretend to die and leave his daughter an orphan.

Would he?

FIFTY-SEVEN

Leo's face appeared in front of Delaney's. "What happened? What can I do?"

Did she dare tell him? She'd grown to trust him. And if Liam was alive, that was sheriff's department business. "I got a call... "

"Yes?"

No. Not yet. You're not even sure. She shook her head. She needed up. She scrambled to her feet, smoothed her pants, swallowed, and licked her lips. "Sorry. I felt woozy. I must be dehydrated."

His brows furrowed. "That's all it is?"

"Yes." She swept back into the hospital room. "Sorry for the interruption. What did you want to tell us, Mary?"

Leo re-entered the room across from her. Delaney refused to make eye contact with him.

Mary let her eyes close for a second before answering. "You aren't going to like it, Delaney."

"It's okay. You can tell us anything."

The woman took a deep breath, held it, then expelled it with force. "It's your brother."

Delaney shook her head. On the heels of the call... that voice... the fishing cabin —what were the odds? *The confirming kind.* "What do you mean?"

"Liam. I think he's still alive. And I think he had Lila killed and wanted me dead to protect his new identity. I know this sounds crazy, but I believe he is the man who calls himself Jefe, that the Delivery Man said is a very bad guy."

Delaney steeled herself not to show that Mary's words were less of a surprise than they would have been minutes before. *Mary thinks he's alive, too. Oh, Kateena.* She stood and started pacing the room. Her brain was on fire. "You believe Liam had his wife, employee, and sister marked for death so he could stay dead himself?"

Mary nodded.

Leo tapped his lips with a forefinger. "He didn't die in the crash."

"I don't think so."

"You're sure?"

"No. But I heard his voice on speaker phone with the Delivery Man. It sounded like Liam's. I'd know it anywhere. I worked directly for Liam for a year. We talked on the phone all the time."

Leo's and Mary's voices sounded far away to Delaney, like they were under a swimming pool full of water, one in which she was making laps and slowly sinking with every stroke.

"So, we might have two unidentified bodies in that crash." Leo wasn't asking it as a question. "Delaney, what do you bet we're going to find out that Clara's missing woman and her missing boyfriend from Casper aren't missing anymore? If Mary's right, they could be the ones who died in the crash in Liam's car."

Delaney nodded on autopilot.

Leo turned back to Mary. "Why have Lila killed, though? Because she knew he was alive?"

She shrugged. "I don't know."

"And why you?"

"I've thought about this a lot. I think it's because of a phone call. From him to me, around the time of his crash. I picked up the call, heard breathing, and then the call dropped or ended or something. Just a few minutes later, deputies were at the bar saying he and Lila were dead. Looking back on it, it seems too fast. Maybe that call to me came in after he was already supposed to be dead?"

"After?" Leo said.

"Maybe. I saved it on my phone. You can check the time it came in against the time of his death, because that's when his phone should have been burned up in the crash. It's the only thing that makes sense to me."

"Holy moly," Leo breathed.

"If I'm right—if he was on the other end of the line on that call—maybe he thought I would figure it out. That he was still alive, I mean. Although I'm not sure I would have. But he didn't know that."

"So, you think you were a loose end," Leo said.

"Yes."

"He had no reason to kill me, though." Delaney stopped, looking at her feet, thinking.

"Jefe never mentioned you." Mary's voice was thin. She cleared her throat. "I think the Delivery Man came after you on his own because I told him you'd find me and because of how angry you would be that he killed your sister-in-law. I don't think he knew about you before then."

Delaney started pacing again.

Leo said, "That makes sense. As much sense as we'll ever make of someone like Robert Brighton, I guess. The Jefe/Liam factor is not good, though. And you said he's a bad guy? What do you mean by that?"

"Besides his connection to the Delivery Man and murder

and kidnapping, I'm not sure. It sounded like he works with some important, scary people."

"Who?"

"I don't know. I'm sorry. But I do know that Jefe was done with the Delivery Man. Telling him to get out of town and not come back."

"And then we heard Brighton telling Jefe to send him help so the cops wouldn't tie them together. Remember that, Delaney?"

Delaney slowed. *All too well.* It had come off threatening when Brighton had said, "I promise. You don't want that." Jefe wanted to sever ties with Brighton. Sicario's death-rattle apology had been to Jefe. And Delaney knew, deep in her bones, that the "help" Jefe had sent was Sicario, who had accidentally solved Jefe's problem for him when he crashed into the sheriff's truck—and that wasn't for Mary's ears. She made a slashing motion across her throat that only Leo could see.

He nodded. "Your phone records speak for themselves. The phone company will have a record of the call. But you are a witness to his connection to Robert Brighton. The only witness. Would you be willing to relocate under a new name to protect yourself and your son? Liam isn't the only one who can fake a death. If I can get the funds to move you, we can announce that you never regained consciousness."

"I'd miss you and Skeeter," Mary said to Delaney.

Her words brought Delaney back. "And I'd miss you. You've become my friend and a valued employee. I was hoping you'd manage the Loafing Shed."

"I appreciate that. But I'd do anything to protect Juan Julio. Would Sicario have to know?"

Delaney returned to her chair. For a moment, her brain took flight again. Liam, the brother she'd idolized until the day he'd refused to take her, was alive. Kateena's *father* was alive, and he was obviously involved in some messed-up things. He'd either killed or used the death of two other people and left them to burn up in a car so that he could be reborn under a new identity. He'd had Kateena's mother murdered. Because of him, Mary was kidnapped, tortured, and next for death.

What game is he playing?

A powerful, volcanic energy bubbled up inside Delaney. Kateena, who was with her sort-of nanny, Skeeter, and Mary's son, had lost so much. She was about to lose more if Juan Julio moved into witness protection. Delaney couldn't let the truth about Liam take another chunk out of her niece. It was too horrible for a girl of her age—of any age—to process.

As far as Kateena would ever know, Liam died in a car crash. End of story.

But she would have to shelve worrying about Liam until later. This was important, here and now. Mary. She looked at Leo. He widened his eyes at her, asking again if she was all right.

Delaney said, "We have some good news and some bad news, Mary. The sheriff and another cop were taking Robert Brighton to jail. They were in a crash with another vehicle. Everyone died."

"I'm very sorry about the sheriff and the other cop, but it's good news the Delivery Man is dead."

"The driver of the other vehicle was Sicario."

She bit her lip, frowning, blinking. Her eyes stayed dry. "That's sad for Juan Julio. But it makes it easier for us to disappear, doesn't it?"

"Yes," Leo said. "I think some of my friends in federal law enforcement might be able to help. I can't make any promises until I talk to them, but if they say yes, you'd have to cut off all ties to your family and friends for your own safety, until Liam is behind bars."

She nodded, her face grave. "I could do that."

Delaney's brain seized on a series of disturbing thoughts.

Liam's odd connection to Sicario, a construction worker, and former drug dealer. The failing construction business and failing bar, yet the homestead and family that stayed afloat. She thought of his expensive, destroyed vehicle. If Liam was getting money illegally, he would have had to launder it somehow. Because obviously, there had been money. Delaney was left with the businesses that were losing money and with the financial responsibility of Kateena, while he rode off into a criminal sunset. How disappointed their father would have been in him. Liam was not the man Rudy Pace had raised him to be. A chill rippled through her. Or was he? Their father had run a failing bar, the site of his murder. What did that suggest about the kind of life he'd lived? About his death? *No. I will not let Liam's choices poison my mind.* For the millionth time in the last twenty-four years, she begged her memory to reveal more. To show her the identity of her father's killer. But nothing came to her. Someday, she would hunt that person down. She would steal justice from the ether. Just not today.

She shook off thoughts of her father and refocused on Liam. Where had his money gone? *With him, of course. But there will be a trail, and I will follow it.*

Liam had said, "If you come after me, I'll be coming for you next."

Take your best shot, big brother.

FIFTY-EIGHT

Delaney stood, ready to leave this hospital room, to escape from the bad news that was not Mary's fault. She needed to wrap Kateena in a hug and never let her go. She started to walk out but stopped when Leo snapped his fingers.

"Mary, have you been to Sicario's trailer recently?" he asked.

"Never," Mary said. "He moved out there after we split up."

"So, you wouldn't have left a pair of panties in his bathroom? And you'd be surprised to find your hair in his bed?"

Delaney knew what he was getting at. DNA testing had identified the hair in Sicario's bed as Mary's. It was a loose end.

Mary's cheeks and neck flushed. Her voice rose. "There's no way. I was never there. Gross. What's going on?"

"We found both there."

Her face blanched. "Someone put them there, then. And it doesn't make sense. Sicario wasn't a pervert. He wouldn't have stolen them."

Leo and Delaney met each other's eyes. He nodded.

Delaney said, "Our best guess is Robert Brighton put them

there. We think he went to your house the day he took you. Maybe he was trying to throw us off his trail."

Mary said, "Ugh. I'm glad he's dead."

Delaney was, too. "Saved the taxpayers a lot of money."

Mary yawned. When she was done, she said, "I guess my painkillers are kicking in. I'm really tired. Thank you for coming, though."

Leo pointed at Mary, then himself. "I'll let you know as soon as I get an answer from the DEA."

They said their goodbyes. Delaney and Leo were walking out when her phone buzzed at the same time as his chimed. Texts. From the department.

Her gut clenched. *Not more bad news.* She read it without breaking stride. *Temporary sheriff of Kearny County announced. Crispin Allen.* There was a link to a press release that had been published in the local paper.

She stopped short.

"Delaney?" Leo said.

"I've got to take care of something. Since we're in separate cars, you go on. I'll see you later."

He looked puzzled but waved and left.

She went back to her phone and read the text again. She clicked the link to the press release. It said Allen had retired to Wyoming a year before but was delighted to be called back into public service.

She felt like she'd been socked in the gut. It was an unusual name. And happened to be the same as that of a certain sheriff in North Dakota who'd had her charged with assault for defending herself against a sexual predator. Granted, with a little more zeal than might have been necessary, but the jerk had it coming.

She hated Crispin Allen, and he was about to be her new boss.

FIFTY-NINE

Leo walked from the hospital to his Equinox, his personal cell phone to his ear. "This is Palmer."

His caller didn't waste a syllable. "Status?"

"That's not why I called. I need something for a victim here."

"Status?"

He hated this woman. "The sheriff was killed."

"I know that. In a wreck."

"I suspect it was more than that. I'm reading between the lines here, but we encountered a bad guy who calls himself Jefe. He faked his own death to create a new identity for himself. Before that, he ran a half-ass construction company and a failing bar."

"Drugs. Money laundering."

"The thought has occurred to me."

"I haven't heard of Jefe. Do you have reason to believe your sheriff was working for him?"

"I think the sheriff was a casualty of Jefe sending someone he'd hoped would assassinate the hit man he'd used to kill his own wife. But that's not the relevant part."

"Don't keep me in suspense, Palmer."

Leo leaned against his little SUV. "My new partner is named Delaney Pace."

"Who's he?"

"*She* is Jefe's sister and the guardian of his daughter. We believe Liam Pace is Jefe. Delaney's father was knifed to death in the same family bar her brother ran, too." He left out the part about the murder occurring right in front of young Delaney's eyes. "Trouble runs deep in this family. In this town."

"Is Delaney part of it?"

"I don't know. I don't think so. But it can't help but find her."

After thirty full seconds of silence, she finally spoke. "Name your favor."

His stomach unknotted. "Two of them."

"Don't be greedy."

"Liam Pace—Jefe—ordered the death of one our victims. We rescued her, but she knows Jefe is alive, and she was a witness to his connection to the serial killer we apprehended. And he knows she knows. We would like to hide her and her little boy. I'd like you to make that happen."

"The second?"

"Let me go home. If I hand you this Jefe, release me."

"Send me the details on your vic. I'll take a look and think about it. But you aren't going back to California until I say you do."

Leo gritted his teeth. She had all the power. All Leo could hope for was the chance someday to treat this woman the way she'd treated him. "Whatever you say, Jefa."

She hung up on him.

He slammed the door of his car with his good arm and drove home with a lead foot, channeling the driving skills of the woman who would never forgive him if she knew her partner was using her to buy his own freedom.

SIXTY

THREE DAYS LATER

Delaney gripped a white rose. The florist had trimmed off the thorns, but her fingers had managed to locate the one they'd missed. It dug into a cut that hadn't yet healed. The physical pain barely registered. It was the pain in her heart that had her paralyzed.

The graveside service for Coltrane Fentworth had ended ten minutes before. It was the last of three in Kearny in the last few days, for the men who had died in the crash that killed Fentworth. First had been Ted Cross's service, then Sicario's modest ceremony. Robert Brighton's remains had been shipped back to Vegas, which was fine with Delaney. She didn't want that killer's body desecrating Kearny ground.

Dr. Louise Watson stood two feet from Delaney. Her eyes were red-rimmed and swollen. Dr. Watson tossed her own flower, nodded at Delaney, and walked unsteadily away.

The silence was complete except for Delaney's breathing as she pushed images from her father's funeral away from her mind over and over again. Another ten minutes ticked by. She couldn't bring herself to drop her rose into the grave. Onto the casket. *Casket. Fentworth is in a casket, like my dad.* It had been lowered into the ground. Six feet down. The man who'd always cheerfully declared that any day on the right side of the dirt was a good day, wasn't ever going to be there again.

"Delaney?" Leo said.

She hadn't heard him approach. She wanted to be alone. But if she wasn't alone, Leo was the least bad of any other option. "I just need another minute or two."

"I understand." Seconds ticked by, then he said, "Your necklace."

She was wearing the heavy medallion on a shorter chain, outside her clothes. She knew it wasn't the most feminine piece of jewelry. It didn't matter to her. What other people did or thought never had. She was numb to the idea of anything about other people ever mattering to her again. Wearing it outside, she could keep a closer eye on it. Make good on her promise to her father.

Leo said, "I'm glad you got it back. It doesn't match your anklet, though."

Nor had the two givers of the pieces matched each other, in the end, but they had come together in Delaney. And Liam.

"That anklet is one of the reasons I had trouble believing at first that you were a cop, after we first met."

"You don't look much like one either." *Maybe the Holly-wood version.*

He touched her elbow. "He loved you, you know."

She whirled on him. "You don't know that. He was right. We had a fight. He was right, I was wrong, and I wasted ten years being mad at him. I never said I was sorry."

Leo shook his head. His eyes held sympathy. She didn't want sympathy. She wanted to punch sympathy in the face. "You were both right."

"How would you know?"

"Because he told me so."

Tears welled in her eyes. She brushed them away angrily. "I

thought I didn't want to come back to Kearny and that I especially didn't want to work for him again. It wasn't true."

"Don't you think he knew that?" Leo moved closer to her. Too close. Into her personal space. She felt uneasy, but it passed. "You were like a daughter to him."

She refused to sob. Bit her lip to stop it from trembling. Her dad, gone. Now, Fentworth. Gone, too. She couldn't say the words. *He was the closest thing I had left to a father. And now I have none.* And she didn't even have a medallion to remember Fentworth by. *But I have the one thing that meant the most to him. A Kearny County badge.*

"Come on. Throw that flower in there for him. He needs you to be able to move on so he can, too."

That, at least, made sense to her. She had chosen a verse for him, and she said it silently as her goodbye. *In the path of righteousness is life, and in its pathway there is no death. Proverbs 12:28.*

Leo cleared his throat. "The Lord is close to the brokenhearted and saves those who are crushed in spirit. Psalms 34:18."

She side-eyed him. "When did you start quoting scripture? I got the impression you didn't believe in that stuff."

"I got the impression it was a comfort to you, so, um, yeah. I looked it up. I thought it might help."

It did, a little.

Delaney stared at Fentworth's grave. She'd thought long and hard about the phone call from Liam. Blood was thicker than water. Just not in this case. Leo was like a mirror into her blind spots. Maybe Fentworth had had a reason for pairing them up. Maybe it was time to trust someone, even though part of her was screaming that the law wasn't enough and that she had to reserve the right to take justice into her own hands if necessary to protect Kateena. With Crispin Allen filling Fentworth's shoes, it sure wouldn't be her new boss.

Her dad would have liked Leo. She believed it with all her heart. Leo was going to be that someone to trust for her.

She turned to him. "We need to talk. It's important."

Leo half-grinned. "If this is about me arresting you, I'm sorry I didn't let you explain yourself. And that I waited this long to say it."

"It's not that. But thank you. I know."

"You know." He chuckled. "Then what is it?"

Delaney shook her head. "Monday will be soon enough." *More than soon enough.*

The two of them walked away from the gravesite, not touching, but close enough that Delaney could feel the warmth of his body beside her.

A LETTER FROM PAMELA

Dear Reader

You're here! At the end of *Her Silent Bones*! With all the choices for and demands on use of your time, I am honored that you spent hours of yours reading it.

If you would like to receive email alerts of all my latest releases, just sign up at the following link. Your email address will never be shared, and you can unsubscribe at any time.

www.bookouture.com/pamela-fagan-hutchins

Honestly, *Her Silent Bones* was a nonstop thrill to write. I'd been imagining Deputy Investigator Delaney Pace, Deputy Leo Palmer, and their rugged Wyoming world for such a long time before I even started writing them that they are constantly in my thoughts. I can't wait to share their next cases and adventures with you.

I hope you enjoyed *Her Silent Bones* and if you did, I would be very grateful if you could write a short review online. I'd love to hear what you thought about it, and reviews make such a difference helping new readers discover one of my books for the first time.

Writing is a solitary experience, and I am somewhat of a hermit anyway. I split my time between two rustic homes. One in—you guessed it—Wyoming, on the face of the Bighorn Mountains, the other on a remote lake in Maine. My companions are my husband and our draft cross horses and sled/ski-joring dogs, with visits from our adult children and grandchild.

So, I *love* hearing from my readers out there in the real world. You can get in touch with me via my Facebook page where I am fairly active, through Instagram, Goodreads, or my website.

Thanks,

Pamela Fagan Hutchins

www.pamelafaganhutchins.com

 facebook.com/pamela.fagan.hutchins.author
 instagram.com/pamela_fagan_hutchins

ACKNOWLEDGMENTS

A few years ago, my husband Eric posted that we were giving away rusty, fire-damaged barbed wire. One of the takers was Daisy, who showed up with her family to claim some to use for a project. We soon learned that she'd given up oil field trucking in North Dakota—and a side gig on a reality series—for taking over the family homestead, raising her second daughter twenty years after her first, and being a service to others through philanthropy and her physical labor. She was a key player in organizing one of the largest agricultural relief efforts in the history of the United States through a huge convoy of truckers, donors, and volunteers after historic fires devastated America's Midwest. She and her family raise (and butcher) a large flock of turkeys every year to feed 300+ people at a free community Thanksgiving dinner. Daisy's the one you want as your second in a knife fight, who could have been a model or actress instead of a rodeo star and extreme trucker, and she's the friend you can knock back a cold one with or take to meet your pastor (after you've done your best to prepare them for the encounter). If by some small miracle you find her in a church, you won't see her sitting in the pews... she's the one standing in the back. She was forged in the kind of volcanic upheaval that can result in smoking rubble or beautiful rocky mountain ranges. Daisy, through character and force of will, is the latter. If you enjoy Delaney as much as I do, it is because of my friend Daisy. Daisy, thank you for agreeing to let me reshape you in fiction.

When it comes to creating a fictional law enforcement

world, you have to start with the real thing. I am so lucky to have Police Chief Travis Koltiska of Sheridan, Wyoming in my corner for this. A fourth generation native of Wyoming (with his kids the fifth generation like Delaney), Travis is a bit larger than life. I know him as the generous guy with the heart for his family and animals, a big laugh, and endless stories, but trust me that you would *not* want to be the perp who faces him! Which is ironic since we met him through his wife after my husband accidentally broke into a house she was listing for sale. (It's a long story that ends in years of friendship, and I swear, it was an accident!) I've included anecdotes, quotes, history, and ideas from Travis in many books. I even have a Deputy Travis who shows up from time to time in several interconnected Wyoming series. This time, he took it a step further and acted as my beta reader and coach. Any mistakes are mine alone. He improved the book immeasurably and put up with dumb questions in texts all hours of the day and night. Please email Travis some love through me as I am praying he wants to continue in this role!! Thanks, Travis, for your friendship and your help.

Huge thanks to my creative, firm, encouraging, brilliant editor Helen Jenner for patiently talking to me about these books for many, many months while waiting for her wisdom and experience with crime fiction to rub off on me and my writing for Bookouture to commence. Helen, you've pushed me through walls I didn't know I'd built to shelter deeply buried writing fears. I'm very lucky to collaborate with you on this project. I hope there are many more to come.

Thanks also to the wonderful team at Bookouture. As a rugged individualist/indie since 2012, I didn't think there was a publisher I would ever be willing to work with. Nimble, lean, flexible, strategic, mission-driven, and reader-centric, Bookouture is everything I was looking for, and I appreciate them taking a chance on me. The support has been incredible, in every step of the process.

Thanks to my husband Eric for brainstorming with me, researching the perfect car for Delaney, teaching me how to adjust engine timing, encouraging me endlessly through some hard times, beta reading, and much more despite his busy work, travel, and workout schedule and truly rough 2022, the year this series was born. And, most importantly, for putting up with my obsession with horses and sled/skijoring dogs!

Thanks to our five offspring. I love you guys more than anything, and each time I write a parent/child relationship like the one Delaney has with Kateena, I channel you.

Finally, to each and every blessed reader: I appreciate you more than I can say. It is the readers who move mountains for authors, and you have done so for me, many times over.

PUBLISHING TEAM

Turning a manuscript into a book requires the efforts of many people. The publishing team at Bookouture would like to acknowledge everyone who contributed to this publication.

Audio
Alba Proko
Sinead O'Connor
Melissa Tran

Commercial
Lauren Morrissette
Jil Thielen
Imogen Allport

Data and analysis
Mark Alder
Mohamed Bussuri

Editorial
Helen Jenner
Ria Clare

Copyeditor
Jennie Ayres

Made in United States
North Haven, CT
13 July 2024

54746755R00232